Eventide

EILEEN ALDERTON

HarperCollins*Publishers*

HarperCollins*Publishers*

25 Ryde Road, Pymble, Sydney, NSW 2073, Australia
31 View Road, Glenfield, Auckland 10, New Zealand
77-85 Fulham Palace Road, London W6 8JB, United Kingdom
10 East 53rd Street, New York NY 10022, USA

First published in Australia in 1994
Reprinted in 1994

Copyright © Eileen Alderton 1994

This book is copyright.
Apart from any fair dealing for the purposes of private study,
research, criticism or review, as permitted under the Copyright Act,
no part may be reproduced by any process without written
permission. Inquiries should be addressed to the publishers.

National Library of Australia
Cataloguing-in-Publication data:

Alderton, Eileen.
 Eventide.
 ISBN 0 7322 5063 3.
 I. Title.
A823.3

Cover by Head Design, London

Printed in Australia by McPherson's Printing Group, Victoria.

9 8 7 6 5 4 3 2
97 96 95 94

Dedication

To the memory of my father, Dr Charles Alderton, formerly Royal Army Medical Corps; and to my husband, Hugh Lynch-Gardner, Rifle Brigade, Commandos and Intelligence Corps in the Second World War. Both served in India during the days of the British Raj. My husband, who helped me with research for this novel, died before it was completed. *Eventide* is dedicated to our sons, Michael and Hugh Lynch-Gardner.

Father, Mother and Me,
Sister and Auntie say
All the people like us are We,
And every one else is They.

From 'WE AND THEY', RUDYARD KIPLING.

All characters are fictitious.
The regiment in India is imaginary.

PART I

India, 1920–1949

Chapter 1

June Barret, born in Australia, daughter of a grazier and mine owner and granddaughter of a Melbourne banker, was twenty years old when Lieutenant Ian Deighton-Gaye of the British Army, stationed in India and on leave, met her holidaying in Europe.

At the beginning of his leave in England, staying in his retired parents' icy Surrey house, he had suffered boredom. It was like a chronic illness that brought on fits of yawning and the inability to rise in the mornings with any anticipation of enjoying the day. His parents remarked that India tended to sap the strength and rest in the country would 'put him on his feet'. They talked of 'good fresh air' and the benefits of wide-open bedroom windows. Fires smoked and doors banged. The bath water was seldom hot.

Ian's parents were as strange to him now as an adult as they had ever been, and with the passing years appeared vague, eccentric, insular and unable to see beyond their noses. Their view was as narrow as Kipling's had been, although Kipling, in spite of bad eyesight, had managed to become a journalist and make a good living from writing books. Leather-bound volumes of his work still lined the walls of the room Ian's father called the library, although no one ever sat in there to read. Beside Kipling was a copy of *The Complete Indian Housekeeper and Cook* (1905, first published 1898). Like Kipling's works, it gathered dust. Ian's mother had never used it. All memsahibs employed a cook.

Ian's life had been mapped out for him. He had conformed. After early years of coddling from native servants he accepted without grumbling the discomforts of English boarding schools. Sandhurst and then a British regiment in India became the inevitable fate of a pleasant, polite, upper-middle-class boy of very average intellect who was, his father said, 'still a little wet behind the ears'.

Just too young to have been involved in the First World War, but keen on 'doing his bit in any skirmish', Ian loved India, gave his regiment unwavering loyalty and accepted without question its beliefs and unspoken prejudices. Apart from short spells of active service, uprisings, riots, the quelling of the followers of Mahatma Gandhi whose passion for non-violence often produced an opposite effect, Ian Deighton-Gaye lived an all-male, sheltered life not unlike school, obeying orders, eating and drinking in the mess where hunting trophies were displayed instead of sporting ones. He slept in a 'chummery' shared with other bachelor officers and was single, not from choice but because suitable (attractive, unmarried) women in India were rare. Mission workers and teachers, dedicated do-gooders with plain faces, were written off as unmarriagable, victims of unkind remarks and pity.

The Eurasian girls, though attractive and some of them well-educated at mission schools, were lumped, along with the despised British Tommies or Other Ranks, as 'beyond the pale', unwelcome in British clubs or at social events patronised by the British Raj. The antecedents of these women were employees of the Post and Telegraph Department, Customs and Excise and the railways. They tended to congregate near railway junctions and workshops, for they had virtually built India's vast railway system and having built it, they ran it. Anglo-Indian parents, self-conscious about their looks (blue eyes and fair skin were priceless prizes for the lucky few) were ambitious for their children and encouraged mating between their pretty daughters and the outcast British Other Ranks, hoping that the dark eyes and sallow skin might disappear in future generations. Mixed blood was despised.

Ian Deighton-Gaye had occasionally taken an Anglo-Indian girl out to the cinema and to tea. He was seen by a senior officer, who told him kindly, 'Look, old chap, that was a charming girl I saw you with—but you really must look out. Honestly, that sort of thing just isn't done.' He explained there would be a black (or half-black) mama behind the girl and Ian would fall into the trap, be hooked like a helpless fish, for an officer was a rare and precious catch. One had to be 'on guard against all that sort of thing'.

The girl—her name was Dorothy—was sweet and friendly and took Ian home to tea, to a little house not far from the railway, with a garish religious picture on the wall and a table set with jelly and custard and pink-iced cakes laid out on paper doilies imitating lace. Here, he realised, was the artificial gentility, the longed-for refinement practised by the Eurasian and mocked by the British upper class. Dorothy's father was invisible but Mama was indeed most visible, very dark and embarrassingly eager that he should 'drop in' whenever he liked, if he was 'prepared to take us as we are', which meant no pink cakes or jelly should she be unprepared for visitors. She showed him a picture of Dorothy's grandmother on her father's side, a fair-haired woman in a high-necked Edwardian blouse. The photograph, gently tinted, was inside a locket of Indian gold with a strand of fair hair hidden in the back. The little locket made him feel unhappy and somehow responsible for these people, though how he had no idea. It did not occur to him—as it did not to any of his brother officers—that the Anglo-Indians bore a stigma that was no fault of theirs. Many were industrious, ambitious, loyal, sometimes brilliant and devout defenders of an Empire that rejected them. Their looks, the blending of East and West, could produce children of astonishing beauty and very often first-class minds.

India, 1920-1949

Ian Deighton-Gaye never went to tea at Dorothy's house again, nor did he take her to the cinema or 'drop in to take them as they were'. He was used to obeying orders. The casual warning of a senior officer made it perfectly plain what was 'definitely not done, old chap'. But he often thought of Dorothy. Even after his marriage he would sometimes remember her, searching for her in the streets, in the bazaar, in the *maidan* where they had taken walks together.

She had been sweet, kind, intelligent, gentle, pathetically hospitable, devastatingly attractive. She had told him, with honesty and not a trace of coyness, told him in the deplored sing-song, chee-chee accent, 'I can say exactly what I am thinking, what is in my head when I am with you, Ian. You understand how things are. I think I would do anything for you.'

He never saw her again, but guilt remained. He would wonder if she ever married, if the determined half-black mama had pushed her into marriage with a fair-skinned British Other Rank; whether she had children, and if they took after her; small, compact, with dark-brown hair and thick arched brows with a shine like silk and high cheekbones and dark, dark eyes, so dark a brown they looked black and deep and in them, if you were not careful, you could drown.

Once, at the outbreak of the Second World War, he had seen a woman in uniform hurrying across the hospital compound. She was coming off the night shift with a crowd of others but she walked apart, and something about her made him think of Dorothy; perhaps the walk, the narrow shoulders, the too-thin legs. A shaft of cruel morning sunlight lit her face like a close-up in a film and he saw a middle-aged Anglo-Indian woman with a sallow skin and black circles beneath her eyes. Not Dorothy. This one was plain and looked like any other Eurasian woman. Many of them were nurses. He walked right past her. She didn't look at him at all.

Never, even towards the end of his life, did he really understand what his daughter Annie believed with anger, with frenetic intensity, for there had never been time to get to know his daughters. 'The Anglo-Indians are the saddest— God, the very, very saddest, most misjudged, most pitiful people on the sub-continent,' the embittered Annie would later say. 'The saddest bloody result of British domination, of imperialism.' So loud-mouthed Annie, drunk or sober, would tell anybody who would listen to her and if they listened they said nothing. Annie Deighton-Gaye was peculiar. She had been expelled from a boarding school in England and finished her education (if one could call her educated) in Australia. It wasn't altogether her fault, poor thing. What else could one expect?

Ian Deighton-Gaye had anticipated his first home leave with some excitement; decent climate, green fields, Scotch beef and Yorkshire pudding, Welsh lamb and fresh mint from the garden, and summer pudding, perhaps, with freshly picked berries and clotted cream. It all proved disappointing and uncomfortable. His parents kept only one elderly housemaid and he was used to being pampered. The 'chummery' had its servants. His parents did not feel the cold and were mean with coal. To the astonishment of the senior Deighton-Gayes, he caught a train to Paris and another to Switzerland, finally booking into a pension on the Italian border. Little English or French or German were spoken here. The language was Italian and it lilted and sang around him. The spring flowers—loaded in buckets and barrows on cobbled streets—were wet and sweet and fresh and went to his head like drink.

He met June Barret in a café by the lake. She was drinking hot chocolate topped with cream.

June was very tall for a girl, and sturdy, with broad shoulders and a healthy skin. Her features were small and neat, her eyes round and china blue. She wore a green flowered dress with a 'handkerchief-point' hem and white shoes with square, stubby heels. Her legs were golden-brown beneath smooth silk stockings. Her fair hair, cut in the modern bob, was held back by a bandeau that matched her dress. Except for little dark-eyed Dorothy—and he had vowed not to think of her—he had never seen anyone so beautiful.

It surprised him to discover that June was Australian. And she, at that first meeting, was careful how she spoke, that no sentence ended in the slight upward inflection that her elocution teacher had told her gave away colonial origins to those educated at Oxford or Cambridge. That he had never been to Oxford or Cambridge did not matter, since he spoke exactly as if he had.

June was rich. He, as yet, was far from rich but his income would rise with rank and captaincy was imminent. June's family owned property; a house in Sydney, another house in Melbourne; a sheep station in a place he had never heard of; an interest in mines; an island in the Pacific; an office in the City of London (they were exporters of precious stones and wool) and 'a dear little place in London'. It was useful, having somewhere in London, if you liked to travel as June and her parents did. Her parents were mad on travel. The little London house was between Hampstead and Highgate and near Hampstead Heath, one of the best areas of London and easy for getting up to town. Did he know it? Oh, yes, he knew it but had never aspired to living there. All his school holidays had been spent with elderly relations, members of the Indian Civil Service or the British Army who had retired in country villages.

He rowed her across the lake; took her to lunch at a café where the streets were steep and cobbled and tobacco was drying in the sun. 'Tell me about India,' said June, china-blue eyes dreamy, imagining handsome princes, Maharajahs, palaces, the riches of the East. 'I'm fascinated by the colonies, of course, being a colonial myself. I come from pioneer stock. My ancestors worked the land.'

India, centuries older than young Australia, could hardly be said to have been developed by British pioneers. His ancestors had never touched the land, only taken possession of its assets and overseen work done by people they considered their inferiors. These facts he could never have discussed, even had he wished to. He belonged to the generation who believed that everything Great Britain had ever done was 'right'. He found her remarks charming and endearing. Within three days, stuttering, stammering, blushing, he proposed to her. June accepted calmly. Her parents were delighted. Ian Deighton-Gaye had 'class'.

They were to be married in London, an expensive wedding paid for from the profits of wool or minerals or whatever else enabled her parents to live the way they did. 'I'm really happy about the marriage,' said her mother. 'She is a very friendly, social girl and from what I've heard of British India the life should suit her very well. She even loves hot weather, would you believe it? She was very bored in Sydney. The boys didn't appeal to her at all.'

Ian's parents were relieved he had found a wife, although they found the Barrets a trifle brash. But no matter. Barrets had fought at Gallipoli and on the Somme and there was obviously plenty of money in the family. A lunch party to celebrate their brief engagement was arranged in London, at Rules in Maiden Lane, so that both sets of parents could get to know each other. Ian's mother wore her tweeds, June's a suit of fondant pink with a frilly blouse. June's mother talked incessantly, Ian's mother was quiet, enjoying her steak and kidney pudding. 'Good old English food,' she said.

Between mouthfuls her eyes were drawn to the Hogarth prints hung slightly crooked on the walls. From time to time her fingers twitched, as if she had a nervous urge to straighten them or, since old habits die hard, suggest to one of the staff that something should be done.

Ian and June spent a short honeymoon in a London hotel, handy for all the shopping June must do before sailing for India. Ian's leave was ending and she was to follow him in two months' time. Her frenetic shopping expeditions, in which her mother joined her, filled him with alarm. The favoured shops were the most expensive, where her mother had accounts. Harrods was the particular favourite.

'The Army and Navy are famous for fitting one out for the tropics,' Ian suggested.

'Not renowned for style,' said Mrs Barret. Thrift was a word unknown to her, as it was to June. Mrs Barret was a smaller, fatter version of June and, unlike her well-spoken daughter, she had a loud, harsh voice. June's father was quiet, morose, until a drink or two set him off chatting about merinos and wool.

Ian, alone with June in their hotel bedroom, felt awkward, clumsy, as if he had suddenly grown an extra hand and foot. He dropped things. He fell over her shoes. He apologised. And he couldn't stop looking at her, touching her. He found himself so engorged with lust he was painfully uncomfortable day and night—and uneasy, unsure. Was she, until their wedding just a week ago, a virgin? Of

India, 1920-1949

course she must have been, an only child, much loved, continually sheltered by devoted parents. How much experience had she had with those Sydney boys her mother said she found boring? He couldn't tell. He wasn't experienced enough himself to know. He only knew that he wanted her and wanted her and couldn't get enough of her; rounded, golden beauty with long sturdy legs and pretty frilly nightdresses he managed to tear as he pulled them up her body, to look at her and look and look, and she, eyes closed when she lay down and wide open when she sat up, reached hungrily for a cigarette which she seemed to need desperately after sex.

Breakfast was sent up to their room. Sitting up in bed, with a little bed jacket across the split seams of the brand-new honeymoon nightdress, she seemed contented and smiled at him and chewed. Diffident, knowing he was scarlet in the face, he asked, 'Was it all right for you? You must tell me. Do you enjoy it? Was it really all right?'

June spread butter on a roll, took a sip of coffee. 'It's lovely,' she said. 'Such delicious jam.'

Ian knocked his coffee over, watched a stain spread across the bed. He felt sweat break out across his forehead and his hands were shaking. 'Clumsy ass, I am,' he said ...

As Memsahib and soon after Captain Memsahib and Major Memsahib, and finally the Colonel's lady, June Deighton-Gaye fitted her role as a pair of costly hand-made gloves might fit her large, square hands. She accompanied Ian wherever he

Eventide

was posted and no one ever heard her complain. She visited the sick, played bridge, gave parties and handed her children, Marjorie and Anne, born within eighteen months of each other, to 'that treasure Ayah'. No trace of an Australian accent remained.

Ian Deighton-Gaye loved his daughters. He saw as much of them as his time allowed. He read to them. He mounted them on ponies as soon as they were old enough and accompanied them on picnics. June, who found small children intensely boring, ordered expensive clothes for them from London and occasionally brushed their hair and 'dressed them up'. Marjorie submitted to the dressing up; Annie suffered it. 'That treasure Ayah' cared for them and loved them. It was Ayah who wept bitterly when they were sent to boarding school in England.

For June Deighton-Gaye the girls' departure was something of a relief. Children, even with servants to do the necessary, were demanding, awkward and interfered with both 'doing one's duty' and social life. 'Oh, how I shall miss them,' she told other officers' wives. Only Ian, for whom their departure was a painful wrenching of the guts, guessed that June, ever busy, would hardly miss them at all and that the weekly letter she would write them was as much a duty as visiting the sick.

Marjorie, calm, obedient, excelling at music and needlework, rose to the rank of head prefect. Annie 'let the side down'. At fifteen, she was expelled.

India, 1920-1949

June wrote to her younger daughter.

1st May, 1937.

Dear Anne,

Your father and I, needless to say, are surprised that your behaviour should have been so unmanageable that one of the best schools in England has expelled you. I noticed on our last leave that both sets of grandparents find putting up with you during school holidays most exhausting. I have decided to send you to my old school in Sydney. It is a convent and though of a Catholic order, willingly takes Anglican pupils without prejudice. My cousin Binnie (you had better call her Aunt) is a widow, at present living in my parents' Sydney house. I have arranged for you to stay with her and she will look after you for a very nominal fee. You will be staying not only near a beach but close to Centennial Park, which is a beautiful memorial to the founding of the colony. You may ride there, although it is not quite up to the standard of Rotten Row. I seem to remember, young as you were in India, that one of the few things you could do well was handle your pony.

You may remember my speaking of Binnie, widowed two years ago. She and her husband were once stationed in Singapore. You will be a day girl for the remaining years of schooling when, of course, you will come out here. Marjorie will be leaving school earlier than expected as the rumours of war are rather alarming and there has been talk of English children being evacuated to the colonies. As the long summer holidays in Australia coincide with Christmas, we shall look forward to seeing you in December next year, or early in January. Marjorie will leave England at the start of the English school holidays, in the previous July.

I have been very busy. We were hoping to spend a little time in Ooty but there has been a most unpleasant outbreak of dysentery and I have been visiting the troops in hospital. The wife of a sergeant in the regiment has recently had a baby who died of this most dreadful complaint at three weeks old. Naturally I did what I could to console her and attended the funeral, which was exhausting in the Hot Weather. One must do one's duty.

I feel very strongly that when you come out here you should be able to do something useful. I have dropped a line to Binnie and the Reverend Mother to see if you can take First Aid classes. India is always short of European nurses. If there is war, the base hospital will need recruits.

Your loving Mother.

Annie remarked to her sister that it was a wonder, with a mother as strict and hard and indifferent as theirs appeared to be, that they had ever been born at all. 'Poor, poor Daddy. I wonder he can stand it,' she added.

Marjorie, silent, looked shocked.

'She did her duty,' said Annie. 'She's such a brick. Opened her legs and thought of England.'

'Annie, that's disgusting.'

'Thought of Australia, the biggest opal in the world or the fattest sheep, but marrying into the British Raj was better. It's called social climbing.'

'You're wicked.'

'Pooh,' said Annie.

She left the English boarding school—and Marjorie—without a pang.

For Annie, with the remains of itching chilblains on her heels, pasty-faced in spite of a long sea voyage and still spotty from several years of badly cooked school meals, Sydney was the most beautiful place she had ever seen. 'Oh, oh, oh!' she yelled, looking from her bedroom window to the beach. The light made her eyes sting. The brilliant primary colours of her first hot morning brought regrets that she had never been interested in art classes at the hated English boarding school.

'I love it, Aunt Binnie,' she said. 'It's beautiful. It makes me want to paint but I can't draw a thing except the back view of an elephant. Can I go out and look around?'

'Do exactly as you like, darling,' said Binnie. 'Enjoy yourself. That's what you're here for, isn't it?'

'Not exactly. I'm here to finish my education.'

'The lovely nuns will see to that.'

Binnie was comfortably fat with a bosom like two unsteady feather pillows and puffy ankles. She wore her grey hair piled up on top of her head, from which hairpins dropped and strands of hair escaped, hanging limp on the sides of full pink cheeks. The backs of her hands were spotted with large freckles, her clothes, made from bright cottons and silks from the East, loose and shapeless. She mixed the colours. Blue clashed with olive green; pink, red, purple fought each other in spots or stripes or flowers. Scarves flew wildly, untidy as her hair. Annie found Binnie's garments fascinating, colourful as a mixture of different flavoured ice-cream. Elderly and vague, Binnie cared not a hoot what Annie did or where she went. She gave her a paintbox and drawing paper and a camera for Christmas. 'You might turn into an artist, who knows? We've had wonderful artists sitting right there on the cliff painting this very view—or you can take photographs. Enjoy! Enjoy!'

Binnie was an odd relation. Nobody in Annie's family had ever suggested that she should 'enjoy'. Putting up with (fog and icy weather), enduring (influenza, measles), facing up to without fuss (boarding school and suet pudding) and being constantly grateful for small mercies (dull holidays spent with grandparents) were clichés spattered throughout her mother's letters, in answer to the weekly letter written by Annie and posted to India.

WHY DID WE HAVE TO BE SENT AWAY TO THIS AWFUL PLACE?
LOVE, ANNIE.

Australia was wonderful. The Barret house in Sydney, a one-storey Federation bungalow of pinkish sandstone, perched above a curving sandy beach. Binnie would have named it Stamford had the property been hers and not merely lent to her by a relation. 'After Sir Thomas Stamford Raffles, founder of a settlement in Singapore in 1819,' said Binnie, who considered herself an authority on the East. Aunt Bin had fond memories of Singapore, especially gin slings in Raffles. 'The finest hotel in all the world,' she said. 'I might even have called this house Raffles, but Arthur said it might look as if we were having one and gambling and if your grandparents turned up—and there's no reason why they shouldn't, the place does belong to them—we would have had to take the name away. The Barrets don't believe naming houses is in good taste, unless it is a large country property, so we must make do with Number 32. At least it is Beach Road. There's a Beach Road in Singapore where Raffles is.'

Annie pointed out that Stamford Raffles had also founded the London Zoo. 'What about "Lion House"?' she said. Binnie shook with laughter. 'Annie, you are a real card. We're going to get on splendidly together. You cheer me up.'

'I'm glad,' said Annie. 'I shall love being here.'

The house reminded her of bungalows in India with verandahs and high, dark rooms. They had lived in several different houses in India, 'moved from pillar to post', her mother used to say, but 'making the best of things'.

This house, which she would always think of as Aunt Bin's, was cool and rather grubby since Binnie possessed few domestic skills and Uncle Arthur, during the short time he had lived there before his death, had never noticed dust. There were no servants. A woman came in every day to clean but rarely touched a duster. She sat in the kitchen with Binnie drinking tea.

Annie went to the beach. She swam. She surfed. She lay in the hot sun, mad to achieve a tan. She went to milk bars and picture houses and rode the trams from one end of the city to the other. She rode harbour ferries, her favourite pastime. She talked to people wherever she went. People were friendly, funny, laughed at her British accent, told her jokes. In the park she rode a gentle mare called Rhona, played tennis and netball and earned herself a reputation for being bright, daring, sophisticated, a 'sport' and not too bad scholastically. She proved excellent at history and chose colonial history as an extra subject, 'because we had to do Willie the Conk and Bloody Mary and Elizabeth and all that lot in England. We never learned anything about India or Australia.'

The girls at the convent were less sophisticated than the haughty pupils at the English boarding school, and the nuns, although insisting on good manners, had soft voices seldom raised in anger. The gentle rustle of their habits, the long corridors tiled in black and white, the statues—the Virgin Mary, blue and gold and silver with a shining halo and waxen face—Annie found calming, restful. She took First Aid classes held by Mother Agnes Peter, who had once nursed in India and had a husky Irish accent and a skin as thin and pale as tissue paper and a high forehead on which tiny lines were etched, conspicuous beneath the linen wimple, as though the tissue paper had been crushed.

Mother Agnes Peter asked, 'What do you remember about India, Anne?'

'Ayah. And my pony and going away to cool places in the summer, to the hills.'

'I taught in a school there for a little time, Indian and Eurasian children. I loved them very much.'

'Did they have to pass exams like us?'

'Some did. Others had no opportunities. They barely had enough to eat. I nursed for a time, in a hospital out there, looking after women and children.'

'Did you like it?' Annie asked.

'I enjoyed my work but there is small satisfaction in results that are so short-time, so brief. One lives in many different levels of society all at once. It is confusing and frustrating. It can break your heart.'

'How?' asked Annie, remembering Ayah and cook and cook's assistant and the bearer and other servants and her mother with apparently little to occupy her time, taking hours getting ready for a garden party.

'The princely states, Anne, where there was richness and often greed and sometimes practices intolerable to Christians. The British Raj—you must forgive me—but their snobbishness is contrary to my beliefs. And then there are the merchants who may or may not make their fortunes but many of them have done very well indeed—and the Anglo-Indians who grow up disadvantaged, looked down upon and so lacking in self-esteem—and the masses and masses, the millions of the poor, who have nothing to look forward to but disease and death. Always the diseases, sandfly

Eventide

fever and dysentery, typhoid, smallpox, rabies. I found the caste system abhorrent. How can a baby be an untouchable? How? Why? It was the inequality—and people like me, the missionaries and the teachers—could do nothing about it, nothing. That was what hurt me most. We are all equal in the eyes of God, but there was little evidence of it in India.' And Mother Agnes Peter opened the First Aid book. 'Forgive me, I am wasting time. Now, Anne, let us see if you remember how to fix a splint ...'

'Why did you get expelled in England?' fascinated schoolmates asked.

'The usual reason.'

'What?'

'Going out with boys.'

'What kind of boys?'

'There was a boys' school nearby and it's difficult not to go out with boys when they're more or less up the road.'

There was a boys' school up the road from the convent but nobody Annie knew would dare be seen with any boy, unless a brother or close relation.

'Did things happen?'

'What sort of things?'

'What usually happens when boys are alone with girls.'

'Nothing of any great importance happened to me,' said Annie. 'There was an old faggot of a headmistress and she wanted to get rid of me.'

'Why?'

'She didn't like me. She preferred my sister. Most people do.'

'What will you do when you go to India? Go out with Indian boys?'

'Can't. It isn't done. Not allowed. I shall nurse the sick.'

'What sick? What's the matter with them in India?'

'All sorts of things, like wounds and snakebites and dangerous fevers. I shall nurse sick soldiers, I expect, in the hospital near where we live in India. I shall disinfect their wounds and give them blanket baths and read to them and wheel them around in bathchairs until they're better.'

'Wounds?' said Annie's best friend, Gloria. 'What sort of wounds?'

'People get wounded all the time in India, shot at or attacked with swords, and they can die of dreadful diseases. Like dysentery.'

'What's dysentery?'

'You poo and poo and throw up and sometimes you dehydrate and die.'

'It won't be very nice, giving baths to men, especially if they poo,' said Gloria. Daintily she placed her fingers against her nose.

'Florence Nightingale put up with worse.'

'You'll see the soldiers without their clothes.'

'So what?' said Annie. 'Bodies are just bodies, unless you're a narrow-minded prude. I'll try and get my parents to invite you to India for a holiday.'

'Mummy and Daddy wouldn't let me, I don't think,' said Gloria, 'not if it's got sick people who throw up and poo. They'd be afraid I'd catch a germ and die.'

'There's a risk in anything you do. If you didn't take risks you'd never do anything at all.'

'We don't take risks in Sydney.'

'Of course you do, every single day. You could be standing waiting for a tram and it could go off the lines and knock you down and squash you flat,' said Annie blandly.

'It wouldn't.'

'It might. It has been known.'

Standing at the tram stop that afternoon Gloria clutched Annie's arm and then her hand.

'You wouldn't be any good in India, not with the tigers and the snakes and the diseases,' Annie said. 'You're such a coward I don't think my father would even want you. He's a colonel.'

'What does he have to do?'

'Prepare for war and lead his men into battle when there is one. See?'

Annie leaped on the tram, one heading for the city, and flung herself into a window seat. She waved and grinned at Gloria, who had to wait for the tram to Watsons Bay. It was a warm afternoon. She pulled her grey box-pleated school tunic above her knees, dragged off the grey felt hat with the school crest on its band and found in her satchel a melting slab of nut-milk chocolate. She would now commit some crimes the nuns had told her no lady must commit. Showing too much leg and eating in public places like a tram or in the street were two of them. Annie displayed as much of her legs as possible and munched with joy.

Chapter 2

The bungalow with its pitched roof supporting the solid columns of a verandah was one of several in a line of married quarters, all of solid brick with rattan shades. It was large and dark and near the barracks, although not too near; quite a distance from the sprawling buildings that housed the British Other Ranks.

The house was far larger than the other bungalows they had occupied when Annie was a child. It had high ceilings and purple shadows in the corners and everywhere was the sound of whirring fans. There were polished floors and Turkish rugs and tables Annie remembered well, carved in uneven bumps to look like lotus flowers. There were brass jugs and ornamental brass and silver trays and silver trophies presented to her father for polo and shooting and a tiger-skin rug with its head left on, its eyes made of glass and its mouth wide open, showing its teeth. There were photographs of men in uniform and of men out of doors wearing topees, and women in long skirts carrying parasols. In one photograph the people were sitting on an elephant that wore robes and jewels. The furniture and the photographs were familiar but the bungalow was different and there were more servants. 'Because Daddy's the colonel,' Marjorie said, 'he gets the best.'

Annie's father looked older and very tired, her mother fatter and rather sallow. But her mother appeared in her element, unaffected by rumours, by the imminence of war. June Deighton-Gaye was 'doing her bit'. Annie studied her sister closely. Since leaving school Marjorie, always a pretty blonde, had become a beauty.

The old gardener, the *malee*, squatted outside the house. Three times a day he swept the verandah and the garden paths where cigarette ends had been stubbed out, where sometimes there was a broken glass and in a flowerbed a heel had trampled on a plant. It was the *malee*'s job to make the garden look like an English garden, with roses and marigolds and a herbaceous border that died in months of drought. Annie discovered on her return that everything, in this place so far from England, must look like England. In the dry weather the old man substituted terracotta flowerpots for flowerbeds and after parties removed spent matches and cigarette ends from his fat red pots, collecting them in his palm and pouring water on his thirsting plants. In cool weather there were jasmine and bougainvillea and chrysanthemums and canna lilies and dew in the early mornings. The verandah, encircling the house, held cane furniture and 'planter's long-sleevers' with pockets for holding drinks. There was a high wall around the house and beyond it the compound, the servants' quarters, a tree-lined avenue with bungalows set well back like theirs and beyond that the cantonment, the parade ground, the barracks, the Church of England school, the garrison church, the graveyard where children were buried, children who had died when they were barely born. Then there was the base hospital where Annie and Marjorie worked as volunteers and the *maidan*, a big park with trees; and a public garden called a *bagh* with a bandstand that had a big round dome; and then the mall with the European shopping centre and the tall commercial buildings and the bazaar and the towering railway station like a gothic castle. Further on was a temple with statues of Indian gods and animals and the smell of smoking candles, and then the little houses near a level crossing and railway lines that forked and twisted, shone, carrying people to the coastal plains and the hinterlands, to the mountains, to the frozen peaks where there was snow.

'Nothing's changed,' said Annie, 'except we have a bigger house.'

'Any reason why it should?' asked Marjorie.

'A lot of reasons.'

Beyond the streets and park, in the quarter where officers' families never ventured, there were back streets and alleys and close-packed dwellings, and stalls selling sticky foods crawling with fat, black flies; and people asleep outdoors, unwashed, stinking; and beggars, and thin children with swollen stomachs—and cripples, lepers, bodies

Eventide

shivering from fever or soaked with sweat. From this no-man's-land drifted a smell that newcomers found most unpleasant. It was the odour of humanity and animals, of excrement and spice, of open sewers and woodsmoke and ghee and chapatties cooked on open fires made from cakes of dried-out dung. From here, in heat-stricken, trembling, glassy light, came the drifting scent that Annie would remember all her life.

'Why don't we do something about those people?' Annie shouted in the middle of a cocktail party, but her voice was drowned in talk. There were always parties; talk. The women who in daylight were sallow after years in India wore thick make-up and looked pink and white beneath dimmed lights. They talked of servants; menus; golf; race meetings; who was at the club; of dinners where protocol was as important as etiquette. Protocol dictated who sat where and next to whom. Menus for dinner parties caused chronic anxiety in case the same dish should, by mistake, be presented to the same guests within too short a time. Long lists were made, stores checked, servants reprimanded. The servants, too, had their proper places, like the dinner guests, except that the servants did not sit at table but served the guests and were known as blacks.

At parties Marjorie was surrounded by young officers, some so young that they looked as if they had never shaved. There was constant smiling, laughing while drinks were poured. Above the voices; the slap-slap of servants' feet across cool, clean floors and the cold, clear sound of ice in crystal.

India, 1920-1949

There was the smell of whisky and of gin and the hiss of soda water siphons. The servants dressed in white and wore turbans and scarlet cummerbunds. They waited, patient, merging with the shadows, holding silver trays in their thin, dark hands.

Annie hated parties, the noise, the growls and screams of mirth, the setting artificial as something in a film. The men greeted each other with remarkable enthusiasm, considering they must meet almost every day. The women tittered, brushed powdered cheek against powdered cheek, mixing scents and silks and showing their teeth and standing away to view each other and admire a dress, a colour, a material. They looked and shook their heads, their voices high-pitched, shrill. Where, where did you find that lovely silk? And the cut is quite exquisite ... Made up here? You are so lucky with your *dirzi*, so lucky.

June Deighton-Gaye had a personal *dirzi* at her beck and call, and an outfit could be made for her in a day. Marjorie, too, always looked so elegant, so lovely. Annie, plump and inclined to spots, was paid no compliments. She sat and listened to her parents' friends talking about the past, the best things, the 'fun', the good times, the highlights of their privileged lives. They belonged to a generation when 'fun' and status and knowing exactly who you were were important, as protocol was vital.

There were rules; unwritten but for generations accepted, unquestioned, except by the colonel's non-conformist daughter Annie, who must be tolerated. She was, after all, a Deighton-Gaye. Oh,

Eventide

but she could drop a brick or two, such as declaring she preferred living in Australia. No airs and graces there. No protocol to speak of, not that she had noticed. One didn't say things like that. It wasn't done. And then announcing that she wanted to train as a nurse and become a theatre sister, like her friend at the base hospital, Sister O'Malley! 'Mallie,' said Annie, 'can teach me such a lot. I'd like to work on her ward and learn. I thought we might have dinner at the club and talk about my future.'

June Deighton-Gaye's mouth twisted until her lips almost disappeared. Later, in private, she spoke to Annie. 'Sister O'Malley, Anne, is Eurasian. You cannot invite her to the club.'

'I could sign her in.'

'You could not. They have their own clubs, Anne.'

'I've never heard anything so ridiculous in my life. Her son's a doctor.'

'That is not the point. It's an excellent idea for you to train to be a nurse.'

'The best nurses are Eurasian, Mother. They work until they drop.'

June turned away. She was arranging a tea party for officers' wives, forming a committee to raise money for the troops. War was declared a week after Annie's seventeenth birthday.

Fund-raising tea parties were events Annie did her best to avoid. Marjorie proved a charming asset but Annie regarded her mother's friends with horror. 'Stupid bitches with their gossip and revolting etiquette,' she said, thinking with longing of Aunt Bin's untidy kitchen, of the jam pot on the table, the way visitors helped with washing-up.

These women, her mother's friends, had servants to wash dishes and employed three servants to do the work of one. They talked of a rather special picnic at Hosur, of a spring meeting in March and 'that rather exciting gymkhana' and a polo match when somebody known as Bonzo broke his neck; and a fancy dress party to which the Deputy Commissioner's wife went as a shepherdess (unsuitable for both her age and size). The D.C.'s name was Platt and the unfortunate shepherdess was called Nina. Oh, they remembered Nina Platt, poor woman, and other poor women who withered away or drank too much or dressed appallingly or flirted so outrageously with young officers they became social outcasts. They whispered as they nibbled delicious little sandwiches and cakes from tiered cakestands. 'Now, Lily, you really shouldn't, should she, Mrs Deighton-Gaye? Lily's naughty—but do go on ... You can't stop right in the middle of a story like that. Tell.' And then: 'Oh, naughty, naughty ... What a scream.'

'They're unkind, vicious,' Annie said to Marjorie.

'I think they're funny, and they do good work,' said Marjorie.

'And eat too much, stuff themselves with cake.'

'I expect they're bored,' said Marjorie kindly.

'We all eat too much while other people starve,' said Annie, furious. 'Three meals a day in the hottest weather, plus those awful tea parties on the verandah.'

'But it's a way of life. You don't have to eat too much. I don't.'

'You leave yours and it's wasted and it would feed a poor family for a month.'

'Oh, Annie, how you do go on,' Marjorie said.

The abundant food was spicy, plentiful as the horde of servants who produced it. There were hot soups and cold soups, huge joints of mutton, assorted curries from mild to burning hot; pickles, chutneys; platters of saffron rice; cheeses and curds; chapatties richly buttered; thin, brittle poppadams; sickly sugared cakes dipped in honey and filling English puddings.

Annie, guilty about the starving in the streets beyond the cantonment, still enjoyed her food.

'You're getting fat,' said Marjorie cheerfully.

'I don't bloody care.'

'Don't let Mummy or the servants hear you swear.'

'The Other Ranks swear all the time. You can hear them in the street.'

'Exactly,' said Marjorie. 'So.'

Chapter 3

Dear, dear Aunt Bin,

I still miss you and Sydney most dreadfully and the house by the sea, although this bungalow which is considered suitable for a colonel (!) is a bit like it, especially the verandah, only bigger. Sometimes Mummy has to entertain 50 people at a time, and more. Did I tell you in my last letter that because of all those muddles we had over booking a passage for me and the panic about Hitler and a war, I arrived here at a most inconvenient time? Mummy was just about leaving for the hills for the Hot Weather! She and several other army wives were going to Ootacamund, which is known as Ooty, and is 7500 feet up in the Nilgiri Hills which are supposed to look like the Sussex Downs and remind everybody of England. The centre of Ooty is called Charing Cross and there are houses with names like Bideford and Harrow-on-the-Hill. I suppose in Australia we've done much the same with places called St Ives and Clovelly and Paddington but Charing Cross in an Indian hill station struck me as very funny. The Hot

Eventide

Weather is much worse than Sydney in January and February. The temperature soars into the hundreds every day. On the other hand there is a remarkable beauty about India, in spite of the ferocious sun. The light is dazzling, brighter even than the Australian light that made me blink when I first came to stay with you after that awful grey place in England. India is full of brilliant colour and awful smells. Unlike Sydney, there is heaps and heaps of pomp here and the women, the memsahibs like Mummy, have nothing to do except give orders to a host of servants who salaam like mad, which I find embarrassing. Can you imagine your Doris bowing to you every time she came to clean and made all those endless cups of tea you shared? I must say we live rather a grand life, never making our own beds or so much as rinsing out a cup! The great superior white race that the brown ones must obey!

If you look beneath the surface here, outside the cantonment where life is most unreal and artificial, the poverty is ghastly and the system makes me ask question after question. I can't accept that such poverty is ignored because it has always been there and little can be done about it. The British turn their backs and enjoy themselves. They do employ a lot of servants, so that may help a little, but thousands are starving and have nowhere to live. Marjorie, of course, fits in perfectly. I think people find me rather odd.

After so long away, I found meeting The Parents again quite difficult. Because of feeling so uneasy I've put off writing you a long letter till now, except the arrived safely bit and some silly prattle. I suppose I'm getting used to things again. Daddy—well, I hardly know him now. He used to read to me when I was little, all the Just So Stories, *'The Elephant's Child' and 'How the Leopard got its Spots' and the stories began, 'Once upon a time, O Best Beloved'. I can't see the same person in the Colonel today, the nice, quiet man I loved a lot when I was young. He has a small moustache and grey hairs and he is what people call 'reserved'. He and Mummy don't seem to have much in common. Unless guests are present, they hardly speak. Everybody salutes Daddy all the time, British officers and Indian ones and all the Other Ranks, of course, so going for a walk with him turns into a series of salutes. He just touches his cap quite casually with his swagger stick, very posh and most superior. When he's inspecting the regiment things are very orderly and grand and very regimented, which I suppose is what regiments have to be, or they wouldn't be called regiments, would they? But everybody treats him as if he was the King. And Mummy, of course, the Queen.*

Since the war started Daddy is always doing something important and we hardly meet. He has just left, taking two battalions on active service, we think North Africa, although nobody ever says exactly where. It was all very calm and unemotional and people call Mummy stoic and a brick. There is a lot of talk about Malaya and Burma and Congress and Independence. Some time, after the war is over,

Eventide

England will have to let India go free, or there will be dreadful troubles. There will be trouble, anyway, because the Hindus and the Muslims are always at each other's throats. And in this war India will have to fight for England, whether they want to or not. (I've heard some don't want to—the rebels, the ones keen on Independence now.) Other colonies— Australia, Canada, New Zealand, South Africa— fight wars beside the English because they want to, because they volunteer and believe in the British Empire, but the Indians have no option. They are expected to obey, to do exactly as they're told. Sometimes I think we treat them like little children.

Do you know the term Man-bap? It means 'I am your father and your mother'. They still believe that, a lot of them, although some of them these days are highly educated, far more so, dear Bin, than you or me. They have degrees from English universities. They make very good doctors and do excellently at law, which makes them almost acceptable in spite of the colour of their skins. Almost acceptable—they are not members of the Gymkhana Club.

I ask lots of questions about Gandhi, poor man, so emaciated in his loincloth and such thin arms and legs. Did you know that in 1930 he walked 60 miles from his ashram to the coast of Dandi to get a little salt, which was illegal as salt was liable to tax? He was protesting and thousands followed him protesting, too. Mummy says he ought to be in prison for good and all, but I disagree. Then there is a man called Nehru who was at Harrow and Cambridge and comes from a rich family here. He is a leader of the Congress Party, the ones that want Independence.

There are still arranged marriages in India and young brides. A girl can be betrothed at twelve to a bloke she's never seen. Their families arrange their lives. One thing that puzzles me now I'm grownup is the way people in trade or commerce, especially trade, are what Mummy would call 'not quite-quite', meaning not out of the top drawer. Is she out of the top drawer herself? I know Daddy is, with his ancestors either in the I.C.S. or the army, but Mummy—I should have thought making money out of wool and minerals was rather the middle drawer of the old colonial tallboy! I shouldn't say these things about my mother, I know I shouldn't, but I've always felt I could say anything to you. Aunt Bin, why does it matter which stupid drawer one comes from? I had an argument with a captain I met the other day— Robert his name is—and I said, Why do you despise people in trade when you took all you could from trade and commerce, indigo and spices and cotton and anything you could get your big white hands on? And he said, Oh, Annie, and you half-Australian, I believe. Your lot shot down anything that moved, and he laughed and said Australia was a colony of convicts and I reminded him about Dickensian England and how people starved and were condemned for stealing a loaf of bread or a paltry chicken and were sent to New South Wales in chains. I told him my maternal ancestor stole a waistcoat and three bodices and four chickens and tried to pinch a horse and he looked quite shocked, although knowing The Parents, he didn't believe a word.

He is quite a good dancer, Robert is, and took us to the club. He gave me a sling which, as you've always said, is perfectly delicious. I thought they only made them in Singapore. You will see from all the above, like my finding out about Gandhi and Independence though I've never laid eyes on Gandhi, that on the ship I read and read, having been warned by Mummy about behaviour and letting down the side if I went wild. A lot of people went absolutely wild and drank a lot. Besides looking up all I could on India, I read a nursing manual on looking after people with diseases and a medical dictionary beginning with Abdomen and ending with Zymosis which means the development of an infectious or contagious disease!!! (No, I didn't read it all!)

While Daddy has changed, I think because he has so much on his mind and heavy responsibilities, Mummy has changed, too. She is much fatter and not very interested in me, but then Marj has always been her favourite. She seems to want to get us married and off her hands. (The above-mentioned Robert seems keen on Marj, certainly keener than he is on me!)

We are both doing voluntary work at the base hospital, and although they don't let us do anything dirty or important—the Eurasian girls do most of the dirty work—I enjoy it and want to qualify as a proper nurse. The sister in charge of the wards I'm on, Sister O'Malley—her first name is Dorothy—is lovely and we are friends, although she refuses to come to the club with me when we go off duty because she has Indian blood. Her son, Henry, is a doctor and after the war he hopes to go to London or Edinburgh or Cambridge to specialise in gynaecology or paediatrics, or both. Indian women find it indecent to have their babies delivered by a man and there are so few women doctors that they rely on midwives. They'll have to get used to Henry. He is a wonderful doctor, but when he has all these extra qualifications he will come back here. Good doctors are needed very badly by the poor, especially for childbirth and caring for young children. He is in the Regiment and has at last achieved the rank of captain, same as Robert and not nearly high enough when he has five times Robert's brain. He is very, very good-looking (now, dear Aunt Bin, don't go getting ideas) and not all that dark—and don't we in Australia scorch ourselves to peeling in order to look darker than we are? Gosh, it's a funny world.

Dear, dear Aunt Bin, I must stop because I have to go on duty (doesn't that sound important?) and you will be getting bored, the way I go on and on.

Your loving, loving Annie.

P.S. Marj isn't working on the wards at the hospital. As she can type a bit she is given reports to sort out and a bit of filing. She looks very glamorous in a white coat, elegant like a film star. When good looks were going around this family Marj certainly got the bonus. I'll send a photograph—the camera you gave me still works like a dream.

Again, all love, Annie.

Eventide

Annie had been on the evening shift when Sister O'Malley, known throughout the hospital as Mallie, delivered a premature baby. The mother, wife of an officer away on active service, would have preferred a pure white midwife but there was nobody on duty to help with an emergency. Mallie managed on her own with Annie. The child, small but perfectly formed, screamed before it fell asleep. 'A very healthy sound,' said Mallie. She ripped off her surgical gloves and scrubbed her hands. Annie made her a pot of tea. She liked it sweet and strong.

'Mal, go home before you drop. Get a long good sleep.'

'Presently. A few things I must do first.'

'You never stop, do you? You and Doc Henry.'

'Henry works harder than I do,' said Mallie, slipping off her shoes, sipping tea.

'He'll be famous like Sir Henry Gidney,' Annie said.

'Gidney was the exceptional Eurasian rather than the rule,' said Mallie calmly.

'What's being Eurasian got to do with it?' demanded Annie. 'He specialised in eye diseases and he's a sir. He's a famous surgeon.'

Mallie laughed into her hot, sweet tea. 'When he was serving in Assam with the I.M.S., he shot fifty-two tigers and four elephants and two rhinos with his own gun.'

'Mal, that's dreadful. The Hippocratic Oath doesn't apply to animals.'

'Not in a society mad on sport.'

'Sport?' said Annie. 'Shooting animals for fun? How could he?'

'How can any of them?' said Mallie. 'They just do. Gidney collects paintings now he's rich, and he did try to help, you know, he with his monocle and buttonhole. I don't just mean people with poor eyesight.'

'Who, then?'

'People like us. Henry and me. Anglo-Indians. He made a speech saying we must get rid of superiority and inferiority complexes and replace them with a complex of equality.'

Mallie rarely talked of her origins, but nor did she deny them. She spoke openly of where she lived, near the railway where a colony of Anglo-Indians had settled years before. She lived in the same little house she had lived in with her parents, 'not far from the level crossing', she said serenely, 'and the trains roaring through the night used to keep Henry awake. He was mad about trains when he was little.'

Mallie had been a widow since Henry was five years old. Over tea and a cigarette she would talk to Annie as she never talked to other nurses. 'We lived in Bangalore. My husband was stationed there. After he died we came back here to my mother's house. She died last year. We didn't get on too well and I wish I had been more tolerant of her funny little ways.'

'What funny ways?' asked Annie.

'Ambition. A rather terrible ambition, Annie, not for herself but for me and for Henry. I wish we could have lived somewhere quieter on our own, but we were rather poor and I couldn't leave my mother. And she was so happy about Henry being clever and not all that dark. My husband's family were Irish, on his father's side. Fair-haired, like you.'

Annie rinsed out the teapot. 'A nun at the convent I was at in Australia worked out here, years and years ago, it must have been. She couldn't accept the inequality. The caste system and the snobbery made her sick. Abhorrent, she called it. It made her sad that there was nothing people like her could do.'

'Or you, dear Annie.' Mallie put down her cup and took Annie's face between her thin hands that smelt of disinfectant. 'And don't destroy yourself trying to put things right.'

'I'm indestructible,' Annie grinned.

'Nobody is indestructible. You can't beat tradition, Annie, any more than you can play tennis on a court without a net, or shoot tigers without a gun. Now, go off home, and thank you for being so helpful.'

Mallie's hands looked tanned, the colour of milky coffee, but in her face there was no colour. She had a greyish look, a pallor deep beneath the tissue as if the pigment from both sides of her inheritance had been drained away, leaving over fine, beautiful bones, a thin covering of skin with less tint than a piece of parchment. Her hair, usually hidden under a starched white cap, was dark with reddish lights. She had long, fine hands with beautiful rounded nails, white, almost luminous against her narrow, milky-coffee-coloured fingers. Her son Henry had good hands too, strong, bony, long-fingered.

Annie liked Henry. She liked his hands, his voice, his gentleness. Sometimes Henry took her out to supper at the China Bowl, a pleasant change from curry. He usually invited Marjorie as well and they would walk together down the mall and in the *bagh*, the public gardens, or round the *maidan* where in the cool of the evening Indian families took their children.

'What will happen after Independence, Henry? It will have to happen, won't it?'

'There will be a changing-over period but eventually it will happen, yes.'

He has a beautiful voice, thought Annie. *You can barely detect the accent as you can with Mal.* 'And then we'll go home,' she said.

'No,' said Henry. 'I was born here. Wherever I go when the war is over I shall eventually come back.'

'Like Gidney did.'

Marjorie asked, 'Who's Gidney?'

Annie answered, 'A top eye surgeon who was born near Bombay. He's a sir and very rich.' Henry laughed. 'I can't see myself reaching those heights, Annie dear.'

'Oh,' said Marjorie, uninterested. Marj, Annie had noticed lately, liked people, men especially, to talk all the time to her. For all her charm and sweetness she liked to hold the stage.

Annie wrote to Aunt Bin in Sydney:

> *Guess what? I've seen a baby born. My great friend Mal in the hospital is a trained midwife and theatre sister. She has handled life-and-death situations which people discuss over drinks and even at the club, though they would never let her in the club, not them. She has a bit of Indian blood and you can't imagine*

how prejudiced people are. Mal has assisted at intricate surgical operations and once saved the life of a mother and baby after a pretty primitive attempt at abortion. I've seen her sit for hours beside an amputee. She's very beautiful and quite worn out and I wish I could help her more. Seeing that birth and the mother in such dreadful screaming pain wasn't pleasant but I'm determined to get used to all the unpleasant aspects of this job.

My friend Mal reminds me of Mother Agnes Peter, the caring and the frustration of knowing so much needs doing that will never, ever be done; and the resignation, the patience. No anger. I get angry. Like Mother Agnes Peter, I have never heard Mallie raise her voice to anybody, although some of the V.A.D.s and Q.A. nurses all la-di-dah treat her like she's not worth much and she knows far more about medical procedures than they will ever learn. If there hadn't been the war they would never have risen to the rank of staff or sister, not those snobbish dimwits who can't wait to go off duty and to the club.

Mal's son Henry lives in a 'chummery'. He is now assistant M.O., the other M.O. being on active service somewhere where Daddy is. Henry started his medical career in the Indian Medical Department which was attached to the army, subordinate to the Indian Medical Service and open only to Anglo-Indians. When he has passed all his examinations in England he might be admitted to the Indian Medical Service. It isn't fair, the way people with Indian blood are treated. I get so angry, Aunt Bin. Nobody seems to care ...

India, 1920-1949

All Indians love children, I think. They cuddle them and kiss them as English people never seem to do, certainly not in public. Some of the women in their saris look beautiful; lovely flowing materials with rich embroidery and vivid colours, wonderful with their dark skins. They wear bracelets and anklets and earrings of shiny gold and some have long, heavy hair, a thick plait like a rope hanging down their backs. The wealthier Indian women have terrific style and move beautifully. Skins are darker here, in southern India, than in the north, Henry tells us. Parsees can be fair-skinned and don't consider themselves Indians at all. They are the descendants of Persians who fled to India to escape Muslim persecution in the 7th and 8th centuries.

Henry is the most interesting person to talk to I've met since I've arrived. He never, ever comes with us to the club. He says he doesn't drink but I wonder if they might not want him, refuse to let him in although some of the most ghastly types I've ever met are members. Aunt Bin, walking between Henry and Marj I sometimes feel a sadness, a peculiar pain somewhere inside my chest when I smell the dry, smarting scent of dust blowing across a land that is old, so old, and its dry, burnt soil holds history and memories and tragedy; a land of beauty and melancholy and patience, acceptance, subservience, appalling poverty—and simmering underneath like a volcano waiting to erupt, there is violence and bloodshed and resentful, bitter pain. Please write to me and tell me I'm not dotty, the way I feel.

Your loving Annie.

Eventide

After working the late shift Robert Harper, who couldn't keep his eyes off Marjorie, sometimes drove Annie home. She was always grateful for the lift. 'I helped Sister Mallie in theatre again tonight,' she told him.

'Oh, her,' he said, and handed her a cigarette. 'Mother of Doc Hank Mal. Everybody knows them. One must admit they're good at what they do.'

'They're experts at what they do.'

'Bangalore Irish,' said Robert. 'Lot of them about.'

'What does that mean?'

'She was married to a corporal. Some Irish in him on his father's side, hence the name. Think he was a corporal. He died, the corporal, or whatever he was, malaria or cholera, not sure, and she came back here and went in for nursing with a vengeance. Worked herself up, cleaner, ward maid, anything she could get, to educate young Hank. He got in the I.M.D. and like a lot of them since the war he shot up mighty quick. R.A.M.C. captain, deputy M.O. Not that he doesn't do a good job.'

'What do you mean, he shot up? He's qualified.'

'He's an Anglo, darling. Half-breed. It doesn't show so much in him but in her it's obvious. Big touch of the tar-brush there. Second generation black.'

'How dare you!' Annie screamed at him. 'Stop the car. I'm going to walk.'

'I shouldn't go round walking on your own at this time of night,' he said, and he drove on fast. She thought, furious: *I hate you, Captain Robert Harper, I do*, and opened the car door, so it swung back and he had to stop and let her out.

The *maidan* was empty, with a soft, warm wind blowing that hardly cooled the skin, had a decadent, lazy quality and smelled of dust and ash and humanity compressed, packed tight somewhere in the darkness, invisible. The sky was brilliant, studded with a thousand stars. Trees, bushes, moved gently, lazy, exhausted by the day. Annie, exhausted as everything around her seemed to be, walked slowly. Her feet were hurting; she had been on them for hours. To the right of her were a house and lights, a bungalow and the church steeple piercing the night sky, reaching for those stars. It was a Norman-looking church, as in England, and its archway was shadowed, black. She could hear voices and laughter and somewhere in the *maidan* her sister Marjorie's voice. 'Yes, yes, yes, oh please,' said Marjorie, 'I've never been there. That would be terrific fun.'

Annie arrived home very late, after helping Mallie with two emergencies. Her mother was sitting on the sofa drinking gin. 'Your father is reported killed in action,' she said.

June was deadly calm. Only from her eyes, which looked smaller and a brighter blue than usual, could Annie tell that her mother had been drinking. 'You had better go in to Marjorie,' she said. 'She has taken it very badly.'

Marjorie was asleep, or pretending to be.

'Marj?'

No answer. Outside rain pattered like footsteps on the verandah boards.

Ian Deighton-Gaye's personal belongings were sent to his wife, June, pitiful relics that could have belonged to anybody: his wallet with photographs of his daughters when they were at school; two brief letters from June telling him trivial local news; no trace of affection, just boring facts. 'The new adjutant seems a decent chap. His wife, Mary, came over for bridge last week ...'

Annie walked round and round the verandah, round the garden. She was soaked by rain. Her head pounded, screamed with pain, with remorse, with guilt, with anger. Her thoughts revolved like spinning tops. *My father was awarded the D.S.O. and there is nothing in this house left of him at all, except a cabin trunk with clothes he will never wear again. The bearer has carried the trunk outside covered in a sheet, to put it somewhere in the compound where it will be hidden and forgotten. My father's medals my mother will hang on the wall in one of those frames covered in heavy glass. The glass will prevent the colours of the ribbons from fading and keep out dust and damp.*

She could not cry during the memorial service and the eulogy and the hymns, and nor did her mother. June's black hat was wide-brimmed and wrapped in veiling, but Annie could see her eyes, blazing bright-blue, dry, passionless as pebbles. Marjorie sobbed out loud and June, very calmly, opened her black handbag and passed Marjorie a perfectly laundered handkerchief. Inside the bag was a little flask with a silver stopper; *our mother's little nip of gin*.

On night duty with Mallie, Annie wept. She howled. Mallie, on her ward round, carrying her torch and treading very softly on rubber soles, stood beside her and held her tight.

'Cry, Annie. Let go. Everybody needs to cry. The stiff upper lip is most unnatural. Well, I think it is. There are many who would disagree.'

'Mal, I wish you were my mother.'

'I wish you were my daughter.'

'I loved my father, but I never had the chance to tell him.'

'He would have known. He was a lovely man.'

'Did you ever meet him, Mal?'

'I've seen him when he visited the hospital, but he wouldn't have remembered me.'

'I don't think anybody could forget you once they'd known you.'

'The C.O. can't be expected to know everybody, Annie, and nurses are coming and going all the time. He was a lovely person and I shall remember him for always.'

'Thank you. Thank you for saying that,' and Annie cried until there was no breath left in her body. Mallie made a pot of tea.

The Christmas festivities began early, even in wartime. The club was decorated with artificial holly and silver streamers. Fairy lights were strung between the trees outside. Red and green and blue blobs of light fell on the courtyard paving. Marj and Annie sat drinking slings with Robert. Outside under the coloured lights couples were dancing. Several people were very drunk. Robert danced with Annie and Marjorie in turn and in between Marj danced with all sorts of people; the adjutant who was paunchy and had a buck-toothed wife; a kilted Scotsman with an incomprehensible accent, who trotted round as if he had a wooden leg; young subalterns with pink cheeks who looked too young to shave. Marj danced close and sexy with her eyes half-closed and her body wriggling. *A sexpot is my big sister,* thought Annie, *a proper vamp. Mummy would have fifty fits if she saw her tonight, drinking sling after sling and sitting like a film star, long legs crossed and skirt crawling to her thighs and her hair, which she wears turned up neatly for work, hanging loose and a little wild; sitting there waiting—and she doesn't have to wait for long—until the next sex-starved, lonely, sweating lad turns up and takes her outside to dance.*

Brushing her long, fair hair, Marjorie said casually, 'Robert has asked me to marry him. There's no time to waste.'

'You want to marry Robert Harper?'

'I've said yes. We want to marry very quietly, no fuss, although I shall wear Mummy's wedding dress.'

'White satin with a train and embroidered pearls,' said Annie smartly.

'It'll clean up beautifully in no time. It's a gorgeous dress.'

'Lace veil, orange blossom, crossed swords, the

lot. Mummy will never allow you to miss out on the trimmings.'

'Robert and I don't want to wait, not with all the flaps we've had since Pearl Harbor.'

'Get married quick, Marj. You know how people talk.'

Marjorie put down the hairbrush and swung round. 'What on earth do you mean?'

'You're over two months late.'

'I am no such thing.'

'You're usually regular as clockwork, except you never remember dates.'

'Don't be so silly, Annie.'

'Think I don't know? When have you remembered to stock up with thingummies? You always borrow mine.'

'Stop it, Annie. You're upsetting me.'

'I left two packets in your cupboard, because you're usually so regular and take time off with cramp. You haven't had a pain in weeks, and the packets are unopened.'

'I've remembered to buy them lately.'

'Tell me another. Is it Robert's?'

'I am not bloody pregnant,' said Marjorie, who never swore, 'and if I were, it would have to be Robert's, wouldn't it? I haven't been out with anyone else for months.'

'Congratulations,' Annie told her brightly. 'Good old Rob.'

Three weeks later Annie watched Marjorie marry Robert Harper, now promoted major. She was chief bridesmaid and felt terrible, ridiculous, in pale blue with artificial rosebuds attached to her unruly hair. Marjorie carried a huge bouquet of lilies and white roses.

And our mother wears a navy suit and a wide-brimmed navy hat trimmed with white and white suede gloves and her diamond earrings. It is a swish affair, a great big turn-out of uniforms and medals and swords and drinks and delicious food and off they go for a few days, somewhere secret, somewhere in the hills, Bangalore, perhaps, where Henry O'Malley was born.

The Japanese are pouring into Burma and Henry is already on his way. No time, no time to say goodbye.

Chapter 4

'Imagine, Marjorie is pregnant,' said June Deighton-Gaye. 'How delighted Ian would have been to have a grandchild. But war is war and one simply must not dwell on grief. We must all carry on as if everything were normal, if only for Marjorie's sake.'

The rest of her bridge eight gathered round her as she poured coffee from a silver pot. 'Sugar? Cream? Do try one of these chocolate peppermint biscuits. I told Cook to stock up every time he went marketing. He found these in the bazaar in airtight tins, so they're perfectly hygienic. There are bound to be some shortages, you know. I've heard rumours of a black market starting up already.'

The bridge players were overwhelmed. 'How perfectly lovely about Marjorie. Oh, the dear, dear girl. We're all so happy for you, June. You're a tower of strength. Marjorie is such a lucky girl to have you for a mother. Who is looking after her?'

'Doctor Rawlinson. She doesn't feel too well. The Hot Weather will be very trying.'

Eventide

June Deighton-Gaye, dressed in navy silk, with her hair just shampooed and set into crisp, tight curls, her back straight as a board and her eyes bright china-blue, smiled, a thin smile not wide enough to show her teeth. She allowed herself a little sigh. 'My goodness, I should know. Anne was born before the Hot Weather was over and I've never really forgotten, although they say, don't they, that you forget in a matter of weeks? I've never quite forgotten what it was like having Anne. Oddly enough Marjorie was easier, in spite of being the first. I'm afraid Marjorie worries all the time about Robert. We all do, of course. Naturally, we're thrilled about the baby.'

Marjorie lay in the 'planter's long-sleever' on the verandah. She wore a huge straw hat and a loose dress of pale-grey cotton. She appeared to be asleep. 'Wonderful,' they said, the bridge players. 'Let the dear girl sleep. Morning sickness already? Poor thing. Such a lovely girl.' Some of them remembered morning sickness very clearly—and evening sickness. 'I thought it would go on for months but, of course, it seldom does, although Marian—remember Marian? They retired in '38— she was sick almost every day for the whole nine months ... Now Beryl, my sister-in-law, was never sick, not once, but her labour was very long ...'

They dealt cards, sipped coffee, nibbled the chocolate peppermint biscuits, and their voices droned on and on. 'Your bid, partner. Goodness me, I'm making some mistakes today. It's the excitement, the wonderful news about Marjorie ...'

Annie had washed her hair and was drying it on the verandah before going on duty. She could hear every word they said but she kept away. 'And you a grandmother, June,' they said. 'You don't look old enough to be the mother of those two girls ... Marjorie will stop her work at the hospital, surely? No good overdoing things, especially if she isn't very well.'

'She gave up work last week,' June announced. 'Actually, I more or less forced her to give up. She was working very hard and standing far too much, I told her. Hard at it behind that reception desk and helping all and sundry and standing by a filing cabinet for hours, I told her she'd get varicose veins if she didn't take things easy. Happily she took my advice and she's putting her feet up whenever she feels tired.'

Annie thought of low-caste Indian women, giving birth in fields or in stinking shacks or in the street and going back to work or squatting, bleeding, cooking meals for families over open fires; and the baby with flies crawling over its mouth and eyes. The appalling inequality, as Sister Agnes Peter said. And nothing can be done.

'Any news of Major Harper?'

'Not for a week or so, but Marjorie is keeping very calm.'

Robert was in Burma. The news was not so good but there were always rumours, and no Deighton-Gaye gave up hope. *Not our mother or those women*, Annie thought. *God, the gushing, twittering regimental wives, the cooing, the excitement, the flattery, the little gifts! The birth of a grandchild might be a little consolation, might help ease the pain of Ian's death and the worry over Robert, though dear June has never been one to wear her emotions on her sleeve. A real brick. And won't Major Harper—Robert, the poor dear boy, fighting in the jungle and the monsoon not far away— won't he be just over the moon about the baby?*

Marjorie, when she woke up, looking white and drawn, was so sweet, so charming, accepting congratulations and presents as she had on her wedding day, as though, once again, she was somebody very special—before sinking back on the 'long-sleever' or lying, curled up, in foetal position, on her bed.

'Marj, shouldn't you take a little exercise? It can't be good for you, lying about all day.'

'I'm too exhausted to drag myself around.'

At night Annie would hear Marjorie crying. Their rooms were next door to each other. In breezeless heat, the slightest sound was audible. The sound Marjorie made was a whimper, like a sick animal, a creature in a trap. Annie went to Marjorie's room, pushed open the door, stood there, an incongruous figure in the top half of faded-cotton school pyjamas.

Marjorie sat up with a jerk, a pale, smudged outline behind the mosquito net. 'What do you want? For heaven's sake put your dressing-gown on. What would Mummy say? What if the servants saw you?'

'Everyone's in bed.'

'Why aren't you?'

'I came to find out what was wrong.' Quietly

Annie shut the door.

'Nothing. There's nothing wrong.'

'Do you feel ill?'

'No more than usual.'

Annie pulled the mosquito net aside and sat on the end of Marjorie's bed. 'You haven't heard bad news of Rob?'

'Of course not—and I do wish you wouldn't call him Rob.'

'Okay. Major Robert Harper. Are you crying because you miss him?'

'Of course,' said Marjorie. 'Why else would I cry?'

'I wouldn't know, Marj. Maybe you don't like being pregnant.'

'I hate it. I absolutely loathe it. Women who say it's so beautiful are liars. I hate everything about it.'

'Soon be over. Not as if you're an elephant. I think they take two years, or perhaps it's eighteen months. Not sure about that.'

'Shut up, Annie. Leave me alone.'

'You want it, don't you?'

Silence; a long pause in which they could hear each other's breathing. This was an invasion of privacy for the elder sister, the quiet ash-blonde who had never given trouble, and growing by the day so like their mother with barriers of respectability and conformity high around her; impeccably behaved, except on those evenings at the club when she had danced like a tart and drank too much.

Marjorie sat up, blew her nose. There was a wariness Annie could feel like something physical, as if thorns were emerging from her sister's skin. Finally Marjorie asked, 'What do you mean?'

'Do you want to have this baby? When it's born, I mean. After all the business of feeling sick and the birth is over?'

'Of course. All women are supposed to want a baby, aren't they?'

'Supposed to want,' said Annie. 'Got a cigarette?'

'Over there on the table. Help yourself. Light one for me.'

'Thought you were told to cut down fags and booze.'

'I'm not drinking much. It makes me sick.'

Annie lit two cigarettes and passed one to Marjorie and drew smoke into her lungs, and slowly blew it out. 'Ah, that's better. I don't think it's necessarily true that all women want children. I'm certain Mummy hadn't the slightest intention of having me. A big mistake.'

'Everyone makes mistakes, even efficient people like Mummy. I'm not efficient, Annie. I'm a fool.'

'No comment,' said Annie kindly.

'No need to be rude.'

'So you don't want it?'

Marjorie lay down again, smoking, staring at the ceiling. The fan made a whirring sound and stirred the smoke, blue fumes from their cigarettes moving slightly and then hanging still, round grey-blue clouds suspended above their heads. 'Oh, look,' said Marjorie, sounding bright and normal. 'I think I blew a smoke ring—or was it you?'

'Marj, do you feel depressed because you were

pregnant when you married?'

Another silence, then, 'I'm not depressed and the wedding has nothing to do with how I feel. The wedding was a great success. Everyone enjoyed themselves.'

And everybody said: Doesn't she look wonderful? Such a lovely bride; the rich satin dress embroidered with seed pearls, the pale face, pale hair, the palest touch of lipstick and tall and thin, but bent over at the waist at the reception, standing for two hours and shaking hands and being kissed and offering her cheek so sweetly and taking guests round to show off the wedding presents, the teaspoons and sugar bowls and cream jugs and teasets and dinner-sets and vases and rose bowls and decanters and wine glasses and tablecloths with matching napkins; Marjorie sagging just a little as the day wore on, exhausted, a drooping flower breaking in the middle on a brittle stalk.

'Never mind the wedding,' Annie said. 'I'm asking you if you want this child.'

'I've tried hot baths and gin.'

'You *what*?'

'And lifting things. I tried to lift the wardrobe. No good.'

'You've tried to lift that great big wardrobe? To get rid of it?'

Marjorie reached over to the bedside table and stubbed out her cigarette and took another from the pack.

'You'll make yourself ill, Marj, hot baths and gin. You'll feel very ill but you won't abort the baby. If it intends being born it will make sure it is, no matter how many wardrobes you try to lift. Why don't you want it?'

'I just don't.'

'Isn't Robert pleased?'

'I expect Robert wants a son. Men usually do, don't they? But if it's a girl he won't mind.'

'Decent of him. Did he know you were pregnant when he married you?'

Another longer pause, as though Marjorie had dropped off to sleep; but her eyes were open and she was smoking. An insect fluttered, hummed in the corner of the room. 'No.'

'Think he'd have backed out, left you standing at the altar, as they say, if he'd found out?'

'Of course not. Robert would never have let me down.'

'Then why didn't you tell him?'

A slow, evasive answer. Annie knew immediately that Marjorie was about to lie. 'We had so little time. I didn't want to spoil things. We only had three days. I'd have felt so awful. It would have been like forcing him to marry me.'

'Well,' said Annie, 'so you were, in the old-fashioned, devious way, what Mummy would call a skivvy's shotgun wedding. Let's hope she didn't know.'

'She didn't, and it wasn't a shotgun wedding. Robert's wanted to marry me since we met.'

'Then why the drama?' Annie, being so calm and reasonable and logical and unemotional and talking very quietly. 'It's as much his fault as yours, if neither of you wanted children. He should have been careful, shouldn't he? Or you should have been.'

'He'll think I've made a fool of him.'

'Because the poor little creature's born a couple of months before it should be? What's he going to do, tell everyone the baby's premature? He won't do that. Robert would expect you to produce a nine or ten-pounder and I bet you do. Only the best for Rob.'

'You've never liked Robert, Annie. Apparently you were very rude to him one night when he'd taken the trouble, made the effort, to drive you home because you were working late.'

'He called the O'Malleys Anglos.'

'But they are Anglo-Indians, aren't they?'

'So what? So what? So might we have been. We could have been sweepers, untouchables. We could have been anything. Luck of the draw, I say.'

'Don't be silly.'

'There but for the grace of God go I,' said Annie.

'You weren't so tolerant when you found out I was pregnant.'

'I was furious that you didn't tell me—and then you lied, most unconvincingly, I might add. Are you certain Mummy didn't know?'

'If she did she's never said a word.'

No, Annie thought, *she wouldn't. She will ignore the unpleasant, pretend it never happened. Ever the colonel's widow with the ramrod back and the gin tucked away inside her handbag; a quick nip when no one's looking.*

Marjorie asked unexpectedly, 'Have you noticed

Eventide

how much Mummy drinks?'

'Of course.'

'Do you know why? I'm sure she didn't drink when we were children.'

'It's the way of life, I suppose. You don't do too badly yourself, or you didn't, before you started feeling sick.'

'She drinks because she's unhappy.'

'She was thrilled to bits about you and Robert.'

'I don't think she was all that thrilled. He wasn't a "regular" and he went to some school she'd never heard of. Before he joined up he was a buyer in a department store.'

'Buying what?'

'Gents' shoes. Of course, Mummy says she likes Robert. She says she's fond of him already.'

'Not quite out of the top drawer, but he'll do,' said Annie drily. 'She dithered about the banns.'

'The banns?'

'She and the padre had a long heart-to-heart about the banns. Three Sundays they should be read, and you only just managed that by getting married on a Monday. You wanted to be married in a week or something. Remember?'

'Of course I remember. Two weeks, actually. Robert knew he was going on active service and we didn't want to wait. I hope Mummy wasn't unhappy about that.'

'If she's unhappy, it's nothing to do with you.'

'I don't want to be like they were, she and Daddy.'

Annie, startled, asked, 'What way do you mean? Rob's not C.O. material, I shouldn't think. One never knows, of course. Promotion's quick in wartime.'

'I didn't mean anything to do with rank. Mummy and Daddy were terribly unhappy.'

'Took each other for granted. People do, after years of marriage. They had their devotion to the regiment in common.'

'Annie, I came back before you did and it was the first thing I noticed. He was so quiet and she would get irritable. I heard her tell him once that he wasn't very bright.'

'Not bright? The regiment thinks the world of him. Thought the world of him. I'm still not used to the fact he isn't coming back.'

Marjorie spoke in a whisper. 'Mummy said he had spent his whole life doing exactly what he was told, what was expected of him. He hadn't the initiative to go further, be a brigadier or a general or something at the top where he'd have to use his own brain and not follow orders from the big brass hats. Once she said to one of her friends, "You wouldn't believe it, but Ian can be such a bore," and the friend said, "Darling, aren't they all?"'

Annie said, 'He was not a bore. Everybody can't be brigadiers or generals. How unfair.'

'They all think Mummy's marvellous,' Marjorie said. 'Don't speak so loudly. She might hear.'

'It doesn't take initiative to be a colonel's lady,' said Annie, refusing to lower her voice. 'It takes a list of dos and don'ts and a stiff upper lip, and she's always had one of those.'

'I think there was someone else.'

'For her or him?'

'Both, I expect, but especially her. She was bored. Somebody called Keith used to ring her up.'

'Keith who?'

'I don't know. He wasn't stationed here. I answered the telephone a couple of times and the name sounded like Keith or Keats. Long distance. Probably somebody she met in Ooty. She loved it there.'

Annie thought of a walk with her father, how, that one time, he had put his arm across her shoulders.

'Think your mother looks all right, Annie?'

'Fine. A bit fatter than she used to be but she looks very well.'

'And Marjorie?'

'Oh, Marj is belle of every ball or whatever gorgeous girls are called.'

'She isn't strong.'

'Strong as a horse, Daddy. Thin people often are. She hardly ever even gets a cold and she's never been a spotty one, like me.'

'I meant strong up here,' and he touched his forehead. *'Not like you. My tough little monster, Annie.'*

And that was all; the only time we almost talked, got near each other, close; the only time since he used to read Kipling to me: 'Once upon a time, O Best Beloved ...' It was a very old book, a sort of purple colour and smelt of mould; and my eyes are burning, blurred with tears; and I am biting my lip and I feel a piece of skin tear away and lie between my teeth. Be a tough little monster, Annie. Tough.

'Annie?' Marjorie's voice, muffled in her pillow.

'What?'

'Could you ask your friend to get something for me, pills or something, or arrange somewhere safe where they'll get rid of it?'

'You mean ask Mallie? I wouldn't dream of it, and she wouldn't. She believes in saving life, not destroying it. And if Robert wants a baby you'll have to have it.'

'People will think I've had a miscarriage. Robert and I can try again as soon as he gets back.'

'But if you mean to try again, why not have this one and get it over and done with?'

'No.'

'Unless it isn't Rob's ...' This was said lightly, a silly joke, but Annie felt Marjorie's reaction, a jolt, a shrinking. 'You did lead them on, didn't you?' said Annie, bright and chatty. 'All those blokes at the club, and you were always going out with different ones, far more than me.'

'People were always asking me out. Usually to the club. There isn't anywhere else much to go.'

Marjorie's bored, blasé voice, but still muffled in her pillow. And then defensive: 'I was just enjoying myself. You'd go out more if you made the best of yourself, but you never bother much.'

'Marj, if ever I saw a girl out to catch a man it was you. I couldn't think what had come over you. Like a cat on heat.'

'It doesn't help me, you being nasty. I've got to get rid of it.'

'Because people are going to talk? Doctor Rawlinson must know, for one.'

'Of course he does but he's the civil doctor and

doctors never betray confidences. He wants me to go to a very nice nursing home somewhere, a place he says is good. Not the hospital here, he says. By the time I'm due it'll be full of troops, sent down from Calcutta and everywhere else, he says, troops from Burma.'

'Do that, then, and come back and say it arrived early or you couldn't stand the heat and were taken into the nursing home early so they could keep an eye on you. Say anything—as if anyone will care in wartime. People have other things to think about than when you and Rob first went to bed, if it was a bed.'

'I don't know what you mean.'

'You were a one for walks in the *maidan*, weren't you? Gin slings and stars and moonlight. Poor romantic Marj.'

'You can't know that unless you were in the park yourself.'

'Walking home one night I went through the park. You were there. Just past the church.'

'I don't go necking in churches, Annie. What do you think I am?'

'Okay, okay. I heard your voice.'

'And who else did you hear that night?'

'Just you. Perhaps you were talking to yourself.'

'And what were you doing there? Talking to yourself as well?'

'Rob had picked me up at the hospital and I walked home after I practically threw myself out of his car. As he told you, I was rude and I walked the long way home.'

'Annie?' Marjorie was sitting up again and crying,

a trickle of tears falling down her cheeks and chin and leaving damp, dark patches on the sheet.

'Stop it, Marj. Nobody's going to know or care.'

'You don't understand, do you? You just don't understand.'

'Tell me.'

'I can't.'

'Of course you can. I'm your sister, remember? So tell me and you might feel better when it's off your chest.'

'It was Robert, actually. You see, we didn't—'

'Didn't what?'

'Robert and I never did-did it, not until we were actually married. Honestly. That's the truth.'

'Immaculate conception, was it? Come on, Marj.'

'How could we, with you or Mummy always there? He often took us out together, remember? Which was sweet of him, considering how he felt about me and—and—then, when we were married ...'

'Go on.'

'It didn't sort of work.'

'Didn't work?'

'I sort of couldn't. I didn't like it. I can't help the way I am. I don't think one could become pregnant from the little that we did. When I didn't want to, he said he ... He said ... He sort of said ...' An enormous, gulping sob.

'What, Marj?'

'Said he couldn't, not properly. Hardly anything happened. He thought it was because we were both a bit nervy with him going away and when he came back that sort of thing would all work out. But it won't. It never will. It'll be like Mummy and

Daddy and we'll put up with each other and never be able to talk about things that matter and he'll go quiet and hurt like Daddy did and I'll ... I'll ...'

'Find another man? Or go off with the baby's father?' A shot in the dark but the arrow found its mark.

Marjorie's voice rose, angry. Her tears had stopped. 'I didn't say Robert isn't the baby's father.'

Annie ignored her and asked quickly, 'Is this bloke married?'

'No. No. No. Who? What bloke? I don't know what you mean.'

'Were you fond of him?'

'Of course I'm fond of Robert. Otherwise I'd never have married him.'

'Not Robert, Marj. You know exactly what I mean. The baby's father.'

Marjorie put her hands against her face. Annie could hardly hear what she said, as if her fists were pushed inside her mouth. 'I adored him. I couldn't help it. I just adored him. I'd have died for him, Annie, thrown myself in front of a train or something if it would have helped him. I would.'

'Throwing oneself in front of trains does nothing for anybody,' Annie said. 'Go on. Now we've got this far I'd better hear the lot.'

'I've never loved anybody before. I didn't know what it felt like. Books don't tell you anything. I went a bit mad, I think. Because I've never cared about anybody except myself before him. I know I'm selfish, self-centred, but I loved him much more than I loved me or anybody else from the first time I saw him. I threw myself at him, Annie. Flung myself at him. It wasn't him that started it. It was me. I loved him, loved him, loved him, I did. I really did and it was wonderful and it was awful and now I want to die.'

'Oh, hush,' said Annie. 'Don't be ridiculous. You're not going to die and don't start howling again, for God's sake. You'll wake Mother up and she'll be in here like a shot.'

'It was fine with him, you see, because I loved him so. It's different when you love somebody, when just seeing them sends you weak at the knees, like a jelly. Honestly. I promise you. You don't mind what they do or what you do, Annie. It's wonderful, if it's somebody you really love.'

'Did he feel the same?'

Marjorie drew in her breath. 'No. That's humiliating, I suppose, because he never said. He'd never lie. I didn't mind. I never felt humiliated, never. I'd have done it over and over as long as he wanted to. You've never felt like that. You've never lost your head. You're not the type. You've never felt-felt sexual passion in your life.'

'Not as yet,' said Annie mildly. 'Not to that extent. You sound like a heroine in *Peg's Paper*.'

'Don't be horrid, Annie. Only housemaids read *Peg's Paper*.'

'I was thinking of those trashy magazines we used to pinch from the maids at school. "He was gone in the morning. There was nothing left of him but the imprint of his head upon the pillow ..."

I always remember that bit. It made me hoot. Of course, they were always married, in secret, or by a ship's captain or they had eloped to Gretna Green. You had to wait a week before finding out where the bloke had gone. It turned out he had been called away to do something noble and ever-so, ever-so brave.'

'Annie!'

'Sorry.'

'Listen to me and stop being funny. I couldn't face doing it with Robert. I couldn't. I couldn't bear it, do you understand? *Do* you? Sometimes I think you don't understand anything, Annie Deighton-Gaye. You're like Mummy.'

'Actually, I'm not in the least like Mummy and I do understand. Does he know, this man? That the baby might be his?'

'Of course he doesn't know and I'll never tell him. It would ruin his life. And I don't know where he is.'

'We can try to find him, for a start.'

'You will do nothing of the sort. You will not try and find him and you wouldn't have any idea where to look. You don't even know his name and I'm not telling. There's nothing anyone can do except help me get rid of it.'

'I'll never help you to do that.'

Now put your arms round her, hug her, tell her you're sorry you made fun of her. Tell her to stop the melodrama. Tell her you'll do anything you can—only not that, not abortion.

Annie said very calmly, 'You've probably got all muddled about dates and things, you know what you're like with dates. Even Doctor Rawlinson could be wrong about the dates. When it's born people are bound to say it looks like Rob. People always do, even if a baby looks like nothing on earth. Or they'll say it's the image of you. Lucky thing, if it's a girl and looks like you.'

'Annie, please go away. Just go away and stop asking questions and making me say things I never meant to say. It's nothing to do with you. Just go away and let me sleep.'

Annie went. She stood on the verandah. Another night of brilliant stars; and under the stars, over the old, dry earth, a choking, smothering layer of sticky heat. Somewhere out there in the city, a light and then another and a voice calling out and someone playing a few notes on a flute—high, pure, painful—like a cry for help blowing across the bay, or an animal calling for its mate, or an eerie welcome to the dawn. And the acrid smell of smoke, the smouldering of early fires, the familiar scent of animals and humans stirring to another day.

What do we do? Annie asked the fading stars, the blood-rippled early dawn. *What? What? Poor Marj. Poor old Rob. And who on earth's the man?*

'Marjorie won't be having breakfast,' June Deighton-Gaye remarked casually as they sat down to scrambled eggs. 'She's not feeling well at all. I shall be speaking to Doctor Rawlinson today to see if we can get her right away until it's all over. Of course, there's been no word from Robert for some time and it's quite natural she should be upset.'

'Poor old Marj,' said Annie, buttering toast.

'After Doctor Rawlinson, I have a hair appointment.'

'See you tonight, then.'

'I'm playing bridge at Leila's.'

Annie, watching her mother drinking coffee, wondered about the telephone calls from Keith or Keats. It was extraordinary to imagine one's parents having sex at all, and even stranger with people they were not married to. Her mother was still a handsome woman, in spite of the extra weight, the increasing puffiness beneath the jaw.

'Why are you staring at me, Anne? Is there something on your mind?'

'Not a thing,' said Annie, 'except that I'm on the day shift and I might be late for work.'

'Not a word from Henry,' Mallie said. She had been on night duty and still she was not ready to go home; her face the colour of putty, the flesh beneath her eyes bruised-looking, almost black. She put her hand against her chest and then rubbed her right arm and shoulder, as if she were in pain.

'Mal, what's the matter?'

'Strained a muscle turning the great big bloke in C1.'

'The sergeant with the leg ulcers in Curzon Wing?'

'Him. Weighs a ton,' said Mallie.

'You shouldn't have tried to cope with him on your own. Go home to bed.'

'I'll be off in half a tick. Your sister heard anything from her husband?'

'Not a line. Mal, I'd like to write to Henry. Do

you think he'd mind?'

'He'd love to hear from you, Annie. He'd be thrilled to bits, I know he would. He thought you were a perfectly splendid girl. Write to him in your lunch break and I'll write mine this afternoon and we'll just have to pray our letters reach him.'

Dear Henry,

(Annie wrote in what passed for a break for lunch) *Things haven't changed much here. I'm loving my work and helping your mother, who is so good to me and has taught me such a lot.*

What more could one say? Henry, please look after yourself and come back soon and get all those qualifications and do better than Sir what's-it Gidney did. I miss you. I miss you and our talks and walks and ... Henry O'Malley, I miss you so. But that would never do.

Look after yourself, Henry, (Annie wrote) *and drop me a line when you get a chance. Marjorie married Robert Harper about the time you went off and he went off, too, after three days' leave. They didn't have much time to get to know each other. Now she's having a baby. Mother and the bridge club go on as if no one's ever given birth before but poor old Marj doesn't feel too good. It's hot, hot, hot, but one does expect that this time of the year and I bet you're even hotter.*

Please write soon and I'll do the same,

All the best, from Annie.

All my love Henry, though I can't say that, not

yet. All the best from Annie will have to do.

But two weeks later—and still no letter from Henry—Annie went on day shift. Mallie, on nights again, was in the sluice room and the water was trickling into a heap of bedpans in the sink and the steam was filling up the room that was already hot and Mallie's thin brown fingers were slipping, slipping, until she let go the sink and fell, fell sideways; lay on the hard stone floor with her eyes wide open and the water went on trickling into the bedpans and spilling over on the floor. And Annie bent over her and felt her pulse and saw her face was blue and screamed.

Two Eurasian nurses rushed in and then one of the Q.A.s and finally the M.O. who pronounced Mallie dead. 'Heart failure,' he said. 'Quick way to go. She wouldn't have felt a thing.'

The M.O. pulled down Mallie's eyelids. Someone covered her with a sheet and they put her on a stretcher and carried her away.

Annie turned the sluice off, stood beside the sink and thought: *I can't bear it, I can't. I can't. She kept having pains, warnings of a heart attack. She kept saying it was muscle strain. She knew all the symptoms of a heart attack—pain across the chest, pain in arm or shoulder ... Why didn't I make her see the M.O.? Why didn't I make her do something? She went on working until she dropped—and it isn't fair. It isn't, isn't bloody fair.*

The Q.A.s talked of Mallie's heart attack. They'd been on duty too, last night. One of them said, 'She had the telegram, of course, about her son.

That could have triggered it off, if she already had a heart condition.'

'What telegram?' Annie shouted.

'After you'd gone off duty yesterday. The Doc was killed, in a First Aid post. We're retreating, so the grapevine says. Hundreds of wounded being flown out of Burma. I expect we'll get a load down here.'

The other Q.A., the one with the drawling accent, said, 'Hellish, but there you are.'

There you are. There you go. Blown up. Gone. Gone. A puff of smoke. At a First Aid post. Blown to little pieces. Was there anything left of you to bury? Was a padre there? Did you die quickly or lie there, in hot sun or mud or in the stinking jungle, bleeding? Did you call out, scream? Did anybody come to help? You will never know about Mallie. Henry will never know his mother's dead. Mallie and Henry, two of the dearest people in the world. I loved them. I loved them both. So much. So very much. I did.

The Q.A.s were making up their faces, chatting. Going shopping in the morning, bed in the afternoon. One of them had the following day off. 'Something to look forward to ...'

'God, yes, night duty absolutely finishes me ...'

'Does the digestion no good at all, supper at two o'clock in the morning ...'

'You should skip it, as I do, and make it up at lunch before going to bed ...'

'I've tried that, actually. Trouble is, I get so peckish ...'

'Ready ...?'

Eventide

'All set ...'

'Let's get out quick ...'

The scent of soap, of their face powder. A door slammed hard.

Annie stood by the sink in the sluice room, washing and drying the bedpans and covering them with clean white cloths and putting them on the trolley, ready for the next ward round.

She washed the huge sergeant in Curzon Wing and dressed his ulcerated legs.

'Gone off duty, has she? The other one?'

'This morning,' Annie said. Off duty forever and forever, dear, dear Mal.

Mallie's funeral; some of the regiment there and most of the hospital staff and 'walking wounded' from Curzon wing, several of them in wheelchairs; and some strangers who had come by train from Bangalore. One of them, a small, bent woman who said she was a cousin, pulled at Annie's sleeve.

'You Colonel Deighton's daughter? The one called Annie?'

'That's me.'

'She would have wanted you to have this.' The woman pushed a small, lumpy packet into Annie's hand and turned away.

'Please wait,' Annie called out. 'Perhaps we could have tea together.'

'I have the train to catch.'

The little hunched figure in black had gone.

In the packet, lying on velvet in a tiny jewel box, was a brooch, the Royal Army Medical Corps badge, with the crown in red and gold, the serpent in tiny diamonds, 'IN ARDUIS FIDELIS' in gold lettering on blue enamel. *Henry must have given it to Mal. Mal must have told that cousin about me. Mal knew, she must have known she was very ill. How dear of her, how lovely.*

There was a second packet wrapped in brown paper; a small photograph in a silver frame, a faded snapshot of a young British officer squinting into the sun, a boy who looked about nineteen. The face was familiar; slightly snub nose, fair hair, features very like her own. Annie removed the picture from the frame and studied it in blazing sunlight. Written on the back, in faded purple ink, were two words: 'Ian, 1919.' So they did know each other, they did, two years before Marjorie was born.

The army retreated, some battalions left with as few as a hundred men. The troops were weak, hungry, uniforms in tatters. The Indians threw away their battered boots and walked on raw bare feet. With them, on a trackless route, went two thousand sick and wounded.

Robert Harper was flown out of Burma on one of the last planes, landed in Assam and was hospitalised in Calcutta, where he underwent surgery to remove a bullet in his back. He suffered attacks of malaria, dysentery, jaundice, raging fevers. He was still in Calcutta when Marjorie's daughter, Lydia, was born.

Marjorie was far from well. Marjorie was too unwell to take notice of the baby. Marjorie rejected the baby, ignored it, did not weep but lay still and silent, indifferent, uncaring. Her eyes looked glassy, unseeing, as if she were myopic.

Lydia Mary was small and neat and weighed six pounds, enabling June to say, 'A teeny weeny bit premature, I'm afraid, but what else can we expect? Marjorie was under such dreadful stress. But all is well. The baby is improving by the day and Robert will soon be discharged from hospital.'

Lydia had dark hair and dark-blue eyes which the nurses said would soon change to brown. All babies were born blue-eyed.

Annie took her niece from Marjorie, who turned away, refused to feed her, said, 'I can't stand that screaming. Just take her and tell them to give her a bottle or whatever they're supposed to have,' and Annie held her, staring into the small, pale face, which had no colour even when she cried; into the large dark-blue eyes which would soon turn brown.

'Not a bit like Marjorie,' said June Deighton-Gaye. 'Marjorie was so blonde—and Robert has red hair. It's far too soon, of course, to tell who she takes after. Maybe somebody on Ian's side. His mother, as far as I can remember, had dark hair but she was quite grey when I met Ian, so it's difficult to tell.'

And Robert, thin—down to ten stone, his florid face a dirty yellow and his back giving him constant pain—returned to find Marjorie unwell and seeing the army psychiatrist. This appalled him. 'So my wife's gone mad.'

Even June was silent; went off, presumably for a drink, and returned with a christening robe across her arm. 'Marjorie is suffering from a depression which is quite usual after having a baby, Robert. She is by no means mad. We'll postpone the christening until she's well, but I thought I'd get the robe all ready. This was Marjorie's. Look, my dear, isn't it beautiful? All made by hand.'

Robert said nothing. Even as his health improved and he went daily to the barracks to a sedentary staff job, his silence was worse than any outburst of rage. He kept away from Lydia. Neither Robert nor Marjorie wanted anything to do with Lydia Mary and a fat, middle-aged ayah took charge.

'A beautiful tiny baba that is needing something of the extra feeding for pleasantly fattening up,' Ayah said to Annie. 'She is a most unusually beautiful bay-bee. She will be growing up most auspiciously lovely. Isn't it?'

'I think so,' Annie said. 'I'd like to steal her and take her to Australia.'

'You will be making exceedingly funny jokes, Annie Mem?'

Annie put Lydia in her cot and bent over her. Already the blue eyes were darkening and looking at her, staring, trying to focus.

Lydia Mary blinked and belched.

'I love you,' Annie said. 'You're beautiful. Why aren't you mine?'

Annie, who had never considered herself a maternal type, began to love, an outpouring of affection which the baby immediately returned. Every day Annie told herself: *I must not get too fond of Lydia. Marj and Rob will get used to her in time. She's their child, no matter who her father might have been. Lydia Mary Harper will never belong to me.* But

Lydia Mary Harper clung to Annie and loved her back. From the beginning, she might have been Annie's child.

Chapter 5

The war in Europe was in its final stages but in the Pacific the Japanese were fighting on. In India the annual migration to the hills was no longer a tradition, could be considered something of an indulgence, or foolhardy. Travelling on the sub-continent was unsafe. Rumours of riots abounded and wave after wave of civil disobedience was reported. Rebels disrupted communications. A train might be derailed, a stone, a rock thrown through a window. The slogan QUIT INDIA was scrawled throughout the city, appearing on the wall of a cinema patronised by British troops, in a side street near the bazaar. Most people on the station, military and civil, were staying where they were unless ordered to another posting.

Lydia Harper had started talking, asking questions. 'Tell me, tell me,' she screamed at them. They ignored her, suggesting a tonic or a change of diet. She was nervy, wilful, spoilt. They told her nothing. They looked at her and looked away, except for Annie who had to go to work.

Lydia refused food. Meals produced tension,

bouts of nausea. Sitting at table with her parents she ran retching to the bathroom to be sick and was held gently by her ayah and then led to the nursery where ice cubes wrapped in towels were placed against her forehead. The M.O. dropped in for a drink and looked her over. The M.O. was in the regiment, part of her parents' world. She cringed when he touched her. 'A light diet,' he said. 'Plenty of fresh air. Pity you can't take her to the hills.'

Marjorie, her mother, said without conviction, 'She will soon improve. This is just a phase.'

Lydia indulged herself in this illness by refusing all food except dry water biscuits. She was banished from the dining-room, confined to the nursery or back verandah. When visitors were expected she was sent to bed.

She was aware of something she did not understand. She felt it, as she felt searing heat and drenching rain. The house was full of it but it was not apparent to visitors. Like some diseases, there were no symptoms. The growth could not be seen, so it festered, undiagnosed, ignored. Annie understood but could not explain. Before going off to the hospital to work, Annie made her promise to eat. 'Just something. Please. Promise?'

'Not blancmange.'

'Then something else. Ask Ayah.'

A disgusting, slippery pudding considered nourishing for growing children, a mould or 'shape' made from milk and cornflour and daubed with jam, appeared regularly on the nursery table. Lydia swallowed two mouthfuls, because she had promised Annie.

'Child, eat, come, eat,' said Ayah. 'Girlie, leaving all the good nice food is not the thing to be always doing. Eat, Lydia baba, and I am loving you. Isn't it?'

'Isn't it?' said Lydia, sticking out her tongue.

'Tomorrow we will be walking to the sea, baba, so eat.'

Lydia finished her pudding and waited for Annie to come home.

Ayah took her walking, to the *maidan* and the *bagh* and the Marina, and along the Esplanade. Ayah made her wear a hat and polished shoes and clean white socks and a cotton dress so starched its collar cut her neck. 'Look child, will you, just look now, isn't it? The Bay of Bengal! You hear me? Eh?' She saw sand, and water, and heard a hushing sound. The sun rose over the sea and the sand was stained dark red and gold. The wrinkled, heaving water with its frill of foam stretched away forever. There were people at the water's edge, washing themselves and scrubbing clothes, soaking their saris and their dhotis, squeezing them, wringing them.

'Why?' asked Lydia.

'Sea water I am telling you is cleaning the person and the garments with the salt,' Ayah said ambiguously. Ayah's clothes were shiny, starched and crisp as the pastry topping of a pie.

It was imperative that Lydia went for a walk every day, early in the morning, before the sun was high. Everybody rose early before heat sapped

Eventide

energy, and the unpleasant, unmentionable sweat began to ooze and torpor spread a glaze of lassitude that stifled, a malaise that exhausted and weakened so the body ached to sleep. Lydia's father was bathed and dressed before dawn.

Ayah held her hand. 'Look, look, child, here is Parry's Corner ... Isn't it?' The walks varied a little but not the conversation. 'There is the Popham Broadway ... There. We must be walking slowly, baba. The heat today is growing to a dampness. It is called the humidity that will be making you feeling tired.'

It was always hot, except between October and December when there was rain. 'Child, do you see where we are going? Isn't it? Look now, baba. It is the Mount Road.'

Three years old and Lydia was learning to read. She spelled out Mount Road and the name stayed somewhere in her head years after she had forgotten what Mount Road looked like. 'M.O.U.N.T.,' said Lydia, 'R.O.A.D.' Ayah looked puffed and proud. She was the shape of a loaf of bread, freshly baked and squashy with a dent around the middle; a dark loaf made with unbleached flour. 'Kiddie, you are a clever kiddie, auspiciously most clever if you are to be comparing with the other kiddies, but what will happen, now, if you refuse to eat? You tell me, child, what happens when girlies angrily and unpleasantly refuse their food?'

Lydia grew thin, pared down to her narrow bones. She liked herself that way. Her rejection of

India, 1920-1949

her meals was the only way she knew to retaliate, to bite back, to scorn, to spit and hurt. Hurt who? Her large and padded widowed grandmother who sank into sofas as though part of the chintz covers bought from the Army and Navy and on which Lydia must never put her feet? The sofas were green and pink, splashed with fat roses exposing spiky yellow hearts. Her grandmother buried herself in these chintz roses, holding a glass of gin that tipped over, spilled, if she fell asleep. A servant mopped up the gin, so Grandmother never knew a drop had been spilled. And wasn't there always gin at hand? Plenty more, along with whisky and sherry and brandy and something called liqueurs. One drink known as a liqueur was deep green and very sweet (Lydia once took a secret sip) and the ladies were fond of it. 'Delicious,' they said, dreamy, as if about to faint. 'Perfectly delicious,' they said, and fanned themselves.

Did Lydia want to hurt, to bite her vague, indifferent mother who once, before a children's party she was told she must attend, rubbed her cheeks with a piece of cotton wool dipped in powder rouge and called her Putty Face?

'I rather liked this yellow silk,' her mother said. 'Well, when I chose it I thought it might do. Yellow throws up a sort of pinky tone. I read that somewhere. Isn't yellow a complementary colour of red or pink?' Her mother pulled at the frilly skirt, frowning, kneeling on the floor. The yellow dress was edged with lace and had puffed sleeves and a sash. 'No. Perhaps I'm wrong and yellow reflects more yellow. Is the skirt too short? Stick legs, oh, dear.'

Her grandmother looked Lydia up and down and turned away. 'Marjorie, my dear, can't you do something about that hair?'

Lydia's hair was thick dark-brown with golden lights and in sunlight it glowed with the faintest tint of red. It was heavy hair, straight, fine, so fine it tangled. 'Such layers of hair,' her grandmother remarked, as though Lydia were one of those long-haired dogs that constantly needed clipping and was quite unsuited to the climate. 'Not coarse, oddly enough,' and once held a piece of Lydia's hair beneath a magnifying glass, examining it as if it were a bug. 'Finer than yours or mine,' she said. 'How odd. I think you had better leave it. Impossible for curls.'

'An Alice band?'

'I don't think so. The face is not suited to a band.'

Lydia's mother let out her breath, a soft whisper of a sigh.

Her mother had pale-fair hair, not as thick as Lydia's but not the kind that tangled. It stayed in place; neat, tidy, as if it had just been brushed and combed. Marjorie, her mother, was considered beautiful. ('How is the lovely Marjorie? Is she bearing up?') Her mother was quiet, except when they were discussing clothes.

'It is the grieving for the great sahib, her father, your grandfather,' said Ayah. But her mother, sent away to school at the age of eight, had not seen the great man, her father, for many years, and when they were reunited their time together was very brief. 'Colonel Sahib was an auspicious gentleman and most mightily important in the regiment,' said Ayah. 'It is a terrible thing that great important gentleman will be dying in such a place called the North of Africa.'

Lydia knew nothing about North Africa and very little about the war but she had already learned to hate—her father (Major Sahib), her pale, fair-haired mother (Major Memsahib), her grandmother (Colonel Memsahib, auspicious widow lady), the doctor they called the M.O. who prodded her stomach and inspected her tongue. But you could not hate a colonel person you had never met, a dead one still held in reverence by the regiment. She had never known her grandfather. Was he horrible like her father, unfriendly like her grandmother, unloving as her mother or boisterous and noisy like Aunt Annie? In photographs he stood awesome as a statue while soldiers marched by saluting him. There was an oil painting of him in the drawing-room, in full-dress uniform that few wore these days, Ayah told her, not now there was a war. There was another picture of him, a bigger one, on the wall of what was called the Mess. Lydia had never been inside the Mess but her Aunt Annie had a good look on Ladies' Day and told her about the trophies and regimental silver 'and those poor stuffed animals, a beautiful tiger hanging on the wall. How dare they shoot animals that have never done them any harm?'

'Perhaps it was hungry and would have eaten them.'

'Nonsense. They hunt them. They can't leave anything alone.' Annie had grown hot and angry. 'The stupid rites, all the damned silly ridiculous taboos ... The Mess isn't a place for females, darling. It is an outdated inner sanctum for unimaginative, blinkered men.'

Lydia did not know what a sanctum was nor what blinkered men might look like, and she would have been terrified to meet a tiger, but Ayah, steeped in the regiment and its traditions and treated more kindly than other servants, answered back bravely, loudly, indignantly. 'Annie Mem, I do not understand how you can say these most unpleasantly improper things and to a little child,' and Annie laughed loud, raucous. 'When the war is over I'll take my Lydie away with me,' she said.

'She will presently be going to school in England, isn't it?' said Ayah.

'Not England, Australia.' Annie tossed her small, fair head. Like Marjorie, her hair was blonde, but darker and wavy and inclined to be untidy. Aunt Annie was not considered beautiful but possessed something called 'character' and 'a mind of her own'. 'Of course,' added people significantly, 'she can be a very silly girl ...'.

'England,' Ayah said firmly. All her charges had eventually been sent away to school in England. It was the only place suitable for an education. Over each departure she had suffered sickening, secret heartache. She was unsure where Australia was but

India, 1920-1949

sensed it to be a most unsuitable place for the memsahib's daughter to be taken by her eccentric aunt. 'Major Sahib will never be allowing such an unfortunate thing to be happening, I am telling you, Annie Mem.'

'As if he cares,' said Annie.

Like Ayah, Lydia had no idea where Australia was but knew her father might well agree to her going there, to be rid of her. Her absence might please her mother, too. Who could want to keep a Putty Face with stick legs and knotted hair who looked terrible in yellow silk and was unsuitable for an Alice band? Her father ignored her. He wore khaki shorts and had red hairs growing up his freckled arms. Her father's name was Robert but he was referred to, even by her mother and her grandmother, as the Major. He did not fight in deserts shooting Germans or in jungles trying to kill the Japanese, but worked in the barracks at a desk, what Annie called 'some staff liaison job'. He had 'limped out of Burma, never to be the same again', according to her grandmother who described her son-in-law as 'such a brick'. There was a bullet hole somewhere in his back. People asked, 'How is the old wound going?' and, 'Does the poor chap's back still cause him pain?' Lydia imagined her father's back, concealed beneath a khaki shirt, as made of brick, hard, red, with a piece scooped out leaving a small, round hole. Annie visited him in his office after her shift at the hospital and they had a drink together at the club.

The Major, drinking a tumbler of whisky and ice

on the verandah, once called her *kutcha butcha*. She asked Annie what *kutcha butcha* meant. 'I've no idea, my love,' said Annie, 'I expect it's Hindustani or one of the strange languages they speak, and I don't understand one word.' Lydia asked the *malee* what *kutcha butcha* meant. He told her it was half-baked bread.

He talked to her, *malee*, the ancient gardener, although she was not allowed to mix with any servants except her ayah. She sat by *malee* among his flowerpots, sometimes in drenching rain. Although he told her little she could understand, she watched, entranced by the movements of his narrow, fleshless arms, the gestures of his double-jointed blue-black fingers, the brown-pink colour of his dry, lined palms. Until Ayah called out, 'Child, you will be coming in at once. What do you thinking you are doing out there?' and dragged her up the verandah steps and inside to the nursery and washed her and dried her and combed her hair and pestered her to eat.

Lydia woke up in the night and beat her head against her pillow. The bed shook, moved across the floor. *Bump, bump, bump*, went Lydia's head. There was a red mark on her forehead in the morning.

'I am telling you,' said Ayah, 'it is stupid to be banging at the one and only head and there will never be another on the way. The day will be coming when it will be breaking open and most unpleasantly there will be some blood. Girlie, I am telling you, you are having a big, red bruise.'

'Tell me ... when I was a baby ...'

'I am telling you, baba, you are about to be asking stupid things.'

'About Mummy.'

'Your mummy is the wife of the Major Sahib, as you are knowing very well, an important, auspicious lady. Isn't it?'

What could Ayah tell her? Ayah did not know or was too scared of the auspicious sahibs and memsahibs to give away a secret. 'Auspicious' and 'important' were Ayah's favourite words to describe the Major Sahib and Major Memsahib and widow Colonel Memsahib, grandmother of Lydia. They employed her, fed her, paid her. The pale-skinned British were her father and her mother, she was told when she was Lydia's age: 'Man-bap'—'I am your father and your mother ...' Ayah believed this even though there were rumours that the fathers and mothers might soon return to the auspicious place from where they came, the place they still called Home.

Only Annie told Lydia things. 'I don't remember much about when I was your age,' Annie said. 'I loved my pony. When I heard them beat retreat, I used to cry. I cried when they played "Abide With Me".'

'The band,' said Lydia.

'The regimental band.'

With Annie, Lydia listened to the band, saw the uniforms, heard the click of rifles, the marching feet. The long burnt day died; 'Abide with me; fast falls the eventide; The darkness deepens ...'

Darkness was thick and purple and rich with smells.

'You like India?' Lydia asked.

'I like listening to the band.'

'Why don't you like India?'

'Imperial pomp.'

'What's that mean?'

'Snobbery and smugness and racism. The bloody British Raj. It isn't all bad, Lydie. Some of it is good.'

'Do you like my mummy?'

'Of course. She's my sister.'

'And my daddy?'

Annie's small, pointed face was blank. 'Poor bloody Rob,' she said.

Lydia was shocked. She knew only the British Other Ranks used bad language, like bloody. She had been told many times that good manners and etiquette were vitally important. It was like playing lines and squares and you had to be careful where you placed your feet; right in the centre, firmly, with courage and conviction that what you were doing was right. Her grandparents and her parents had lived between these narrow lines, behind high walls, shut away in comfort well away from the other people who had nowhere to live at all, and slept in the streets without undressing. Annie took her to see those people, in secret. It was a secret she and Annie shared. Annie hired a tonga or a taxi or drove a borrowed car and they went out far beyond the cantonment and hordes of dark faces pressed against the car and waved and shouted and even wanted to touch them. They asked for money. 'A drop in the ocean,' said Annie, tipping out her purse. To be surrounded by so many dark people who waved and pushed and refused to go away was frightening. Lydia wanted to be taken home but was afraid of Annie's disapproval. 'They are there, there, there, everywhere, millions of them,' said Annie. 'They exist. They are human beings as we are. They are living and they are dying, dying by the day—and we do nothing, nothing.' Annie was not afraid of the pushing people, the dark faces, the outstretched filthy hands, the dirt, the smells. She said, 'We tell ourselves how honourable we are, how they will suffer when we go. They suffer when we're here. We've taken what we can from places that don't belong to us. That's colonisation, Lydia, but never tell I said so. Promise. Promise you'll never tell.'

Lydia promised although she did not understand. 'Annie Mem is a little odd, isn't it?' said Ayah, 'a little mad. Nobody says those things, isn't it?'

Nobody but Annie drove through filthy streets and gave away money and cried—for Annie, a grownup with a resounding laugh, a nurse 'doing her bit' at the base hospital, could cry, and as loudly as Lydia.

'I love Annie,' Lydia said. For Annie she would even eat some food.

'Eat then, for Annie Mem,' Ayah sighed.

Lydia's grandmother did not love her. June Deighton-Gaye, the Colonel's mourning widow, dressed in navy blue or black looked, on social occasions, a different person, a different shape from the flabby woman resting on a sofa after lunch. Lydia watched her, buried in rose pink chintz and swallowing gin. When visitors were expected her back was straight, her flesh held together, pinned, pushed upwards, restricted by iron-like spikes Annie said was 'an Army and Navy Twilfit corset, lightly boned with four suspenders'. Annie and Lydia found this funny. Annie had never worn a corset in her life and was unable to show Lydia what a 'Twilfit' looked like.

When there were no visitors June Deighton-Gaye's face, without its mask of make-up, was the colour of a rotting mango. The flesh hung loose beneath the chin like a soft, squashed purse. Most of the older women had sallow faces, yellower than the people called Eurasians they despised, so Annie said. The Eurasians, the half-breeds, the quarter-breeds, the ones with 'just a touch of the tar' were so attractive, Annie said, but they said 'Cheerio' and 'Pleased to meet you,' which were unacceptable to the British Raj. 'Would you believe it, the way they put up with the way we treat them? Like underlings, but they wave the flag and pretend they're no different from the rest of us. They want to be exactly like we are, God knows why, and we treat them like bloody dirt.' Some of Annie's best friends at the hospital were Eurasian. 'One of them was the loveliest person I've ever known,' said Annie. Lydia saw with horror Annie's streaming tears.

When the Hot Weather ended and it began to rain, it seemed to rain forever until suddenly, in the evening, the sky cleared and turned pink and green and acid yellow, before the flow of water began again. Lydia, the child, listened to the rain, imagined God up there weeping, the tears splashing on a dark-brown face like *malee*'s, although she had already attended church and knew from the stained glass windows that God, like all superior, proper people, must be white.

In wet weather the house was dark and damp. It was the same house they lived in when the Colonel was alive, a 'grace and favour house,' said Annie, 'because Rob will never be a colonel. He'll never go higher than he is.' Only Annie called the Major 'Rob'.

Lydia knew about 'rank' and at a very early age understood the difference between the officers and the British Other Ranks. The uniforms were different and B.O.R.s did not employ a host of servants—cook, cook's help, bearers, *dirzis*, *dhobis*, *malees*, ayahs, sweepers and young servants who ran everywhere and were known as Malee's Boy or simply Boy. B.O.R.s seldom had Married Quarters and never came to tea. They spoke badly, said her grandmother, and they swore. Dreadfully common, most of them, boors. 'But naturally we couldn't do without them. Of course not. One must be fair.'

When the weather cooled around Christmas, invitations for picnics and parties arrived. Lydia stayed behind with Ayah. She hid inside the folds of Ayah's apron until Annie came home from work.

When Lydia was four years old there appeared a baby called Sonia. Everyone was mad about the

Eventide

baby, even her father who had ignored Lydia for as long as she could remember. He was devoted to the baby and so was Ayah. It was a horrible, dreadful, pinkish baby with thin, white hair. The baby screamed, propped up on silky cushions and chewing its fists and bellowing. 'Bay-bee is so beautiful, bay-bee, come, beloved,' cooed Ayah. 'Now, child, I'm telling you, you take care of bay-bee and I bring tea. Hot tea coming, isn't it? I'm telling you, you be careful of Sonia baba.'

Lydia would have liked to spill boiling tea on Sonia baba's red and furious face. Ayah's apron smelled of the baby's soap and talcum powder and its dirty bottom. 'Best beloved,' crooned Ayah to the dreadful baby and sang it hymns. 'Now the day is over; Night is drawing nigh ...'

'Shut yer bleedin' mouth,' said Lydia in cockney, in imitation of B.O.R.s she'd heard yelling in the street.

Lydia was aware as she grew older that Ayah had a sing-song way of speaking that all-white people abhorred. Lydia was reprimanded for speaking badly, for imitating Ayah's accent. 'That child sounds positively chee-chee,' said the Major, and bounced Bay-bee on his lap and sang and sounded ridiculous. 'Mares eat oats and does eat oats but little lambs eat ivy ...'

'Lydie, try and love the baby,' Annie said.

'Do you?'

'Of course.'

'More than me?'

'I don't love anyone more than I love you.'

'Promise?'

'Promise.'

They stood on the verandah as the day died in flames and the band played, the sound swelling in a dusk of purple, of indigo, of heavy air and sweat. 'Change and decay in all around I see; O thou, who changest not, abide with me.'

'Abide with me,' sang Lydia out of tune and Marjorie, standing beside them sipping gin and tonic, turned away, ignoring her. Lydia's face was contorted, wet with tears.

Annie put her arms around her. Annie, too, was crying.

'Us cries,' Lydia said with interest.

'Oh, yes, us does.' Annie picked her up and hugged her and burst out laughing.

On 6 August 1945 the first atomic bomb was dropped on Hiroshima and on 15 August the Japanese surrendered unconditionally to the Allies.

'Where's Annie?' Lydia asked constantly, as she would ask for many years ahead.

Annie worked double shifts at the hospital. The wards were overflowing, with beds wheeled into corridors and verandahs. Ayah told Lydia, 'Annie Mem nursing, isn't it?'

Lydia was five years old and her sister Sonia fourteen months when India's twentieth and final Viceroy flew to Delhi to wind up the British Raj. Lord Louis Mountbatten and Jawaharlal Nehru, soon to be the first independent prime minister of India, were photographed together, apparently the best of friends. The popular Mountbatten wore a perfectly cut suit. Nehru was dressed in his white tunic-coat and familiar little cap. Edwina Mountbatten had become as popular as a film star. 'Such a stylish woman,' said June Deighton-Gaye. 'They both are. Of course, Lord Louis is a cousin of the King's.'

Before Independence became a fact, thousands of Anglo-Indians left the country, afraid that if full-blooded Indians ran their own nation, there might be reprisals. They had for decades clung to the British side of their ancestry, accepting such small privileges as were available to them as underlings of the Raj. Annie read in the newspaper that more than 25,000 Anglo-Indians were determined to make new lives for themselves in Australia, Canada and the United States.

Civil war had broken out in the Punjab. Amritsar and Lahore were smoking wrecks. 'Partition,' said Robert, 'will never work, with the line running right down through the Punjab. The bloody Hindus and Muslims and Sikhs will butcher each other. The sooner we get out the better.'

Robert had put on weight, was red-faced, swarthy and drinking heavily, both inside the club and out of it.

'I'm staying on for a bit,' said Annie.

'You want your head examined.'

'Yes, Rob, but I'm staying.'

On 14 August 1947 Mountbatten signed away his paramountcy and the flag that had flown over the Residency at Lucknow since the Mutiny was lowered, the flagpole wrenched hard from its foundations.

'It'll take a little time to clear things up,' said June Deighton-Gaye. She had plans—England, the little house near Hampstead Heath where her parents, now both dead, had made their base. It had been hit by a rocket, 'one of those nasty V2 things,' and she was waiting to hear 'from those terribly slow and inefficient war damage people. I shall go home and supervise repairs, of course. Naturally, everything will need redecorating. I can't imagine what England will be like under this Labour government. What came over them all, voting for Attlee and treating dear Winston as they have?'

She spoke of the Mountbattens as Louis and Edwina and of Churchill as 'dear Winston' as though they were relations or dearest friends. Aunt Bin, her cousin, had died. This fact upset Annie but left June unmoved. A letter had been sent by Binnie's cleaner.

We was drinking our tea as usual and having a good laugh when she sort of fell forward into the tea cozy of which she was very fond since she has it since in Singpaw. She did not suffer, I do not think. I am popping in once a week to see the house tidy should any of you wish to return now the war is over. The garden tho is overgrown.

With deepest sympathy, D. Dunn.

'What an illiterate woman,' said June.

June Deighton-Gaye was now considerably wealthy. All her parents' money had been left to her. She had inherited a sheep station, shares in the wool business, the mines, three houses and a Pacific island.

Robert, still complaining of his back, faced a bleak future. 'How the hell am I to find a job in England?'

'Oh, you'll find something,' said June dismissively. 'Perhaps the place you were in before the war would have you back. Boots, was it, and shoes? I can't remember where you said it was.'

'Balham,' Robert said as if he was spitting. His parents had been killed in an air raid in Balham, a direct hit on a shopping centre.

'I'm not very familiar with that area of London. I'm sure things will work out,' said June.

'You expect me to spend the rest of my life, with two girls to educate, selling bloody shoes?'

June had had an early morning nip, as Annie noticed, an earlier-than-usual nip. She told Robert, 'I've been thinking a lot about you, Robert, and the future. I sent a letter off to Bernard. He's in oil.'

'Who the hell is Bernard?'

'Bernard Bryson, old family friend in Sydney. I'm certain he'll find you something really interesting in oil.'

'I know nothing about oil, and why should I live in Sydney?' said Robert. 'I'm English, not a bloody Aussie.' He had long given up showing courtesy to

June. She was no longer the C.O.'s wife. The old boy had been dead for years.

'And I shall let you have my house, where Binnie lived, at a nominal rent until you can afford something of your own.'

'I can find my own house, thanks.'

'It's a beautiful house, very suitable for children and close to some good schools. It's quite time Marjorie had a place of her own in a pleasant climate. You should be thankful, in spite of your wound and your aches and pains, that you have married into an established family who can help put you on your feet when you are demobbed.'

'Jesus Christ,' said Robert.

'Don't swear in front of the children, please. Anne, find Ayah and tell her to see to the girls. Immediately, Anne, please.'

'Yes, ma'am,' said Annie. She picked up Sonia and took Lydia by the hand.

'We going to Australia, Annie?'

'Don't know, Lyd, but if you do, you'll like it there.'

'Not without you I won't.'

'I'll come and see you.'

'When?'

'As soon as I possibly can. Promise.'

'What's being in oil?'

'A job of some sort.'

'What's a job?'

'What we have to do to earn some money.'

'Won't he be a soldier any more?'

'I don't think so, no.'

Lydia said clearly, 'Hate him.'
'You mustn't say that, Lyd.'
'Will. He hate me. I hate him. Hate. Hate. Do.'

Rob did dislike Lydia, and it showed. She was bright, over-sensitive. She refused to eat. Often she was sick, soaking up the tense, bitter atmosphere like a sheet of blotting paper in a puddle. The bungalow was sour with hatred. There had been some sort of artificial reconciliation between Robert and Marjorie, who now hung on every word he said and called him 'darling' and 'my sweet'. He was barely civil to her, often downright rude. Even the birth of Robert's precious Sonia had done little to lift the tension, the anger, the boiling resentment that Lydia should be there at all. Sonia was quite unmistakably all Robert's, fair and pudgy and already far too fat. She was remarkably heavy. It made Annie's arms ache to carry her around. She put Sonia on the floor.

'Annie, I'm not going to anywhere,' said Lydia, 'not 'less you're there too.'

'I'll try, Lyd, but I've work to do here first.'

'You could work in oil.'

'Not bloody likely,' Annie said.

'Annie.'

'Yes?'

'Don't swear in front of children.'

'Sorry, Lyd.'

'Don't say sorry. I don't bloody mind.'

June Deighton-Gaye left first, for England, where

she remarried. Her new husband was a retired Scottish brigadier she had met at Ooty. His name was Peter Keating. He had been married but his wife had returned to England just before the war and now they were divorced. June and the Brigadier were married at Caxton Hall and moved into the now-renovated house near Hampstead Heath. She wrote that she had never been happier in her life. She had chosen some beautiful wallpapers and carpets and curtains and the place looked just like home. 'I told you,' Marjorie said, 'I told you there was someone else and he used to telephone her.'

'Sounds as if she's glad to be rid of us,' Annie said.

'That's unfair. Mummy always did everything she could.'

'Did her duty.'

Annie took the snapshot of her father from the back of her dressing-table drawer where she kept it hidden beside the little brooch. *You did your duty, too—but did Mallie make you happy for a little time? Did she? I bet you didn't let her, you with your principles and prejudices and rigid rules. Mallie would never have made a colonel's lady in British India. Mallie was more a lady than Mother could ever be. Mal was a loving, gracious lady to her thin milky-coffee fingertips. But never a colonel's lady. Oh, dear me, no.*

And the old, familiar anger rose like bile.

Annie sat with Robert in the club. He drank whisky, she gin and lime. 'You could get a grant, go to university, make a new career.'

'University? Not bright enough.'

'Stop feeling sorry for yourself, Rob. If your parents were alive, would you go back to England?'

'No.'

'Weren't you fond of them?'

'I suppose I was. They weren't your class.'

She put her hand around his wrist. 'Don't start that class distinction stuff with me.'

'A cuckold,' Robert said. 'Can't you understand how that feels?'

'You and Marj will be all right.'

'If it weren't for the baby I'd take off.'

'Don't take your frustrations out on Lydia. That isn't fair.'

'I can't help myself.'

'She's a lovely child.'

'You can have her.'

'I wish I could.'

'Then take her.'

'You know I can't do that. Pull yourself together, Rob, and stop drinking so much. You're drinking yourself to death.'

'Pity I got out of Burma.'

'Don't ever say that. You were very lucky.'

'Annie—'

'Yes?'

'You're worth ten times your bloody sister.'

'Don't ever say that either, because I'm not.'

PART II

*Australia,
1950–1982*

Chapter 6

Growing up in the sandstone house in Sydney; attending the local school and then the grammar; Lydia, dark, sullen, thin, a 'swot' who must come top in examinations; obsessively competitive, with a driving ambition to be the best; Lydia who loved the sun but was told not to lie on the beach covered in 'that nasty oil'. Her mother asked each summer, 'Aren't you black enough?' Her skin was on the greasy side and never burned, and was slow to turn darker. She was told by other girls, with envy, that she looked tanned all year round.

'Where's Annie? When is Annie coming?' It was no use asking. Her parents refused to discuss Annie or life in India before Lydia was born. Annie never wrote.

'Is Annie dead?' Lydia asked her mother.

'Gracious me, no,' said Marjorie. 'Why should she be dead? Of course she isn't dead.'

Sonia, fair, plump bay-bee, once Ayah's pet, showed musical ability; at four years old expressed a desire to learn the piano and the cello. The baby grand in the drawing-room was tuned and the

Eventide

Major came home with a small-sized cello. Sonia made a terrible sound, banging at the piano keys and scraping at the cello. Marjorie, too, took piano lessons, in order to play accompaniments for Sonia later on. Marjorie had been quite a good pianist when she was at school but it was a long time since she had touched a keyboard. She started off practising scales and exercises which Lydia found excruciating. The music teacher, who gave lessons to both of them, came from the North Shore by ferry and by tram and charged extra for her fares and travelling time. She was called Miss Utting and she smelled of fish, sardines. One of her side teeth was black. The smell of Miss Utting was revolting.

Sonia asked for singing lessons and a bigger cello. Everything Sonia wanted she got. She went to a private school where music was an important subject, a school that had produced pupils who had gone overseas and performed at such places as the Albert Hall in London. The fees were high. Sonia cost far more than Lydia, even when it came to food. Lydia no longer starved herself but her appetite was small. Sonia ate everything put before her and nibbled between meals.

Marjorie made changes to the house once occupied by Binnie. She had the walls painted white and bought reproductions of paintings by Australian artists. Lydia's favourite was a Charles Conder, 'Departure of the Orient, Circular Quay 1888'. Everything was damp, wet, with people holding up umbrellas. There were touches of green and mauve, like a wet-weather Indian sky and warehouses and tall commercial buildings. Lydia thought of the waterfront where Ayah used to take her walking. Her other favourite was 'The Railway Station, Redfern', painted by Arthur Streeton in 1893. It was a street scene, wet and grey with horse-drawn carriages and a sprawl of railway buildings. 'I think I love the rain,' Lydia told her mother in the middle of a drought. Marjorie answered, 'Then it's a pity you keep going outside in the sun and getting black.'

Marjorie threw out the old furniture, except for an antique desk and a dining-table. She liked the new Swedish furniture with bright upholstery and splayed wooden legs. She liked glass coffee tables and electric fires with artificial coals instead of open grates, and flowered sheets and pillowcases and bright 'scatter' cushions and wall-to-wall carpets with rubbery underfelt, springy as sponge beneath the feet.

Like her mother, June, Marjorie was a spender. The Major did not approve of her unnecessary extravagances. 'Who wants pictures of wet weather?' he asked, furious at what the Conder reproduction cost. 'Do you think money grows on trees? Or do you imagine people will think you've bought an original? Who is Conder? Who's heard of him?' Marjorie did not answer. If she liked something she bought it and she had money of her own.

And Australia in the 1950s and 1960s was an age of spending, of buying blocks of land and owning property, of moving into luxury apartments or home units. The masses were now able to save enough for a deposit on a flat instead of renting. Huge tower blocks sprang up with balconies that looked like bath tubs stuck on brick. It was the era of smart kitchens with 'breakfast bars' and gleaming workbenches and sinks and draining boards of stainless steel and mixers and grinders and juice extractors, of washing machines and steam irons and barbecues and outdoor furniture and television sets. It was a rich and lucky country and everyone was intent on enjoying themselves, making up for the deprivations of the Depression and the war. If Marjorie did not appear to enjoy herself or have many friends, or a happy marriage, she compensated herself by decorating and shopping. Workmen ground and hammered; vans unloaded gadgets for the kitchen which looked like a picture in a magazine.

Marjorie employed a builder to extend the drawing-room, so now there was a patio—patios had become popular—where she grew plants. She employed a gardener once a week to help. The garden, neglected by Binnie, bloomed with colour. There were wisteria and jasmine, camellias, a magnolia tree, a frangipani and an orange tree with small, bitter fruit. A high wall kept out the strong gales blowing off the ocean. Marjorie, besides her patio, had a new sunroom extending from the dining-room. It was warm as a conservatory and thick with plants. There were cape honeysuckle with delicate, tiny flowers; and zebras with white markings like fishbones on the leaves, and pale-green calatheas with broad dark-green stripes. The stripes were bold, flamboyant, thick as brush strokes of olive paint. Umbrella trees grew up and up until they touched the ceiling. 'Like a bloody jungle,' the Major said.

'Poor, poor Daddy doesn't like his job,' said Sonia.

Robert had changed jobs several times. He and Bernie Bryson of the oil company fell out; a very nasty argument that almost came to blows. Robert then worked in the public service as a clerk. The salary was poor but large cheques arrived for Marjorie from her mother in England. So Marjorie spent.

June Deighton-Gaye was apparently content with her elderly brigadier and devastated when he had a stroke and died; and she began to liquidate her assets. The sheep station and the house in Melbourne were sold; so were some wool and mineral shares, although she intended to keep her interest in the mines. The Sydney house was given to Marjorie. The deeds were now in Marjorie's name; Robert did not need to pay rent. A few hundred pounds were put in trust for the education of the grandchildren. Sonia must be sent to London and enrolled at the Royal Academy of Music. Would Marjorie please consider coming to England to live? It would be so pleasant having the family to share the Highgate house.

Marjorie said, 'Not just yet,' for she could not bring herself to take Sonia away from Robert—nor

Eventide

would he allow her to—and she could not bear to leave the Sydney house, which was hers by right. It was not Robert's house. Marjorie's personality, restrained but modern, elegant and artistic—so she saw herself—was stamped throughout.

Marjorie was doing what she could to enjoy a little social life in Sydney. She joined the local tennis club and forced Lydia and Sonia to join too. Sonia quite enjoyed the tennis club although she did not play particularly well. Lydia hated it. She did not excel at sport. She disliked anything at which she proved mediocre and she was a mediocre tennis player. Lydia was excellent at English, literature, history, drama and an avid reader; a photographer—when she could afford to have her films developed—and starred in school plays nobody in her family bothered to attend. 'How can you like Shakespeare?' Sonia asked her. 'I can't make head or tail of the silly funny language.'

Her school reports were good, her marks high. Her teachers praised her work, but they found her remote, dreamy, unsociable, and wrote on the end of her reports: 'Not a friendly girl. Must learn to mix,' a point her parents noticed immediately, while ignoring the high end-of-term examination marks. Every weekend she wrote to hospitals and nursing agencies, asking the whereabouts of Annie. Anne Deighton-Gaye, hospital sister, address unknown.

'Mother, you must have an address for Annie somewhere, or a telephone number.'

'How can I possibly have a telephone number

when I have no idea where she is? She could be nursing pygmies in Africa for all I know.'

'Can't you help me find her?'

'Your father feels we should keep out of her affairs and I agree.'

'But why?'

'Lydia, there are reasons your father and I would rather not discuss. Now, please don't mention your aunt again. I've no time for these discussions. I have too much to do.'

'Could I have some stamps?'

'Why?'

'I want to post a letter.'

'On top of my desk,' said Marjorie irritably. 'And please do not take the lot.'

Marjorie sat on committees to raise money for the poor and homeless, to clear the slums, to help the elderly. She arranged fetes and balls. Like her mother, she had an instinct for organising social events. She also believed in 'culture', thin on the ground, she said, in Sydney. She took Sonia to concerts at the Town Hall and to art exhibitions and to the theatre. She invited neighbours in for coffee, when Robert was at work, but never for tea or dinner in case he came home drunk. Robert was drunk most evenings and very unpleasant when he was; rude, with slurred speech, before going off to sleep. Marjorie and her daughters watched a lot of television when he went to bed. Lydia was mad on television plays and serials, wanted to learn about photography and writing dialogue and narrating for documentaries. She still had an old box camera

Annie had given her years before but she had replaced it with an up-to-date model. She photographed the frangipani at several different angles, which Robert said was a bloody waste of money, a waste of film, to say nothing of the cost of having the photographs developed. They all looked the same.

'But they do not look the same,' said Lydia. 'The angle of the light is different in every shot and in one you can actually see the oozing sap.'

Lydia implored her mother to let her join the new television school. 'We'll see,' Marjorie said, and the Major shouted, 'Make her learn shorthand and typing and get her off my bloody hands.'

'I am not *on* your bloody hands,' said Lydia. 'This is Mother's house and we use her money—but I'll get out when I've found a job. Don't think I'll stay here a week longer than I must.'

The Major slapped her across the mouth and she yelled, 'And I don't believe you're my bloody father. You can't be. So!'

Marjorie intervened. 'Lydia, why are you so awkward, so difficult? What an extraordinary thing to say.'

'Where's Annie?' asked Lydia again, again. Just as they never spoke of India, they refused to discuss the whereabouts of Annie. Annie was something unmentionable, like a dirty word. 'I want to know where Annie is.' Exasperated, Marjorie said when the Major was snoring in a drunken sleep, 'There was a row to do with money. Annie behaved very badly. She borrowed money from your father and never paid it back.'

Lydia did not believe a word of this, and she persisted: 'Is Annie still in India, nursing? Or did she go back to England? Is she somewhere here in Australia? She so loved Australia and this house.'

'We have no idea,' said Marjorie. And if she had, she would never say. Oh, but the secrets were still there, hidden pieces of a jigsaw, and Annie's laughter and her crying, her swearing, the dark faces in the squalid streets—and Annie's anger.

'Mum, tell me about India and where Annie went.'

As always, the usual answer, the no-reply. 'I don't know, Lydia, and it has nothing to do with you.'

When she was not at school, Lydia walked. She walked miles, into the city, to Circular Quay where old men dug into garbage containers for scraps of food and seagulls screeched and circled and street musicians, with a cap or hat or violin case open at their feet, played popular tunes. Some of them played quite well, better than Sonia ever could. A few people coming off the ferries dropped coppers into the hats or violin cases. One man who looked very old played a saw, high and sweet. He played 'Abide With Me' and Lydia threw some of her sparse pocket money in his hat and turned away because she didn't want him to see that he had made her cry. She walked to the wooden wharves to watch the big liners berthing and the container ships loading and unloading, and back again along the quay to Farm Cove and the Botanic Gardens where the Moreton Bay fig trees, gnarled and ancient, threw a little shade, their thick roots spreading beneath the ground; and to the stone seat carved out of sandstone, ordered by Governor

Eventide

Lachlan Macquarie in 1816 and known as Mrs Macquarie's Chair. Here his wife Elizabeth would rest while she enjoyed the harbour view. Lydia climbed into the chair and the hard stone felt warm, even in winter.

Winter in Sydney was beautiful; cold, with cloudless skies. The branches of the coral trees were like thin black arms with red flowers growing on the fingertips. Bottlebrush and banksia thrived in the park above the beach and in her mother's garden and during high winds knocked against the windows. Marjorie told the gardener everything must be cut back. 'Those trees and bushes spoil our view.'

Lydia walked on the beach below the sandstone house. There were few people on the beach in winter. The sea was smooth, in calm bands of green and blue until a storm came up, the wind screaming round the corners of houses, blowing dust along the streets and almost lifting Lydia off her feet. Walking along the seafront she had to touch the old sea wall, to lean against it to regain her balance. High tides left reddish-yellow seaweed slimy on the sand and there was a smell of rotting kelp. The sea no longer looked like silky ribbon-bands of blue and green, but turned an angry bottle-green. Stranded bluebottles lay at the water's edge, gelatinous, translucent-white, broken, dying, their gas-filled bladders bursting liquid the colour of purple ink.

Lydia climbed up the steps from the beach and walked along the cliffs extending along the coast to the next bay, and the next. They were steep and crumbling. Their tops zigzagged in and out, like carvings of prehistoric faces; bulbous noses, battered jaws, raw slits of mouths. Where the sea broke and seaweed clung and barnacles, the cliffs eroded, rocks falling, splitting open, exposing the underside of sandstone, pale pinky-beige, flesh-coloured, lacerated, raw with wounds. Lydia stood at the handrail and watched the boiling sea.

At sixteen she passed matriculation and took shorthand and typing classes, for which her mother paid, although the Major took the credit. The first job offered to her was in an engineering firm. She typed about bricks of all shapes and sizes, even new ones coming on the market called convict bricks with imitation thumbprints. This was an architect's idea to make raw new buildings look old, to give character to the spread of housing developments, square three-bedroom boxes that, from the plans, looked identical, as if they were coming off a production line in a canning factory. She typed about concrete foundations, drip beads, outlet pipes, gratings, air vents, air-conditioning systems and tabulated column after column of figures, tenders and quotes and measurements. It must have been the most boring job in the world but they paid her to be bored. The other girls were bored, too, but slower. Lydia made no friends; and spent her lunch hours with a book.

Coming in from work on a blazing December afternoon, Lydia found the Major sprawled face down on the plushy wall-to-wall. *Drunk*, she thought, and went to her room to change and then went out for a walk along the beach. When she returned Sonia was sobbing, her mother, back from shopping—there were parcels on the table—was weeping too. A doctor had rung for an ambulance to remove the Major from the floor.

'Didn't you see him when you came in?' screamed Marjorie.

'I thought he'd fallen over drunk.'

'But didn't you help him up? Couldn't you see he was ill?'

'How was I to know? He's fallen on his face before.'

The doctor and the ambulance attendants looked shocked. Lydia went to her bedroom and locked the door: if the Major should die it would be her fault.

The Major died that night in hospital. Lydia did not go to the funeral. Marjorie was quiet, distant, and plans for Christmas were cancelled. Sonia refused to speak to Lydia for a week. Lydia spent Christmas Day on the beach, alone, surrounded by people playing Happy Families. Playing. Happy Families is a card game that bears no relation to real life. She came back exhausted by the sun and faintly sick. Now, at home, the Major was rarely mentioned.

Sonia was attracted to boys, and they to her. Lydia was a loner, reading, taking photographs, dreaming of what might happen to her in the future when she had saved enough to get away from drip beads and bricks, when she had found the sort of work that would interest her—and she could live away from home.

Marjorie accepted invitations to dances for her daughters: a social life was so important. At these dances to celebrate a birthday or an engagement, the girls huddled at one end of the hall, the boys at the other. Sonia forced Lydia to attend these social functions with her, 'because Mummy worries so when I'm out alone ...' Sonia loved dressing up. 'You'll enjoy yourself,' said Sonia. Lydia knew she would loathe every minute.

At somebody's birthday party in a hired hall Lydia met a boy called William Napier, who actually asked her to dance. Boys had never taken much notice of Lydia, nor she of them. After the first dance he returned and asked her to dance again, and to have tea with him. Could they go to the Art Gallery together? Or to a film? He was an actor who had already played small parts in television and in locally made films. Tall, fair and good-looking with deep blue eyes, he had graduated from the television school and wanted to 'get in' on the production side. *A waste*, Lydia thought, *for a fellow with a matinee idol face. Perhaps he's choosing production because he's not much good at acting. You don't need to act well to play small parts on television.*

Wearing her dull navy chiffon (she felt conspicuous in bright colours) Lydia looked small, neat, pale. The sallow skin was matt with foundation cream and powder but would, inevitably on a warm evening, ooze grease. She knew her face would sweat; it always did when she was nervous. She wore bright red lipstick. Her mouth was too wide, Sonia kept telling her, as if she had chosen it herself. 'It's a slit.' Sonia had what the Edwardians called a rosebud mouth, full, sulky. Lydia studied her mouth, rubbed off the lipstick, put on more. The dark dress made her eyes look black. Sonia wore powder blue with a wired and swirling skirt. The boy, William Napier, appeared to be as nervous as Lydia, and his palms were wet. He had remarkable eyes, the colour of dark sapphires. If men could be beautiful, this one was very, very beautiful. William of the sticky palms was so beautiful Lydia could hardly breathe. He started talking immediately, excitedly, without a trace of shyness, in spite of the sweaty hands. They pushed each other around the wood floor made slippery from chalk, and his voice, as beautiful as he was, rose above the thumping of the band.

'Australian films and television will be this country's biggest assets in the future,' he said. 'And the tourist industry. I want to make documentary films to show the world what we've got right here.'

'Not many tourists will travel to this end of the earth, I shouldn't think,' said Lydia. 'Not just for a holiday.'

'Oh, they will. Distances will shrink as the airlines develop, and they're developing all the time. You see if I'm not right. I want to start a company of my own. What do foreigners know about the Northern Territory, the desert? Or the islands?'

'My family owns an island.'

'Where?'

'Near the Barrier Reef.'

'What's it like?' He looked interested, fascinated,

not by her, of course, but at meeting somebody whose family owned an island.

'I've never been there.'

'You're going to develop it?'

'It belongs to my grandmother.'

He stopped dancing and held her by the elbows. They stood almost nose to nose in the middle of the dance floor. 'Tourism,' he said. 'Boat trips, fishing trips, swimming, diving, looking at the underwater world. Coral. Beautiful. Living. Did you realise coral is alive until people tear it up and turn it into necklaces and bracelets? An island! Gosh! Can we go and look?'

'I don't see how we can. I think somebody lives on it.' What a remarkable idea. Did he mean they should go together, up to Queensland?

'Is it a hotel?'

'I don't think it's as grand as a hotel. I don't know anything about it. I haven't seen my grandmother for years.'

'Where's this grandmother, then?'

'In London.'

'Write to her.'

Lydia backed away, heading for the table with the lemonade. He grabbed her elbow, then her hand. 'Please don't run away from me,' he said. 'I don't often talk to girls and you're so nice.' And Lydia felt like a beast. But what on earth had her grandmother to do with him?

Sonia started to slim down just a little and had a boyfriend. Clive Baird, seven years older than she was, worked for a London-based import-export company. He travelled through the Pacific basin and to the United States and Europe. His company dealt in materials, cottons and linens and Thai silks. He was brown-haired and not particularly tall, about five feet ten, barely taller than Sonia who was five feet seven without high heels and who towered over Lydia. He was pleasant and ordinary with a well paid job—but he was not beautiful at all. He was mad about Sonia, or so she said. She admitted she was very fond of him. He was sophisticated, she said, and would like to settle in London, where she wanted to live herself, she and Mummy, eventually, when she was ready to complete her musical education in England.

Lydia and William Napier went out together regularly. They walked a lot. William was short of money, waiting for his agent to find him something in a new television series. Lydia invited him home to dinner, which amazed Marjorie. Men rarely noticed Lydia. Sonia didn't like him. Far too handsome, she said, and didn't he know it?

Marjorie found him 'enchanting'. 'Such good looks—that fair hair and those incredibly blue eyes. I wonder if he has Scandinavian blood?'

'So what if he has?' said Sonia. 'He seems very uncertain about what he really wants to do, act or produce films or what. At the moment he isn't doing anything at all.'

'He'll do very well in the artistic world, I think,' said Marjorie, 'with those magnificent looks—like a Norseman, a Viking.'

'Producers are always looking for leading men to

play Vikings, of course,' said Sonia with spite.

'Scandinavian, I'm certain,' Marjorie said, under her breath, a remark Sonia found extraordinary. 'When a man like that marries, his children are likely to be blond.'

And Marjorie encouraged William; fussed over him, went twice to see a film he had played in, a small role, so small that Sonia, who went to the cinema with her, only just recognised him. Nevertheless he was brilliant, said Marjorie. Her praise astonished Lydia and Sonia and even William himself.

She invited his widowed mother to lunch and tea and dinner. Ethel Napier was a domineering woman who adored her son. William seemed deeply devoted to his mother. Lydia found Ethel Napier overpowering, terrifying, but Ethel Napier, too, seemed to want this friendship to continue.

Marjorie said to Lydia, 'You're lucky he is so interested. A man like that must have a string of girls chasing after him—and his mother seems to approve. He will do, I think. Your father would have approved.'

'Why would Daddy have approved of William?' asked Sonia. 'Wouldn't he have approved of Clive?'

'Clive is very, very nice, Sonia, ideal for you.'

Clive Baird was mild and friendly with grey eyes and not dangerous. William Napier was dangerous and beautiful. Clive wasn't beautiful at all.

'William is quite dangerously beautiful,' Lydia said to Sonia.

Sonia giggled. 'Mind he doesn't bite.'

Eventide

Sonia and Clive were married on Sonia's twenty-first birthday. The reception was held on the patio and in the garden and Lydia swallowed champagne in gulps and held William's hand and her face was sallow, taut, the cheekbones prominent; her hand hot, when they said goodbye, burning, dry; a fire burned inside her, a blazing fever. And she began to change, grew cat-like, stealthy, determined, consumed by this fever that ate away her flesh, leaving her limp, exhausted. She shed whole layers of skin—her youth—and became a woman. 'I've never had a woman,' William said. 'You will be the first.' She found this alarming; she knew little about men. *But if I'm the first I shall make sure I am the last—and my mother and my grandmother will be happy. Our children will be blond. Not kutcha butcha. Not half-baked bread. When William and I have children they will be Viking-fair.*

William gave Lydia an engagement ring and Ethel Napier announced their engagement in the newspaper. William said there was no hurry about getting married. They both had careers to consider, not the kind of boring work she did, shorthand and typing and filing and dealing with paperwork like writing invoices. She must learn something about films and television.

Instead of leaving home, as she had intended, she continued living with her mother and spent her savings not on a flat for herself—and hopefully for William to share—but on fees for the television school, on drama lessons, on photography courses.

She and William met each weekend, either in her mother's house or his. 'William, we're both too old to live at home,' she told him. 'I don't get on well with my mother. What's the point of waiting?'

William, religious, he said—or his mother was—disapproving of the promiscuity of the 1960s and anxious not to hurt his mother, refused even to spend a night with her. She wondered whether he had other girlfriends and what he did when he went away on television courses and seminars. As far as she could tell there were no other women, and William's mother endorsed the remarkable fact that William had never been serious about a girl until he met her at that dance. 'Although,' said Ether Napier, 'many girls have chased him. Wouldn't leave him alone. He's so attractive to women but William is particular, fastidious. He cannot bear women who throw themselves at men.'

William's friends, said Ethel Napier, were highly educated men, ambitious men, talented actors, photographers, artists, directors, producers. 'You are a very lucky girl,' his mother told her proudly. 'William will be faithful to you. He will be a wonderful husband. I hope you will be as faithful to him as he will be to you. My William is a perfect gentleman.'

Lydia, disliking Ethel Napier more and more, her possessiveness, her smugness, burned with lust, frustration, wondered whether all perfect gentlemen subdued their sexual instincts and treated their girlfriends like sisters until after marriage. She knew perfectly well that they did not, not these days. Sonia and Clive long before they were married stayed out late. Sonia had admitted to 'necking like mad', in the cinema or in the car. Wherever Lydia went she saw couples entwined, clinging to each other as if their mouths were glued. She felt she might be unfaithful as a whore with anybody available (and men, she had discovered, were available, liked her, were confused by her rebuffs) if she and William did not fix a date to be married. William hugged her, kissed her but not in the way that other men had tried to do. He never made what Sonia would have called a 'pass'.

'Why, William? Don't you want me?'

'Of course I want you. I love you. I just want us to get a bit of money together and then we'll go into partnership and work together.'

'I want to get married, William. Soon.'

'Okay,' he said, sweet William with his lovely voice. 'We'll get married soon. We'll fix a date.'

Sonia and Clive lived in an apartment on the North Shore, travelled interstate and overseas for Clive's company and seemed to enjoy themselves. Sometimes they came to stay with Marjorie, who greeted them with open arms, came to life as she never did alone with Lydia. When Sonia was home they went out, playing in a chamber music group or going to concerts. Clive, not interested in music, went to the local pub. But one night, two years after Sonia and Clive were married, when Marjorie and Sonia were out, involved with an amateur quartet, Lydia was at home, in bed with a cold and reading a book on photography. Clive brought a mug of cocoa to her room.

She was wearing William's ring, a sapphire the colour of his eyes. She was looking deep into her dark-blue ring surrounded by tiny diamonds and wearing brushed nylon pyjamas with wide legs and daisies embroidered on the pocket; the kind of pyjamas schoolgirls wore. Clive stood shadowy in the doorway with the hallway light behind his head and his brown hair, his ordinary mouse hair a little paler than the cocoa. 'You are remarkably beautiful,' he said, 'and intelligent and special and somebody should have married you years ago. You need a man.'

'I've got a man,' said Lydia, twisting her ring.

'I could love you very much.'

He put the mug of cocoa on the bedside table that was painted white and the cocoa left a stain. 'Don't do it,' he said and took her ring away from her and put it on the table beside the mug of cocoa. 'They won't be back for hours,' he said and climbed into bed beside her and unbuttoned her brushed nylon pyjamas. 'You're not going to marry William Napier, not this year, next year or ever. I am going to love you very much. I will never let you marry William Napier. I won't let you do it.'

But he let me do it and how could he—my brother-in-law—ever stop me? I married William. Sonia and Clive gave us an expensive wedding present—silver in a baize-lined wood canteen. A southerly blew up on the afternoon we were married and when people threw confetti at us it floated back at them and fell inside their champagne glasses. Their drinks were sprinkled with little spots of colour like hundreds and thousands on a children's cake.

Chapter 7

And then, and then—but then was now; there was no before, no after, just now, now, and it was terrifying. *Like in a train going too fast, hurtling through darkness, stopping at a station with a blue light, a red light blinking, warnings at a station that has no name; and then on and on, rushing, rattling, roaring, screaming on through blackness; like a nightmare, except that you are wide awake. You are pregnant and the child is not Sweet William's. It is Clive Baird's.*

I think of Clive, kind, ordinary, unbeautiful Clive with a funny habit of looking down or sideways, as though embarrassed. He avoids my eyes. Clive is Sonia's devoted husband who came to my bed and told me not to marry William. Clive's face is there, beyond the windows of this nightmare train, in a corridor dim with shaded lights, on a station platform—a flash of familiar features; gone.

And I look at William. 'An infatuation that's wrong, a good that's misdirected. You deceive yourself ...' Who wrote that? I read it somewhere, in a play. Who was deceiving whom? We all deceive each other and ourselves. An infatuation that's wrong ... wrong ... wrong ... Only fools deceive themselves.

Australia, 1950-1982

William knows this child cannot possibly be his but he says, 'So what? I like children.'

'But don't you mind?'

'Why should I mind?' says Sweet William. 'I wouldn't mind if you had six children. You have as many children as you like.'

That makes me cry. He really doesn't mind. 'We get on well,' he says. 'We're friends and we've made our mothers happy.'

'Getting pregnant was a mistake. It just happened,' I tell William.

A beautiful mistake that mattered not a jot to Clive. Perhaps he sleeps with women whenever the opportunity arises—a whim, a passing attraction, like a pleasant day out when the sun shines; or a rich five-course dinner not to be repeated too often because greed is so ill-bred—and Sonia will never know. Perhaps he keeps different women in different compartments of his life. Men can do that, especially businessmen who travel across the world importing and exporting materials, Irish linen and Indian cotton and bales of rich Thai silk. 'Clive is so young to hold down a job like that,' says Sonia. She never mentions that the business is a family one and the sales directorship earmarked 'Clive' from birth.

'Your being pregnant is not my business,' William says. 'We won't discuss it any more.'

We didn't discuss it after that. He never asked about the father. Not his business, so he said.

And so we travel, on terrifying Ethel Napier's money. We are a company backed by Ethel. She has bought William expensive camera equipment with special complicated lenses and reels and reels of film. London first, to see my grandmother, and then Paris and somewhere in Italy where William is meeting a producer he calls Janno. William says he cannot do without me, will never have to be without me, never again. He says I am his friend. 'You are my best friend, my business partner,' he says. 'I hope you and Janno get on well.'

'Oh, I'm sure we shall. Who is he, exactly?'

'Janno Polanski, the entrepreneur.'

Sweet William. Beautiful sweet William. I shall get on with Janno. Of course I will. I will do anything Sweet William wants. Sweet, sweet William who married me.

In London, June Deighton-Gaye looked frail and very old and thin, the puffiness of jaw turned to hanging skin; but still determined, autocratic, insisting they go off without her to see the sights. Except for breakfast they had to eat out, manage for themselves. She had no live-in help and did little cooking—just a few small necessities delivered each week, which had to be made to last. She hadn't entertained since the Brigadier died. But, oh, she managed, she managed perfectly well.

She said pointedly to Lydia, 'I'm leaving this house to your mother. She can sell the place in Sydney if she likes. I know your mother and your sister want to live in London and Clive's head office is based in London with subsidiaries across the world.' And then a very casual tailpiece to those remarks. 'I'm leaving you my island, Lydia. Do with it what you like. It is just a lump of grey rock and coral in the Pacific but you might find it useful, for what, I cannot imagine. The climate is disgustingly hot.'

Lydia asked, 'Where's Annie?'

June Deighton-Gaye shrugged her bent shoulders. She had a hump like a camel's on her back and had lost height. Once she had been tall, buxom, upright, with plenty of surplus flesh. Annie had said the flesh was held up by Army and Navy corsets. Now it sagged, hung loose from chin and neck, from beneath her arms. 'I have absolutely no idea about your aunt. Gone to the dogs, one might assume. Annie was a dreadful trial.'

The Regency house was beautiful, with tubs of spring flowers outside a door painted blue with a brass knocker; and bow windows and a narrow iron balcony upstairs, but the central heating had been turned off since Easter. William admired everything, expressing no surprise or particular interest that Lydia would in time inherit a Pacific island. 'You mustn't talk about things like that,' he said to June. 'Just look at you! Sprightly as a girl.'

Sweet William was a liar.

There were traces of India which Lydia remembered in that house; the tiger skin rug, the table carved with lotus leaves, brass and silver trays, brass jugs filled with flowers. Their bedroom had no heating, not even the smallest electric stove. Lydia slept in thick pyjamas and a jersey and shivered all night long. *William, speak to me. Why can't we talk?* They lay in single beds in a room with Regency-striped wallpaper and matching curtains and all the furniture was heavy, carefully waxed to a deep rich shine. 'Elegant,' William said. 'I like it better than the modern stuff your mother

Eventide

buys. We might go in for some antiques in the future.'

'I love old things, too,' Lydia told him.

'Grandma seems a rich old girl,' said William, shrewd.

'William, I'm cold. I'm coming into your bed.'

'Not here,' he said, sitting up, alarmed. 'Not in the old girl's place.'

'William, love me.'

'I've got a sore throat. Been feeling pretty awful all evening. Go to sleep.'

'I'm not sleepy.'

Foreboding. A feeling of inadequacy. *He doesn't want me, not the way Clive did. Give it time. Everything takes time. He's never had a woman, he said. He wants me as a friend.*

'William.'

He was a hump beneath the bedclothes, fast asleep.

They saw 'the sights' in pouring rain, went up the Thames in a rocking launch; plodded up Oxford Street and Bond Street and round Trafalgar Square and looked at the Houses of Parliament and Westminster Abbey and Buckingham Palace and stood in a crowd smelling of damp coats to watch the changing of the guard. They shivered in the evenings in June Deighton-Gaye's drawing-room where conversation was stilted. There was no television. The radio was turned on once a day, for the nine o'clock BBC news.

June put them up for a week before she sent them on their way, but before they left, she said, she must show them Kenwood House. It was her favourite place in the whole of London and William might find it interesting for his film on stately homes. She knew the curator well and he had given permission for William to film anything he liked. Which was kind, Lydia thought. William had only mentioned once that he and a producer friend had plans to make a documentary on stately homes. They would walk across the heath, said June. It would do them good; so healthy, this spring weather, crisp, quite a nip in the air. She walked very slowly. The nip in the air turned Lydia blue. The wind bit through her jacket, stung her to her bones.

There were trees and grass and ponds and a little bridge and daffodils and tulips and a cherry tree in flower. 'Such a beautiful reminder of the past, I always think. Don't you agree, William dear? What an excellent idea of yours, a documentary film on English stately homes. You must write and tell me when it will appear. I might even invest in a television set.'

She was astonished by William, or astonished that Lydia could have caught a man so beautiful and talented.

William filmed everything, the ponds, people walking dogs, children in a playground. Beautiful Byronic-looking William was charming to Grandmother Deighton-Gaye. 'It's Adam architecture, William. I know you will appreciate it. You simply must see the Reynolds, my dear. I know Australians always appreciate art.'

The gallery—and Sir Joshua Reynold's painting

of Lady Louisa Manners; a snooty piece, Lydia thought; but very sexy, in pale gold, silky stuff clinging to her bulging thighs. *Would I be more attractive to Sweet William if I had bigger thighs?* One hand was raised against her face, the elbow bent; the other, plump with short, fat fingers, held some bronze material that matched the sash and trimming on her cloak. 'Isn't it fantastic, William?' said June Deighton-Gaye, and held his arm.

They stood before a painting of a girl who looked about six years old and had bright red cheeks and was dressed in white with lace trimming. One layer of skirt was lifted to hold posies of summer flowers. The child had tight red curls, like a bad permanent wave. On the back of her head she wore a black hat.

'That's very famous. That's the famous Lawrence,' said June.

'She looks consumptive.'

'Lydia, really!' June squeezed William's arm. 'I know you've been brave enough to marry her, William, but our Lydia, if you can put up with her long enough to find out how difficult she is—well, you're a very courageous young man. Our Lydia has always been a worry!'

They stood before a Gainsborough, stood back, peering. 'Because,' said June, 'you have to stand well away to appreciate the detail ...' As if neither of them had ever been in an art gallery before.

The Gainsborough lady wore black shoes with club heels and buckles and a pink dress with grey lace the colour of cobwebs draped over it and a straw hat shaped like a frying pan. Her name was Mary, Countess of Howe. She stood against a background of violent yellow sky and trees and earth beneath the buckled shoes burnt orange. 'I'll remember her,' Lydia said. 'I like her.'

'I'm so glad, darling,' said June, sarcastic.

They looked up, up at a ceiling that curved like the inside of an enormous tunnel, circles and squares of blue and gold and green and pink meshed above their heads. They looked at translucent marble columns and fussy boudoirs that smelt not of potpourri or dried lavender but of cleaning fluid; and a library with a vaulted ceiling and a music room, all the rooms encircled by silky ropes to prevent the proletariat from coming near, from touching; and then, in gusty wind and the start of a thin, cold shower, an orangery without oranges where chamber music concerts were held in the high season.

When they left June's Highgate house she kissed William goodbye. 'Well, William, it has been delightful meeting you,' and she touched his hair. 'It's quite incredible, your colouring. Have you Scandinavian blood?'

'I don't think so,' said William. 'I'll ask my mother. Nobody's ever suggested that I have.'

Lydia felt him tense, sensed a ripple of resentment. She took his hand.

And then trains and coaches and country buses, weighted down by camera equipment; beaches hard with pebbles; bitter winds; and history. They were steeped in history. William shot reel after reel of film. Lydia took notes. Each night he made her read the notes aloud. 'If you're to be a narrator you must pronounce every word perfectly and speak so your listeners are interested in every single thing you say. You speak well,' he told her. 'Very English upper class. But you must work.'

They made love—or tried to—in a cold bedroom in an almost empty boarding-house. Fumbling. Shy, she was, and frightened. William uninterested, as if he were thinking: get this over, because she seems to want it, need it. She wanted it; needed it. But not William. 'I'm exhausted,' William said. 'Can't you wait until we have less work to do?'

Lydia, too, felt exhausted, sore, unsatisfied, puzzled and totally inadequate. *Is there something wrong with me—or him?*

'There's more to life than sex,' William said. 'There's friendship and working together and affection.'

Yes, yes, yes, William. Yes.

Ham House in Surrey, built in 1610. Marble dining-room, gilt-leather hangings. Cedar tables, brassbound boxes for keeping jewels. Sudeley Castle in the Cotswolds, built on a prehistoric settlement some 4000 years old, or so they said. Katherine Parr lived here briefly in 1548, died here that same year. Hever Castle in Kent; Anne Boleyn stayed here, lived here, wrote letters here. Elizabethan panelling, suits of armour, a plaster ceiling reconstructed in the style of the sixteenth century. And beautiful, rich green country, sodden, battered by heavy rain ...

And now up the east coast to Norfolk; bitter winds, high seas, sand dunes, thick sea mist; thatched cottages and cobbled market squares and narrow twisting lanes and pavements so narrow you had to walk in single file. Blickling Hall with huge fireplaces, tapestries, a moat and lawns and a lake as smooth as slate and the clock tower and Dutch-type gables like pen and ink sketches against a sullen sky.

Staying in country pubs; wooden stairs, low beams, rough hairy sheets on creaking beds; a strange smell, different from any city smell; of damp and dogs, silage, chickens, ducks; bacon and eggs and greasy fried bread for breakfast and crusty bread and cheese and pickled onions for lunch and different regional accents in the bars; old men drinking huge glass mugs of beer.

Lydia scribbled names and dates. 'Everything must be checked and double-checked,' William said. 'Janno will cut and edit and a lot of what we do may not be used at all but we must give him all the facts and details available. You'll be spending hours in libraries.' *I don't mind. I don't mind. I'll spend days in libraries, hours and hours anywhere you say. Tell me what I must do. I'll do it.*

More trains and a Channel steamer pitching, and another slow train (second class, third class?) with wooden seats and people eating garlic sausage. At last, Paris in the spring, and unseasonably cold. They booked into the Pension Belle Louise and never discovered who Belle Louise might have been. Stone staircase leading to a little room with wooden shutters; no heating; remember, this is spring. Moonlight like frost across the cobbles and a neon sign, brazen in red and purple, flashing 'Pension Belle Louise'. Downstairs the concierge coughed all night and spat.

Lydia sat with William in a pavement café, eating flaky croissants and strawberry jam, and suddenly the sun broke through cloud, tepid, thin as watered honey, but warmer, warmer, piercing their winter clothes, falling on their faces, on their deep bowls of milky coffee. Oh, lovely, lovely! Sun! Lydia watched William drinking coffee in a pool of golden light.

And watched William late at night, when the moon was icy, a strip of steel on boulevards, on rooftops, on William's hair. She could not stop looking at William, Sweet William; tall, blond, Byronic, and in the moonlight there was a greenish tinge to his fair hair. He had the body of an athlete, a sprinter, fleshless, hard. She could imagine him a trapeze artist hanging upside down and swinging from a bar without a safety net.

Their room in the Pension Belle Louise was colder than the streets, which now smelt of spring and flowers. It faced a grey brick wall. William's skin was warm and smooth with golden hairs. William's head had a bump at the back which meant intelligence, didn't it? She touched the bump. 'Don't do that,' he said.

William was strong bone and golden skin and beauty and the frozen strip of moonlight fell between the close-packed houses and slid across the floor and touched the bed. 'Read to me,' William said. She kept her thumbed and grubby book of Matthew Arnold's poems beside the bed.

> Ah, love, let us be true
> To one another! for the world, which seems
> To lie before us, like a land of dreams,
> So various, so beautiful, so new,
> Hath really neither joy, nor love, nor light,
> Nor certitude, nor peace, nor help for pain.

'Let us be true,' Lydia said to William. 'Let us be true and honest, honest, William, please.'

William moved away across the bed. 'You're cold,' he said. 'Covered in goose pimples.' He turned his back.

William's back was warm and smooth and gave out heat.

Lydia read:

> Soon will the musk carnations break and swell,
> Soon shall we have gold-dusted snapdragon,
> Sweet-William with his homey cottage-smell
> And stocks in fragrant blow.

Sweet William was asleep.

Italy—and at last the sun was hot. 'We're going to make beautiful films together,' William said, 'you and me and Janno. This is the most beautiful country in the world.'

Secret gardens and canals with willows weeping into cloudy water, and worn-out damp-stained houses with little balconies and geraniums flowering scarlet and washing dripping. Lydia felt starving hungry and her ankles ached in heat.

Eventide

I am pregnant, disgustingly, sickeningly pregnant. William never mentions my pregnancy although I told him. I was honest. I was. I was. He knew but he didn't care. I'm certain his mother Ethel guessed. Ethel was delighted when we married. Extraordinary for anyone of her generation to be so pleased and Mother had no idea, but Ethel Napier was thrilled. 'All I have ever wanted is for William to settle down and have a family with an intelligent well-bred girl who will back him in his career,' she said.

William said: 'You have as many children as you like.' Remember that. William likes children. He talks to children in cafés and in the street; little dark Italian children smile at William and he smiles back and pats their heads.

An *albergo* in Italy; hot sun outside and somebody playing a guitar and the scent of garlic and coffee and William lying there on the bed.

'William, please love me.'

William turned away.

'William, William ...'

William no longer sweet; William vicious. He shouted. He screamed. 'You're like a shark,' he said. 'You'll devour me, eat me up. I can't stand it. You swallow me. It's like trying to swim and drowning in the dark.'

'What is, William? What?'

'Inside you.'

'But you never want to. You turn away. Is it because I'm pregnant?'

'It's nothing to do with your being pregnant. I'm

glad you are. That's good. Good enough for me. But don't ever try to get me into bed again. It makes me sick. Sick, do you understand me? It nauseates me, so don't you ever try again.'

'If you find me so nauseating, why did you go through with marrying me? Because your mummy said you should?'

'Bitch,' he said, spitting. She felt his saliva spray against her face. 'Insensitive, stupid cow.'

And Lydia wiped her face, asked very quietly, gently, 'Because your mummy was delighted to think you'd got somebody pregnant just to show you could?' And she held her hands carefully against her stomach, because he was standing up and she ducked before he could smash his fist against her body.

'Half-caste cow,' he said. 'Devious cow, with a devious nasty family all trying to get rid of you. Your hypocrite of a mother, my God. Her. The elegant Marjorie Harper. She hooked me like a fish to get rid of her half-black unwanted daughter. Your snobby mother must have gone right off the rails in India to produce a child like you. *Like a Norseman, like a Viking, William dear* ... God almighty, what a way to talk. And I fell for it because I was fond of you.'

'Fond of me?'

'Of course I was fond of you. I liked you the first time we met, at that bloody awful dance. I like going out with you, talking to you, working with you. You know I do.'

Lydia shouted, 'I'm not responsible for my birth

or for my mother's hang-ups. I'm not responsible for her prejudices or for the narrow-mindedness of the British Raj.'

'I'm Australian,' he said. 'I know nothing about the British Raj. Don't want to. I just don't understand how you got born into that peculiar family, looking as you do.'

His eyes were so blue, so cold, so bright. So beautiful.

'You think I'm hideous?'

'I think you're rather beautiful. Different. Foreign-looking. I like photographing Asian women. I prefer you to your fat, insipid sister. I couldn't stand her for half a day.'

'You can't stand me, either.'

He looked as if he hated her, despised her, or loathed and despised himself.

'I've tried. With women. I can't. I thought you must have known.'

'No, William. I didn't know.'

'I thought I made it quite obvious.'

'No.'

And now his face screwed up, an unhappy, frustrated mother's boy. He was crying.

'Don't, William. Don't, don't, please. It's not your fault.'

'Get out,' he said. 'Go for a walk or something before I wring your neck.'

The next day they went to Bassano to meet Janno. 'I'm sorry,' he said, 'sorry I said those things. I cried all night.'

'Me, too,' she said.

Lydia cried and a voice sang somewhere, calling

out across the sleeping city under stars. A church clock struck every hour.

They walked through the little town where boys screeched down cobbled streets on motorbikes, careless, uncaring, bold-eyed, stealers of handbags, muggers of old women. Boys gathered on the bridge at Bassano, drunk on *grappa*, scorching, burning, cheap fire-water of the hills made from the refuse of the grape. Boys eyed girls with liquid chocolate eyes. Lydia and William crossed the bridge and looked at the ceramics in the shops, dishes and baskets of huge, shiny fruits, pears and apples and purple grapes and cherries that looked real; candlesticks and plates and bowls and vases. And there were food shops with salami and cheeses and dozens of varieties of pasta and cake shops with pastries bursting cream, and vegetables of every size and colour; aubergines swollen-fat and shiny; artichokes with purple centres and bases creamy like candle wax. Boys and girls were singing. A festival of some sort, it must have been. They drank *grappa*, too. It was like swallowing a taper, a burning torch. And everybody sang and sang.

> Sul Ponte di Bassano
> Noi ci darem la mano
> Noi ci darem la mano
> ed un bacin d'amor.
>
> On the bridge at Bassano
> We held hands
> We held hands
> And then we kissed.

Eventide

We kissed, Sweet William and I, the sort of kiss he would give a child, sexless, pure as soap. We stood on the bridge looking at the shallow greyish water and the willows.

Janno was waiting in a café and singing along with all the rest. He wore a big bush hat.

She knew then, knew for certain what she had pushed away somewhere to the back of her mind, rejecting, because she didn't want to know, to believe what any woman with more experience, any normal woman less wracked with the need to love would have guessed at the beginning. William was homosexual.

Janno was William's lover.

Janno Polanski was, before he took Australian citizenship, Hungarian-Russian. He and his mother escaped Russian tanks with a loaf of bread between them. On that loaf they had survived a week. Janno claimed his interest in food had died in the 1950s, a defect of the taste buds beyond reviving. Most food but grain and vegetables and fish, which he liked almost raw and salted, was impure, and meat disgusting. He drank goat's milk and ate goat cheese and drank *grappa* and brandy and pernod and rough red wine. His neglected body appeared to thrive. Janno was never ill.

Janno's voice was beautiful, persuasive, a dark-red velvet voice; a deep cello voice, vibrating, each word plucked like a cello string or joined to other words as if he spoke through a smooth sweep of horsehair bow lightly drawn across catgut string. He was thin, double-jointed, cracked his knuckles—

a disgusting sound. He had long, thin legs and bent them as if he had built-in hinges at his knees. He had a long, thin body that seemed to stretch, elastic-like, through arched nose and pointed beard and fleshless flanks to long, thin feet in leather thongs; as though his stomach muscles and his spine were joined by a narrowed network of shrunken, ironed-out intestines, leaving him flat, a hollow tin container of a man, undernourished because the body's cavities were too shallow to contain normal solid food. His hair was thin and dark, tied back with a ribbon and receding above a high shiny forehead like a dome. He was deeply tanned and wore oriental clothes—full butter muslin trousers with elastic at the ankles and embroidered jackets and rows of beads. Sometimes he wore gold hoop earrings. He smelt of sandalwood, of dope. He looked like any other hippy but his eyes were never glazed or dreamy, like the eyes of people hooked on dope. His eyes were hard, shrewd, and neutral, the colour of dried-out mud.

Janno Polanski was gaining a reputation as a director, with a devoted crew who accepted his eccentricities, embraced him for what he was and put up with often unfair criticism, put-downs, spasmodic work and sometimes spasmodic and meagre pay. They were a close-knit group, the kind of people Lydia had never met before; shabbily dressed, talented, noisy, self-centred extroverts mad about their work. If Janno backed a production he came out in the black—just. But he needed money. He absorbed William's and Lydia's company (and William's mother's money) as easily as he might have bought a consignment of out-of-date canned goods from a warehouse; cash on delivery. William and Lydia were now his partners so long as they delivered what he wanted and how he wanted the goods presented.

Janno had plans. After the documentary on stately homes and the travel piece on Europe there was to be a long documentary on Australia's indigenous people, on pearling, mining, on Far North Queensland and the Barrier Reef. Australian television channels were interested, as was the BBC. He had, too, contacts in the United States. For years he had been fascinated by the Barrier Reef. Lydia's island might make a convenient base.

Lydia wondered whether her island and her grandmother's wealth—which she had mentioned to William long before he had even met her grandmother—were reasons why William had married her; and his mother, of course, who must have been determined to disprove any ideas people might have had that William was homosexual. Her pregnancy and her grandmother's island were good enough reasons for marrying a *kutcha butcha* girl; an ignorant, confused, sex-mad girl who could have as many children as she liked, so long as William Napier played no part in their conception.

Her feverish, frustrated passion, her obsession with Sweet William flickered out and died; hot coals hosed away, doused with cleansing water. Gone forever. 'It's all a delusion, everything you feel ... An infatuation that's wrong ... You deceive yourself ...' But for years they worked together and were friends.

Chapter 8

Before returning to Australia they went back to London. Janno was to talk to the BBC and to commercial television stations, to literary and theatrical agents, and to attend a conference of scriptwriters.

Janno arranged a voice test for Lydia at the BBC. In a small glass box she read aloud, narrating some of the script from *Stately Homes*, which was greeted with faint approval—'If you can call "quite pleasant, thank you," a sign of approval,' she told Janno. 'They don't go overboard, the English. They put you down in the politest way which is more crushing than downright rudeness.' Janno decided that he and William would both narrate and appear on-screen in documentaries. Lydia would do research and see to location arrangements, accommodation bookings, salaries, expenses and, unfortunately, tax.

'You are so efficient and practical, darling,' said Janno. Perhaps he felt her face not right for the small screen. Viewers might reject the 'touch of tar', in those days still not quite acceptable. What viewers might think of Janno's face was not discussed.

In London he discarded his hippy clothes and wore a lightweight suit; cream linen with a striped cotton shirt open at the throat. He did not own a tie. But he had had his hair cut in honour of the BBC. He kept his beard, a shortened version. Lydia was not sure whether he looked worse or better, but he was still the kind of person who attracted a second look.

William and Lydia, early in the morning—it was now summer and London was hot and grey and stifling—called at her grandmother's house near Hampstead Heath. The plants in the tubs outside her blue front door looked thirsty, half-dead. They knocked and there was no reply. Lydia peered through the bow window and saw the familiar tiger skin rug, the framed photograph over the fireplace of a man in uniform, the second husband, the dead brigadier, who had watched them each night from above the empty grate while they listened to the news; and on the Indian table carved with lotus leaves and flowers enlarged photographs of Sonia and Clive on their wedding day and Marjorie standing beside them, smiling beneath her wide-brimmed mother-of-the-bride straw hat.

They knocked. They rang the bell. A shaft of sunlight through the bow window fell on furniture with a layer of dust. A woman came out of the house next door wearing a dressing-gown and slippers. She bent down to collect a pint of milk and a newspaper. It seemed odd, seeing somebody in this smart street in a dressing-gown, but it was early in the morning and even the rich must collect their milk. She stared, the milk beneath her arm, the newspaper against her chest. She looked in her fifties or early sixties and a little worn, as middle-aged women do first thing in the morning without make-up.

She said in a harsh cockney accent—*which just goes to show*, Lydia thought, *you only need money to live in a smart street like this*—'She's gorn, Mrs Gaye 'as. You relations?'

'Is she on holiday?'

'Passed away,' the woman said. 'Poor dear. Poor old dear. Over a month ago, it was. You the relations that came to stay a while ago? I sawed you goin' in an' out from time to time.'

'I'm her granddaughter. Do you know what happened?'

'Gorn ever so sudden. Went into 'orspital and never got out.' The gilt top on her milk bottle caught the sun like a winking eye; blink, blink. 'I goes to see her in the 'orspital. They did what they could. Private room she 'ad, in ever such a nice place, so yer can't blame National 'Ealth. They operate, yer know, exploration or wotever. They give 'er one of them.'

'Exploratory.'

'It wasn't a bit of good. The liver. Once it's gorn, it's gorn, worse luck.'

'Something was the matter with her liver?'

'Large it was, ee-normous, but yer'd never know, 'er being so thin. Lost weight every week and couldn't eat a crumb. I used to be on at 'er—stop it, I said. You just stop.'

'Stop what?'

'The vodka. She liked 'er drop of vodka lately, rather than the gin. Lonely, she was. I'd just pop in. Lot of empty bottles she left outside round the back, where the bin is, but they wouldn't all fit in. Put some of 'em in mine. Don't care for bottles left about. I explained to the dustmen all them bottles was next door's and I tipped them—well, you 'ave to tip. They expect it, like their Christmas box, although they 'ave that notice on their rubbish vans saying no gratities.'

Gratuities, she meant. 'Tell me about her illness.'

'Well.' The woman shifted the milk bottle from under one arm to the other. 'Well, when I first knew 'er, when 'er old man was alive, that army fellow, they drank gin, plenty of it. Pink. Like they do in India, she used to say. She'd invite me in for a noggin'. I'm not a drinker. Nice lady, she was, your grandmother. Reel refined. Used to talk a lot about India. Must have been orful, when they all got kicked out—in 1947, was it? Used to tell me about the parties and the goings-on. You too young to remember, I expect.'

She looked hard at Lydia, 'You born in Australia, were you? Or was it India?'

'I was born in India.'

'Well.' *Smelling a rat. I should wear a sari. Always wanted to wear a sari but didn't dare.* 'Mustn't keep you, dears. Sorry to be the one to break bad news. A very nice lady, yer poor old gran. Gettin' on. No chicken. If we 'ave to go, we 'ave to go. If it's not one way it's another. That's life. A reely nice neighbour, she was. Quiet as a mouse. Never no complaints. Never 'ad a cross word since we moved in. Used to pass 'er *Lady* on to me.'

'Her what?'

'*The Lady*. The magazine. A bit old-fashioned I thought it was. Remember me mum used to take it. Respectable, not like some of 'em today. The ads were good, 'oliday 'omes and boarding 'ouses and au pairs and nannies wanted, that sort of thing, and a recipe or two. And the knitting. It was the adverts that caught the eye.'

She sighed, pulling the dressing-gown across her chest, clutching the milk bottle which looked unsafe, about to smash into pieces outside her door and make a mess. That wouldn't do at all. Spilt milk is difficult to wipe up, far messier than getting rid of empty vodka bottles.

'See you again, I expect. The solicitor 'as a key. She didn't give one to me. A very private type of lady. You want to go inside?'

'No, thank you. We're going back to Australia soon and we've a lot to do before we leave.'

'I dunno,' she said. 'India, Australia. We go to Devon every year. Dawlish. Been goin' there now for years. Never leave England, we don't. Can't see why people go mad about abroad. These days they're all goin' to Spain. For the sun. Can't see anythink the matter with our climate. Been a lovely summer, once it got started proper. Suddenly got all nice an' warm.'

Lydia looked into a sultry sky that held a touch of yellow. The pavement felt hot beneath her feet.

She fumbled in her shoulder-bag for money. 'Let me settle up with you for the tip you gave the garbage men.'

'The wot?'

'Dustmen.'

'Wouldn't dream of takin' it,' she said, outraged. 'It's the least a person can do for a neighbour that's passed away,' and she looked at Lydia's stomach.

'You expectin'?'

'Yes.'

'Best of luck. Sorry about your gran. Deepest sympathy and all that.'

She went inside her house and shut her door. They were aware of her watching them through nylon curtains.

'We can take a taxi,' William said.

'But we always go everywhere by tube.'

'I don't know how long probate takes, but you'll soon be rich. We'll go mad and take a cab.'

'Of course I won't be rich.' *I wish I could feel sorry, that I could grieve for my grandmother. I feel nothing, nothing at all. But I remember; the bungalow in India and the parties, the chintz sofas with pink roses and the glass of gin and the way she used to look at me, telling my mother to do something about my hair.*

'You'll own an island.' William took her arm. 'Think of all that lovely coral.'

'I don't think we should start dreaming about coral yet.'

'Come on, Lydia. She was a dreadful old bag. I knew she drank. Held it pretty well, I'll say that for her. Didn't fall about.'

'She never smelt of drink, not when we were staying.'

'Vodka doesn't smell.'

'Doesn't it? I didn't know.'

'You don't know much, dearie.' His silly voice; his getting-round-her, facetious voice.

No taxis. They took a bus and then the Underground. The train was packed—people going to work, tourists with rucksacks and suitcases. Other people's luggage scraped her ankle, their elbows dug her bulging stomach. There were no seats, no floor space. It was airless, hot. The train stopped in a tunnel. Outside the windows, a wall of black until another train with lighted windows packed with faces behind newspapers rushed past. A nightmare, another nightmare. Lydia grabbed the strap above her head and shut her eyes.

Clive and Sonia were on a business trip together; a business trip for Clive and a shopping spree for Sonia; Bangkok, Singapore, Hong Kong, London and a week in Ireland, looking over some flax factory in Belfast. 'Wonderful Sonia has had a chance to see the world,' said Marjorie. The sandstone house in Sydney, with its patio and modern kitchen and spongy carpets had a FOR SALE notice outside. Marjorie was moving as soon as possible into her mother's London house. William and Lydia rented a flat that Marjorie considered 'a bit dark and old-fashioned and no garden or ocean view. I wouldn't want to live in it myself. I don't think I would like living in a flat.'

'You've never lived in one,' said Lydia, tart.

But it was big and had five rooms so Lydia could use one of them as an office and there was a small bedroom which would do for a nursery. Outside, in a narrow courtyard, a eucalypt grew high, blocking out the light, its dusty silvery leaves shaking, rustling. It gave out a faint medicinal scent. Marjorie, packing up, wrapping newspaper around dishes and pictures and glass and placing them in containers, said casually, 'You and William could have lived here, you know. I'd have leased it to you. Too late now, but it would have been preferable to that depressing flat.'

'I quite like the flat.'

'Eventually Sonia and Clive will buy a place in London big enough for a growing family.'

'They haven't got a family.'

'They're hoping for at least four children.'

Oh, Clive, Clive Baird, the family man who walks into his sister-in-law's bedroom with a mug of cocoa and makes love to her, makes love like mad with his wife's sister.

'I thought Sonia wanted to be a professional musician. I thought the whole idea of going to London was her musical career.'

Marjorie said, 'Sonia has changed her mind about the academy. She wants to be a wife and mother, and that's exactly what Clive wants her to be. She will join an amateur orchestra or chamber music group and a choral society, no doubt. London has so much to offer. Clive doesn't want his wife to work. He believes he should be the sole breadwinner and I entirely agree.'

'But if she's mad on music it wouldn't be like work.'

'Work is work,' said Marjorie. 'Sonia and Clive have decided that careers and motherhood just don't mix, and there is much evidence of that.'

'What evidence?'

'Statistics.'

'Statistics?' said Lydia.

'The divorce rate is rising all over the Western world, especially now these new laws are coming in, the no-fault divorce. They will make things easier for the promiscuous.'

'Why should working wives be promiscuous?'

'Propinquity,' said Marjorie crisply. 'I've never worked since I was married. One hears of so many broken marriages. And not just in America. I don't mean Hollywood and people like that. Everywhere. Sign of the times, an unfortunate sign. Women are leading such selfish lives, marching about and protesting. So stupid and unnecessary, and just look at them—badly dressed, unwashed. No wonder no man would look at them. They've only themselves to blame. I've been very lucky. My marriage lasted until the Major's death.'

And how!

'Will Sonia and Clive live near you, Mum?'

'Not too far away. Clive has his eye on a house in a place called Gospel Village, or is it Gospel Oak? There are some lovely old houses in an area that is coming up.'

'You mean it used to be a slum.'

'Several suburbs of north London that used to be considered slums are now being cleared and the houses are being bought and beautifully renovated by professional couples. Delightful little corner, Gospel Village, quite countrified. And so nice and near the heath.'

Lydia imagined Sonia pushing a pram across that freezing heath, a string of toddlers behind her; children pink-cheeked, overfed, strong like Sonia, an outdoor family who never felt the cold.

'Do you think you'll ever come back to Australia, Mum?'

'For a holiday, perhaps. You and William can always come and stay with me, and the baby, of course. You must send me photographs immediately it's born.'

Big colour photographs so you can see the colour of its skin? 'We have a business to run.'

'Ah, yes. When I've sold this house I'll put some of the proceeds into your business, Lydia. I feel I must. William's mother has been such an enormous help.'

'You don't need to give me money, Mum.'

'It's your grandmother's money. She would have wished her savings and investments to be distributed round the family. She was always very fair. And remember, she has left you her island. I think that was very fair.'

'You wouldn't want an island on the Barrier Reef and nor would Sonia.'

'That, Lydia, is not the point. I am merely emphasising that in her will your grandmother has been generous and fair. I think you might at some time go up there and investigate its possibilities. A nice hotel, perhaps, a holiday resort? I'm sure you will manage to turn it into a going concern.'

'What do I know about hotels and holiday resorts?'

'You could turn your hand to most things, if you tried.' Spoken grudgingly, resentfully.

'Mum, why do you have to go to London now?'

'I want to help Sonia settle in. It's a big step for a young wife, moving to the other side of the world. And they want me to house-hunt with them.'

Next month I shall have a baby. Isn't that a big step, too? Don't you want to help me settle in? Don't you want to help me adjust to being a mother?

No. You never adjusted to being a mother yourself, not to me. Sonia was different. Sonia was the prize.

'Mum, why won't you tell me who my father was?'

And Marjorie wheeled around, holding in her hand a Chinese vase, one of her clever buys at a recent auction.

'Lydia, I am so tired of your ridiculous questions. You have been asking silly questions like that for years. The Major was your father, as he was Sonia's father. He was my husband. Would you like some of my pictures, Lydia?'

Not the rose prints or the watercolours of the Sussex Downs; or the photographs of Sonia or the Major; or the wedding pictures, Sonia and Clive, William and me. No thanks.

'I thought you might like the Conder and the Streeton.'

Yes. I would. I would. 'Don't you want them, Mum?'

'I've grown bored with them. I'm rather fond of change.'

Lydia hung the Conder and Streeton reproductions in the big, bare flat. Wet weather; umbrellas, cloudy skies. Every time she looked at them they gave her a sense of contentment, of joy. *My mother remembered I love the Streeton and the Conder. She remembered. And I remember when she bought them and the Major made a scene. My mother has given me two of her favourite pictures. She must care just a bit, a little bit. I like to believe she cares just a little about me.*

William and Janno were away on location; Ballarat and Bendigo and Castlemaine, the old Victorian gold-mining towns; to Portland to film the seaport and its ancient inns and through South Australia, to Port Augusta and Port Pirie, and across mile after mile of spinifex to the dry red sand and the opal mines at Coober Pedy; on to Ayers Rock and the Olgas and to Alice Springs, where the Todd River is a bed of dried-up mud. They sent her postcards and she followed their journeys on the map. 'Who says we haven't any history?' wrote William. 'The bloody Brits, of course. They're not the only ones with stately homes and museums and art galleries. I think what we're doing will bring them here in droves, and the Yanks as well. Keep in touch with Imogen Smythe, will you? And give her all our love.'

Imogen Smythe was an out-of-work actress, once a member of Janno's crew, with a face well-known from advertisements for toothpaste. She visited Lydia almost every day, brought fruit and flowers and wine and if they watched television together went into hoots of laughter at herself, a woman in a bathrobe cleaning her teeth and with a rapturous, gleaming smile, proclaiming, 'Fame! Fame fights caries. Fame is recommended by dentists for guarding against decay!'

In the flesh Imogen looked little like the beaming beauty in the toothpaste commercial. Broad, tall, with short shiny hair the colour of horse-chestnuts, she wore faded black stretch jeans in which, she said, one could travel the world in comfort without betraying the fact that the bottom half of one's body was too big and square to match the top and that one's legs were on the thick side. With her jeans she wore silk shirts faded from many washings and a frayed denim jacket slung across her back. Out of work, 'resting' she might be, but she was happy, radiantly theatrical; talked rapidly and incessantly and smelled deliciously expensive; French scent, of course, she would explain to Lydia, bought in better days when producers sought her out and offered jobs; or presents from ex-husbands with whom she remained firm friends. Imogen had two ex-husbands and four children, lived in a decayed weatherboard house round the corner from the block where Lydia lived with William and earned a little money from running a private child-care centre and looking after hordes of other people's children besides her own.

Such warmth and affection were difficult to resist. She and Lydia became friends.

'Of course, I simply adore your William, and

Janno is one of my very favourite people. If they ever get the backing for a feature film I know they won't forget me. They're not the sort to forget their friends. They really are the dearest people—and so are you, Lydia darling. When you've had this baby we'll all have a terrific time.'

Doing what? Lydia wondered, looking at the company's expenses, attempting to keep the neglected books. *Where, where does all the money go?*

It was Imogen, frank, tactless (or trying to be helpful?) who explained where some of the money went. 'Darling, now you and William are married I do feel you should keep an eye on him, a very careful eye. You don't want the company to go broke and it does happen, oh, dear me, yes, it happens.'

'You mean they're fiddling tax?'

Imogen pushed at her ruffled auburn hair, twisted her fingers together, then waved both arms. 'Darling Lydia, please don't be offended but I have known them both for many years. You must keep William away from gee-gees.'

'From what?'

'From the horses, sweetie, from the racecourse. He can't help it. It's a bit like drink. Some people just can't help themselves. There's been quite a bit of research done lately. Doctors now look on it as a disease.'

'Putting a bit of money on a horse is a disease?'

'If you can't stop it is. You see, they tell themselves they're doing it to help their business or their families. They kid themselves they'll stop tomorrow—like people trying to give up grog or drugs. And the government does absolutely nothing because of all the revenue it gets from gambling. There've been suicides, you know, and it's all swept under the carpet because nobody wants to know.'

'William is hooked on gambling?'

'Addicted. Addicted is the term, but I believe he's been a bit better since knowing you. And the company is on its feet, isn't it? Since William's mother and your mother helped. I mean, Janno's taken both of you as partners. Before you came along, Janno thought the world of William, of his work, and William is absolutely, absolutely brilliant, but Janno doesn't like taking risks.'

Imogen's arms stopped waving. Her hands were folded in her lap. 'Perhaps I shouldn't have told you, Lydia.'

'I'm very glad you did.'

'Don't mention I said anything. I'm certain William's mother doesn't know.'

'I won't say a thing.'

'And now William's married and you're going to have a family, life will be quite different. He'll be leading a proper normal life.'

Not quite he won't, and nor will I.

Lonely. I have never lived alone before. The half-empty, high-ceilinged rooms of this old block ring with emptiness and I miss listening to the sea, to wake up in the night and hear the tide. When Imogen has left, noisy, so talkative she wears me out, and her scent hangs in the air after she has gone; after the security doors downstairs have clanged behind her, it is lonely. I switch on lamps, beautiful ones given me by my mother from the old sandstone house. I sit on the sofa (my mother almost threw it out) and look at the Conder and the Streeton. I clean and scrub—they call it the nesting instinct—and when the waters break, at four o'clock in the morning and the bed is soaked and there is a trace of blood I ring for the ambulance and go to hospital alone, with bath towels wrapped round me to smother the water leaking from my swollen body.

And it is now very, very lonely; all alone; strange faces with razors and measuring instruments and rattling trolleys and in the receiving ward the woman beside me groans. This is a very animal procedure, undignified. The other women have husbands and mothers and sisters waiting outside but I have no one and perhaps that is the best way, because nobody can help you but yourself; but when they've shaved me and peered at me and told me to have a bath, they leave me alone beside this groaning woman who does not notice I am there lying on a bed beside her, and the loneliness is terrifying. I want to run away, run and run; but run where in a hospital gown with a grotesque, distorted, leaking body? When it all starts in earnest and they wheel me into the delivery room I will not shout and scream like some of them. I grunt till my throat is sore and stare at a big round light in the ceiling and I won't scream, I won't, won't, won't, although it feels like boots with spikes dancing on your back and then as if your body will tear, break in half; it is like being on a rack and tortured, and they bring sheets and towels so you cannot see the blood but you can smell it; blood has a most peculiar smell. And then they say just a few more pushes—we can see the head—and I ask very calmly, 'Is it dark or fair?' and somebody answers, 'Fair, I think, but it's hard to tell.' The gas and air they give doesn't work with me and I push the rubber thing aside and push and push and grunt and at the very end they put me out and just before they do I call out, 'Annie!' I know I did, because afterwards one of the nurses asks, 'Is your sister called Annie?' And I say, 'No, Annie is my aunt.'

They roll me on my side and show me Adam who is lying on a sheeted table beside the bed. I chose that name. Adam is my favourite name. I touch him, his face, his bloodied head. I say, 'Hallo.' They take him away to wash him and strap my legs for 'just a little stitching'. More indignities. Imagine my mother and my grandmother putting up with such a messy, basic carry-on. This is procreation. This is the way the world goes on. The Lord might have thought up a pleasanter way, less primitive. Adam has ripped me wide open. Adam has fair hair.

I think: I must write and tell my grandmother Adam is fair-haired, fair-skinned, not a bit like me, and she may believe that at last I have done something right and proper. At last! At last! And then I remember my grandmother is dead.

When it is all over and I am in a ward with two lines of beds containing what looks like dozens of other women, I start to cry. It is impossible to stop. They tell me this is perfectly natural and may go on for a day or so and won't it be lovely when my husband visits? They have rung the flat but there was no reply.

'I think he's in the Red Centre somewhere,' I tell them. 'He makes films.' They find that fascinating. 'Ooh,' they say, 'what fun.'

Chapter 9

Adam loved her, at the start he did, trusting, all-dependent, needing her, wanting her, following her with his eyes, turning his head; questioning: *don't leave me; don't go away*. Frightening, this primitive love, this clinging to the womb that had discarded him in a short nine months. His needs went beyond the physical. He was comfortable, clean, fed. Lydia found, surprisingly, that domestically she was quick, competent, organised. His emotional needs were harder. She had to work.

'Imogen, they want me to go to Broken Hill with them. Will you have Adam?'

'Any time, any time,' cried Imogen, ecstatic.

'Im, I've got to fly up to Proserpine and then catch the launch to the island. The launches only run twice a day. It'll be a dreadful rush. I can't possibly take Adam.'

'Of course you can't take him, darling. He'll be exhausted, poor lamb. Leave him with me. He loves staying here with all the other kids.'

Imogen, arms wide open; Mother Earth.

The island; Nodding Blue Island it was called. In the poor sandy soil the nodding blue lily used to grow. Now the vegetation was sparse, the coral dying. The island, from the water, looked uninhabitable—a grey lump of rock, of wasting coral, like hollow lumps of coke, slag-heaps of coral clinkers. A jetty, warped, creaking, thrust a heaving finger into a brilliant sea. Lydia walked up an uneven path to find the house; saw peeling paint, a sagging roof and a line of wooden cabins partly concealed by exhausted palms, deformed, colourless, dried out, dying of thirst. In hot, steamy silence insects hummed, a butterfly landed on a patch of dry grass, poised, lifted, flew away. The departing launch blasted its hooter and Lydia jumped. The door of the main building hung open on a broken hinge.

Inside, a large room that must have been a kitchen, with a broken stove, a sink piled with cracked, unwashed crockery and bent knives and forks and a wooden draining-board black with ants. Rubbish. Stacks of rubbish bulged out of plastic bags and swarmed with flies. A gap in the ceiling exposed a slice of sky and a tin bucket stood beneath the gaping hole, with the remains of stagnant water at the bottom. A broken golf club; several dirty, very ancient saucepans; a frying pan coated with grease and mould; empty baked bean cans; a comb with broken teeth; half a red bikini hanging on the stove. And dozens of beer cans, crushed by an unknown fist, and a wine flagon, lying on its side and several more flung in a corner; cigarette stubs and empty packs of cigarettes and a broken radio; a dirty hairbrush holding long dark hairs. And silence except for the buzzing flies. Eerie.

Who stayed here? Hippies? The drawling, sun-baked Queenslander driving the launch told her that fishermen had once rented cabins on the island, but nobody went there now. Nobody had been seen for months. There had been rough types, squatters, some time ago. His company delivered supplies to other islands, but never stopped at Nodding. No point. No holidaymakers asked to be put off at a broken-down wreck with nothing to look at, no amenities, not even a café. He would pick her up later in the afternoon on his way back to Proserpine.

Lydia, thirsty (the water had been turned off, if there ever had been much water) and feeling slightly sick, sat on the sagging verandah and smoked. Smoke, she thought, might keep away the flies but flies still swarmed round her, sticking to her T-shirt, creeping round her eyes. Dirt. Decay. Heat. Smells. No wonder nobody wanted this place. No wonder her grandmother had left it to her. Someone had to have it. Lydia would do. She could develop it or sell it. Who cared? Who had ever cared about Lydia? Only Annie, who had disappeared.

Now don't you go feeling sorry for yourself, Lydia Napier. Get going and think.

She walked round the island, looking out for snakes. There were little paths, slight hills where the view of the sea was beautiful. Everything was dry, scorched.

She went down to the wharf, sat smoking, waiting for the launch to take her back to the mainland.

The island had possibilities; grey, gaunt, wasted, a clumsy, shapeless lump rising from a glittering sea into blazing, brassy picture-postcard sky. She visualised healthy palms and coloured lights, a dance floor, tables with bright umbrellas; good food, wine, a band, seafood sizzling in garlic sauce, pineapples and pawpaws, mangoes, fresh, luscious fruits and vegetables arriving daily on the launch, and tourists tanned and happy with bulging wallets. Why not, even if the nodding blue lilies had disappeared? *People will come here. Of course they will. The Great Barrier Reef is one of the wonders of the world and one little piece is mine.*

Back in Sydney, Adam turned away from her, wound his arms round Imogen's legs, clung to Mother Earth. 'Oh, please let him stay,' said Imogen.

The first words Adam said were, 'I loves Im.'

Quotations from builders, plumbers, electricians, were exorbitant. The bank manager, willing, like most bank managers at that time, to lend money for business enterprises, demanded security, collateral. Lydia had had money of her own, money placed in trust for her and for Sonia by her grandmother for educational purposes. Sonia's had been spent on music lessons but Lydia's had been barely touched. She had put it into the business. But like the money invested in the company by Marjorie and by Ethel Napier, it had been spent; vanished.

'Films are expensive,' said Janno in his most velvet voice. 'You should know that by now.'

Lydia sat at the kitchen table with bank statements and a calculator. 'One doesn't start a business for fun.'

'And one doesn't expect to make a profit from the arts,' William told her sourly. 'My mother isn't asking for a return on her investment.'

'And nor is mine, but I want some money for the island.'

'Your island,' said Janno, 'will have to wait.'

She often thought about her island; deserted; a lump of rock and coral, frying, dying in the sun.

Adam grew broad-shouldered, stocky, fair hair darkening to mouse-brown; an ordinary-looking boy with a violent temper. Pre-school teachers found him unmanageable, aggressive, violent with other children, who avoided him. William ignored him. 'He's nothing to do with me, thank God.'

'Everybody thinks you're his father, William. Your mother loves him.'

'She does not. She finds him impossible. So do I. Janno can't stand the sight of him.'

'You'll have to help me look after him in the holidays when Imogen's away. She's closing the day centre for two weeks.'

'So Janno and I have to have that monster.'

'You want your scripts typed, don't you? I haven't finished the one on pearling. I'm a month behind. I can't work when Adam's here.'

Adam wrecked what little furniture they possessed. He tore up manuscripts, bashed his fists on Lydia's typewriter. He screamed.

Sweet William of the deep-blue Viking eyes had a look like flint, and Adam stuck his tongue out and then smiled and looked away, looked down and sideways; Clive Baird in miniature.

Unmistakable. *Are mannerisms inherited? Is it possible that Adam can inherit mannerisms from a man he has never seen?*

William, who had said how fond he was of children, had patted Italian children on the head and smiled at them and teased them, avoided Adam. 'Thank Christ,' he said, 'you only had the one.'

Work was time-consuming. The documentary on pearling took six months, a film on gemstones eighteen months. Lydia seldom accompanied the company on location now, but they sent her notes to decipher, on amethyst and beryl and topaz, on turquoise and tiger-eye, on opal matrix from Andamooka in South Australia and matrix opal from Queensland. 'Do not mix these up,' they wrote.

There were pages and pages on simple cuts for transparent gems—standard brilliant, half cut or 'chaton', drop, octagon or emerald cut, marquise ... 'Any inaccuracy of angle or position of any facet on the stone can cause a diminution of the total light ...'

'Get on, Lydia,' they said, standing over her while Adam screamed. 'Get *on*. It's easy enough. It's only a draft narration. All you have to do is simplify what we've given you for the semi-educated masses who like finding or buying gems. Preferably finding them, for free.'

'The masses are our bread and butter, if we had any.' Lydia, like Adam, banged her fists on the typewriter and yelled, 'Leave me alone.'

Imogen told her, 'Everything will work out. Just wait and see.'

Adam grew fast, a difficult personality, noisy, restless; at times sullen, sitting on the sofa swaying, backwards, forwards, making an odd humming sound. Then again the restless energy would begin, body on the move, legs kicking, arms swinging. Janno bought him roller-skates. 'No,' Lydia said. 'He'll kill himself or somebody else.'

'You're too protective,' said Janno. 'He can take them to Imogen's backyard.'

On the way to Imogen's, Adam clattered ahead of Lydia, went faster, faster. Lydia tore after him, shouting, 'Stop!' Just before he reached a set of traffic lights Adam knocked down an elderly woman who was waiting for the lights to change. The woman fell heavily and broke her wrist. She was taken to hospital by ambulance. Lydia went with her with the screaming Adam, the roller-skates in the gutter.

The woman said she was sixty-five years old and had broken a wrist before. Her bones were brittle. She was a kindly woman who disliked trouble. 'Had five of my own,' she said. 'My grandson skates. I think they should be banned. Lucky for me the other grandchildren are girls.' No further steps were taken.

Lydia shouted at Adam. 'How many times did I tell you not to skate except at Imogen's?'

'Fuss, fuss,' said Janno, in the flat as usual with amendments to a script. 'If old women can't see a boy approaching on roller-skates, they shouldn't be let out.'

'She was waiting to cross the street—and he should respect older people and be careful not to hurt them.'

'If you weren't such a mother hen he might

behave a little better,' said Janno in his smoothest velvet voice.

'Hardly a mother hen. I'm always working.'

Adam stared up at Janno, looked him up and down, up and down, like a Geigercounter detecting metal; a curious stare of defiance, triumph, and a hint of fear.

Janno gave Adam a pair of penknives. Lydia locked them away and hid the key. Adam screamed. William took no notice, as if he were stone deaf. William never gave Adam presents; said he was too busy and too broke.

At school Adam threw tantrums. Teachers found him restless, lacking in concentration, a troublemaker but bright, oh, yes, brighter than the average, if he tried, if he made an effort. Adam rarely made an effort, his energies directed at causing distraction, chaos.

'He's so disruptive, Mrs Napier,' said Adam's teacher, a pleasant woman in her forties, untidy, with bitten fingernails. 'Is there some trouble in the home?'

'No,' said Lydia. 'Of course not. We're very busy. We have to work.'

The head teacher, a young man with a pink sunburnt neck and a short fair beard, demanded an interview with Lydia. 'I'm not going to mince my words,' he said in a resounding voice that sounded as if he were bellowing in her ear. They sat in an empty classroom that smelled of chalk and bananas and wool socks. He explained loud and clear that Adam was very exhausting for the staff and not good for the other children. They were frightened of him. Even the teachers were frightened of his tempers. Adam, at nine years old, was very strong. He could knock down somebody twice his height. Perhaps a child psychologist or a psychiatrist might help? Or one of the special schools? Adam was far too disruptive for a normal school. An appointment with a child psychiatrist was advised.

Lydia ignored the advice. The idea of a psychiatrist horrified her. There was nothing wrong with Adam, nothing. If only she wasn't always busy ... If William would occasionally look after him ... If they weren't always worrying about money ... If the company could pay its way ... If the bank would stop writing those threatening letters about the overdraft ... If. If.

A social worker called to inspect the flat, to assess Adam's sleeping accommodation and his diet and talked, too, to Imogen, declaring her private child-care centre perfectly adequate by council standards. How lucky Lydia was with her big flat and child-minding facilities just round the corner. How charming was Imogen Smythe, her friend. Mrs Smythe had such a way with children. 'Oh, yes, indeed, my friend Imogen is quite wonderful. What would I do without her?' Adam was no trouble, just normal and energetic and a little wild at times, said Imogen, but a little wildness in a boy was healthy. Imogen Smythe stood outside her weatherboard house from which layers of paint were peeling, before a strip of grass with paddling pool and paints and empty margarine cartons and

Eventide

cardboard boxes painted with doors and windows; with a swing and a see-saw and shrill voices, ever-demanding, scalpels behind the eyes; standing, big, tall, grubby, in disarming chaos, with a pile of washing-up in her greasy sink, with mugs and sticky spoons strewn around her kitchen; Imogen wearing a smock stained with paint and jam and baby food and God only knew what else, the familiar toothpaste smile flashing, warm, friendly, giving out a radiance of welcome, of love.

God, to be like that—the ease, the casualness, the calm. The social worker, sniffing love, ignored the squalid kitchen. And Imogen, apologising for the mess, because children must make a mess, otherwise they wouldn't be children, would they? swore as soon as the last one was collected she spent the evening clearing up. She never did. Surprisingly, nobody caught infections in Im's place. Never mind the flies.

The social worker questioned, probed. 'You work in your husband's business, Mrs Napier?'

'We have a film company.'

'And you often go away?'

'Sometimes I go on location, not often. I cope with a lot of paperwork at home and at the moment I'm trying to develop a property on the Barrier Reef.'

'Gracious, what a heavy schedule. Who looks after Adam at weekends?'

'I do, or his father and his friend.'

'Your husband's friend?'

'His business partner. Sometimes they have him or he stays with Mrs Smythe.'

'Over weekends, too? So he doesn't see a lot of either of you?'

'He's perfectly happy with Mrs Smythe.'

In spite of the social worker's approval of Imogen and her impassioned defence of Adam—she absolutely adored him as if he were one of her very own—Lydia was sent with Adam to the children's hospital. No point in refusing, ignoring them, William said. They could take him away, put him in care or something. 'One never knows,' said William. 'Mother would be devastated.'

'Sod your mother,' Lydia said. 'Tell her to get stuffed,' and William looked bland, uncaring, as if he couldn't wait for Adam to be taken away by strangers, except that darling Mummy must not be upset. Mummy had a heart condition and the slightest worry produced palpitations and soaring blood pressure.

'Oh, such pretty language you use, for such a well-bred girl,' said William. 'My mother has done so much for us and you ignore her. Treat her like dirt. And Imogen, you take advantage of Imogen all the time. Adam would be better off with Im. Pity she can't adopt him. Perhaps she will.'

'He's my child.'

'Obviously,' said William. 'You're welcome to him. Just keep him away from me.'

Is this William, Sweet William whose good looks are already blurring, fading, merging into something indistinct, something strange and foreign, someone I hardly know? This is Sweet William, my friend, who married me and gave my child a name. Sometimes I hate him. I think I do.

Eventide

A green arrow pointed to a block of single-storey huts marked CHILD PSYCHIATRY. Inside was gaudy brightness; rocking-horses, dolls, toy soldiers, books, paper, crayons, rubber balls, coloured bricks; children's drawings on the walls; matchstick figures with yellow hair and crooked arms and legs, big mouths, half-moon shaped, curving upwards in incongruous grins with uneven teeth. They waited half an hour. Adam refused toys, books; tore drawings from the walls, kicked a small girl sitting on her mother's lap. The child sobbed quietly against a flat-chested teenage mother who wore a cheap ring on every finger.

Look around, no, don't. Behave as if sitting here is the most normal way of spending a sunny morning. What can be wrong with these other children, most of them quiet, some silent? Hyperactive, brain-damaged, retarded, backward readers, poor-sighted, deaf? There were pamphlets on autism, allergies, asthma, hearing problems, diabetes, diet, Down's Syndrome and support groups for families to get together, exchange ideas, to help each other. Into which category would a psychiatrist place Adam, who could read and write and do sums and had sharp eyes and ears and looked the healthiest of the lot? Adam stamped his feet, circling the room, shouting, 'Go home! Let's go home!' meaning, of course, to Imogen's; and the thin teenage mother looked at her many rings and then at Lydia. 'Geeze, you've got a handful there.'

'Sit still, be quiet, Adam, just for a little while. Read that book. Adam, please ...' Adam's foot came out, kicked her on the shin. Pain, shame, anger made her want to shake him. *Don't, don't, don't, in case they think you ill-treat him, in case they think you're the monster and he the victim. Adam, don't look at me like that—Clive Baird's eyes—evasive, devious, a little sly, until you smile, a loving smile that can break my heart except that it doesn't mean a thing. It means you have won the battle, your will always fighting, battering at mine. And you win, leaving me exhausted and ashamed; ashamed because I have lost control.*

A woman in a white coat took Adam by the hand and told Lydia that doctor would see her now, on her own, please. Presently he would see the boy, and then both of them together. *And the boy will kick your shins, dear girl, but never mind. You are paid for enduring abnormal children. It's your job and I don't envy you but Adam, for a little while, is all yours.*

Lydia, back straight, concentrating on keeping her shaking body steady, walked through the open door.

The psychiatrist had thinning dark hair and a round bald patch and thick black eyebrows meeting above his nose and big, plump hands and a fleshy body; and framed certificates on the walls from several countries. A soft voice with a trace of an accent, slightly guttural. Jewish? German? Austrian? Polish? Escaped at an early age from the holocaust? Parents flung into a gas chamber? Brothers and sisters disappeared? Liquid eyes, sad eyes, sharp eyes, slightly slanting; Slav eyes beneath puffy lids; polite, charming, interested in every word she said, or pretending to be; a short, thick-set podgy teddy bear of a man who had begun with the odds against him and who was now rich, well-fed and highly qualified. He uncapped a fat black pen.

'How does Adam get on with his father?'

'Very well,' said Lydia automatically, a little robot sitting there, her handbag in her lap, her fingers playing with the clasp. 'My husband has always been fond of children.'

'Does Adam object to your working?'

'If he does, he's never said, and I have to work. We need the money.'

'Does Adam miss his father? Is he unhappy when his father is away?'

'Difficult to tell. His father is so often on location.'

'Being in films and television must be hard, and all boys need a father around, at least at weekends. Do they have pleasant outings together? Picnics? Going to the beach—that kind of thing?'

'Oh, yes, when it's possible. Of course we do.'

How to explain that any outing—and outings with Adam were very rare—inevitably included Janno, that William had no domestic or paternal instincts; that his indifference was in itself a form of cruelty? So Lydia lied, calmly, convincingly, as the plump little doctor went through Adam's file.

On a school outing Adam had broken light bulbs in a railway carriage, punched another boy in the face, broken his nose, showed no remorse, just a fascination at the pouring blood.

Adam at school was disobedient, noisy, rude, impossible to discipline, and had made no friends. 'Now, why would that be, Mrs Napier? Have you any idea why Adam has no friends? Is your marriage happy, Mrs Napier? What about your sex life? Do you enjoy sex? Have you a lover? Do you suspect your husband has a lover? Do you fight, argue, before the boy? Did you have a happy childhood yourself? Have you any idea if your husband's childhood was normal, happy?'

Like skating, twisting, turning, skidding, avoiding pitching forwards or backwards, skirting, shirking direct answers, thinking carefully, speaking slowly, clearly, replying to every question with a convincing lie, like stepping over mines or a well of deep water, a bottomless chasm; like sliding on a cracking sheet of ice. 'As far as I know my husband had a happy childhood. He is devoted to his mother. She was delighted when we had Adam and she has helped us a great deal with our company. So did my mother, of course. We've been very lucky.'

'And your own childhood, Mrs Napier? Can you describe what that was like?'

'Perfectly normal. Pleasant house. Good schools. We were, I suppose, what people would call comfortably off. No complaints. I'm sorry to be unhelpful but I can't think of anything that might help you over Adam. Not a single thing.'

Lydia and the psychiatrist stared at each other over the notes detailing Adam's short, traumatic life. 'You have told me the absolute truth, Mrs Napier? It will do the boy no good at all if you hold back facts.'

'Of course.'

'You love your son?'

'I love him, but I'm aware I'm not a very good mother.'

'It is a mistake to believe that all women are born

to motherhood. Sometimes it takes time and patience and professional help.'

'I've come here for professional help.'

He asked, 'Do you eat properly yourself?'

'Like a horse.'

'Have you ever suffered from anorexia nervosa?'

'No.'

'You know what anorexia nervosa means?'

'Of course. I do read, you know.' Furious. She could have hit him.

Hasty, hasty; now he's annoyed. Irritation shot like an electric current through pads of fat concealed beneath his dark, expensive suit. 'I'm sorry,' he said mildly. 'I didn't mean to be offensive, but you are very underweight.'

'I've always been what people call underweight.'

'Not neurotic about your figure? No hang-ups about keeping slim?'

'No.'

'Could we make an appointment for your husband to come in with you? Perhaps next week?'

'I'm afraid not. He's shooting a documentary and has very tight deadlines.'

'Perhaps when the documentary is finished?'

'Perhaps.'

'In the meantime I can give you a list of schools that might help your son. He's a bright boy. Keep in touch, Mrs Napier. You're not alone, you know. Hundreds of parents come here to talk things over. A support system is very often the answer for a family in crisis.'

'We are not in crisis.'

The verdict after an hour of questioning, Lydia

alone, Adam alone, then both of them together—a session that produced not one word from Adam—was insecurity, hyperactivity, a nervous disposition. A good boarding-school—'highly recommended and yes, quite expensive, unfortunately'—might do the trick; a school with small classes, one-to-one coaching, individual attention and weekends at home, of course, unless that might entail stress within the family, or a weekend once a month.

'Think about it, Mrs Napier, and make another appointment to see me before you leave. Please try to fix the date so that your husband can accompany you.'

Lydia dragged Adam from the waiting-room where a social worker who looked about nineteen had been encouraging him to draw a picture: 'Mum, Dad, Me,' said the social worker. 'There! There you go, the three of you.' Happy Families. The traditional game.

Sonia and Clive now had two children, one of each, Diana and Duncan. Photographs sent by airmail; 'Outside Grannie's house after Duncan's birthday party'. Fair hair, fringes, stocky, serious, very clean and tidy, eyes screwed up, looking into the sun. *The plants in Grannie's tubs are flowering. The house looks just the same. Do these children kick and scream and break noses and watch the blood? Do they need a special school? Of course not. Such a normal happy family.* A scribbled note from Sonia. 'C and I are coming to Sydney, business trip, in October. Mummy is to have the kids. She so enjoys them. So see you soon.'

They can't stay with us, not with William and me in

separate rooms and Janno always in and out and Adam such a monster. But by October Adam will be sent away, to a special school I can't afford and we shall both be working. They can stay in a hotel—on expenses—can't they? Of course they can.

She sent a telegram to Sonia. 'Sorry can't put you up. Workload huge. Shall I book hotel?' and the answer came back promptly: 'Company booked us Menzies. Will ring.'

William and Janno were interested in finding out whether Clive's company would invest some money in a film. 'Lydia's brother-in-law is stinking rich, so we believe,' said William. 'We'll take them on the harbour, one of those evening cruises.'

'Why should Clive invest in us?' asked Lydia. 'He knows nothing about films.'

'He doesn't need to. As long as he knows about finance.'

'I shall feel embarrassed.'

'You never feel embarrassed,' said William coldly. 'You've a good head for business. If anybody can find some money to get our company on its feet, it's you.'

'It should be on its feet by now. *Stately Homes* did very well, so did the travel stuff. The Yanks are interested in pearling and gemstones. So are the Canadians. What I'd like to find out is where all the money goes. And why we can't get a grant.'

'We were considered too wealthy for a grant. We had capital.' Janno cracked his knuckles. 'I find applying for grants degrading.'

'Me, too,' said William.

'You'd rather go bloody broke.'

'You could sell the island and put the money into

the company. You haven't done a thing about the island, for all your talk about quotes and builders.'
Janno, looking angry, cracked his knuckles twice, and then again.

'I'm keeping my island. It's all I've got.'

They walked out of the flat and left her there among the bills.

While Lydia was away in Queensland, talking to builders, architects and bank managers, William went into a private clinic for aversion therapy.

'He's had a sort of breakdown,' said Imogen on the telephone. Imogen understood. Imogen visited every day, brought fruit and flowers.

'Lydia, you must see him. It's so awful for him. They won't let him out alone. They locked his outdoor clothes away. He has to wear pyjamas and a dressing-gown unless a staff member goes out with him, a psychologist.'

'Sounds like a nuthouse,' said Lydia. 'Who got him into a place like that?'

'Janno. It's all for the best.'

'The best for William or for Janno?'

'Don't be silly, Lydia darling. It's a wonderful place, very, very efficient. Naturally there are some very sick people there. Some of them are on anti-depressants and all sorts of drugs. You can tell. They walk around, some of them do, if they're up to it. William isn't on medication.'

'Does Janno visit William in this place?'

'Janno keeps away. He doesn't like hospitals. They make him ill.'

'But what is William in there for? Therapy for what aversion?'

'Gambling, of course, darling.'

'Gamblers don't get put in funny farms like basket cases.'

'But they do, and it isn't a funny farm, darling. It's a private clinic with a very good reputation. The people in there are very sick.'

Lydia, irritated, asked sharply, 'What do they do to him?'

Imogen talked on and on, husky, breathless, theatrical. 'It's like this. He listens to tapes, to help him relax and then he is told to pick his horses and get his money ready and he and the psychologist place the bets.'

'In his pyjamas?'

'No, no. When he's going out with the psychologist she gives him back his clothes. As soon as he bets, he has to put the money back in his wallet and then the psychologist takes him out for a cup of tea and back he goes to the clinic. It's hard for him, very hard. Gambling is exciting. It's a disease, like alcoholism or taking drugs. To bet brings on a high, a sort of euphoria, a bit like sex.'

'Fancy that,' said Lydia drily.

'So they say. An addicted gambler can't stop gambling. They need therapy. They're sick. When William has to come away without placing any bets he feels very ill. He's getting better but he must go back for follow-up every six months. You must make sure he does. Honestly, Lydia, it's wonderful, this treatment, a sixty per cent success rate. William will be fine, so long as he keeps all the follow-up appointments. Only you can see to that.'

'I can't make William do anything he doesn't want to do.'

'Oh, darling, of course you can. You're his wife!'

'You did say a private clinic, didn't you? What does this place cost?'

'Lydia, how can you talk about money at a time like this?'

'Easily,' said Lydia. 'We're broke.'

Lydia looked at William, lying sweating on a narrow bed and listening to some tape that told him to relax his facial muscles and his jaw and then his shoulders; to let go the muscles in his back, his legs, his ankles and to imagine he was somewhere beautiful, on a river or a lake with his fingers trailing in the water. The background music sounded Indian or perhaps Chinese. He reached for her hand. 'Thank you for coming. You're my best friend. My very best friend, Lyd. You are.'

She withdrew her hand and looked at her palm and rubbed it as if William had left a trace of something sticky on her skin. His hand was burning hot. He looked thin, yellow. 'You're feverish, William.'

'Some bug. Hospitals are always full of other people's germs.'

'Get them to give you antibiotics, something.'

'Nonsense.'

'You look as if you have jaundice.'

'I'm perfectly well. I was a bit tense, stressed, but I'm getting better every day.'

On the way out she saw other patients. Some of

Eventide

them were in dressing-gowns staring into space. Most of them were smoking. Two, fully dressed, played Scrabble. All of them looked drugged. They took no notice of Lydia and she tried not to look at them. The clinic was comfortable, expensively furnished and full of flowers. The staff did not wear uniform. Little cards with photographs and first names identified them as nurses or psychologists.

A blackboard in the foyer outlined the day's activities from 8am to 10.30pm. Breakfast; Exercises; Relaxation; Morning Meeting; Morning Tea. Group Therapy (all groups, Rooms 1 to 7); Lunch; Afternoon discussion on Feelings (Room 2); Discussion on Assertiveness (Room 3); Afternoon tea; Painting (optional); Dinner 5.30 pm; Supper 8pm; Hot drinks 10.30pm; visiting hours 6pm to 10pm; Weekends 11am to 10.30pm; AA and NA meetings 6pm sharp; Transport will be provided.

Lydia picked up a pamphlet titled *Gamblers Anonymous*. Imogen must have read it. Gamblers Anonymous held regular meetings and was linked to Alcoholics Anonymous and Narcotics Anonymous. There were also groups for the families of gamblers. Gambling was an addiction about which governments did nothing. The revenue from gambling was too high. Gambling was a disease. Gamblers convinced themselves that what they were doing was a harmless hobby. In stage two they convinced themselves they were gambling to save their businesses, their homes, their families. Gambling caused broken homes and suicides. When gambling became an addiction, professional help was vital. The pamphlet gave the addresses and telephone numbers of Gamblers Anonymous in every State.

Behind a vase of flowers, the receptionist smiled at Lydia. Lydia smiled back, put the pamphlet in her handbag and headed for the automatic doors.

William will never get better in this place. William will never get better. And the company is broke.

Clive and Sonia arrived in Sydney on a day of pouring rain. Lydia booked a harbour cruise, invited Imogen to make up a convenient number: she and William, Janno and Imogen, Clive and Sonia. Lydia attempted not to look at Clive.

Sonia had put on weight. She looked pink and white and fleshy with a little fold beneath her chin. She wore a very English summer outfit, a green and white silk dress with spots and white shoes, and carried a cardigan. Her fair hair was white above her forehead and her hair looked thin. Her arms were milky, strong and fat.

'I imagined I was coming back to a decent climate,' said Sonia, pulling the cardigan round her shoulders. 'When we lived here it was always hot.'

'Of course it wasn't always hot.'

'I really liked California, you know.'

'Didn't know you'd been there.'

'We did a lot of travelling together, before Clive got this assignment confining him to the Pacific Basin. I've been sending you postcards for years.'

'Yes, of course.'

Already there was an atmosphere, resentment, Sonia pouting.

The harbour cruise was not a success; Imogen, in an Indian dress that reached to her ankles, embroidered with tiny sequins that looked like an electrician's screws, and bangles and earrings and open-toed sandals and wild red hair, recently permed, standing out from her head like wire; Janno dressed like a hippy in an enormous hairy sweater, his scant hair tied back in an elastic band; Clive in an expensive business suit and his old school tie. *We are an odd lot*, Lydia thought.

Sonia looked at Imogen. 'You run a play centre for children? You look after Adam when Lydia is working?'

'A private day care centre. I have him in the holidays. I miss him terribly now he's away at school.'

'Ours will never go to boarding-school,' Sonia said. 'What's the point of having children if you're going to send them away?'

Clive ordered pre-dinner drinks and wine and insisted on paying.

'Our treat,' said Lydia.

'Just let me do the drinks.'

Janno cracked his knuckles. Sonia stared in astonishment at Janno's bony hands.

The harbourside houses slid by, lit up, luxurious, although the affluence was obscured by rain. They helped themselves to the 'carvery' and Sonia said, 'Rare lamb? Lamb in England never oozes blood.'

'Have the beef,' said Lydia, the hostess.

'It's something,' said Sonia, greedy, 'that one can apparently come back for more.'

'As much as you like,' said Lydia, 'and the salads are wonderful. Rockmelon, watermelon, avocado, pawpaw, kiwi fruit, not just dreary lettuce.'

'We grow our own vegetables in Gospel Village.' Sonia sounded smug. 'We take some goodies every week to Mummy.'

Sonia had two helpings of everything, and trifle, and chocolate cake, and when the dancing started on a tiny floor like a handkerchief, Clive asked her if she would like to dance.

'You know I did my knee in tiling our extension. No.'

So Clive took Lydia's hand and led her to the small round floor. She felt light-headed, not from drink, which she had not touched. His presence, Clive in the flesh, at last; comforting, broad, stocky, looking at her with kind grey eyes; looking at her with affection, with love. The look of years before, the night he brought the cocoa to her room. Currents like hot needles passed between them, through their arms and shoulders, through hip and thigh and fingertips. She felt the almost-forgotten stab, the curling pain deep inside her, in her womb. At first they danced far apart, hips wriggling, then close, bodies together, bodies apart, again together. They looked at each other, straight between the eyes. They looked and looked. Sonia watched. Lydia, in her straight black dress and black stockings and flat black shoes, her sallow face touched up with colour, her thick hair falling to her shoulders, swinging, flying, was 'different'. Diners looked at her, although she did not see them. Her body was elastic, every movement sinuous, sexy. 'Lyd,' Clive said, 'now this is my specific area I'll be back. We'll see each other. Would you like that?'

'Yes, yes, yes,' said Lydia, her body bending, stretching, arms and legs and shoulders moving to the beat. 'Yes, yes, oh, please. God, this is wonderful. I haven't danced in years.'

'I do love you, Lyd.'

'I love.' Two words she said above the thumping music. Two words she had never said before. 'I love.'

'When I get back here we'll go away together.'

'We can't go anywhere together.'

'We'll go away.'

'No.' But Lydia was weak, shuddering, damp with lust. *I love.*

Back at their table Sonia was talking loudly to Imogen, so loudly her voice could be heard above the band. 'I hate career women,' said Sonia. 'I always have. I can't imagine what Lydia thinks she's doing, working for a company that's broke.'

'She has talent,' said Imogen.

'It isn't fair on that poor child.'

'Adam is at a very good boarding-school.'

'And they can afford it?' Sonia turned on Lydia. 'Can you afford this special boarding-school?'

'No,' said Lydia frankly.

'Adam is a lovely boy,' said Imogen. Sonia looked at Imogen, a summing up. Not her type; bit of a freak, the huge hoop earrings, the gaudy Indian dress, the frizzy hair.

Clive pushed back his chair. 'Hot in here. Going on deck for a breath of air.'

'Darling, you'll get wet. It's pouring.' He took no notice and Sonia watched him leave, shrugged, continued talking, high and shrill. 'I think we should take Adam back to England, to be brought up along with my two. Of course, you can come over and see him and stay with us or Mummy whenever you like.'

'Thanks, no,' said Lydia.

'You're being very selfish,' said Sonia. 'I know Mummy would be pleased, and so would Clive.'

'I can't imagine how you can know anything of the sort. They've never seen him and nor have you.'

'You sent photographs. He looks very like my two.'

Across the table Janno again cracked his knuckles. The sound was like a door hinge needing a squirt of oil. Sonia shuddered, reached for her cardigan. Her face was scarlet. Imogen took Janno's hand and they joined the others on the dance floor. Sonia sat, fat arms resting on the table. With her cardigan hanging from her shoulders, she went to the servery and asked for profiteroles. They were delicious, thick with chocolate coating, swollen with whipped cream. Outside the rain beat against the windows.

Back at the table opposite Lydia—fork piercing a profiterole, a spurt of cream—Sonia spoke rapidly, loudly. 'If your business is broke and you're going to develop the island, do you honestly believe that is a normal life for Adam?'

'He is at a very good boarding-school.'

'Which you say yourself you can't afford. And does he realise that his father is ... is a bit odd, to say the least? My dear, it's so obvious. Those two, your husband and the fellow who cracks his knuckles. Lydia, don't be such a fool.'

Shocked; stunned. She guessed. How? Lydia, feeling sick, wondered: *Is it so obvious? Has Clive told her he warned me about William, said don't marry him? He couldn't have. Even Imogen hasn't guessed about William—or if she has she hasn't said a word. Sonia isn't the kind of woman to recognise homosexuality. William and Janno don't speak like queers. William doesn't look like one. Janno looks a bit unusual, but so many people do. Nobody would know when they're together. They hardly look at each other. They never touch. How could Sonia tell? Perhaps she has queer friends. Perhaps the Gospel lot is full of queers. What have I ever known about Sonia and her friends? Nothing.*

Lydia's head was pounding. She said quietly, 'William and Janno are brilliant at their work.'

'So brilliant they've gone broke.'

Silence. The band was quiet between dance numbers. Rain lashed at the windows. *Clive must be soaking wet.*

'Think about it, Lydia, you really should. I honestly believe that if you don't agree we could take the case to court.'

'What case?'

'You aren't a fit mother for Adam.'

'How dare you, Sonia? You know nothing about our lives.'

'Tonight was an eye-opener. I don't mean to be beastly, but really ... and that funny woman who looks after him ...'

'Imogen is an actress and my friend.'

'Yes, well. That's as maybe. What I'm trying to say is we can give him so much more in England. And there are blood tests, you know. I think we might prove that William is not Adam's father. I'm going to talk to Clive. I might even have a word with Mummy.'

'I'd rather you didn't. It's not your business.'

'But you admit William is not Adam's father?'

'I've admitted nothing of the kind.'

Sonia smiled. 'Clive is the most understanding person. He'd never condemn you for anything you've done. He's not like that and he'll do anything to please me, and Mummy, too, of course. He's very fond of Mummy. Clive is so good with children. Ours absolutely adore him.'

'I'm sure they do. He's their father. Could we stop this conversation, Sonia? You're our guest and I don't want to be insulting.'

Sonia ignored Lydia, continued talking, raised her voice so people at the next table turned and looked. 'And Clive's so generous, generous to a fault. There—you see? I can't guarantee we'll ever be able to back films or documentaries or whatever you lot do, but we can help expenses by taking Adam into my family.'

'No,' said Lydia. 'Will you please shut up?'

'Where is this expensive boarding-school?'

'On the south coast. It's a three-hour drive.'

'What's it called?'

'St Luke's. Why?'

'We thought we might drop in and take Adam out. We've hired a car. We could take him out for a great big lunch or for a picnic or something, if the weather clears.'

'No, thank you, Sonia, and they wouldn't let him out midweek.'

'Nonsense. We're relatives. We've every right, and I promised Mummy I'd tell her all about him. What's the headmaster's name?'

'Howard, but I don't think he'll agree and I can't come with you. I'm editing a script this week. It's urgent.'

'You don't have to come with us. I'm his aunt and Clive is his uncle. This Howard man can't object. Have you got the telephone number?'

'Not on me.'

'We can look it up or ask directory enquiries,' said Sonia, determined. Her jaw and the little fold of fat beneath it moved.

'I'd prefer you didn't visit Adam.'

'Why? Has he two heads or something? Is there something wrong with him? Is that why he's at this special boarding-school? Is he backward? Retarded? What are you trying to hide?'

'I'm not hiding anything, and there's nothing wrong with Adam.'

'Well, then. Now, where's Clive? I've had enough of this evening. Let's go home.'

'You can't until we dock, unless you'd like to

swim. Go on. Jump.'

'Funny,' said Sonia, and pointed at the desserts. 'Might as well have another one of those. There's nothing else to do.'

'I hope,' said Lydia clearly, 'you throw up. I hope you're sick all night.'

Chapter 10

Stupid to have been so rude, childish, furious with Sonia, thought Lydia three days later. They had not telephoned to thank her for the evening out nobody enjoyed. She had not rung them. Even Imogen, always lavish with thanks and appreciation, did not ring.

Nobody can take Adam away from me, thought Lydia, vehement. *Adam is mine. Maybe Sonia was trying to be kind because she pities me. Maybe she has guessed Adam is Clive's child. Maybe our mother has been nagging her to find out all about me.*

Maybe. Damn Sonia. By next weekend they'll have flown away and I never need see either of them again. Clive will be coming back but I don't intend to meet him. Can't. Mustn't. Wicked. Mad and bad.

Somehow I'll find the money to pay Adam's school fees and when the island is ready I'll take him there; send him to the local school on the mainland or teach him myself. Nobody, nobody in the world will take Adam away from me.

She was alone in the sparsely furnished flat and the weather had turned warm. She pulled down the canvas blinds and sat at her electronic typewriter, a recent extravagance, but necessary; Adam had broken the other machine and he tore up scripts. She was editing a script on a new ballet Janno hoped to film in Melbourne. It was the last of their assignments, based on a half-promise that the film might be featured in an ABC arts programme on a Sunday afternoon. By the time the clips appeared, if they ever did, the company would be bankrupt.

William and Janno were both in Melbourne. While Janno negotiated with the ballet company, William was auditioning for a role in a new soap opera. He hadn't much chance of landing the role he wanted, a suave father of four with a roving eye. William had been on the production side for too long to get back into acting, to break through the new breed of young ambitious would-be stars. William had begun to look middle-aged and sick. William was still gambling. Lydia could now guess from the company bank statements where the money went but there was nothing she could do. To discuss it with Janno would have been unthinkable, disloyal.

Janno and William still went everywhere together but they were not as close as they used to be. Janno was restless. There was a space around him, a void. Most of his film crew was deserting him, looking for jobs with some degree of security, although security was never guaranteed in the profession. The crew knew this, but still it deserted. Only fools cling to the wreckage of a sinking ship, and Janno had never employed a fool.

The morning mail brought a series of disasters. A

Eventide

Queensland bank had agreed to lend her money to renovate the island, but the collateral was the island itself, and now it belonged not to Lydia but to the bank. She was behind with interest payments, due two weeks before. When, they asked, would the development on Nodding Blue Island be complete? It had hardly begun. A building company had started on the roof. The builders wrote, asking for a downpayment. Cost of materials had risen. The building had been empty and neglected for so long. Such neglect, she must realise, would increase time and labour. Plumbing proved a problem. Fees were owing to an architect, an engineer, an electrician. Schedules were behind due to bad weather. It was most unfortunate that the foreman had been off sick. They assured her of their co-operation.

She telephoned them immediately to tell them she had never authorised in writing the advice of an architect, and asked them to outline in detail any other problems. The telephone was answered by a girl who had no idea who Lydia was or what she was talking about. Everybody was out, 'on site'.

Whose site? Mine? The girl did not know. She was new to the job. Lydia left her telephone number. Would somebody ring her back today, this morning, as soon as possible? She would fly up to see them when she could but she wanted some answers to her questions immediately. The girl, who sounded confused and half-asleep, promised to give the deputy foreman the message. Chances were she would forget.

Australia, 1950-1982

In the mail, too, was a brief reply to one of the many letters she still wrote in her continued attempts to find Annie. She had written to nursing associations, to hospitals, clinics, nursing registration boards; to the Red Cross; to missions, to aid and relief organisations, to Amnesty International, to health and community services and to the Department of Aboriginal Affairs. Some of the letters remained unanswered. Others stated briefly that no nurse by the name of Anne Deighton-Gaye could be found in their records. That day's letter, from an Aboriginal mission in the Northern Territory, informed her that several years ago a Sister Anne Dayton had worked in the children's eye clinic but was now retired. This was the only name similar to the one mentioned. They had no record of a Deighton-Gaye, nor the present address of Sister Anne Dayton. They sent their best wishes, hoping her search would be successful.

Lydia filed the letter with all the rest and returned to Janno's script. A needle in a haystack, Annie was. *She could have changed her name or married. She could be anywhere in the world.*

When the entry phone buzzed she took the receiver from the wall and heard a squeak.

'Let me in.' It was Sonia. 'Let me in Lydia, please. This is urgent.'

Lydia pressed the buzzer, opened the front door and waited. Sonia, after climbing two flights of stairs, looked hot. She was dressed in white and carried a large sunhat.

'Well, let me come in,' she said, and Lydia stood

aside. Sonia glanced quickly round the sitting-room. She sat down on the sofa that used to be Marjorie's, looked at Marjories's pictures on the wall, at the fraying blinds that kept out the blazing morning sun, at the carpet stained by previous tenants and Adam's propensity for throwing plates of food. 'You're not going to like what I'm going to say.'

Lydia sat opposite her in the only armchair, bought second-hand with a loose cover that had never fitted and a shawl draped across its back. 'I'm sure I'm not, but carry on. Would you like some coffee?'

'No, thanks.'

'Go on, then.'

Sonia was flushed, uneasy. Beads of moisture broke out across her forehead. 'We saw Adam. We took him out. We spent two days with him. The headmaster was very glad to see us. Apparently you don't go down to see him. You never see him.'

'It isn't easy. We haven't got a car. Janno's the only one who has a car. He and William have been down there and I took Adam at the beginning of the term by train. It's a hell of a journey without wheels.'

'*God*, Lydia.'

'What exactly does that mean?'

'Why haven't you got a car?'

'I had. We sold it.'

'You let those two visit Adam on weekends?'

'They've been once.'

'And that knuckle cracker, you have no idea what he does to Adam?'

'Janno doesn't like him. That I do know. He did give Adam roller-skates and penknives but he has no time for children.'

'Services rendered,' Sonia said.

'What on earth do you mean by that?'

'That Janno has plenty of time for little boys.'

Wait. Wait, now. Does she mean what I think she means? Lydia heard the hum of traffic from the street and the eucalypt in the courtyard rustling in the hot, dry wind. She said, 'Janno hardly notices Adam exists,' and Sonia began to shout: 'How can you be so blind? We talked to Adam. We talked to the headmaster, Mr Howard. Adam isn't normal because he's been abused.'

'Abused? That's nonsense.'

'By that knuckle cracker.'

Lydia, too, felt sweat break out, on her forehead, her face. Her heart was thumping, a drum inside her body. A trickle of moisture ran down her back. Her jeans felt pasted onto her thighs. 'You're talking rubbish, Sonia. If anything like that was going on, Adam would have told me.'

Sonia pulled a tissue from her handbag and wiped her face. She leaned forward. The sweat continued to trickle from her forehead and down her nose. 'Adam told us. It's been going on for as long as he can remember and if he doesn't tell you things it's because you haven't the time or the patience to listen. You've always left him to that actress person who is most unsuitable. You don't know what you've done, Lydia, to your own child. You let it happen.'

Lydia shouted, 'I did not let anything happen! I don't believe you!'

'Ask Adam. He talked to us. He took to us immediately—and he's the spitting image of our

Duncan, which upset us. We imagined such an awful thing happening to our son. I don't know how you can live with yourself, Lydia. I don't understand.'

Lydia took a long, deep breath. 'I don't think Adam has been alone with Janno in his life.'

'No? Do you think your husband is always with them? Do you believe that sleazy actress really cares what Adam does, where he goes, who takes him out? Not a bit of it. Your husband goes to the races and your actress friend is always busy with other people's babies and her men. The knuckle cracker does what he likes to Adam. Adam said. He told us.'

'Does what, Sonia? What did Adam tell you?'

'That dreadful creature, Janno or whatever his name is, takes his trousers down. He says "Look at this" and makes Adam touch him and Adam is too frightened to tell a soul. He threatens him. Adam is a victim of appalling child abuse and I gather it's been going on since he was two. And the answer isn't to send him away to a boarding-school miles away. He needs medical attention, proper treatment—and love, Lydia, the kind of love Clive and I can give him, and Mummy, and his cousins. Di and Duncan will do him the world of good.'

Keep calm, Lydia, calm. She's making all this up. For some reason she wants to take Adam away and she's telling me lies to frighten me.

'I don't believe you, Sonia. I don't believe a word. What I can't understand is why you should make up such a disgusting story.'

'Adam told us.'

'Kids make things up. They look at too much television. Adam doesn't like Janno and Janno dislikes Adam. Adam must have told you stories. Wanting your attention, I expect, trying to shock you.'

'He had all our attention. He talked and talked. He even told us that actress has several husbands in her bed.'

Lydia stared. 'I don't believe that. Imogen has been divorced for years. She hasn't any husbands, only two ex-husbands and she's on good terms with both, but they never come to stay.'

'How would you know who comes there at night when you're working? She's taking students as live-in boarders, as well as all those kids in day care. Adam has seen men, different men, in bed with her. Is that a healthy atmosphere for a boy of Adam's age, or for anybody of any age, come to that? The woman is a whore.'

'I didn't know Imogen was taking boarders.'

'You don't know anything, Lydia, about your so-called friends—and an odd freakish lot they are, Sydney's artistic cream.'

'They don't think of themselves like that.'

'I'm not interested in your husband or his friends. I'm interested in Adam. I love him already. I've telephoned Mummy. I told her everything. She was terribly upset. Clive wants to tell the police. We both intend going to the police but it seemed right to tell you first.'

'How dare you, Sonia?'

'How dare you condone your child being sexually abused?'

Eventide

'He has not been sexually abused.'

'Ask him. We've brought him back with us. He's staying with us in our hotel. And the headmaster agrees we should tell the police.'

'You told the headmaster all this?'

'Of course we did. What else could we have done? The headmaster knew something was very wrong with Adam. Apparently you took him to a psychiatrist because he was making trouble in his school here. The headmaster has the psychiatrist's report and reports from welfare officers. Everybody knew there was something seriously wrong with Adam, except you. You even told the psychiatrist a pack of lies.'

'I did not.'

'You told him you had a normal, happy marriage.'

'William and I work together. We get on all right. He calls me his best friend.'

'Bisexual, is he? I suppose he must be, although nothing will convince me he's Adam's father.'

'Why, Sonia?' Shouting, 'Why?'

Sonia was again dabbing at her face. She said, 'Because,' and gave Lydia a look so full of hate that Lydia sat back in her chair and turned from hot to cold, shivering, her hands clasping the knees of her shabby jeans. 'Tell me what you mean.'

'I think you know exactly what I mean.'

'You're going to tell the police and cause a filthy scandal.'

'I'll see that knuckle cracker safely locked up in jail.'

'You've no proof.'

'We can get a doctor's evidence.'

'Adam had a medical at school. There was nothing wrong with him.'

'Perhaps not physically as yet. We don't know, do we? We're going to have him tested, Clive and I. But what about his mind? Have you no idea of what child abuse can do to a child's mind, Lydia? What do you know of Adam's mind? Have you ever given it a thought? Too busy being the career girl, working your guts out to keep two poofters who should be in jail. Clive is coming to see you this afternoon. I'm going now. I feel too exhausted to discuss this dreadful business any more.'

'I'll be out this afternoon,' said Lydia shortly.

'I don't think you will be out this afternoon. I'm taking Adam to the zoo and you'll stay in and wait for Clive, who is skipping an important meeting just to see you, to make you see reason. You wouldn't dare go out.'

'Sonia, wait.'

Sonia strode to the front door, banged it hard behind her. In the quiet of the morning Lydia heard the security door slam hard, and heard the leaves in the courtyard moving in the hot and dusty wind, like someone rubbing the dry cracked skin of their palms together. The sound reminded her of something—India—*malee* rubbing his black hands together, pinkish palm against pinkish palm; and Annie, laughing, crying; 'Now, Lyd, never tell I said that ... You're coming to Australia with me, Lyd ... One day, one day ... I love you, Lyd ...' And the black faces, hands outstretched, begging, and the smell of heat and spice and dung.

Annie. The only one who loved me. The only one who could have helped me. Gone.

Chapter 11

Clive, in an expensive lightweight suit, arrived at half-past two. He smelt of soap, and kissed her cheek and put his arms around her hard and kissed her mouth. 'Oh, Lyd,' he said. 'Lydia, Lydia, Lydia, what are you going to do?'

'Make you some coffee.'

He followed her to the shabby kitchen, watched as she laid out two mugs and a carton of milk on the oilcloth-covered kitchen table. 'Lydia, we're so shocked—'

'Sugar?'

'Please. Two. Lydia, you must face facts. That bastard has committed an atrocious crime.'

'You're wrong. He wouldn't. Janno wouldn't. Sorry, I only have instant coffee.'

'I could do with a drink.'

'Again, sorry. There isn't any. Can't afford it.'

'You couldn't afford that harbour cruise.'

'Special occasion.'

'Christ,' he said. 'What an awful mess.'

They sat together on the sofa, sipping scalding coffee.

'You'd no right to take Adam away from school. You've no right to keep him in your hotel. I want him back here, tonight.'

'Sonia's taken him to the zoo.'

'She told me this morning. She has no right to take him anywhere without my permission.'

Clive looked hurt, astonished. 'We're family. The headmaster was in complete agreement.'

'And you're going to the police. If you don't bring Adam back by six o'clock I'll go to the police myself.'

'We haven't kidnapped him, Lydia. We're only doing what we feel is best.'

'Who are you to judge what's best?'

He moved a fraction on the sofa, picked at a piece of loose cotton on the arm. 'Listen to me, Lyd.'

'Don't call me Lyd. The name is Lydia.'

He spoke slowly, soothingly, as if she were a child. 'Just listen to me before flying off the handle. I don't want to make things worse for you than they already are. I want to give you some advice.'

Lydia put her fingers against her mouth as though smothering a laugh. 'You? After all these years? You imagine I'd take advice from you, or Sonia, or from my mother? I suppose you know Sonia's rung our mother and told her all?'

'She felt she should.'

'It was a despicable thing to do.'

'She meant it for the best.'

'That's what nosy, interfering people always say when they poke about in other people's lives.'

Eventide

She heard Clive sigh. He sat eyes half-shut. Exhausted. *Dislikes trouble, arguments, always has. Wants a peaceful life.*

'You must leave that fellow, Lydia.'

'Leave William? And do what?'

'Come back with us. We want you back. All of us. We want you and Adam.'

'You may want Adam, but nobody wants me. Not Sonia and not my mother. Nobody in my family has ever wanted me except Annie.'

'Who?'

'My mother's sister.'

He passed his wrist across his forehead, then stroked his chin as if he had grown a beard. 'Get out of this film company. Forget it. Get out while you can. And you must sell the island. That's my advice.'

'Advice or threat?'

'I'm not threatening you, Lydia.'

'You already have, or Sonia did, saying you were going to the police.'

'I'm telling you what's best for you and Adam.'

'The island isn't saleable. It isn't even habitable.'

'It's land in a prime position. It must fetch something.'

'I'm not giving it away for whatever I can get. It belongs to the bank, not me. I've had to get a loan.'

Alarmed, he asked, 'Are you in debt?'

'I'll pay it off eventually. The island could be a goldmine. I'll make a go of it, if it's the last thing I ever do.'

'Your family took little interest in it.'

'My grandmother left it to me. She hated me.'

Again he sighed. 'Oh come, Lydia, your hang-ups. I never knew your grandmother but I'm sure she didn't hate you.'

Her teeth came together with a click. 'Let's get this straight. I am not coming to England and nor is Adam. I will not become a satellite, not again. All my life I had a bellyful of Sonia until I broke away. I'll do my own thing, and nobody, not even you, will make me change my mind.'

She felt him wriggle beside her, uncomfortable, uneasy. 'The catering business, tourism,' he said. 'Such a waste. I hate waste. You were one of the brightest girls I knew. I can't understand why your business is going broke. We saw your documentaries in the UK and your name on the credits. I felt very proud. I thought you were doing well.'

'We went broke because William gambles. He can't stop himself. It's an addiction. He's had treatment but I don't think it worked.'

'Treatment?' Clive's eyebrows shot up. He said roughly, irritably, 'What rubbish. You make backing horses sound like taking drugs.'

'It's much the same. If you've never been hooked, you never understand.'

'Couldn't you have stopped him?'

'You can't stop people. They have to want to stop. Addicted people have to help themselves.'

Lydia lit a cigarette and felt him wince. 'You've stopped smoking, Clive? Well, I haven't. We all smoke like chimneys.'

'I noticed that the other night. I stopped because

we have so many singers in the house and it isn't good for children, seeing their parents smoke. Sonia loathes the smell.'

'Does she now? What different lives we lead, Sonia and I.'

He looked down, at his feet, at the carpet, glanced at her and looked away. 'I don't understand anything about your life. I told you not to marry William. I told you. You wouldn't listen. I wanted you so much, Lydia. You'll never know how I felt when you married William.'

'So you could have both of us? Sonia and me? One can't do that, not with sisters. Nobody could have coped with both of us.'

'Things would have worked out.'

'Of course they wouldn't. Sonia and I are caviar and cake.'

'What the hell do you mean by that?'

'She's all pink and white with icing. I'm half-black, wholemeal bread, half-baked bread, or a chapatti. Do you like Indian food?'

'Stop it,' he said. 'Stop muckraking. You're being ridiculous.'

'You don't know what it's like growing up in a house of lies—the little innuendoes, the evasions, the deceit.'

'How can it matter after all these years?'

'If it didn't matter, you wouldn't call it muck.'

'I didn't mean it like that.' Red-faced, embarrassed, he stared at Marjorie's pictures, at Marjorie's lamps.

'William called me a half-caste when we were on our honeymoon.'

'What your husband said is of no interest to me whatever. I came here to discuss your son.'

'I'll never give him up.'

'If you refuse to come back with us and bring Adam with you we'll have to take further steps.'

'That *is* a threat, and why do you want him? He's mine.'

'And mine,' he said. 'I knew as soon as I saw him. Adam's mine.'

Lydia put her coffee mug on the floor. Her head swam, bending down. A trickle of coffee soaked into the carpet. 'Have you told Sonia?'

'Of course not.'

'I think she knows.'

'Sonia does not know. She wants to take Adam because he's family. She's a wonderful mother, always on the go, always busy. She practically runs the Gospel orchestra and the choir and she makes all the food for the musical evenings. She never stops. If it's not gardening it's decorating or practising with the orchestra or driving the children or your mother here and there. She did her knee an injury tiling the hall and the extension and then when she was gardening she hurt her back. She's mad about gardening. Very green-fingered.'

Lydia said mildly, 'What an admirable woman. You are lucky, Clive. She can't possibly want another child, especially as he's mine.'

'She's quite willing to take on another child, and she'll treat Adam exactly as she does the other two. That I can promise you.'

'A paragon,' said Lydia. 'It's remarkable how busy people are when they don't have to make a crust, when all the crusts are brought home free.'

'That's unkind and spiteful.'

Lydia rubbed the spilt coffee into the carpet with her toe and put the mug on a scratched, unsteady table. 'You love her.'

A terrible silence; teetering on a cliff edge, waiting.

'Yes.'

Reluctant to admit it. Remorse. Poor Clive. He said, 'It doesn't make any difference to what I've always felt for you.'

'You hardly knew me.'

'We produced a son.'

She interrupted, fierce and angry, 'You can't prove that.'

'I don't want to prove anything. I just want to make sure his life isn't ruined, that he doesn't grow up a nervous wreck. He's very highly strung, very intelligent, and a mental mess.'

'Is that what Sonia said about him?'

'I agree with her.'

'I'm going to get to the bottom of it. I'm going to ask Janno face to face ... '

'You think the filthy bastard would admit a thing like that? If he has other convictions the police will know.'

'Clive, not the police, please, please.'

'Frightened of publicity? It's not as if any of you are famous.'

'Janno and William are well known in the profession. We've sold our work overseas. Janno is a brilliant director.'

He spoke with a trace of acid, as if he were tasting something sour. 'You seem to get involved with very odd, unsavoury people.'

'People like you always find creative people's lives are odd. You live in a different world. Sonia can spend her time working for some amateur orchestra or choir or whatever it is she does. You don't find that odd.'

'The Gospel lot may not be over-talented—I wouldn't know—but they don't embezzle money to back horses. They raise money for deserving charities.'

'Point taken. Do-gooders. I find do-gooders quite a pain.'

'They do not molest young children.'

'You really do believe what Adam is supposed to have told you.'

'Not supposed to have told us. Did tell us.'

'Did he mention William?'

'Hardly at all. He wouldn't talk about William. We gathered he was no perfect father.'

'You don't believe William has been molesting Adam?'

'I've never liked William but I don't think he's a paedophile. I do believe every word Adam said about that hippy creature and if you don't do something about it, Lydia, if you continue to wear blinkers—'

'You'll go to the police. As Janno's partner William will be involved, and it'll kill his mother.'

'I remember that woman. I remember her at your wedding. So the old girl's still alive.'

'Just.'

'You fond of her?'

'No, but I don't want to kill her off.'

'Lydia.'

She waited. 'Yes?'

'Are you still fond of William? You were mad about him once.'

'I'm fond of him, in a way. Sometimes I hate him. Sometimes I'm sorry for him. Sometimes I feel affection for him.'

'Do you ... do you ... you and he ...'

'The word is cohabit. No, Clive. William doesn't care for sex with women.'

'You could have been divorced years ago. That's grounds enough. Why have you never tried for a divorce?'

'No point. We work well together. If I ditched him he might spend every cent on gambling. He might starve.'

'Let him.'

'I wouldn't want him to starve.'

'You've led a life of celibacy.'

'More or less.'

'Lovers?'

'Not really.'

'What does that mean?' Sharp. Interested. *He can't be jealous, surely?*

'One of the camera crew, once or twice. Didn't mean a thing. A publicity bloke we met in Melbourne. That didn't mean a thing, either. Maybe I'm meant for the very occasional one-night stand, but I wasn't born to be a nun.'

'Don't talk like that, Lydia.'

'You asked me.'

'I don't know how you've coped.'

'I haven't, not awfully well.'

Turning to her, taking her by the shoulders, tearing at her T-shirt, pulling at her jeans. 'I do love you, Lydia. I do. I do.'

'Don't, Clive.'

'Are they coming back, those poofters?'

'They're in Melbourne.'

And Sonia is at the zoo.

Chapter 12

'Clive.'

'Hmm?'

'You'd better go.'

'Not yet.'

'You've got to tell Sonia I want Adam back tonight.'

'Not yet,' he repeated, blinking, yawning, rolling over in her bed, glancing at his watch.

'I'm expecting a telephone call from a builder.'

'He can wait.'

The telephone was ringing. 'That must be the builder. Or Sonia.'

'Leave it.' He tugged at her hair, pushed it back, drew it forward across her eyes. 'Terrific stuff. Incredible hair. I love your hair.'

Lydia sat up. The telephone stopped, rang again but when she picked up the receiver the line was dead.

'Just leave the damn thing. If it rings, it rings.'

'Clive, promise me you'll bring Adam back tonight?'

'All right. I promise.'

'And you'll do nothing about the police, not yet? If anyone goes to the police it will be me.'

'Yes, yes,' he said, turning away from her. 'Can I have a shower?'

'Of course. Clean towels in the cupboard just inside the door. They're a bit worn. Sorry.'

Clean Clive, washing away the smell of me before returning to his wife. Maybe Sonia will smell of zoo.

She heard the water running, watched him walk back into the bedroom wrapped in one of her stringy, faded towels. She asked, 'Remember the sandstone house where we used to live?'

'What about it?'

'Painted bright pink now and divided into flats. They've put a swimming pool in our mother's patio.'

'Things change.'

'Annie loved living in that house.'

'Who?'

'My aunt. When she was at school she lived there with somebody called Aunt Bin who died. Don't they ever speak of Annie?'

'Not to me.'

'She disappeared after we left India.'

He was dressing quickly; business suit, hotel-laundered shirt, silk tie. 'Christ,' he said, 'it's hot.'

'No air-conditioning here. Sorry.'

'Oh, stop it, Lydia. Stop apologising.'

'Have I been apologising?'

'Yes. For your instant coffee and not having any grog and now your towels and lack of air-conditioning. Trivia.'

'Sorry.'

'There you go again.'

'Will you try to find out for me where Annie is?'

'I'll try, but they'll think it odd when I never met the woman. Your mother's sister, did you say?'

'Yes. Please try.'

He was in the hallway, standing by the door. She saw his face, flushed, bewildered, stricken.

'Lydia.'

'Yes?'

'I'll see you soon, my darling, darling.'

She touched his face and found it wet with tears.

Sonia brought Adam back at six o'clock, saw him up the stairs and refused to come in. She kissed him. He wound his arms round Sonia's neck. Sonia said, 'Goodbye, pet. I'll pick you up tomorrow. Uncle Clive has work to do, some boring meeting, but you and I will go somewhere nice.'

'Where?'

'You decide.'

'The beach.'

'Okay, the beach it is.'

She turned away, walked downstairs. Lydia noticed her step was not quite steady. She held the handrail as she went down.

They faced each other, Lydia and Adam, over cooling plates of bacon and baked beans.

'I want the truth, Adam.'

No reply.

'Adam, speak to me. I want to know exactly what you told Sonia and Clive about Janno.'

'No.'

'Why won't you tell me?'

'I want to go to England.'

'I want you here. If you don't like being away at school, we'll go to the island together. You'll love it there.'

'No.'

'There's no need for you to see Janno. I'll take you right away.'

'England.'

'But why? You know nothing about England.'

'Hate it here.'

'You can't possibly hate Sydney, darling. It's one of the most beautiful cities in the world and the island's going to be even better.'

'I'll hate it.'

'Do you hate me?'

Kicking his feet against the kitchen table. Knock. Knock. Knock.

'I'm speaking to you, Adam.'

He looked up, looked down, continued to kick the table.

'I'm your mother, Adam. I love you very much. I want you here with me.'

The plate of bacon and baked beans was pushed away, flung across the room. Adam kicked the table hard until it tipped over. He threw himself on the kitchen floor. Baked beans streaked tomato sauce down the wall, the door.

The screaming and kicking began.

'Stop it, Adam, stop it! You're behaving like a baby!'

Louder screams. Somebody in the flat downstairs

banged on the ceiling. Adam's fists and heels thudded against the floor. His eyes were running, and his nose. Lydia hauled him to his feet. It took all her strength to lift him. 'Tell me what Janno did.'

'No.'

'Tell me.'

'Can't.'

'Where did he touch you?'

'Go away.'

'Try to tell me what happened, what he did to you.'

'Put me on his knee.'

'He put you on his knee?'

The screams began again, piercing, hideous. Fear. Anger.

'You're not lying to me, Adam?'

His face was dark red, almost purple. She thought: *I should get a doctor. There's something very wrong with him. Something did happen with Janno. What Sonia told me must be true.*

One word came clearly through the screams. 'England.'

This is Sonia's doing. And Clive's. If Janno has corrupted him, so have they.

'Adam! Get up off the floor and speak to me.'

He sat up, stared at her glassy-eyed, as if unsure of who she was. When he spoke it was like an adult insulting her. 'Get off my back.'

The childish tantrum began again; clenched hands, thrashing legs, head turning from side to side, body stiff. His rage was like a cyclone, beating, screaming. She could not move him, he was far too strong. *Is he epileptic? Can children his age have a seizure? Is he mad?*

She rang the hotel where Clive and Sonia were staying. They were at dinner, they would be paged. When Sonia eventually came to the telephone Adam's screams were deafening, terrifying. With every scream his body heaved. Sonia's voice was inaudible. Lydia held the receiver away from her ear and she, too, screamed. 'Help me!' She left the telephone receiver dangling and went into the bedroom and shut the door. Downstairs someone thumped the ceiling and shouted: 'Can't you keep that child quiet? Make him shut up, will you? We're trying to hear the telly.'

Lydia lay flat on her rumpled bed until the entry buzzer rang and then got up to let Clive and Sonia in.

So they won, Sonia and Clive. Adam went to England for a year. Clive saw to passport, air ticket, all necessary documents. He contacted people who would help speed up formalities. The trip was described as a holiday with his mother's relatives, and there was no need to ask William's permission for Adam to leave the country. Adam would go to school with Diana and Duncan. He would have the best medical attention, the top child specialist. Privately, of course. Clive and Sonia would pay. They said they would write regularly letting Lydia know how things were, and she could fly over to see him whenever she liked. Clive offered to pay her fare. 'You can stay with us or with Mummy,' Sonia said. 'Mummy would love to have you and she has so much space.'

Pain was a scalpel in her chest, her stomach, in her head. The pain was unbearable and Lydia began to shake. Her body trembled and her hands, so she was barely able to sign her name.

William telephoned from Melbourne. He had been given the role of Piers in the new series, *Summer Nights*. The pay was good and he and Janno had taken an apartment in Melbourne. Lydia could hardly comprehend a word he said. She remembered nothing of packing Adam's cases or the airport or the farewells. She remembered nothing for several days. Lydia was sick, bleeding profusely, blood trickling down her thighs.

Imogen took her to her own doctor, 'A charmer. Nothing he doesn't know about women's private parts.' The doctor could not find anything organically wrong. He took some routine tests. 'Women cry through their wombs,' he said. 'They bleed.' She had a pap smear and a mammogram. He prescribed a sedative which she refused.

William's mother died, fell down dead with a heart attack as she left her doctor's surgery after having her blood pressure checked. She fell on the path between the surgery entrance and the gate. Lydia had heard stories of deaths like this but had never known of an actual incident. She did not attend the funeral and was not surprised when William suggested divorce. The solicitor's fees would not amount to much.

Everything William and Lydia possessed had to be divided equally between them, but they had no possessions worth dividing. Furniture had already been sold to pay the bills and they had never bought a house. Lydia kept the island, as it was solely in her name. She might also keep her mother's pictures although William said he wouldn't mind the lamps. The Family Court awarded Lydia custody of Adam and accepted that he was on holiday with her relatives. William did not want custody, nor 'reasonable access'. He was now settled in Melbourne and the soapie he played in had top ratings. In a few months it became so popular that his fan mail was more than he could handle, so he told the press. His photograph appeared in magazines, along with those of his television 'family' and the television 'wife' who endured his unfaithfulness, his affairs with younger women. He was devoted to his 'children', Sandy, Greg and Paul. The wife's name was Patricia. The dialogue was appalling, the storylines predictable. The cast wore shorts or sun-dresses or swimsuits and the sun shone every day. The masses loved it.

Lydia cleaned the flat, handed over the keys and flew up north to argue fiercely with the builders. Standing on the quay waiting for the launch to take her to the island she met Enrico. The bleeding, suddenly, stopped.

Enrico sat near her on the launch. He talked. What was she doing? Was she on holiday? Had she walked on the reef, been in a glass-bottomed boat to see the ocean bed? What was she doing alone? 'So beautiful,' said Enrico, 'such a splendid shape, but the Almighty left a bit off when he was making you. Such a tiny bum.' Lydia considered moving as far away from him as possible but the launch was packed.

Enrico was Italian, born in Rome. He was swarthy, attractive, undoubtedly devious; probably an illegal immigrant or a crook or both. Fifteen years he had lived in Australia. He spoke fluent English with an Italian accent and hideous vowels. Once he lived in Sydney, he and his girlfriend, Maria, who came from Fiji. They were hairdressers, Enrico 'hair stylist'.

'And why did I give up my salon? Because the taxes. I work and work to pie the taxes. Never. Not agine.'

He smiled at Lydia. 'Now I tike any sort of work, for cash. I cook and wait at tybles and I clean. I pint houses. I lie bricks. What do you do?' She told him she was developing an island and was on her way there to confront the builders. Which builders? She told him the name of the company who were weeks behind their schedule. She even told him about the increasing costs. 'You employ those crooks? I will work for you. Tell them to stick their invoices up their arseholes and I will work for you.'

He helped her off the launch and accompanied her to what she hoped would be a building with a roof. The work had hardly been started. Enrico promised to see to everything and employ cheap labour. He could find her new showers, said he would paint the cabins, find her staff. 'Six months, if I can live here. It will be band-aid job.'

'What sort of job?' Lydia asked suspiciously.

'A quick mike-over for the tourists who will mike

their messes so that presently we have to start agine. A pint job and somebody to clear the undergrowth and I shall mike a pool.'

He had contacts, 'mites' who gave him discounts. 'I know people in the tride, in several trides,' he said, sounding almost shy. What she must have in her motel was a little café and a little shop selling trinkets, scarves and sandals and sunhats and necklaces and earrings. His beautiful Maria from Fiji was very good at selling trinkets to tourists; she had worked in the Strand Arcade in Sydney. 'Sarongs,' said Enrico. 'Cheap. Toys, for bambinos. You do not want luxury. You want a family motel, with drinks. I mix drinks, cocktails. I give swimming and diving lessons to bambinos. I shampoo and blow-dry the visitors when they come, so long as they pay in cash. My mamma send me products from Rome. No duty. No stupid taxes. Trust me. You must trust.'

Lydia decided she would not trust him further than she could throw him, which wasn't very far. He was large and strong. But he could be useful. He patted her bottom. 'Such a little bum. You stay here with me?'

'No,' said Lydia and moved away. 'I've booked in on the mainland. And if you intend doing some work for me, please do not paw.'

He grinned at her. 'What is paw?' He had very white teeth, a deep tan, dark brown eyes that reminded her of the Italian boys in Italy, in Bassano; reminded her of the day she and William met Janno sitting in a café in his hat. She pushed thoughts of William and Janno, of Adam and her family, away. Lydia was learning to close her mind.

Enrico wore nothing but swimming trunks and a gold chain with a cross that lay in the middle of thick black hair growing on his chest. He was a Catholic, he told her, a devout one, although he had no time to go to Mass. 'My mamma thinks I go early every die. I would not tell her. She is old-fashioned. She believes in hell.' When Lydia was looking at the chaos left behind by the absent builders, he ran down to the beach and returned, water dripping from his body and gathering round his toes which were big with rounded nails; the toes of some ancient statue alarmingly bare. She felt off-balance viewing at close quarters these slices of male anatomy; feet and toes and solid calves, a sculpture cast in bronze. 'No worries,' he told her. 'I do everything. You tell those builders you will report them if they don't return your money and then you leave everything to me.'

'What do you charge? How much an hour?'

'Nothing, until visitors are coming off the launches for holidays. No counting hours. You just pay for little things we buy. Then we share the profits. Ten per cent for me, and I also cook. You must do advertisements because I cannot spell.'

'Advertisements already?'

'Opening night six months.'

Returning to the mainland she wondered where he would sleep and if he had a toothbrush and for the first time for many weeks Lydia began to laugh.

The 'mates' who came to help Enrico were

Vietnamese, two men and a woman, thin, wiry, energetic. They spoke little English. Boat people, Lydia wondered, who have escaped the immigration net? She could not ask them about their passports or their work permits because the language barrier produced nothing but blank stares and mumbles in a foreign tongue.

Enrico and a Vietnamese he called Jo-Jo brought huge parcels to the island; bedding made in China, towels from Taiwan, cheap plates and cups and saucers with no identification on the back; sarongs from Fiji and thongs and sandals and coral necklaces and bracelets that were not real coral but some metal or plastic painted brilliant shiny pink. A huge freezer arrived and was stocked with food bought wholesale, and a dishwasher which looked far from new but worked. A little wooden hut was erected and Enrico, who had been a sign painter in his time, named it QUICKIE SNAX, either intentionally or because he could not spell. Lydia liked it. Every time she looked at the sign she laughed. Another hut had a counter with the souvenirs displayed. Trees were chopped, unruly bushes pruned, sprinklers and hoses revived the wilting palms and tables and sun umbrellas suddenly appeared. Worn-out Christmas tree lights were washed, rewired and hung among the trees. Verandahs were patched and covered with artificial grass. Every cabin was painted, the walls varnished a shiny brown. It was tasteless, crass, turning day by day into a holiday resort for people with pot bellies and loud voices who would never miss an episode of *Summer Nights*. And that, said Enrico, showing her invoices that were frighteningly low for his purchases, was what people wanted. There was now a bar with plastic padding on its wall and a huge television set found on a rubbish dump and reconditioned by 'a clever mite'. The same 'mites' produced reconditioned fans, and built a swimming pool.

Lydia knew Enrico was a crook and told him so. 'If things go wrong I tike the rap-tit,' he answered proudly. 'I am the chef and manager and you the proprietor who asks that things get done. And they are done, eh? And quick. No worries, little bum-bum.'

'Don't you call me that.'

'It is a love name because I love.'

Lydia wrote a cheque for the sheets and pillowslips that Enrico, holding out a calculator, made her alter, deducting ten per cent. The ten per cent was his.

She moved to the island, did what she could to make her cabin comfortable, bought on the mainland English Breakfast teabags and imported vintage marmalade, the dark, thick kind with chunks of peel. Tea and coffee for the visitors and staff were the cheapest available and the marmalade a runny jelly. Enrico's girlfriend, Maria from Fiji, moved in too.

Maria dressed in shorts and strapless suntops, her flesh bare where most people would have worn a belt. She was exotic, pagan, voluptuous; bizarre, this girl, weighed down by necklaces and bracelets, metallic baubles glistening against coffee-coloured skin. She appeared half-asleep but knew exactly what she was doing. She walked tall as though, like her ancestors must have done, she carried produce on her head. There were times when Maria aroused in Lydia excruciating jealousy. Maria from Fiji oozed sex.

Two waitresses arrived, both used to waiting at table but unemployed for months. Dorrie came from Brisbane, Miriam from some country town beyond the Glasshouse Mountains. Enrico lured them to the island with promises of tips. Dorrie was young, fat, spotty, with a foghorn voice; Miriam, in her forties, worn and thin and quiet. Lydia pointed out to Enrico that these waitresses were not being paid enough. Their wages were well below the award. 'Free food and tips and an island holiday,' said Enrico. 'Who cares about awards?'

Occasionally Lydia wondered if in the not-too-distant future she and Enrico might go to jail.

Chapter 13

She wrote to Adam every week, chatty letters telling him about the island and the new swimming pool and how the tourists enjoyed themselves. She sent him presents—a book about Australian fauna ordered especially by telephone, because there were few shops on the mainland except for food. She sent him a rather garish T-shirt and a cotton sunhat and a wool scarf for winter which would most likely not be worn as it might not 'go' with the new school uniform.

About every three months Adam wrote back, a short note enclosed in a letter from Sonia and obviously dictated by an adult.

Dear Mum,

I am very well and like my new school very much. I play football and cricket and we had a good sports day. I won a race.

Hope you are well, with love from Adam.

Sonia wrote once a month. Adam was doing very

well indeed. He was under a psychiatrist, a professor—a friend, really, and neighbour. Such luck discovering him. He was a tenor in the Gospel choir. He had two children of his own and Adam did not think of him as a doctor. He made house visits, so there was no need to go to his consulting rooms in Wimpole Street. Adam's health had been thoroughly checked out and he was pronounced fit. No physical damage had been done by that ghastly pansy, but Adam still needed help. 'Improvement in these cases is always slow,' wrote Sonia. 'We take one day at a time and we know all will be well eventually.'

Which sounded, Lydia thought, as if the tantrums were continuing, and she wondered whether Sonia would stand the mental stress, the draining fatigue of looking after Adam. Sometimes she hoped Sonia would send Adam back. She hoped and hoped, for surely any child would enjoy living on the island? At other times, exhausted by hard work, for the season had already started, she knew Adam would be too disruptive. *Later*, she thought, *next year, the year after, they must send him back*.

'Clive is covering the Pacific region. I expect he'll ring you and give you all our news,' wrote Sonia.

Clive rang from Melbourne. He rang from Sydney. 'Meet me tomorrow, at the Wentworth. I'll pay your fare.'

'I can't, I can't. We're too busy.'

'Darling. Just for dinner.'

'We have two package tours arriving this afternoon.'

Eventide

'Two what? What did you say?' As if she were welcoming a boatload of lepers. He sounded exasperated. 'Christ, Lydia, I'm only a short flight away.'

'I'm sorry, I'm sorry. Is it something about Adam?'

'No, it isn't. Adam's fine. Tomorrow. Around seven. The Wentworth. Ask for me at the desk.'

Yes, yes, Clive. Yes.

This was the beginning, no, the continuation of what had happened long ago. Staying all night with him brought mixed sensations, fear, curiosity, triumph. *I love. I love.*

They didn't mention Sonia. They barely talked of Adam. Adam was now very well. Adam enjoyed school. Adam was very good at sports. They all went ice-skating on Saturdays. 'Come over soon and see him, darling.'

At breakfast, in a room with glass walls and indoor trees and silent waiters, he talked of their going to Bangkok and Singapore.

'You can take a holiday, darling.'

'I can't take a holiday. Not just now.'

'Bangkok,' he said. 'Air ticket on the way.'

They took a cab to the beach suburb where he had married Sonia, she had married William. A quiet, grey day, subdued, no glaring sun, a different sort of day from Queensland. Broad sands, still sea, the broken promontories of rock. Colours muted; azure, silver, grey. The old Federation house looked taller than it had the last time she had been here.

'It isn't divided into flats. It's a duplex,' he said. 'They've stuck a bit on top. Would you like to live here again, Lydia?'

'I wonder if they've changed the carpets. Must have, after all this time.'

'Why are you wondering about the carpets?'

'The Major died on the wall-to-wall, in the drawing-room.'

'Oh, darling. They've done a good job of it, haven't they? The new bit blends in well. I like the lacework on the upstairs balcony. Would that be original Federation ironwork, would you say?'

'I shouldn't think so. Mother's magnolia's still alive.'

'I can see you living here again. The top half? No, the downstairs bit near the pool and trees.'

'There was no pool when we lived here. The pool was Mother's patio.'

He began talking about Federation architecture, the way skyscrapers had sprung up—and what was the actual date of the opening of the Harbour Bridge? Inconsequential chatter as though he sensed her mood, the sudden smothering depression. *Sad, sad, coming back here. Oh, sad.* 'Cheer up, darling. We haven't long. I've a meeting this afternoon.'

Clive was sensitive but he didn't care for moods. He liked everything smooth and easy. He was looking at her uneasily. 'Lydia?'

'When we lived here I couldn't wait to get away.'

'We were all like that,' he said. 'Youth. Couldn't wait to leave home and see the world.'

Standing shoulder to shoulder against the sandstone wall, they could hear the sea.

Eventide

'Your lover?' said Enrico, hovering behind her with a scrawled piece of paper, today's menus he was waiting for her to type. She was the only one of the staff who typed. He saw the air tickets on her desk.

'Just a friend. Wants me to have a holiday.'

'You deserve,' said Enrico. 'You deserve a holiday with the lover. You are pale and thin. We manage. I give you hairdo before you go.

'I'm not going anywhere.'

'The lover will come up here and stay with you?'

'No, Enrico. And it's nothing to do with you.'

'When Little Bum-Bum goes white and shaky I know it is the lover.'

'Shut up, Enrico. Go away. I'm busy.'

Nodding Blue Island was doing well. Enrico, Maria, the Vietnamese and the two waitresses worked well together. The Vietnamese men were known as Jo-Jo and Pan-Pan and the woman was Lalah. All three wore black trousers and T-shirts and sunhats. Lalah was never seen without her hat, even out of the sun or indoors. Bookings poured in; a tourist agency arranged for a party of Japanese; Australians from the south, from Victoria and Tasmania, came seeking tans and sunshine. Queenslanders, tanned already, were curious to see an island only recently advertised as a resort.

Lying in bed in the early morning, Lydia saw the newly painted ceiling already stained with insect blood, and humidity blurred the mirrors. The furniture felt sticky, with a bloom like the skins of grapes.

Enrico was already up. She could hear him singing by the pool. *Enrico is ghastly. Enrico is competent. Enrico has made this business a success so that even the bank manager has ceased writing nasty letters. I must be grateful to Enrico.*

She dressed in cotton trousers, T-shirt, sandals. Six-fifteen and the sun was already strong. Next door gentle snoring; along the verandah in the largest cabin (FACILITIES FOR CHILDREN OF ALL AGES) a door banged, a child screamed.

Lydia sat on her verandah drinking coffee. Outside Enrico uncoupled chairs, opened sun umbrellas. He called out to her, 'We have twenty-five arriving and you are lite.' He stood beneath her verandah, grinning. 'Fatty in Number 10 wants extra milk for her smelly kids.'

'Give her extra milk.'

'And the husband wants prunes for breakfast for his constipation.'

'We give them bran.'

'Order prunes on the next list, Little Bum. We cannot afford for our guests to have the bowel trouble.'

Lydia blinked and reached for her dark glasses. Out there it was hot, hot, hot. Out there beyond the island the coral was alive. It was moving. Hideous fish swam above an ocean bed secret and treacherous and filled with swaying reeds, weeds, bloated plants. A cannibalistic ocean bed where creatures prowled, searching for other creatures they could eat. At low tide, when the reef exposed its hedgehog back, the tourists climbed from launches into glass-bottomed boats and stared between their legs at the greedy world down there; and were unloaded to pick their way across salty puddles to photograph the living coral which was a curious colour, pale, anaemic, like watered blood and quite unlike the artificial pieces painted pink and red for souvenirs. A treacherous place, the seabed, the spiky reef. Lydia typed out notices underlined in red and headed WARNINGS. She put them up in every room.

> WEAR A SUNHAT ON THE REEF. EVEN IF THE DAY IS CLOUDY YOU CAN BURN. REMEMBER TO TAKE SUNSCREEN WITH YOU. ALWAYS WEAR SANDSHOES IF WALKING ON THE REEF. YOU MAY CUT YOUR FEET ON CORAL AND BECOME INFECTED. THIS IS IMPORTANT. DO NOT TAKE RISKS BY WEARING ORDINARY SHOES OR SANDALS.

Already the staff was up. The Vietnamese had cleaned the kitchen and were heaping trolleys—stolen from some mainland supermarket—with clean towels and cakes of soap. Dorrie and Miriam laid out breakfast. It was a help-yourself breakfast; cereals, bacon and eggs from a hotplate, toast, fruit juice, tea or coffee. Sometimes there were sausages if Enrico found a bargain lot. By the time everyone had helped themselves the eggs and bacon swam in grease. Nobody so far had complained.

Just below her verandah she saw Fatty, a baby at an enormous blue-veined breast, and heard the baby sucking. It was huge, a toddler, and it made a noise like water gurgling down a drain. Fatty wore a cotton dress, faded blue with buttons down the front. She smiled at Lydia and shifted the baby onto the other swollen breast. Fatty had a rough-red country face; contented, mindlessly becalmed.

'Okay about Len's prunes?'

'I'm ordering prunes.'

'He gets very constipated when we go away. Not that we don't like it here. It's super. Don't mind me feeding Brett out here in the sunshine, do you? His vitamin D ration for the day, because later it gets so hot.'

'Go ahead.'

'More and more people are going in for it these days.'

'Vitamin D?'

'No, no, dear, breastfeeding. Len's all for it. He actually enjoys seeing me breastfeed Brett. We have a very good association, very active, where we live.'

'Where do you live?' Lydia asked politely.

'Near Cairns. We're a very small community but very lively, very active. I'm on the committee and I work hard. It's an interest. I'm totally involved.'

'The committee?'

'The breastfeeding committee. There are branches right across the country. He's on solids, too, of course, Brett is, but I let him go on feeding at the breast because he likes it and so do I. I can manage it so easily. I've plenty, you see, plenty of good milk.'

'He looks very healthy,' Lydia said, trying not to look at the sated, burping baby.

'Oh, he is. Brett is wonderfully healthy. We all are, except for Len's constipation.'

'Don't worry. You'll get your prunes.'

'Very lightly simmered, he likes them, with plenty of juice.'

God, what an awful woman but a boon to a Third World country; in the middle of a field, milk at the ready for any passing village child; wet nurse in a paddy field, a drinks machine flowing with uncontaminated goodness, the right amounts of protein and carbohydrates to make healthy teeth and bones. Teeth. The baby already has some teeth. Does he bite, the awful creature called Brett? Does the Fatty woman mind?

Lydia finished her coffee and went into her stuffy little office. She switched on the fan and started writing out the bills and adding up the books. *Adam, would you have been easier, more placid if you had been breastfed? I was too busy. I made up bottles in advance and sometimes as I fed you I read scripts. I fed you without looking at you. I never had the time to give you love.*

At lunchtime there was hilarious screaming by the pool. Enrico set up a poolside bar and mixed mysterious cocktails in tall glasses sugar-crusted around the rims. Enrico was wonderful with drinks; gin and rum and whisky and slices of fruit and drops of bitters and secret herbs. Enrico used up a great deal of Lydia's gin.

In the post-lunch torpor she bullied teenagers into the shade and distributed sunhats donated by the State Cancer Council and leaflets describing the dangers of sunbaking without protective cream. Maria sat on a stool in the little shop, folding T-shirts stamped with 'Nodding Blue Island'.

She wore a sarong today, an orange one tied low,

with a slit that showed her legs. She sat beneath a fan, among shells and necklaces and bracelets, the beach towels and sarongs and tea towels with pictures of the island; and the sandals and the beach shoes and the cheap shiny scarves; all the paraphernalia of tourism. But people bought things from the shop. Maria was worth looking at. Husbands bought sarongs for wives who should never have worn garments that expose the flesh. The Japanese were reticent. They wound the sarongs around their waists like skirts and wore T-shirts on top. Stock was growing low. The goods they sold were cheap.

'Doing all right?' asked Lydia.

'Last week we made a profit. Doing good.'

The fan stirred Maria's black, frizzy hair.

In the late afternoon Maria moved—or glided—to the Quickie Snax, where she sold sticky cakes and ice-cream and Lydia sat inside the shop. She made a list of depleted stock and wrote a postcard to Sonia.

Trade on the island is very good indeed. You will be interested to hear that William and I are being divorced. I look forward to seeing Adam—and all of you—next year.

Love Lydia.

As the day cooled, the Christmas lights glittered in the trees. The two package tours had arrived and unpacked. Enrico was cooking dinner. Dorrie, screeching, ushered new arrivals to their tables.

'Glass of wine? Red? White? On the house. Welcome to Nodding Blue Island. Hope you enjoy your stay.'

Lydia mashed boiled pumpkin sprinkled with black pepper, drained carrots, pounded mashed potatoes and flung dried mint into boiling packet peas. Two earthenware casseroles bubbled with cheap stewing steak into which Enrico poured the dregs of flagon wine. 'Want a gin?' he asked.

'No, thanks.'

He served portions of meat and vegetables straight onto the plates, rather small ones, carefully spreading the food so that each helping looked larger than it was, and decorating each one with a sprig of parsley that took up space. Dorrie stood at the hatch to receive the food. She balanced plates, four at a time, twisting round the tables in spite of being overweight, her little fat feet bursting out of pink rope-soled sandals. She stepped as neatly as a cat, avoiding backs of chairs and handbags on the floor. Miriam poured the wine and offered the wine list as the 'glass on the house' was finished.

Enrico squirted topping on glass dishes of tinned fruit salad. 'Here, Dorrie, here, quick.' He carried a load of dirty plates and cutlery to the sink, loaded the dishwasher. The reconditioned machine trembled, groaned. He washed his hands and dried them and patted Lydia's bottom. 'What are you thinking and so soulful? Tell. Truly.'

'I don't think we're giving them enough to eat. We're swindling them.'

'It is not criminal to make profit. It is absolutely

normal and everyone is, everyone who is anyone. I will have more gin.'

'Be my guest,' said Lydia sourly. Once, years and years ago, Sonia and Lydia drank gin and lime together. They were very sick. 'We must hurry dinner, darling,' yelled Enrico. 'Miriam, get coffee ready. It is the time almost for *Summer Nights*.'

Twice a week the visitors gulped their sweets to watch the television. Dorrie and Miriam, who had a little set between them, departed to their cabin. No demanding guest could tear them away from Piers and his family and his young girlfriend, Carmel. 'It'll go on forever, it's so bad,' said Lydia and began to wipe the dining-tables.

In the lounge the guests watched the flickering screen. The reception was not good, but you couldn't expect everything on what amounted to a desert island. The sea whispered just outside and the moon was huge. Lydia stood in the doorway and heard William's familiar voice. 'I can't give you up. I can't ...' Carmel sobbed. 'It isn't any use going on.' Somebody whispered, 'Her mum threw her out, see? Last week. Hasn't he got lovely hair!'

William's hair had been touched up and in some shots the ends looked tinged with green. Beautiful Sweet William was growing old.

In the commercial break Imogen appeared, not worrying about her teeth but informing viewers that even an older woman might look years younger if she used Moss Milk Moisturiser. 'They say I look so young—know why?' Imogen put her finger to her mouth. 'Hush!' she whispered, holding up a smart bottle tied with ribbon. 'Remember Moss Milk if you care about your skin. It really works.'

So she's had some work at last, Lydia thought, *an ad for the older woman. We are all growing old, Im, William, me.*

Imogen telephoned just before midnight. 'Had to wait for the cheap time, sweetie. How's things?'

'Saw you on the box tonight.'

'We made that ages and ages ago. It's awful, isn't it? Quite degrading. Awful for the morale, the self-esteem. The things one does for money. Lyd, you never ring or write. William keeps in touch.'

'Good.'

'He's not well.'

'He doesn't look too good. I saw a bit of that moronic soapie. Didn't mean to look at it. An accident.'

'It's lovely,' said Imogen. 'The UK have bought it and one of their stations is running it every single afternoon in the slot before the news. Do you suppose Adam watches?'

'I wouldn't know.'

'William told me about Adam.'

'I expect he did. You could have warned me about Janno.'

'What about him? You must have known he was homosexual. You're not silly, Lydia. I know heaps of bisexual men like Janno and darling William. They're my greatest friends. I wouldn't mind being married to your William.'

'Not *my* William. You may have him.'

'Your ex-William, darling. How could I have

warned you about Janno, Lydia? How was I to know he'd shoot through? I thought those two would stick together forever.'

Lydia didn't know what Imogen was talking about. 'Shot through where, Im?'

'I thought you knew. I thought that was what you meant about warning you. I thought perhaps you wouldn't have gone ahead with the divorce if you'd known they'd split.'

'William and Janno?'

'It's rather awful, actually.' Lydia could see Imogen at the telephone, waving one arm round in circles, or holding the receiver in her shoulder so that she could wave both arms at once. 'Janno's in Greece, in the Greek islands, with his ballet dancer.'

'His what?'

'A dancer he met when he was filming that ballet. They went off. It broke William's heart.'

'Oh, well,' said Lydia, indifferent.

'A mere boy, Lydia.'

'I'm sure. I've got to go now, Im. Very busy. Thanks for ringing.'

'I met that lovely brother-in-law of yours when I was in London.'

'Didn't know you'd been to London.'

'Just a quick trip. Exhausting. Took the kids. My ex paid, of course.'

'Which one?'

'Number one. Met Clive in Oxford Street, would you believe it? We went off and had a bun in one of those dreadful Wimpy places.'

'Was Adam with him?'

'He was all alone looking at the Christmas lights.

Eventide

I felt quite sorry for him, looking at the lights alone.'
'I'm sure you cheered him up. Goodbye, Imogen.'
''Bye, sweet.'

In the morning there was a telegram. 'Bangkok meet airport 14.15 on 9th.'

Chapter 14

Bangkok; steaming; air so thick walking in the streets was like wading through condensed milk. Every afternoon it rained and children surrounded them trying to sell them raffia unbrellas.

Expensive hotel with a curving marble staircase and several bars and restaurants and beautiful Thai girls kneeling beside the tables as they served them drinks. 'Gorgeous girls,' said Clive.

'Gorgeous room,' said Lydia, unpacking. It was gold and green and white with a huge bathroom and a chocolate and a flower on their pillows every night.

'Heavenly food,' said Lydia, eating duck and ginger and wild cabbage, a dish called *Khao na phet*.

'Lyd, go out and buy yourself anything you want while I'm working.'

There was nothing she wanted, nothing, except Clive. But she went to the shopping arcades because they were air-conditioned, freezing cold. Thai silk was beautiful in ice-cream colours and smoky autumnal rusts. The dresses and jackets were high-necked, eminently respectable. Everything she tried on fitted because she was so slight. *And where, she wondered, would I ever wear such elegant, beautifully-cut understated clothes?* Never on the island. Here, of course, dining in air-conditioned luxury with Clive; and the next time she met Clive, and the next time and the next. She bought a dress and jacket; and shirts and ties for Clive who had dozens of shirts and ties and he said, laughing at her, 'You're spending bahts on me as if there's no tomorrow.'

Maybe there is no tomorrow. So.

With a guidebook in her hand, she walked. The streets were filthy and pollution left her breathless as if clumps of dust tipped out of a vacuum cleaner were clogged inside her throat. The traffic crawled and people hung onto the outside of buses which had no windows. The smell of Bangkok was strong; fish and spices, industrial waste, dirty water.

She walked in and out of temples, leaving her sandals outside along with all the other tourists' sandals and remembered:

Advice to foreigners. Never touch a Thai on the head, not even a child. In Thailand it is considered an insult. Never point your feet towards a sacred image.

Lydia looked at temple after temple, at lines of Buddhas, careful of her bare feet and walking like a crab. She read all the tourist literature she could, in order to talk intelligently to Clive in the evenings but Clive, who had seen it all before, had no interest in the Emerald Buddha Chapel (the *Wat Phra Kaeo*, which she was unable to pronounce) or in the *Wat*

Arun which meant Temple of the Dawn. She would remember later that they hardly talked at all. There was only touching, breathing, panting, sweating, shuddering, loving.

Lydia stood on the tiny balcony of their expensive room, letting in the smells of the east. *Is this*, she wondered, *the scent of my childhood? Did India smell this way?* India smelt of dung and unwashed people and smoking fires. Bangkok smelt of fish and stale milk and vegetables and flowers and the dirty river. But something about the smell was similar and she breathed in the filthy air.

She closed the balcony doors and switched the air-conditioning on high. The touching and the breathing and the love began again. 'Lyd, I do love you,' Clive said in the middle of the night.

Remember that; remember every word and touch and scent. Nothing so beautiful can last.

'Singapore next month,' Clive said at breakfast.

'Please, Clive. Yes. Yes. Yes. I'll get away from the island somehow.' Lydia, the besotted, unable to say no.

At Singapore he sent a car for her to the airport with a Chinese driver with amber skin and spotless shirt. A hot, still night and purple-dark. Wide streets; huge trees still as in a painting; a smell of flowers. He had booked at Raffles. It was faded, a little mouldy and soon it would be renovated, modernised. It was not flashy or luxurious like the new hotels in the part of the city where business executives like Clive would stay. Raffles looked just like it did in old picture-postcards; white, gracious, elegant and Lydia loved it. The palms were like tall, skinny people wearing feathered hats. On its lawns she could imagine men with sideburns and the swishing skirts of women wearing bustles. Room 160 was dark with inadequate air-conditioning and outside there was a courtyard but inside, with the shutters closed, they would have to turn on lamps to see each other. The wallpaper was damp. It was a shabby room with elegant cane furniture that needed painting.

He was late, detained at some meeting. He took her to the bar which was open until midnight. He drank scotch and Lydia swallowed mango juice in gulps. She read the notices on the wall:

Malayan Dinner and Show from 7pm; Rijsttafel Thursday; Tiffin Curry Luncheon Sunday. No tipping please. Singapore time is eight hours ahead of Greenwich. Please be fire conscious and use ashtrays.

'What would you like?' Clive asked, reaching for her glass.

'You,' she said.

She felt ashamed of the damp and crumpled bed next morning, the smell of semen and female juices; the unmistakable acrid scent of sex. Clive said, 'They're paid to clean up after everybody. They won't bat an eyelid.'

She thought of Chinese eyelids batting as they changed the sheets and wondered how many affairs he had had besides the one with her. She wondered. She never asked.

They ate fruit for breakfast, looking out over

gardens and the swimming pool and brilliantly coloured birds sang in gilded cages above their heads. Lydia disliked seeing birds in cages and wanted to set them free.

They walked hand in hand in thick, wet heat, up and down Beach Road where there was no beach, no water but towering buildings and factories and yawning gaps in the pavements where renovations were incomplete. They walked and lost themselves. They found food shops beneath crumbling houses, the fruits and sweets exposed to flies. Old men lay sleeping, their heads on grubby embroidered cushions. 'In a couple of years this will be about the cleanest city in the world. All the old buildings, all these shop-houses will be demolished,' said Clive, as if he had a part to play in the reconstructions. Lydia found the idea of rehousing these people in ugly high-rise blocks sad, because the inhabitants of the shabby shop-houses seemed happy, smiling, friendly—those who were awake—and who wouldn't want to sleep in heat that lasted all year round? 'Can't they renovate a little instead of demolishing?' she asked.

'They're building a fine new modern city, Lydia.'

'But they shouldn't pull down the past.'

He smiled at her, indulgent. 'Progress, darling. If you had your way people would still be hurling their slops in the street and catching typhoid.'

'I didn't mean people should be dirty.'

'Come on, darling. Lunch.'

They hailed a cab and went back to the hotel.

Eventide

'Asia suits you,' said Clive over curry.

'You mean I should wear a sari?'

'Or a sarong or absolutely nothing. You have stunning looks. Beautiful.'

'A quarter black and sallow.'

'Don't be ridiculous,' he said. 'You should see England these days. People of all colours, all races. The old prejudices have gone.'

'Not in my family.'

'Lyd, you're so silly and you're beautiful.'

A north country family with children was having lunch beside them. They could recognise the accent. There were few English-speaking visitors staying at Raffles. 'Do you know them?' she asked him.

'No, of course I don't.' But he looked afraid. He glanced at them sideways, devious, and looked away.

They drove to Mount Faber to see the view and up there she saw a familiar face, a woman who had worked on continuity with their company in a film. The woman greeted Lydia like a long-lost friend and hugged her and kissed her cheek and then rushed off to catch her coach.

'Who was that?'

'Can't remember her name. Comes from Melbourne. Met her when we were on location years ago.'

'She'll talk,' he said, furious.

'About what? To whom? She's on a stopover before going to the UK for a holiday.'

'People always talk.'

'You're paranoid,' she said. She could have strangled him.

'I do love you, darling,' he said, as he always said, defying her to contradict him, making an excuse.

In the Botanic Gardens the paths were like a maze. Orchids grew in pots, massed together, flamboyant, exotic clumps of pink and apricot and red and yellow. They saw no one they knew. Everyone looked Chinese.

'I really do love you, darling,' he said. 'I'd like to buy you orchids. Masses and masses of those orchids.'

'You can't,' she said, 'and I don't like them much. They look as if their mouths are open, voracious, ready to eat you up.'

'Lydia, you're so sweet, so funny.'

'Funny? Me?'

'You're a voracious type yourself.'

'Clive, I don't eat you up.'

'In bed you do and it's wonderful. Out of bed you're sensible and calm.'

'Calm?'

'You give me a sense of peace. Peace,' he repeated. 'Nobody else does that for me.'

She whispered: 'Peace'.

Two months later she took more time off. 'The lover,' said Enrico, 'is erratic, unreliable. Two days here and three days there and always going by plane. It is no holiday for you. Tell him to take you for a month.'

'I can't go away for a month, Enrico. Don't be silly.'

And Clive would never have a month to spare. If he had he would go home to Sonia.

Eventide

They met in Sydney at the airport in the middle of the lunch-time rush. They saw nobody they knew but he looked uneasy. They flew first class to New Zealand. It seemed extravagant to Lydia but in business class or economy he might have seen somebody who recognised him. He was terrified—and she knew he was—of being seen with her.

Christchurch; beautiful with wide streets and trees and parks, it reminded her of an English cathedral city; on to Queenstown in a little plane battered by a gale, flying above snowfields and glaciers and mountain peaks and staying in a hotel on Lake Wakatipu and eating roast lamb and sleeping wrapped round each other in heavy blankets and then flying to Auckland where he had meetings. He left her alone for three long days before they drove north in pouring rain to the Bay of Islands. Roaring seas and settlements with fascinating names—Waitangi, Paihia. 'Wouldn't mind some game fishing up here,' he said. 'Pity there's so little time.' In a glass case in their hotel there was a stuffed marlin, a huge striped creature, a monster, with evil eyes. 'No,' Lydia said and thought of the tiger in the Officers' Mess that had made Annie angry and of her grandmother's tiger skin rug with it s awful eyes.

'We'd better have a look at Cape Reinga before we leave,' said Clive. 'It's the most northern point of New Zealand.' From Cape Reinga, where there was a kiosk, he bought a postcard to send the children and she could not stop herself from reading what he wrote:

Took a day off to see the sights. Am standing on the most northern point of New Zealand. Terrific. Home soon. All my love.

She watched him stamp and post the card. 'I'll be back before it arrives, I expect,' he said, 'but it's the thought that counts, they say. Fantastic coast, isn't it?'

'Wonderful,' said Lydia.

It was wet and cold and beautiful and lonely and tears streamed down her face. She asked, 'What are we going to do?'

'Put up somewhere comfortable for the night before it's dark,' he said. And he said, 'You must get back to your island, mustn't you? Or the profits will be down.'

Dismissed. The future, if there ever had been one, dismissed.

On their last night she asked him, 'Clive, try to find Annie for me. She's the only one who can tell me who I am.'

'You're you. What does it matter where you came from?'

'It matters to me. Everyone has a right to know their origins. I've always been told a pack of lies.'

'Oh, nonsense, darling. I did mention your Aunt Annie to your mother once. The last anybody heard of her she was in Africa or India or somewhere awful, nursing people dying in a drought. They never talk of her. Gather she was a black sheep.'

'Annie was no black sheep. I loved her.'

'Yes, well,' he said, 'I never knew her and I expect you've loved some funny people in your time.'

'Like you.'

And he laughed and they made love and he went back to England and Lydia returned to her job as proprietor of the Nodding Blue Island Motel. That was the last time they went away—until the very last time which was in the future.

Sonia wrote that Clive, at last,

has done with all the awful travelling. He will be based permanently in London, I'm glad to say. Managing Director, at last, at last. He used to say the only good bit about all the packing and unpacking and the air travel was getting home. Couldn't wait to land at Heathrow and get inside the door.

Lydia read the letter twice and she wondered: *did he really feel like that, couldn't wait to get home? Did he feel like that when he left me, flew off without me? Of course he did, because he loves her. He said he did. I just get the crumbs.*

Chapter 15

'One day,' said Enrico, 'I will buy you out.'

'One day I might be quite glad to sell, overdraft and all.'

'And the lover can have you all year round.'

'The lover, as you call him, is settled in the other hemisphere for good and all.'

'He will come back because you are a lovely little Bum-Bum. If he go away, he is a fool.'

'Shut up, Enrico. And don't call me that.'

'Try to love yourself,' he said, like a sentence lifted from a book on self-esteem.

'Go see to the puddings.'

'Desserts.'

'A pud is a pud as far as I'm concerned.'

As usual, the visitors gobbled their desserts to watch the television; Sweet William still starring in the most popular soapie ever made.

But that night visitors, gathering in the lounge and bar, were quite distraught. William had been written out of the cast. Piers, the philanderer, had driven his car off the road, crashed into a tree. Piers was dead.

'A wonderful actor ...'

'So good-looking ...'

'Not a sympathetic part, of course. Such a one with the women. But charming.' Somebody announced, 'I only watched it because of him. I sort of understood why he chased those other women. Wouldn't mind if somebody like that was after me.'

If they only knew.

Imogen rang weeks later. 'Lydia, William is very ill. He's got this new disease they're going on about in America. Acquired Immune Deficiency Syndrome they call it. You get it through needles and from other people's blood. It's a sexually transmitted disease, Lydia, and it's attacking homosexuals right across the world.'

Lydia's stomach pitched. Enrico's dessert, green jelly and too-sweet topping, rose to her gullet so she could taste it, sickly-sour. Imogen's voice came over the line loud, theatrical, as though she was onstage addressing a live audience. 'Lydia, are you there? It's so sad. William's in and out of hospital with infections. Now he has pneumonia. People are dying from this disease. You can carry the virus for several years but eventually you die. Haven't you read about it, Lyd?'

'Yes, but what can I do about it?'

'You could come down and see him.'

'I can't. We're too busy.'

'And you must get tested yourself, and Adam. In America they're testing children who've had blood transfusions or been on drugs.'

'Adam hasn't had a blood transfusion and he's not a junkie.'

'Darling, William is Adam's father. You must both get tested.'

'We are not sick.'

'They all say that,' said Imogen, drawling, 'until they find they are. I think you should see William. Visit him in hospital or at least leave a message.'

'I'll see. I'm very busy here.'

'You always seem to be going away. I've rung you several times and been told you were on holiday.'

'I've had a few short holidays.'

'Overseas, one gathers, but not to the UK to see Adam.'

'I'm going to the UK to see Adam soon. I can't think what it has to do with you.'

'We're friends, aren't we? Or we were, all of us. I loved Adam and he loved me but your relations took him away before I could even say goodbye.'

'I've got to go, Imogen, I'm sorry.'

'Goodbye, Lydia. I'm sorry for you.'

'You have no need to be.'

'I think it's sad you've grown so hard. You sound absolutely heartless. William being so ill just breaks my heart. My heart is breaking, Lydia.'

'The heart is just one of the body's organs. It doesn't break.'

'Very funny,' said Imogen. 'Goodbye.'

William, unexpectedly famous through a soapie voted one of the most popular television programmes in the Western World, was caught in the teeth of the British tabloid press. Somebody had talked to somebody who had talked to somebody who had told the press. AUSSIE ACTOR VICTIM OF GAY PLAGUE. A few days later Marjorie was on the telephone, her voice faint, with long pauses between sentences. Marjorie might be speaking from Mars.

'Lydia.'

'Hallo, Mum.'

'Before you come here to visit Adam I want proof that there's nothing wrong with you. We had Adam tested and he's clear, but you ...'

'What about me?'

'How do we know that you're not going to bring some dreadful contamination into the house? There's Diana and Duncan to consider and Sonia and Clive, and all of us here who have always led perfectly respectable normal lives.'

'You don't think I've led a normal life?'

'You married a homosexual and now the whole world knows.'

Lydia shouted, 'We're divorced. I don't know anything about him. I haven't laid eyes on him for a year.'

'One never knows for sure. A cut finger ... blood ...'

The word *blood* echoed hollow on the line.

'The virus dies as soon as it is exposed to air, Mum. You should know that.'

'Nobody knows much about it yet, not even doctors and scientists. Did William take drugs? They say dirty needles, that these drug addicts share needles ...'

'William is not a drug addict. He did not use drugs, Mum.'

But Janno did. I always knew Janno used drugs, but not William. William never even drank, or hardly ever. His addiction was not drugs.

Her mother's voice became louder. 'You there, Lydia?'

'I'm here.'

'You were married to him, Lydia.' The line crackled, spluttered. 'Now, promise me you'll get tested.'

'Mum, William and I never lived together as other married couples do.'

'You must have done, at the beginning. You honeymooned in Italy. You had Adam.'

'Years ago.'

'This disease can take a long time to develop, so they say.'

'Okay. I'll fly down to Brisbane and get tested.'

'I could arrange something here, if you bothered to stir yourself and fly over to see your son.'

She knows how to throw her darts, my mother. Perfect aim; right on target; a bull's-eye. 'Mum, I've been very busy. We had a hectic season. I'm trying to take some time off to visit you. It'll be this year, definitely, perhaps September or October.'

'I suggest you make it in the immediate future and be tested by somebody our doctor recommends.'

'Sexually transmitted disease clinics here are as good as any in the world.'

'Please yourself,' said Marjorie. 'I'm sure there's more of it where you are, per capita, naturally, than over here.'

'Per capita I think the figures are much the same.'

The line went dead.

Lydia's test was negative. She rang her mother.

Eventide

'Thank God, thank God,' Marjorie said fervently. 'Now that's over, you get over here and see your son.'

Sonia wrote that September would be fine for Lydia to visit so long as it was after the 9th. They were all going to Scotland during the school holidays. 'The children will be going back to school in September, but you'll see them in the evenings. Mummy says you're to stay with her. The Gospel Chamber Orchestra is putting on a Mahler concert in September and I shall be very busy.'

Lydia wrote back: 'I'm staying a night or so in a hotel because I expect I'll have most frightful jet lag. Will ring you soon as I arrive.'

Her last night before flying to England. Zipper bags and a large handbag packed; her cabin clean. Her last night, purple with a reddish moon, Dutch cheese with a corner sliced off and pink light like watermelon instead of silver on the sea. Lydia sprawled on her bed in her dressing-gown, hair lustrous from Enrico's efforts with shampoo and conditioner, face colourless compared with Enrico's and Maria's. Enrico held up the gin bottle. 'Maria and I will hold the fort while you enjoy yourself with Mama and sister and your little boy.' He had ceased inquiring about her lover. Nobody had asked if she were related to William Napier, the dying actor. Napier was a city in New Zealand and not an uncommon name.

Dorrie and Miriam crunched crisps, lay on the floor drinking gin and giggling. The Vietnamese were in bed. 'Such a celebration,' Enrico said, 'our boss going off to England for a proper holiday and leaving us to run the place. Have a good time, Little Bum, a lovely time.'

There was a smell of salt and chips and vinegar and gin. Enrico, too, smelled of salt, sea salt, invisible crusty tang on hair and skin. The chain with the cross around his neck glittered in the moonlight. Enrico, bronzed womaniser, slum boy from Europe, saving money, determined to make good. In Italy she had seen many boys with Enrico's face.

> On the bridge at Bassano
> We held hands
> We held hands
> And then we kissed.

Poor Sweet William who will die.

'Go to bed, Enrico, and take the others with you. And the empty bottles. I need some rest.'

The others left but Enrico stayed. He opened the window and the watermelon moonlight was a lacquered solid on the sea. *I lie here, light and empty, floating on neat gin.*

Enrico, beautiful, demanding, sulky; crooked; a taker, a hungry animal. And I'm hungry, too; ravenous Lydia, amoral in her dressing-gown, up half the night in her bedroom with her chef.

'Goodnight, Enrico.'

'Goodnight,' he said, outlined reddish in the doorway which swung open, letting in a draught.

And off he went, along the verandah, down the steps to Maria's cabin. *Do I fancy him? How could I? How could I fancy a spiv like that? Just sometimes, when Clive is far away and there's a waning moon.*

PART III

London, 1982

Chapter 16

Sonia Baird sat on the bottom step of her dusty staircase, doodling on the telephone pad and talking to her mother. She rang her mother each morning, although they met almost every day.

Sonia and Clive lived in a once run-down suburb of north London, in an Edwardian villa with rising damp, draughts, ivy climbing up the brickwork, a carriage lamp in the porch and a front door painted canary yellow with a heavy brass knocker. Their neighbours were professional couples with children, overdrafts, creative tendencies (music and pottery and renovating antiques). They called their suburb The Village, although it was remembered by earlier generations as the slum near the railway bridge and the unhealthy Vale of Health. There was, of course, a smattering of coloured people and an Indian emporium where the owner's wife wore a flimsy sari even when it snowed. Sonia and her friends filled their spice racks there and were devotees of curry.

Marjorie, living in the house once occupied by her mother in the most expensive part of Highgate,

ate curry only when invited to her daughter's house. She had provisions delivered, declaring she detested supermarkets and crowded shops. She enjoyed her house, her little garden, walking on the heath and occasional trips by cab to Harrods. She expressed surprise when Sonia's friends complained of the proliferation of coloured faces in the area. 'I live in the last little piece of country left in London,' she would announce. 'I have a pond outside and ducks and trees, and what more could anybody wish for at my age?' Asked about the years spent in India, she would look vague, misty-eyed. 'I was spoilt, of course. We never had to lift a finger. Life changed after 1947 but what must be must be. And then we went to live in Australia and the Major died.' Asked for more details, she would shake her head. 'I'm happy here in London. This was my mother's house. It's lovely for me, being near Sonia and the children.'

This morning, two days before the arrival of Lydia, she murmured on the telephone to Sonia, 'I am seriously disturbed. You can't imagine how I worry.'

'Stop it, Mummy.' Sonia doodled frantically on the telephone pad, stick men with arms and legs, seagulls, clouds, a square of dots. 'You always say she must come over to see Adam.'

'But Adam is ours, darling. He is one of us.'

'So, presumably, is she.'

'She has never been one of us.'

'She's your daughter, Mum.'

'And I'll have to put her up.'

'She'd be quite happy in some hotel. She wants

London, 1982

to spend her first night in a hotel—to get over jet lag, she said in her last letter. She isn't asking us to put her up. You offered. You told me to write and say she must stay with you.'

'It wouldn't be decent for her to be in England and stay in an hotel.'

'Oh, Mum! If it's going to upset you, don't have her. I'll have her, although it isn't easy with the concert coming up. I can't spend much time with her. We've rehearsals and the hall to fix. One of the second fiddles has broken her wrist and we've got to find someone to stand in for her.'

'Oh, dear, who?'

'I don't know yet. I've got to look around.'

Marjorie asked sharply, 'What does Clive say about Lydia coming here?'

'Nothing. Why should he? It won't make a scrap of difference to Clive if Lydia stays with you or me or on the moon.'

Sonia, in bedroom slippers, wriggled her toes, rubbed one bare ankle against the other. It was a chilly day. She wore a caftan and a thick cardigan over her nightdress. Her hair hung down her back, its strands held together with a slide. Her face was flushed. Sonia was prone to blushing. 'Is your physio coming today, Mum?'

'I expect so. Few people come when they say they will but the physio is an exception. The man never came about the television. You said you would remind him.'

'I did remind him.'

'If the television is working properly it might be a diversion when Lydia's here.'

'I doubt that. They do get all the English programmes in Australia, just as we get their rubbish. Not that I've watched *Summer Nights* or whatever that thing was called. The kids watched it; unfortunately.'

'You shouldn't have allowed them to.'

'Adam was interested.'

Marjorie sighed, a whistle along the telephone line like an asthmatic's wheeze. 'I expect Lydia would like to come and hear the Gospel orchestra.'

'I doubt if Lydia appreciates Mahler.'

'I suppose you're doing the catering for the supper.'

'I've done all that. Everything's in the freezer.'

Sonia tore the page from the telephone pad and screwed it in her fist. 'Look, Mum, I'm freezing sitting here and the house is disgusting. I must get on.'

'You do too much, my darling, always on the run.'

'Somebody has to do things.'

Marjorie sighed again. 'Darling, you're such a clever girl.'

'Mum?'

'Yes, Sonia?'

'What's the matter?'

'I'm a trifle scared. That report in the newspapers, Sonia, I suppose we have to introduce Lydia to people as Lydia Napier.'

'It's her name, unless she's changed it.'

'I shall suggest she changes it back to Harper.'

'She wouldn't do that. You know how she felt about Daddy.'

'Or Deighton-Gaye.'

'I suspect the Australians don't go in for hyphens, Mummy. Do stop worrying.'

'It's all so disgusting and unhealthy. It would be most unpleasant for the children if the word went round the school that their aunt was once married to a homosexual. He actually talked to a reporter and admitted it, one paper said. So brazen.'

'Some people,' said Sonia slowly, 'might find that brave.'

'Suppose she insists on taking Adam back with her?'

'She can't. She'll be going back after school's started. She's only staying three weeks. She can't possibly take him away at the beginning of the new school year when the fees are paid.'

'Hardly worth the effort, three weeks,' Marjorie said.

Sonia bit the end of her pencil. 'She will, I expect, want him back sometime and we'll have to let him go.'

'We can fight.'

'No, Mum. We can't fight. There's nothing to fight about. She's divorced, she's running what appears to be a healthy business and William Napier's dying.'

'He's your child now. He calls you Mum.'

'Only because the others do. He's still Lydia's child.'

Marjorie shouted, 'But you love him and he loves you and Clive.'

'He's very fond of Clive,' said Sonia vaguely.

'He adores you, darling.'

'Mum, don't keep on. Let's see what happens when she arrives. She may not want him on her island or he may not want to go. She may intend remarrying.'

'Who on earth would she marry?' asked Marjorie in alarm.

'We don't know much about her, do we? See you later, Mum. I must get dressed.'

'I don't know which room to give her. The green bedroom, do you think?'

'Does it matter?'

'No,' said Marjorie, firm. 'It doesn't matter in the least. It's only for three weeks.'

'Funny,' said Sonia slowly, 'how you and Lydia have never got on.'

'You two have never got on either.'

'She isn't easy.'

'No,' said Marjorie fervently. 'Nobody could call Lydia easy.'

'Nor is Adam,' Sonia said.

'Sonia, he's a perfect darling.'

'Sometimes. I'm going now, Mum. See you tomorrow. Half-past ten, your hair appointment, isn't it? I'll pick you up at ten.'

'Thank you, darling. I'll be ready.'

Sonia drew another seagull, then tore the page in half and flung the pad across the hall.

Chapter 17

Dirty, stale, this first glimpse of London after so long; some strike holding up passenger flights so that people lay asleep on the airport floor beside rucksacks and suitcases, and Indians and West Indians swept around them, whisking straw brooms and looking bored and gathering up plastic mugs to throw in overflowing garbage bins.

But there, just beyond the barrier, Clive; and Lydia's trolley, rattling with 'duty free'—whisky for Clive, gin for Sonia—swung and swerved and bumped her knee and headed towards him, uncontrollable, as if it knew he was waiting there. Her stomach heaved, an elevator hurtling from a top storey to the basement. 'Lydia,' he said. 'Oh! You!'

He held her in big tweed arms and kissed her cheek; as any man would kiss his sister-in-law, his wife's only sister, arriving in England from the other side of the world.

'Me,' Lydia said, standing very still in her grey tracksuit with yellow piping, her old denim jacket, her face and hands gritty, a feeling of dehydration in her skin. Familiar, so familiar, Clive; smelling of soap; big—he had put on weight since she had seen him last—and not affluent-looking although he must be affluent. He wore a tweed jacket and a striped shirt from Marks and Spencers, the kind actors often wore in British television films. 'We'll have to take a cab. Where're you staying?' he asked.

'The Thames Arcadia.'

'Why there?'

'Cheap. Cheaper than most hotels in Central London. Nice and near the Savoy.'

'Hardly the Savoy.'

They stood in a line of people and suitcases and carry-bags while cabs drew up, luggage was pushed inside. 'Funny old London cabs,' she said. 'You didn't bring Adam with you.'

'It wasn't possible.'

'You didn't say you were meeting me?'

'Well, no. Here, move on. Two more to go and with luck we're there.'

'And where, Clive, are you at this precise moment supposed to be?'

'In the office.'

'Lies, lies, lies,' she said brightly. 'How did you know when my plane was landing?'

'From what you said when you gave the date to Sonia. I rang the airport in case there was a delay. There's been some strike. If you weren't on this flight I'd have met the next.'

In the cab they sat apart. She stretched out her hand, drew it back. 'Thank you for meeting me. Lovely surprise.'

'I wanted a chance to talk to you alone.'

'Talk away.'

'Not now.'

Everything felt different, looked different. Clive was different, in what way she felt unsure. She stared out of the window. 'What horrendous traffic—and the flyovers. How can you bear to drive in London?'

'I don't much. Sonia has the car today. They're buying new school uniforms for the kids.'

'Don't you have a company car?'

'I don't use it much. It can take two hours crossing London—more. God, here comes the rain.'

'I don't think I could bear to live in London.'

He sat very still, staring at the driver's head. Attempting conversation, she said, 'I can't remember anything about the area round Heathrow.'

'You haven't missed a thing.' He leaned forward, slid back the glass partition and instructed the driver on a quicker route. The driver appeared deaf. 'Twenty quid, I bet,' said Clive, peering at the meter. 'At least.'

'That's dreadful. We should have caught the airport bus or the tube.'

'God, no,' he said and shuddered. Rain spattered against the windows.

The taxi leapt, crawled, turned in and out of side streets and finally brought them to Trafalgar Square. Familiar; the lions; the Nelson Column; the National Gallery; a line of bright red buses. Lydia

Eventide

babbled, 'Now I know exactly where we are. It's much busier than it was when William and I were here. It'll be funny staying in my grandmother's house again. My mother's house. There used to be a very cockney next-door neighbour.'

'Your mother's next-door neighbour is a doctor.'

'Clive, what a mass of people. Lines of them at the bus stops.'

'September,' he said curtly. 'Still the tourist season.'

The Thames Arcadia, a blaze of artificial lighting, looked as tired and beige-coloured as the tourists sitting by their luggage in the foyer. Her room would not be vacated until twelve. They were short of rooms—renovations—and the place was full. The noise was a roar; several languages babbling on at once and over the top a Boston drawl. Reception, manned by a black boy—ebony-faced with ivory teeth—checked her reservation. 'Twelve, please,' he said. 'Sorry. Sorry. Your luggage will be out the back. Please wait until twelve.'

'I want a bath,' said Lydia.

Clive muttered, 'I don't think that's possible until you get your room. What about breakfast?'

'I think I had it on the plane. Clive, could we walk, a long, wet walk?'

'Walk where?'

'By the river? Anywhere. Please, Clive, let's walk.'

Pale, wet light, a dirty colour, the sky a grey and sodden blanket hanging low. The river, said to be cleaned up now and almost fit to drink untreated, looked muddy. Matchsticks and a cigarette carton and an ice-cream paper bobbed by. The trees were still in heavy leaf, dusty London green scorched brown at the edges, ready in a week or so to fall, to rustle and clog the gutters. Autumn. The buildings looked old, dirty, decaying, the new tower blocks across the water disorientated, raw. Rain began to soak her hair. *Here we walked, Sweet William and I, so long ago, sent out by Grandmother to see the sights. Sweet William and I, best friends, walked along the Embankment hand in hand.*

They leaned against the parapet, a wide space between them. 'You'd better ring your mother and Sonia when we've had some lunch. Sonia is expecting you to dinner.'

'I can't.'

'You must. I shan't be there. Your mother has your bedroom ready for you. It's all right to spend one night in a hotel if you're jet lagged and exhausted but you must move to your mother's place tomorrow.'

'Must?' Sharp, hard, she knew she sounded.

'You're here to see Adam, aren't you? And your mother and Sonia? So why make difficulties as soon as you arrive?'

'Where will you be tonight?'

'At a meeting.'

'How's Adam, Clive? Tell me truthfully. I'm nervous—can't you understand? I haven't seen him for two years. I'm terrified.'

'There's nothing to be terrified about. You did the right thing, letting him come to us.'

'I don't think I ever do the right thing. I never know what the right thing is.'

'Stop that, Lydia.' And suddenly, gentle, husky, 'I love you. Remember? I love you very much.'

'And a right proper mess you'd find yourself in if anybody heard you say so.'

'It's a secret, isn't it?' he said. 'Between you and me.'

'We can hardly tell the world.'

'I've got to get back to the office. Let's have lunch.' He took her arm, pulling her from the parapet. The rain had stopped.

They lunched in a wine bar, sitting outside under an umbrella that held quivering raindrops on its rim. He picked up the menu. 'Choose. What would you like to eat?'

'Fish and chips,' said Lydia and looked at his face and laughed.

Little round tables and bright-red tablecloths and a menu ink-smudged, pretending to be French; fillet of sole and French fries and raspberries and cream. 'How perfectly delicious. On the island I give my tourists awful food—all my package tours.'

'Lydia, we were very shocked ...'

'I bet.'

'That awful TV series and then the gutter press writing filth. Did the Australian papers make a meal of it?'

'They took a nibble. They weren't unkind. He was popular.'

'He must have made a heap of money. Let's hope he leaves some of it to you.'

London, 1982

Lydia took a chip between her fingers. 'We're divorced and he hasn't any money.'

'He must have. I've heard actors in those puerile series make a packet.'

'Not William. He wasn't in the soapie long enough to make much money. Even if he had money, I'd never touch a cent.'

'You'll let him leave it to that freak.'

'William's not dead yet, Clive. They may find a cure. The freak's run away.'

'Run where?'

'Gone away with a ballet dancer. They're somewhere in Greece.'

'A male ballet dancer?'

'Yes, Clive. A boy.'

'Good God.'

'Yes, Clive,' and Lydia grinned.

'You find it funny?'

'Only your expression and the way you said, "Good God".'

'Drink your wine,' he said, looking round him at the people at the other tables; afraid their conversation might be overheard; afraid somebody he knew might see him. *This is like it always is; Clive afraid of being seen with me. Worse for him in London where he must know heaps of people. He was jumpy enough in Singapore.*

'Eat up, Lydia. I haven't got all day.'

She ate, fast. 'Beautiful raspberries, beautiful.' She licked her spoon. 'Clive, apart from seeing Adam, getting to know him all over again, finding out if he wants to come back and live with me ...'

Eventide

'We'll talk about that later. Not now.'

'I'm determined to find Annie.'

'She never contacts your mother. They haven't said a word to each other in years. I did ask your mother a few questions. Not very forthcoming, your mother.'

'Did she tell you anything?'

'Only that they fell out over money but you know all that. Annie swindled money from your father.'

'She did not. Is she in England? Did my mother say?'

'She's in London.' He was pulling notes from his wallet to pay the bill. 'Some dreadful suburb—Colinwood I think it is—end of the Northern Line by Underground. I believe she drinks.'

'I'll find her. She must be in the telephone book.'

'She never answers her telephone, that I do know. Your mother had her number once but there was never a reply.'

'I don't believe she drinks.'

'The British Raj was famous for alcohol consumption.'

'Annie wasn't part of the British Raj, only by birth. I remember some of the things she used to tell me and how she loathed the way we lived, with servants waiting on us hand and foot, and about the beggars and disease.'

He switched the subject, smiling at the waitress, leaving what seemed to Lydia a gigantic tip. 'Want to look at the shops?' he said. 'I'll buy you something glamorous.'

London, 1982

'No. You won't.'

'It's up to you.' His shoulders moved; a casual shrug. She sensed in him a sudden weariness, boredom. Wanted to be rid of her, to go back to whatever he had to do in his managing director's office.

'Is your office very grand?'

'Not particularly.'

'Where is it?'

'Ludgate Circus.'

'Not all that far from here.'

'No.'

She peered in shop windows. Handbags and shoes, sandals, bracelets, chunky Cleopatra chokers, heavy leather belts; skirts in crumpled cheesecloth; Indian dresses with gold and silver threads, like Imogen wore. A wonderful bookshop.

'Clive? Can I look?'

'Don't be long. I've work to do.'

'I've brought some books for all the children. Australian history and flora and fauna.'

'History? Ned Kelly, some cricketers, a handful of tennis players. And convicts.'

'Don't you knock Australia. It's my country.'

'It is not your country. You were born in British India, as you never let anyone forget.'

'My grandmother was Australian, and both her parents.'

'You didn't care much for your grandmother, and the great-grandparents probably died before you were even born.'

'That's not the point.'

'I don't know what the point is.'

'Are we quarrelling, Clive?'

Again, the impatient shrug. 'Lydia, it's after two o'clock. Your room must be ready by now. If you refuse to allow me to buy you anything, let's go back to the hotel and get you settled.'

Her room was a single on the sixth floor and faced a grey brick wall. While Clive tipped the porter—she had forgotten the British tipping system—she pushed open the window. Greyish nylon curtains blew against her arms. There were side curtains of beige rep tied back with tassles. Everything smelt of cleaning fluid. Outside traffic hummed, builders hammered and the rain poured down again.

Clive sat in the only chair. He looked at the beige carpet and the beige walls and a picture of a tree and some grass titled 'Hyde Park'. His eyes were restless; *he's nervous. He's nervous being alone with me.*

She unzipped her bag and hung a skirt and jacket and a shirt on hotel hangers, reaching up because they were the type attached forever to the hotel's wardrobe, defying theft. She looked in the tiny bathroom and laid out sponge bag and make-up and then sat on the narrow single bed. She sat primly, feet together. 'Bath, no shower. I must get them to iron that shirt before I meet my mother.'

'You haven't brought much to wear.'

'I don't possess much to wear.'

'Trust you brought a sweater.'

'In the other zipper bag. Don't tell me the evenings are drawing in.'

'Well, they are.'

'You said you wanted to talk to me alone.'

'I did. You don't appear in a particularly receptive mood.'

'Go on, talk. But not about the seasons and the evenings drawing in. It's spring in Australia, you know.'

'Lydia, what is the matter with you?'

'I told you. I'm scared stiff. I'm bloody frightened. I'd like to run away.'

'Just listen to me, will you?' He looked not at her but at the picture of Hyde Park. There was a film of dust across its frame. He cleared his throat as if about to make a speech. 'We want you to sell that island and come back and live like other people.' He wriggled in his chair, uncomfortable.

'I don't know how other people live.'

'We all want you back.'

'Nonsense.' She kicked off her shoes and lit a cigarette. 'Sorry. I remember you've given up. Do you mind?'

'It's your room.'

She lay on the single bed, lifting one leg and then the other, as if exercising, with the cigarette burning in the ashtray on the bedside table. 'Of all the hotel rooms we've been in, this one is about the worst. I did love Raffles.'

'No more trips now I'm based in London. Doubt I'll get farther than Belfast.'

'You be careful there. Managing director, Clive, my word. I forgot to congratulate you.'

He said, 'I'm going in for property so the kids

Eventide

inherit something that will keep increasing in value. They'll all have some bricks and mortar when they reach eighteen.'

'Why do you say inherit? You'll be around when they're all eighteen.'

'One never knows.'

'Of course you will. Is something wrong with you?'

'Not that anybody's discovered.'

'Well, then. What sort of property? Not high-rise office blocks?'

'Nothing like that. I've bought a cottage in the west country and another in Wales and an ancient place in Norfolk—thatched roof, heavy doors with latches. That one's for Adam.'

'That's rather wonderful of you, Clive.'

'Not until he's eighteen. Then he can do with it what he likes. I want you to come up there and look.'

'What does Sonia say about it?'

'She hasn't seen the Norfolk place. Nobody has. I want you to be the first. I'll book you on a coach to Cromer and meet you at the bus station.'

'And what do I tell my mother and Sonia?'

'That you're visiting friends, film people, tourist agents, anything. They'll believe you.'

'And where will you say you're going?'

'We have several branch offices. There'll be no problem about my getting away.'

'God, Clive, you tell lies just like the rest of them.'

Ignoring her, he continued, 'You can't go wrong with land and bricks and mortar. You'll enjoy a few days in Norfolk. It isn't comfortable, not yet, but it has character. You'll love it.'

'I expect I shall. Now I'm going to have a bath.'

He looked quickly at his watch. 'I must get back to the office. Now, Lydia, ring your mother and Sonia. You must.'

'You're sure you won't be there tonight?'

'Quite sure. Take a cab. That duty free weighs a ton. Here, have a taxi or a minicab on me,' and he put some notes on the dressing-table.

'No, Clive. I can manage the duty free. I'll get the tube and walk to your place from the station.'

'You don't know where it is.'

'I'll find it. I do have a London map.'

'Don't be absurd,' he said, irritable.

'You're leaving money on the table as if I were a tart and we haven't even been to bed.'

'Stop it, Lydia.'

'You're not afraid of catching a nasty sexually transmitted disease?'

He went to the door, opened it, closed it very quietly. She was alone in the ugly room. In the bedside table locker were telephone directories stacked beside a Bible.

Gaye. Deighton-Gaye. Not a single Deighton-Gaye but many Deightons though not in Colinwood. Gay ... Gaydon ... Gaye. Gaye A, furrier. Not Annie, that one. She would never have become a furrier. Used to be angry about the tiger in the Officers' Mess. Lydia ran her finger down the page. Gaye G. 15 The Shrubberies, Colinwood. Right suburb, wrong initial. Lydia dialled the number. No reply. She rang all afternoon. She rang several other Gayes. Either no reply or a strange voice saying, 'You've got the wrong number,' or 'Nobody of that name here.' Gaye I, who lived at 2A The Crescent, Colinwood, eventually answered the telephone at five o'clock. A man's voice, breathless, as if he had just run upstairs, said, 'Ian speaking'. No one called Anne or Annie lived there or had ever lived there as far as he was aware, and he had been there for twenty years.

Annie never answers her telephone, Clive said. Tomorrow or the day after I'll go to Colinwood and find 15 The Shrubberies and if nobody answers the door I'll ask the neighbours if they know her. Gaye G. Maybe she changed her name. Annie, Gaye G of Colinwood must be you.

Chapter 18

Lydia walked from the Underground, down the slope of Gospel Village; over an intersection with traffic lights and past a new supermarket and the pale yellow bulk of a block of flats. She wondered: *Was all this here last time, when I was in London with William? We walked back this way, I think we did, the day Grandmother took us to Kenwood House. The Gainsborough lady, Mary, Countess of Howe. I'll always remember that painting; beautiful light; reddish earth and her little shoes. And William's flash. William's excitement and being so charming to Grandmother and she being so nice to him and rude to me. No. We didn't come this way and even if we did, everything has changed.*

There was a pancake restaurant, a steak house, an Indian emporium, still open at half-past six and take-aways—Chinese and Indian and hamburgers and chips, the smell of frying, thick, sickly. The grease felt solid, touchable in the damp evening air. And here, at last, was Sonia's street, full of trees and shrubs and flowers—late roses, double dahlias bursting red and yellow. Dahlias, in England, meant the end of summer.

Eventide

Stopping by the gate she fumbled in her handbag to find a comb and tugged it through her hair. A lamp shone in the sitting-room window. Already? It was still summer, only September, and the northern evening should go on and on. Where had the twilight gone? It was a sad, a desolate English evening but the rain made the flowers smell strong; night-scented stocks, lavender, roses overblown. Sonia, the green-fingered.

The front door opened, and there was Mother. Cheek touched cheek; the familiar waft of the expensive scent she had always used; fair permed hair, beautifully arranged. Cold hands. Marjorie wore a brown skirt and a cream silk shirt and bronze shoes with little heels. Elegant as ever, Mother.

'You've brought very unsummery weather with you, Lydia. The children have nasty colds.'

Sonia's hall; ceramic tiles she put down herself and an antique hatstand invisible beneath a heap of garments. Lydia put the parcels of duty free on the floor. 'A little booze and torrid froggie pong, Mum.'

'Thank you, darling. Sonia, Lydia's here.'

Sonia emerged from the kitchen in a wrap-around cotton skirt and clog-type sandals that slapped the ceramic tiles like hammers. Her hair looked dusty fair and dusty white above her forehead. The whole of Sonia appeared dusty, as though she had been filling bags of flour. Only her round pink cheeks glowed, a blush that swept upwards to her hairline. Embarrassed seeing Lydia again? Wished she hadn't come?

'Sorry Lyd, not being ready. Been a hectic day. We rehearsed until half-past five.'

'Some duty free for all of you. I've a few things for the children.'

They brushed cheeks, barely touching, the conventional gesture that meant not a thing to either of them; and then stood away from each other, looking into each other's faces, wary as two animals, two dogs; bitches waiting for a fight. Sonia was the first to look away, diving into the bags of duty free. 'Ta ever so. All contributions gratefully received. Whisky, eh? I'm not keen on Clive getting into spirits but I suppose the occasional nip won't do much harm. He drinks too much when he's away on these ghastly trips but now he's based in London I'll keep an eye on him. Sorry he's not here to welcome you. Some boring old meeting that'll go on forever. Rang to say he wouldn't be back for a meal.' She clattered back to the kitchen. 'Must check my pie. Made it in such a hurry. Hope it'll be all right.'

'I've never known you make a bad pie yet,' said Marjorie.

'Can I see the children, Sonia?'

'In the television room. Half a tick and I'll be with you.'

Postpone the moment of seeing Adam, who is now twelve years old. Half a tick. *And where is Clive?* Lydia wondered. Bet he hasn't got a meeting. Clive will be sitting in an empty office waiting for this get-together to be over. Or dining somewhere expensive on his own? Or actually at some meeting? She will never know and will never ask. Remember he said this afternoon: I love you, I love you very much.

Her mother led her not to the television room to

Eventide

see the children but to Sonia's drawing-room; grand piano, sheet music heaped on the floor; knitting on a chair and a biscuit and a cat and over the fireplace invitations to parties and stunted candles in pottery candlesticks ingrained with crimson wax; and scattered around the room three music stands and Sonia's cello. Everything, in spite of extensions and renovations, looked dusty, dirty. Funny Clive could stand the mess; Clive, so clean, fastidious.

'Sorry it's a bit untidy but we've been so busy,' called Sonia from the doorway. 'Give Lydia a drink, Mum.'

'Sherry?' asked Marjorie. 'Medium dry?'

'Thanks, Mum.'

The room was full of leaping shadows and a shaft of lamplight lit her mother's face; creamy foundation, rouge, bright red lipstick; green eyeshadow flecked with silver; fingernails painted to match the lipstick; the figure still firm and slim; legs, too. Expensive Mum. Only the hands, speckled, slightly arthritic, gave Marjorie's age away.

'Sit down, Lydia.'

'I want to see Adam, Mum.'

'In a minute. They're engrossed in some dreadful television programme. It's useless so much as speaking to them until it's over.'

Lydia sat in a lumpy armchair that smelt of cat. 'The children?' she asked, sipping sherry, a drink she disliked. She repeated, 'I want to see Adam, Mum.'

Outside Sonia yelled, 'Turn it down. Turn it off. Lydia's here,' and appeared in the sitting-room doorway. 'Come and see the kids,' she said. 'They've already eaten, so we'll have some peace at dinner.'

The children, Diana, Duncan and Adam, looked alike. Adam was the tallest. Lydia rushed towards him to hug him, to hold him and felt him squirm away. 'Hallo, Mother.'

'Adam, oh, darling, it's wonderful to see you. I've brought you a few things—T-shirts and some books and a few little things for Duncan and Diana.'

Fumbling with her parcels, dropping things. 'Here, Adam, this is specially for you. Australian birds. See? There's an emu on the cover.'

'It's an ostrich. From Africa.' He sounded husky. A cold? Or was his voice about to break?

'No, it isn't. It's an emu, an Australian bird but it doesn't fly. It can run very fast, though.'

'All birds fly,' said Duncan.

'Not emus or ostriches. They're known as fast-running flightless birds.'

Adam took the book, glanced at it, put it down. Duncan and Diana inspected the contents of their parcels and put them aside. All three said, 'Thank you,' without enthusiasm. Sonia remarked, 'More T-shirts, good gracious me. You must have about fifty each.'

'These are ones we sell on the island. There's a painting of the island on the back. Nodding Blue Island. See, Adam?'

Eventide

'Yes.' He unfolded the T-shirt, shook it, glanced at it, folded it neatly and put it on a chair. He looked up at her. 'I'm watching something special on TV in a moment, if you wouldn't mind ...'

All three of them sat on the floor, backs turned to her. Adam and Duncan were alarmingly alike; Clive's eyes, his eyebrows, his stocky shoulders.

Adam turned the television up high. They talked among themselves in faintly cockney accents through heavy colds. *My goodness, things have changed*, thought Lydia, shocked. *In our day we had to be so careful of our vowels. Adam doesn't want to talk to me. I am a stranger, dropping in for supper. Adam doesn't care a damn. This is a family; I am an invader of a unit, excluded from a close group that includes my son.*

'Come along, Lydia, leave the TV addicts and have another drink.' Sonia smiling, friendly, but Lydia sensed resentment, tangible as the scent of meat and pastry from the kitchen.

The dining-room was an extension of the drawing-room, big and chilly, furnished with antiques that needed dusting. The huge dining-table, Marjorie explained, would seat ten when it was extended. 'Sonia rubbed it down to its original grain and polished it herself.'

'Elbow grease,' said Sonia airily.

'The Victorian dining-chairs were picked up in a funny little shop in Islington. Sonia did the seats herself. Did you know, Lydia, that Sonia is now doing upholstery and tapestry?'

'No, Mum. I didn't know. They're beautiful.' Touch them. Pat them.

London, 1982

The sideboard, laden with antique plates and glass. In a big fruit bowl some of the bananas were turning black. Sonia served steak and kidney pie and cheesecake with whipped cream and talked about the Gospel orchestra and the Mahler concert and of people Lydia did not know. 'Tony insists we all wear black, so I'll have to run up a new black skirt, Mum. We'll go out and look at materials tomorrow, that is if Lydia doesn't mind.'

'I don't mind one bit,' Lydia said briskly.

'You will move in with me tomorrow morning at coffee time,' Marjorie told her. 'It is perfectly ridiculous your staying in an hotel.'

'Yes, Mum. Thank you.'

'And finish your dinner, Lydia. Everything in this house is homemade. Nothing take-away or tinned, not in Sonia's home.'

'It's quite delicious.'

'Are you still peculiar about your food?'

'Peculiar? No.'

'It used to drive us mad when you were young, the way you wouldn't eat.'

'I eat like a horse, promise.'

'And still thin as a stick. It isn't attractive, Lydia, although you may think it is. As women grow older they need a bit of flesh. Sonia, now, is just right, I always think, nicely rounded and the sort of face that won't age.'

'You think I've aged?'

Marjorie paused, fork halfway to her lips. 'Who wouldn't, on an island in that climate? Australia has one of the harshest climates in the world.'

And Lydia ran her fingers across her forehead

and her cheeks and chin and wondered; *If I'm that bad he won't want me any more. He'll prefer the nicely rounded Sonia with her fat arms and legs and untidy house. He married her. This is his life. He wants things to stay the way they are. He loves her. Maybe he loves all sorts of women and I'm not the only one.*

'I believe you've had a successful season on your resort.' Marjorie collected plates, then stood at the sideboard, knife ready to cut the cheesecake.

'We've done quite well.'

'Who is running the place while you're away?'

'My chef. He's Italian. I think he wants to buy me out but I'm not selling yet.'

'Mafia money,' said Sonia idly. 'What staff have you got besides him?'

'Two waitresses and a girl from Fiji and three Vietnamese.'

'Vietnamese?' Marjorie looked faintly shocked.

'Very multicultural.' Sonia smiled, pouring cream. 'What kind of people stay there?'

'All sorts. We've had a party of Japanese.'

'Nips,' remarked Sonia, mouth full.

'The Major,' murmured Marjorie, 'would turn in his grave,' and Lydia refrained from pointing out that the Major had been cremated. 'Young honeymooners mostly, Mum, mad on taking photographs and very sweet.'

'No Jap is sweet in my book, Lydia.'

'The young ones weren't born during the war. They know nothing about it.'

'History books burnt and no proper history taught in schools, like Hitler's regime, I expect.' Marjorie's mouth looked thin, lipless.

Lydia said gently, 'Thousands of their grandparents must have suffered radiation sickness.'

'And serve them right.'

Stop. Switch the conversation. Ask her something about herself. This is important. She must answer. 'Mum, isn't your second name Julia? I'm sure it is.'

'I'm surprised you don't remember, Lydia. Marjorie Julia. Julia after a great-aunt on the paternal side.'

'What was Annie's second name?'

Marjorie paused, frowned as though unable to remember. 'Georgina. Actually, Georgina is her first name, Georgina Anne, but Mother didn't think she looked like a Georgina. She was named after a great-great-grandmother on the maternal side, who was believed to be very beautiful. Annie wasn't beautiful, so they called her Anne.'

'Lovely names.' Lydia's head began to swim. Marjorie turned to Sonia. 'That cheesecake was delicious. Now tell me, is this girl you've found for the second fiddle's desk going to be any good?'

'Not what one could call experienced, but she isn't bad. I must remember to tell her about wearing black. Remind me to ring her.'

Georgina Gaye. Georgina Anne Deighton-Gaye. Gaye G. Lydia suddenly felt so exhausted her head drooped above her plate. 'Sorry. Jet lag caught up on me. I'll get a cab.'

'You be at my place by half-past ten,' said Marjorie. 'Coffee and a chat before Sonia and I go shopping. Perhaps you'd like to come with us?'

'I don't think so. I loathe shopping. There's never anything I want to buy.'

Marjorie looked at her—jeans, cotton shirt, denim jacket and those dreadful running shoes; like a teenager at forty. No sense of style. 'You could do with a few good outfits while you're here.'

'I don't go to places where people wear good outfits.'

Marjorie carried out the half-demolished cheesecake. 'No, Sonia, I'll clear up and see the children into bed. Cough syrup for all of them tonight and some aspirin wouldn't hurt. You put your feet up, just for once.'

Sonia leaned forward, elbows on the table. Her upper arms were dimpled and white as milk. 'Don't you go anywhere? I suppose you can't, living on an island in the middle of nowhere. Have you got a car?'

'No point. No roads, just footpaths. People like it that way. Bushwalkers find it bliss.'

'No airstrip?'

'Not enough space. It's a very small island, Sonia. We get to the mainland by launch.'

Sonia yawned. 'Poor old you.'

'I've grown very fond of the island and it's doing well. I want Adam to come out for the Christmas holidays. There's diving and swimming and wonderful boat trips to see the coral and the other islands and there'll be children his age to play with. It's a family motel. We've put "Children Welcome" in the ads. I'll have your two as well, if you'll let them come.'

'Cross the world on their own? Not likely.'

'The cabin crews are used to looking after

children. I'd fix everything. They'd be perfectly safe.'

'I wouldn't dream of it, Lydia. Sorry.'

'Come with them.'

'We're going to Austria this winter, skiing. Clive's already paid.'

'I want Adam for Christmas, Sonia, please'

'You'll have to talk to him yourself. By the way, don't forget the concert, Friday, eight o'clock. That is, if you want to come.'

'Of course.'

She approached the television room again. All three children were almost asleep.

'Adam.'

No answer. *Shake him. Wake him up.* 'What?' he mumbled, red-nosed, red-eyed.

'Will you come over to Australia and spend Christmas with me in the sun?'

Now wide awake, he looked appalled. 'Can't. Going to Austria.'

'I want you to come and stay with me.'

'Sorry. I want to go to Austria.'

Stubborn mouth, eyes looking downwards, sideways, and Duncan and Diana sat up and shouted, 'We're all going together, so Adam's got to come.'

'I'm your mother, Adam. It's so long since I've seen you. Over two years.'

'Yes, Mother, I do know that.'

Shut out. Unwanted.

'Think about it, Adam, and let me know.'

'Okay.'

He won't give it another thought. So back in a taxi to the hotel, to the dreary beige room. Into bed and look at the picture of Hyde Park Clive kept staring at. Listen to the traffic going up and down the Strand. The traffic noise went on all night.

Lydia lay staring at the ceiling and the neon lights that stabbed her room with beams of colour, reflected, bounced, against the brick wall outside. *Tomorrow Mum for coffee; and shopping, and Friday this concert at which Sonia will star. But I must find Annie. I will. I must.*

The early hours. *What are you thinking, Clive, lying in bed in Gospel Village with Sonia? In Australia it is already afternoon. It is tomorrow.*

Sounds in the street; rattling dustbins and an early bus grinding to a halt outside. Dawn between beige curtains and the street lights going out. *I feel cold and tired and sick with dread. I must pack my things and pay my bill and move to Mother's. We will drink coffee and make strained conversation and Sonia will take us shopping. Can't. Won't. Must.*

Fit in. Try. They are your family. They have your child. The bed is freezing cold.

Lydia, now wide awake, jet lag turned to nausea, sat up and found the telephone book and again went through the Deightons and the Gayes. Gaye G., Georgina Anne. *It's her. It must be. Gaye G, 15 The Shrubberies, Colinwood.*

At six o'clock in the morning she dialled the number and there was no reply. She dialled again at seven. No reply. *Never mind, Annie, I'll find you. I will. I must.*

London, 1982

Lydia packed her bags and paid her bill and took a cab to her mother's house in Highgate.

Chapter 19

'Those tubs outside the front door,' said Lydia, placing her zipper bags carefully in her mother's hall, 'I've always remembered them.' They stood firm, solid, on either side of Marjorie's front door. In the drawing-room two armchairs upholstered in pink chintz faced each other across a round Indian table carved with lotus flowers. The tiger skin rug was there, with its bright glass eyes; so were carved brass vases from India, brimming with dahlias and roses. Elegant room, elegant as Mother who this morning wore a light tweed dress, heather-coloured, with an expensive leather belt.

'I never liked that carved table, Mum. It used to come out of its slots and collect the dust.'

'Hand-carving like that, my dear, is precious. It must have taken a craftsman at least a year.'

'Some starving craftsman, some one-legged beggar sleeping out.'

'Gracious me, what nonsense. You have never lost the habit, Lydia, of trying to discuss matters you know nothing about. You simply don't understand how things were.'

London, 1982

'I understand why the British were kicked out of India, why there isn't an Empire any more.'

'We were not kicked out. We gave India independence and look what's happened since we left. Bloodshed.'

'There was plenty of bloodshed when we were there.'

'Are you anti-British, Lydia? A Communist, perhaps?'

'I'm not anything political.'

Coffee poured from a silver pot into fragile cups, Coalport, pink and green. The coffee was not instant. Marjorie disliked instant coffee.

'People mixed up with films and ballet and homosexuals—and you must admit there are a lot of homosexuals in the arts—people like that are so often left wing, causing unnecessary trouble for the rest of us.'

'I'm far too idle to involve myself in trouble, demonstrations, that kind of thing, if that's what you mean by trouble.'

'Are you going to live on that island for the rest of your life?'

'I've no idea how I'll spend the rest of my life. Lovely coffee, Mum.'

'No chance of your remarrying?'

'No.'

'Nobody available?'

'Not a soul. I wouldn't remarry if there were.'

'You were mad about William when you were a girl. Couldn't keep your eyes off him.'

'He was beautiful.'

'He was handsome, I admit, and he came from a good family. His mother was a charming woman.'

'She was not. Ethel Napier was a proper bitch.'

'She helped you with your business, and don't speak ill of the dead, Lydia. I won't have that.'

'Mum, why can't we talk without arguing? I wanted to ask you so many things.'

'Such as?' Marjorie's eyebrows lifted, arched brows, perfectly plucked.

'I want to know exactly who I am.'

'You always upset me, Lydia. You always have. The Major and I did everything we could for both of you. He was a very sick man after the war, when we went to Australia, a very sick man indeed. He worked himself into the grave to provide everything he could for you and Sonia.'

'It was your money, Mum.'

'And when he died on that hot afternoon, you left him there, flat on his face on the floor. Poor Sonia was beside herself.'

'Yes, well, he was her father.'

Marjorie picked up the coffee tray. 'We'll go for a little walk now. It's a lovely day. Sonia will pick us up at twelve for shopping. There's a wonderful new shopping complex in Finchley with space to park. I suggest you buy some clothes.'

They walked across the heath. At least nothing here seemed changed. A swan glided across a pond with cygnets in her wake; and moorhens and ducks dived and fluttered. Dogs lifted their legs against benches and trees. Once round the pond and back to wait for Sonia. Sonia's car—or Clive's—looked brand-new. Lydia sat with the children at the back, but not next to Adam. Next to her sat Diana with a stuffed-up nose.

'Swish car, Sonia.'

'The company car. Clive lets me have it. It's so awful crossing London these days—much quicker to take the tube. Now he's based in London he actually has a space in the office car-park. He doesn't use it much. Clive says he's buying me a runabout for shopping, a little car but new. Clive doesn't trust second-hand cars. He says I can have a little sports car if I want one, lucky old me. But where would I fit the kids?'

Lucky Sonia Baird.

The shopping mall; plate glass and chrome with a dome of gold and red and many moving staircases and at least three floors; Lydia's idea of hell. People, so many people, and shopping trolleys and food piled up everywhere; raw meat and fish and bread and cakes and even live crabs in a tank with a water sprinkler and a notice: DO NOT TOUCH. CRABS BITE. The children hung above the crab tank and Sonia shouted, 'Come on, come on. Skirt material and some curtains for Di's room while we're here and a joint for the weekend.'

Lydia leaned against the counter while the shop assistant measured materials. Snip-snip went her scissors. Lydia's legs felt weak. Her head began to pound. From all the shops the noise burst like gunfire; rock music from boutiques, somebody singing high and shrill from the record shop. The children rushed off to buy ice-creams. Sonia doled out money. 'And darlings, a cone each. No more.'

Eventide

They returned, licking, voracious as animals. Sonia was careful to keep the children together. There was no chance to talk to Adam. Lydia sat on a wooden bench outside the café where Sonia suggested snack lunches for everybody.

'I'll wait here.'

Marjorie asked, 'Don't you feel well?'

'I'm all right. Not hungry.'

'It'll be a day,' said Marjorie, 'when you eat like other people.'

Waiting for them in this noise—in this swarm of people, inside a glass box filled with music coming from several directions all at once and clashing, a hideous, discordant, deafening mixture—this was a nightmare. *How long will they be with their ghastly shopping?* When they at last came to get her they were laden with shopping bags. 'I'll take that, Mum,' said Sonia. 'You give me the heavy one and the kids can carry the other things. What a successful morning.'

A morning of sheer hell.

'You're certain you don't want to buy anything, Lydia?'

'Certain, thanks.'

'Did you pack a skirt?' asked Marjorie. 'You can't come to the Mahler concert in those jeans.'

'I packed a skirt and a top and decent sandals.'

'Not those dreadful runners, or thongs?'

'No. Sandals.'

In the afternoon Lydia slept, long and deep in the room she once shared with William. Two single beds and waxed furniture and pretty striped wallpaper to match the curtains and fluffy bedspreads in cream.

London, 1982

She slept for four hours and dreamt of Enrico. He was wearing his gold cross and smelt of salt.

'Hi, Lyd,' said Clive. 'Long time no see. Good flight? Not too jet lagged?'

'I'm feeling fine.'

She wore a green cotton skirt that her mother had insisted that she iron and a white cotton shirt and her respectable sandals. They stood together by the tea and coffee urns in the Gospel church hall where a remarkably enthusiastic audience had endured an hour and forty minutes sitting on hard wooden chairs. The audience clapped and cheered and yelled, 'Bravo!'

'And so the last note dies away, thank God,' said Clive disloyally. 'What did you think of it?'

'Several chairs being pushed across a polished floor. Squeak, moan, squeak. Are they supposed to be good, this lot?'

'Very good, I'm told, for amateurs. Almost up to professional standard.'

'Who says?'

'The local paper, friends. People are always saying how good they are.'

'Quaint,' murmured Lydia. 'Which one is the stand-in second fiddler?'

'Not sure. Think the one over there being congratulated. Red hair. Known as Timps.'

'Why Timps?'

'Used to play the drum or a triangle or whatever orchestras call timps.'

'And cymbals.' Lydia giggled. 'Look at all that lot round Sonia.'

'She's a very good organiser, like her mother.' Clive sounded calm, placid. 'Mahler isn't an easy chap to play. Not that I know anything about music. I know nothing whatever about Mahler but I'm told his work isn't easy to interpret.'

'Why don't they try something they can interpret?'

'They've given many performances of the popular works. Nobody was quite sure how the Mahler would go down.'

'Apparently very well.'

Sonia was shaking hands and being kissed and patted on the back; the leading cellist, her great instrument firm between her fat knees like a fortification against rape. All these people thought the world of Sonia.

Clive whispered, 'You look lovely, darling. Could you sneeze or something and get a tissue out of your handbag?'

'Why?'

'I want to give you something.'

Lydia coughed obligingly and fumbled for a tissue from her ancient leather shoulder-bag. Clive pushed something in an envelope inside it and turned to the coffee urn.

'What is it, Clive?'

'Coach ticket, return. Victoria bus station to Cromer. I'll meet you Tuesday half-past four.'

'I can't. I mustn't.'

'You must. Don't let me down.'

A drop of scalding coffee burnt her toe in her only decent sandals and she moved her feet away and people surrounded them, hard, harsh British voices, drawling voices, affected suburban voices, and accentless upper-crust voices belonging to women in shapeless cotton dresses and vague-eyed men who could be professors. The coffee urn hissed, spat.

'Something wasn't quite right in the slow movement,' said Sonia. 'Do you think anybody noticed?'

'Nothing was wrong. Technically perfect, my dear. You did wonderfully.'

Sonia pushed between them, her mouth full of curried egg. 'What are you two whispering about? Help serve the tea and coffee.'

Everybody was praising Sonia, the food delicious, the performance exquisite. Clive disappeared, carrying a plate of curried eggs. Just behind Lydia, Marjorie stood smiling. 'I know Sonia is my daughter but I can't help being proud.'

'You have every right to be,' said one of the men who looked like a professor.

Lydia bent down and rubbed her reddening toe.

'I've a couple of people I must see, Mum, if you wouldn't mind—advertisers, travel agents. I might be out all day. We're getting the Brits interested in our islands.'

'British,' said Marjorie. 'I *do* dislike being referred to as a Brit.'

'Sorry. British.'

'You're seeing business contacts on a Saturday?'

'I fixed up a few things before I came away. You don't mind?'

'Why should I mind? Sonia is bringing the children to tea. They're going to help in the garden. They're always ready to do little jobs for me around the place.'

'I'll be back in time for tea.'

'The music critic has promised the concert a good write-up in the press.'

Lydia asked curiously, 'Which newspaper?'

'The *Gospel Village Weekly*. It comes out on Tuesdays.'

'The local paper.'

'And a very good one it is. They always send a music reporter to our concerts. He thinks the world of Sonia. She's been photographed for the *Gospel* several times. There's one of her in evening dress I like. I'm asking for a print so that I can get an enlargement made.'

'Everybody around here appears to think the world of Sonia.'

Marjorie, clearing the breakfast table, snapped, 'And you, my dear, have always been jealous of her.'

'I am not jealous of Sonia.'

'You have been jealous of your sister since she was born.'

'We're very different, but that doesn't mean I envy her.'

'Lydia, do you take me for a fool?'

And what does she mean by that? 'Mum, I must go, if you don't mind.'

'Do as you please, my dear. This is your holiday.'

'I'll wash the breakfast dishes before I go.'

'Please don't bother, Lydia. I am perfectly able to manage a little washing-up. I am quite used to living alone.'

'I'll see you at tea-time, then.'

No answer. Both the kitchen taps were turned on hard.

Lydia walked to the Underground. A misty morning with the promise of heat later in the day. Shafts of smoky sunlight punctured the canopy of cloud. The Underground was filled with tourists, rucksacks and foreign tongues; German and French, Swedish and a noisy party of youths and girls from Denmark. Lydia stood on the platform, watching the lit-up indicator. Northern Line; Morden via Charing Cross. The train arrived with a rush of air and noise. No desperate rush-hour on Saturday. She found a seat. From time to time the train stopped in tunnels and outside there was nothing but blackness and inside somebody's laboured breathing. She read the advertisements again and again, for bras and slinky underclothes, for jobs at employment agencies; courses for receptionists, holidays in Spain and Portugal.

Kennington, Stockwell, Clapham North, Clapham Common, Clapham South, Balham, Tooting Bec, Tooting Broadway, Colliers Wood, South Wimbledon ...

At Colinwood the mist had cleared, the air was thick and hot like high summer. The ticket collector, a West Indian, looked blank when she asked him the way to The Shrubberies but a woman with a brimming shopping trolley buying *Woman's Own* at the bookstall knew it well, described the route and walked beside her. 'Next on the left, second on the right. Can't miss it.

There's flats on the corner, where the old dairy was, when this was country.'

Was this ever country? A long line of bungalows stretched each side of an empty street. Annie's house—if this was Annie's house, Number 15—had a crazy paving path with weeds growing between the paving stones. No flowers, no lawn, like the other dull, neat houses in this street. Lydia went up the path and rang the doorbell. No answer. Perhaps the doorbell didn't work. She lifted the knocker and banged three times. There was a curious silence, hot, steamy, a feeling of being watched. She banged the knocker, again, again.

A voice called through the letter slot.

'Who is it? Go away.'

'Lydia.'

'Who?'

'Lydia. Your sister's daughter. Lydia. It's Lydia. Annie, please let me in.'

A window opened next door. Somebody unseen was listening. A long wait but a rustling sound behind the door. Bolts slid back, a chain rattled. The door opened, a crack, then wider.

There, looking at her, was a wizened replica of her mother. She made a peculiar noise, this woman with her mother's wide-spaced eyes and small, straight nose. The noise was a strangled scream. 'Oh, God, Mallie,' she said. 'Mal. Mal. Mal.'

Chapter 20

'Annie, don't you remember me? It's Lydia. Annie?'

Annie fumbled in the pocket of a loose, shabby cardigan and produced a pair of steel-rimmed spectacles. They rested loose, slipping on her nose.

'You gave me a shock. Thought you were somebody else, somebody who's been dead for years. Come in. Shut the door. Bolt it. And there's a chain.'

Her voice and body shook. Lydia asked gently, 'What's the matter? You frightened somebody might break it?'

'Habit. I like to be locked away.'

Lydia closed the front door and bolted it and slipped the chain into its slot. Annie watched her, small, bent, standing in the narrow hall, her fingers against the wall as if she had lost her sense of balance, as if one side of her body were lighter than the other. Her skin was furrowed, deep lines, crevices down her cheeks and around her mouth. She was a sickly grey. Only her head had colour. Her hair was strawberry-blonde and curly. Bright gold-pink curls tipped across her forehead. 'My God,' she said, her voice hoarse, strangled as her scream had been, 'how old were you when I last saw you? Five? Six?'

'I've been looking for you ever since.'

Lydia went to Annie to take her in her arms, to hug her. Annie stood there, unresponsive, her hand now flat against the wall. Holding her was like clutching at a bag of bones hidden in a worn, frayed cardigan, a small turkey or a chicken that had been stripped of meat, used up in a stock pot and ready to be thrown out wrapped in rags. The incongruous mass of curls moved, slipped. Annie wore a wig.

'A lot of good it will do you now you've found me, Lydia. Your mother know you're here?'

'Nobody knows I'm here.'

'Come in. We'll sit in the front room. Don't use it much. I sit in the kitchen near the telly.'

It was a narrow house stretching backwards into gloom, a corridor with closed doors and a smell of dust and stale cigarette smoke and another barely discernible smell like the scent of a circus or a zoo where animals are in captivity. Ill health? Annie looked very ill. She pushed open a door. 'Sit down, Lydia. Staying with your mother, are you?'

'Yes. I'm only here three weeks.'

'Want a drink? Tea or gin? Haven't any coffee. You smoke?'

'I'm afraid so. Yes.'

'Me, too. Like a chimney. Lot of nurses do. Or did, when I was working. Sure you don't want a drink?'

London, 1982

'No, thank you, Annie. I just want to talk. You don't seem very pleased to see me.'

Annie reached into her sagging pocket for a crumpled pack of cigarettes, lit up awkwardly, her hands unsteady. 'Haven't you found out yet the futility of turning back the clock?'

Not a good beginning, after all these years. This wasn't the Annie she remembered. This was a sick old woman who didn't want her there. Lydia dug into her shoulder-bag for her cigarettes. They sat looking at each other, smoking. Strangers.

The small square room, papered in faded cream and green, faced the street. Curtains were drawn and behind them yellowish blinds. The light was greenish-yellow, the colour of a stagnant pool; an unused room with a cheap two-seater sofa and a fireside chair. No pictures, no ornaments. Annie sat in the fireside chair. Her knees protruded like knives through a worn grey skirt. In this light her hair looked a peculiar pink. Lydia, trying not to stare, found her gaze drawn to that head of hair, to the wasted body, the shabby clothes.

'Annie, I want to know where you've been all these years. Why did you disappear?'

'I stayed on in India after Partition and then I went to other places.'

'What places? You promised you'd come to Australia. You promised me. You always loved Australia and you used to swear you'd take me there.'

'You weren't mine to take.' Spoken roughly, curtly, the curls blurred by clouds of smoke.

'Where did you go?'

'After India? Nursed in north-west New South Wales and then the Northern Territory. Aboriginal children. Lots of work.'

'So you did come to Australia. We were in Sydney, Annie. Sonia and I were at school there. You could have come to see us.'

Annie looked at her, blue eyes faded, the surrounding whites a bloodshot yellow. She pushed at her spectacles, blinked, tugged at her remarkable head of hair. She began speaking quickly, jerkily, hoarsely. 'I often thought of coming. It wasn't possible. I loved Sydney and that house you all lived in, where I lived with old Aunt Bin. Went to the convent in Sydney. Adored it. Learnt First Aid from a nun who had worked in India. Said it distressed her, the inequality, the prejudices, the poverty.'

She stopped, drew in her breath as if her lungs were short of oxygen and went on talking, in rapid spurts, with breathless pauses. The old vitality was there still, and the bitterness, the anger. 'She once said to me: "How can a baby be an untouchable?" I've never forgotten that. When I went out to join the parents I found all that out for myself. Made myself quite unpopular defending the Eurasians. Most spurned, unlucky, pitiful people, the goddamned saddest result of British imperialism. Misfits. Neither one thing nor the other. Not quite acceptable. Not "quite-quite".'

Lydia waited. Annie lit another cigarette. 'Used to write long letters to Aunt Bin about India and the snobbery. But it got at me, India did. Asia does

London, 1982

get at people. Aunt Bin was dotty about Singapore. You've been there.'

'Once. For a very short time. You sound as if you knew I'd been there.'

'I suppose I know a thing or two,' Annie said ambiguously. 'They ever speak of Bin?'

'I don't think so. Wasn't she some cousin of Grandmother's?'

'Yes. Not "quite-quite", as your grandmother was fond of saying. Drank tea in the kitchen with her char.'

'After Australia, Annie, where did you go?'

'Back to India for a time, then Vietnam, Kampuchea. London. I worked here for several years, worked for an agency. The money wasn't bad. Retired. Had to. Can't go on forever.'

'You were in Vietnam?'

'One of the last out of Saigon, but people who were there never talk about it. Ever met anyone who was in Vietnam who will tell you what it was like?'

'I suppose not, no.'

'A catastrophe. A catastrophic waste. So don't ask me.'

'I heard you were working in disaster areas. That's all I knew.'

'Who told you that?'

Clive had told her. 'Can't remember who told me, but I wrote to so many hospitals and agencies. I tried so hard to find you. There were no Anne Deighton-Gayes. Not a single Anne Deighton or Anne Gaye. Did you get married?'

'God, no,' said Annie, lighting her third cigarette.

'I only just found out by fluke your other Christian name so I stuck pins in the London telephone directory until I found you. Georgina. Nice.'

'I like it. Wearing another hat. People call me Georgie. They would. I didn't care for being called George. So butch.' A raucous laugh; coughing on the cigarette and spilling ash.

'You were in Australia at the time we lived in Sydney,' said Lydia flatly. Annie hadn't wanted to see any of them again, not even her.

'I expect I was.'

'But why didn't you contact us?'

'It wouldn't have been wise. Better I kept away. Like a drink? Not tea. Something stronger.'

'A bit early. No, thanks. Just tell me what happened to you.'

'Mind if I have a drink?'

'Of course not.'

Annie pulled herself out of the fireside chair. She knelt awkwardly beside a cupboard in the wall and produced a smeared tumbler and a bottle of gin. *She drinks, Clive said. Annie drinks.* 'Mind if I remove my hair? It tickles in this hot weather. They have a wig library in the local hospital and they gave me this. Difficult to fit, I was. Small head. I'm rather partial to the colour. Barmaid blonde.'

She put the wig on the floor. Lydia saw she was almost bald. Dry-looking grey hairs sprouted from her scalp like seedlings. 'Annie, you've been ill.'

London, 1982

'You could say that. After I retired. Radical mastectomy. Had a tit cut off and all the glands removed. Chemo. Sends one bald. All right now, bit lopsided. Like to work again but far too old. Your mother's getting on as well but I expect she's just the same. Elegant and vain.'

'She's very elegant, yes.'

'The beautiful Marjorie Harper. I rang her after the op. Told her she should have a mammogram. Sisters should, half-sisters even. Breast cancer runs in families, so they say. She hung up on me.'

'I'm sure she has regular check-ups. Mum is careful of her health.'

'You had your tits x-rayed?'

'Some time ago. I wasn't well after Adam left Australia.'

'Get them looked at every year. I'm warning you. Adam your son? I heard you'd had a son.'

'You heard but you never wrote to me?'

Annie drank her gin as if it were a glass of water. She swallowed, said crisply, 'No point. I knew both you and Sonia had married. My friend Jeannie used to keep me well-informed. After your sister married Clive Baird Jeannie told me lots of things.'

'Who's Jeannie?'

'We nursed together. Got out of Saigon together. Good friend. Her daughter worked for your brother-in-law's company and Jeannie would tell me all the gossip, the secrets. I knew quite a lot about you, Lydia, more than you'd care to have me know, I daresay. Then Jeannie died and her daughter lost her job just recently, when your brother-in-law became managing director of that place. After all the years of loyalty she gave that firm. Gave him, I'd say. Replaced her with a twenty-year-old. Charming, I heard he is. Makes plenty of money. Loves money. Likes an easy life. Can't stand trouble. Wriggles out of anything. Don't know what you see in him. Nothing to do with me.'

Annie finished her gin, got up to pour another. Lydia ran her tongue across her lower lip. Her throat felt parched. 'You had a friend whose daughter worked for Clive?'

'Small world and getting smaller with all these planes roaring above our heads. Nice girl, Jeannie's daughter. Artistic. Wanted a job to do with screen-printing, materials, that sort of thing. What she got was a dogsbody job, personal assistant to the export–import manager and there she stuck. Believe she had a bit of a thing about your brother-in-law. Believe a lot of women liked him. Your sister puts up with it. Knows where her bread is buttered. Lydia, you've grown up beautiful.'

'I'm not beautiful.'

'By today's standards you are. Not considered beautiful when you were little. My God, the way they treated people, the fucking British Raj.'

Now the ice, the awkwardness, the reticence, was breaking. Annie, her mind stirred to activity through alcohol, looked animated. Lydia said, 'I remember some of the things you used to say, and how you swore, as bad as the British Other Ranks, the B.O.R.s they were called, weren't they? I remember your bad language and Ayah looking shocked and the band playing "Abide With Me" and the places you used to take me and the poverty and the smells.'

'You were a lovely child. I loved you.' Annie flung her cigarette end in the empty grate and lit another. 'Difficult. Wouldn't eat. Sensed every atmosphere. Always listening, watching. You used to bang your head against your pillow until your forehead was bruised and red.'

'Did I? Sometimes I've wanted to go back and see it all again and remember. I'd think: one day when I find Annie we'll go back together and find the past.'

'Nobody can find the past,' Annie said. 'Things change. The smells haven't changed, not when I went back the last time. Everything else had changed. They make the most terrible romantic films in Bombay and Madras and the traffic and pollution—awful. Stinking. Everything industrialised. Tamal Nadu.'

'What?'

'The state of Madras that was. Don't you read the newspapers? Madras is now the capital of Tamal Nadu.'

'Yes, of course,' said Lydia weakly.

'Remember Parry's Corner and Popham Broadway? It's now called Netaji Subhash Bose Road, well, officially it is. Mount Road, which you could spell when you were three, is called Anna Salai. Everything's different. Not better. Not a hope of that. Still beggars and disease. Still floods and droughts and fights and riots and blood. A bloody country but beautiful. It gets you.'

'So you went back.'

'Twice. The second time was supposed to be a holiday. It was before Jeannie died. Took a trip together. Vegetarian in the south. You'd hardly know the British had ever been there. No meat and booze. I kept remembering the club. Strict prohibition in Tamal Nadu. Need a liquor permit to get a drink. Not the place for me.'

Again the hoarse, raucous laugh.

'I can't understand why you didn't even ring us when you were in Australia.' *Make her tell. Make her.*

'To be insulted by your mother? Not bloody likely. I used to get down to Sydney occasionally, when Robert was alive.'

'You saw the Major?'

'From time to time. Used to meet him in the golf club. Your mother never went there. Didn't care for golf. Poor old Rob. Drank too much but he had his points.'

'I can't think what they were,' said Lydia dryly.

'He was generous.'

'Annie, he was mean.'

'Not to me. Used to send me a bit of money when I was broke. Your mother found out and raised merry hell. She didn't need the money. Had plenty of her own. He could do what he liked with his own bloody money. Your grandmother gave your mother a hell of a lot of money, even after she married that brigadier or whatever he was, her boyfriend she met in Ooty. Not a penny came my way.'

'Why, Annie? Even I got a little bit to help with my education, and I inherited the island.'

'Your grandmother ignored anything unpleasant, shut her eyes to it, went on being the gracious lady—between nips of booze—a habit she's handed down to me. But once, just once, she said I was a filthy slut. Immoral.' A wide, sly grin slit the ravaged face. 'So she didn't leave me anything. What do you think of that?'

'Were you? Immoral?'

'By their standards. A first-class whore. By the standards of the nineteen-forties. So was your mother. Again by those standards. Different today. No standards whatsoever these days. Don't think it's made much difference. People always do what they want to do. In those days it didn't do to get found out. Today it doesn't matter.'

'I think you're wrong about my mother. Mum's very prim and proper. She never even swears, like you.'

'Ha,' said Annie and drained her glass and staggered up for more. 'Rob left me this house. It was his parents' house in the days he sold men's shoes in Balham, before he went into the army and got a wartime commission and became the British gent. Your grandmother considered him rather common. Definitely not "quite-quite". Grammar school boy, poor old Rob.'

'The Major left you this house?'

'It was bomb-damaged and then rented out when his parents died. Killed in the Blitz, both of them. He once told me they weren't our class. He was a bloody idiot about class. Inferiority complex.' Annie sat back in the fireside chair holding a half-glass of neat gin between her hands. 'Hell of a job getting the tenants out, but in the end they went. He left me this house in his will and your mother accused me of stealing. Said he wasn't in sound mind when he made his will. We wrote stinking letters to each other, your mother and I. Through solicitors. I won. There was nothing the matter with his mind. He wanted me to have this house. He wanted to give this place to me. Kept on at me to take it. Don't ask me why. For old time's sake, he used to say. He hadn't anything else to give. He told me years before he died he was leaving his house to me. It's no palace. It's shabby and ugly but it's home.'

'I knew there was some squabble over money. That's all I knew.'

'Not only over money. Your grandmother and your mother found out about Rob and me.'

'You—and the Major?' said Lydia, stunned.

'Me and poor old Rob. We consoled each other. He was bloody unhappy and so was I. Used to drink ourselves silly at the club.'

'Annie, I think I will have a drink, if you don't mind.'

'Help yourself. Haven't any tonic. Always drink it neat. It's the bubbles in tonic water that make people drunk. Ever heard that one?'

'No, and I doubt very much if it's a fact.'

'The tap's in the kitchen if you want yours watered down. Kitchen's a bloody mess. I can't get things done these days. Such a bore.'

The kitchen was small, untidy; piles of newspapers and magazines on the floor, a cardboard box

London, 1982

of empty gin bottles, wooden draining-board, stained sink with cups and plates unwashed and more bottles underneath, an old basket chair in front of a large television set, an old-fashioned refrigerator. Lydia looked inside. Needed defrosting. Almost empty. Half a sliced loaf, carton of margarine, slab of cheese, hard, rotting at the edges. *God, she's sick and starves herself. What can I do?*

She heard Annie calling. 'Lydia. Can't you find the tap?'

'Coming.'

Sit back calmly. Make her talk. 'Tell me about you and the Major.'

'Nothing much to tell. History is a repeating pattern. Like you and your brother-in-law. All the telegrams or cables or whatever you call them now. Telling you where to meet him and sending off the air tickets and you went running every time. Carol, Jeannie's daughter, used to send them from the post office in case anybody in the office found out. Sent them in her lunch hour. And every time he flew off and met up with you he got Carol to get a large bunch of roses delivered to his wife. Carol is a great one for discretion. He trusted her. Singapore, New Zealand, and didn't you spend some time with him in Bangkok? I also heard you were divorced and he and your sister have your son living with them. I suppose he's Clive Baird's child?'

Lydia whispered, 'Yes, Annie, yes.'

'Carol told me that one. She didn't think he was

your husband's child from something your brother-in-law let slip. Used to confide in Carol, see? It won't go any further, not through Jeannie's daughter. I watched that telly series. Got hooked on it, like a lot of other people. Then we heard your ex-husband was gay and dying from a virus poofters catch. No wonder you had a lover—several for all I know. Pity it was your brother-in-law. I bet your sister loves you. Mad about you, she must be.'

'Annie, don't.'

'I call a spade a spade.'

'Sonia has never been fond of me, but she doesn't know.'

'Of course she knows. She's not daft. Why would she take your child if it wasn't his? Your mother loathes my guts, your little sister Sonia loathes yours. Understandable. Nobody's to blame. Faults on both sides. Can't understand why you gave away your child.'

'I haven't given him away. One day soon I'll take him back.'

'Can't understand why you let them have him in the first place. Education in Australia's as good as here. These days it is, so they say.'

Lydia finished off her watery gin. She felt faintly sick. 'I'll tell you one day. Annie, who was Mal?'

'Why do you want to know?'

'Because of what you said when you saw me. It gave you a shock. Why?'

'If your mother has never told you it's not for me to say.'

'Oh, yes, it is. Do I look like this person you say has died? Was she a relation? You're the only one to tell me. My mother lies. My grandmother was a liar. It's everybody's right to know where they came from. I know I'm not the Major's child. I've always known. He resented me, hated me.'

'He had his reasons. He shouldn't have taken them out on you and I used to tell him so. Rob was far from perfect but he wasn't all that bad.'

'Who was Mal?'

Annie poured another drink. She lit another cigarette. 'Mal was your grandmother. I've always guessed. Today I knew for certain. You're the image of her. Dorothy O'Malley. Everyone called her Mal.'

'Grandmother?' Lydia could think only of June Deighton-Gaye.

'On your father's side. Your father, Henry, was Mallie's only son. She was a lovely person. A nurse. We worked together. Henry was a doctor, Royal Army Medical Corps. I loved them both.'

'Is he dead, too? The man you say is my father?'

'Blown up in the retreat from Burma. At a First Aid post. Whizz, bang, gone. She was a widow, Mal was. She died the day after Henry got blown up, the morning after she got the telegram. Heart gave out.'

'God, Annie.'

'She was in the sluice room cleaning out bedpans when she died. A trained sister but doing the most unpleasant jobs nobody else wanted and taken for granted. Nobody appreciated Henry either. Anglo-Indians. Eurasians. My best friends.'

Eventide

Lydia felt the gin burning in her throat, sweeping through her body like a flame. Annie's hoarse voice went on. 'Henry was my friend, too. I adored him. Your dear mother swiped him. Your mother made a point of snatching any man who looked twice at me. She always pinched my men. Looked as if butter wouldn't melt in her mouth when your grandmother was around, but my God, give her a sling or two and she was off, throwing herself around as if there was no tomorrow. A sexy piece your mother was. What used to be known as a girl with lots of "oomph". Looked like Rita Hayworth. Know what Rita Hayworth looked like?'

'I've a rough idea. You and Mum are quite alike. Same eyes, same nose.'

'She blind as a bat like me?'

'She wears glasses for reading.'

'She looked sexy.' A torrent of words poured from Annie. Hoarse; excited; short of breath. 'I said she looked sexy. Didn't say she was highly sexed. Had to be the centre of attention. Funny thing, women like that often don't like sex. She didn't, except with my poor Henry. Flung herself at him. She told me she'd met her dream boy, her great romantic dream. I didn't know it was Henry, not then I didn't. She was pregnant. She was engaged to Rob. Nobody knew she was pregnant except me. Henry was in Burma when she married Rob. Huge wedding. All the trimmings. She swore you were Robert's child but one night she let out to me that you couldn't be. She didn't like it, not with Rob. Sex with Rob disgusted her. They only had three days before he was sent on active service and nothing happened. Not enough to conceive a child.'

Again the grin; a hint of malice. 'She couldn't stand him near her and he couldn't get it up. Sorry if I'm vulgar. He never had that problem when he was with me. Then he went off to Burma. Got wounded. When he came back you were born and your mother was seeing the regimental shrink. Poor old Rob was horrified. Your natural father never knew about you and nor did Mal.'

'O'Malley, O'Malley,' Lydia whispered. 'That should have been my name. Not Harper. So my mother and the Major didn't want me.'

'Your mother was afraid.'

'That I'd turn out black.'

'Not black. Half-and-half. Mal looked distinctly half-caste. Beautiful but an obvious touch of the tar-brush. She was married to an Other Rank with an Irish father but he had a touch of tar on his mother's side. What were they supposed to do, British and Irish Tommies, in a country short of women, in a society where pure white women despised them, treated them like dirt? They used to be called "the fishing fleet" before the war, the English girls coming out to India looking for husbands. They wouldn't go near a half-caste, not them, the bloody snobs.'

Annie was panting. There were tiny spots of red on her cheekbones, above the sunken cheeks.

'What happened to Mal's husband, my other grandfather?' Lydia asked.

'Died. Some fever when Henry was a kid. Mal worked her guts out to feed and clothe and educate Henry. Rob and I had a row once because he called them Bangalore Irish. A lot of them about, he said, as if they were scum. That's how things were.'

Lydia shouted, 'Why didn't my mother abort me if she was so afraid I'd look like scum?'

'In India? In those days? Dangerous. I wouldn't let her.'

'Did she try?'

'She lifted a wardrobe once.'

'Would my father—Henry—have married her?'

'I expect he would, if he'd known she was having you. Honourable type was Henry. But Marj was engaged to Rob when she was pregnant. Henry had already gone to Burma when they married. But Marj could never have married a Eurasian.'

Lydia demanded, 'Why?'

'Not the colonel's daughter. The great man's lovely daughter married to a half-caste? Dear, dear me, no. Out of the question. Not done.'

'Did Henry love her?'

'She said it was all on her side but I suppose he did. He was no philanderer. Didn't drink. Would never come inside the club, not even with us. Because they wouldn't have let him in, although they did relax their fucking rules a bit in wartime. I never had the chance to ask him if he loved her. He was attracted to her. A lot of them were. She led them on. Henry was my friend. We'd talk and talk. If we went out together she saw to it that she came too.'

'Did you love him, Annie?'

'I'd have married him like a shot.'

'You were a colonel's daughter, too.'

'Pooh to that,' said Annie. 'The colonel, your grandfather Deighton-Gaye, was dead. Killed in North Africa. What your grandmother and the regiment thought wouldn't have worried me one scrap. I'd have gone to the ends of the earth with Henry, if he'd wanted me. He didn't. Thought I was a jolly good sort. That's all.'

Lydia took a swallow of her watery gin. 'I can't imagine my mother ...'

'Losing her head? Going all weak at the knees over the most unsuitable man she could have picked? Unsuitable in those days, see? You have no idea what it was like.'

Lydia said, 'That's what Mum says when people ask her about India. "You have no idea what it was like." Don't cry, Annie,' for the tears were pouring down the crevices in Annie's face.

'Want to hear the whole story? Of course you do. That's why you came here, digging for the truth.'

'I wanted to find you.'

'Oh, I'll tell you. I'll tell you everything now I've started. I'll show you the past.' Annie rubbed her nose against the sleeve of her cardigan. Then she poured them both another gin.

There were photographs, in albums, or pushed carelessly into envelopes. Her mother and Annie riding ponies; a faded picture of her grandfather: Ian, 1919. 'Mal took that one. They'd met, my father and Mal. One of her relations gave me that picture after her funeral.' There were photographs of Ayah and the gardener and of her mother lying on a verandah pregnant and several of men in uniform and girls in summer dresses sitting around a swimming pool with drinks. There was an enlarged photograph of Grandmother Deighton-Gaye dressed in a smart 1940s suit and a big straw hat. There were several snapshots of the Major; khaki shirt, sleeves rolled up. Lydia remembered the ginger hairs growing up his freckled arms.

There was a little gold brooch with gold leaves and a crown and a snake in diamonds in the centre and the words IN ARDUIS FIDELIS stamped in blue. 'Henry must have given that to Mal. A relative of hers said she wanted me to have it.' Annie put it back in a little box lined with velvet. She began gathering up the photographs. Annie's treasures. 'Here's one of you, Lydia, a photograph of you with Ayah.'

A thin, sullen child in a frilly skirt holding the hand of an Indian woman. *I remember, I remember. The pieces of the jigsaw fit.*

'Take anything you'd like, Lydia. Do you want the brooch?'

'No, Annie. I'd rather not. It's yours.'

'Please yourself.'

'Annie, I'm going to take you out to lunch.'

'Never eat lunch.'

'I'll go out and get some take-away.'

'Couldn't eat a thing. I sleep in the afternoons.'

'I'm going to that shopping centre to buy some food. You haven't anything in the house to eat.'

'I have enough to eat.'

London, 1982

Lydia said roughly, 'You look half-starved.'

'I do all right. I've a pension and enough money for a bit of booze and I have the house. You go back now, to your mother's. They'll be wondering what's become of you and I'd rather you didn't tell.'

Lydia knelt beside the fireside chair. 'You're coming back to Australia with me. In two weeks, Annie. I'll fix everything. We'll have a stopover in Singapore so you won't be too exhausted.'

'Barmy,' said Annie. 'Flying across the world? Not me. Done with travelling. Besides, I have my treatment here.'

'You still have treatment?'

'A bit of radiotherapy now and again. That's no bother. Get a bit tired for a day or so. They pick me up and bring me home. I don't want to talk about illness, Lydia.'

'You can have treatment in Australia.'

'Be no different from National Health. People grumble about the queues. People always grumble. Doesn't worry me.'

'I'll see you get all the treatment you need. I'll get you to the best hospital in Brisbane and you can have a long holiday on the island. You'll love my island. Annie, please, I'm not leaving you alone in this house.'

'There's nothing wrong with my house except that it is dirty and ugly and has no architectural merits,' said Annie distinctly, with drunken dignity.

'You shouldn't be alone. You're not well. I'm going to defrost your refrigerator and buy some food.'

'You'll do no such thing.'

Lydia took her purse out of her handbag. 'I'm going to the shopping centre near the station. Annie, will you please not lock me out.'

'I might,' said Annie and shut her eyes. Lydia removed the cigarette from her fingers and a heap of photographs from beneath her feet. She laid them, and the brooch, beside the atrocious wig.

Hot outside; not a breath of wind. A scorching London day; heavy sky; hint of a storm. The supermarket was crowded. Tea, coffee, bread, butter, milk, cheese, eggs, bacon, chops, cream, two frozen quiches. A tin of asparagus. Tins of soup. Weighed down with shopping, she walked back to The Shrubberies. The woman next door was watering her front garden. She didn't look at Lydia. In the house on the other side a curtain twitched.

Annie was still asleep, lying crookedly, her elbows and knees exposed. They looked like panes of broken glass.

With the shopping, Lydia headed to the kitchen. *Find some rags—can't see any. Look under the sink. Ah, an unopened pack of cleaning cloths. Boil a kettle and find some bowls and put them on the refrigerator shelves until you get the bloody ice to melt. Wash the kitchen floor while the refrigerator defrosts; clean the sink and the draining-board. The freezing compartment is tiny. Push the quiches inside. They'll just about fit in. God, the time. I said I'd be back for tea.*

No time to do the bathroom. Must come back another day.

'Annie.'

Annie snored. Lydia bent over her. 'Annie, I've bought some food. Look in the refrigerator. I'm going now, but I'll be back next week.'

Annie sat upright, wide awake, reached for a cigarette. 'I told you not to go buying food.'

'I have, and you're going to eat it. I'll come again as soon as I can, and I'll book your flight to Australia. Where's your passport? And you'll need a visa.'

'Haven't got a passport. Don't go anywhere. Why would I need a passport?'

'You must have had one. Find it. If it needs renewing I'll get that done, or we'll get you a new one.'

'I don't go bloody anywhere. I don't go out. I'm not flying off to Australia. Too old.'

'You must go out sometimes. Otherwise you wouldn't have the gin.'

'They deliver.'

'It's a pity you don't get somebody to deliver food. Cut down on gin. Promise me.'

'You're a bully. Go away.'

'I'm going, Annie, but I'll be back.'

'Lydia.'

'Yes?'

'Some Eurasians inherit the best from each—the best from East and West. Some get the worst. That's the law of averages. Mal inherited the good, the very best selfless caring, and so did Henry. Perhaps the same applies to you.'

'I'm not a good person, Annie.'

'You've got whiter hands than Mallie had. Hers

were the colour of milky coffee. And you've got some freckles.'

'A right odd mixture.' Lydia picked up her shoulder-bag. She bent down to kiss Annie, smelt sourness and gin.

'Be careful of that main road, Lydia. Use the pedestrian crossing. People have been knocked down there.'

'I'll be careful.'

'Everyone I've ever loved has died, except for you. I did love you, Lydie. I'm sorry I kept away.'

'Don't be sorry about anything, Annie. Just get well.'

Walking back along the street she could feel eyes, the neighbours', boring into her back. She crossed the main road at the pedestrian crossing. *'Everyone I've ever loved has died, except for you ...' Annie, oh, Annie, Annie.*

The Underground again, and an almost empty train. Rattle, rattle, swerve and sway, Annie's gin fiery behind her eyes. *Crying. Can't stop crying. People staring. Can't stop. Can't. Find dark glasses. Henry O'Malley, my father. Son of half-caste parents. Blown up. Whizz-bang. Blown to pieces. Gone. Dead in a stinking war. Never knew of my existence, Lydia O'Malley, half-caste bastard. Who cares about bastards these days? Who cares about the colour of your skin? Born into the wrong age, I was.*

Annie and the Major. Unlikely pair. That shocked me. Annie and the Major consoling each other with booze and bed.

London, 1982

Mother knew. Grandmother Deighton-Gaye knew. Annie knew about Clive and me. She says Sonia must know. Stop crying. Think. Do something. Must blow my nose.

Annie in her horrid airless house, drinking herself to death. Nearly bald and thin and dirty. 'Everyone I've ever loved has died,' she said. Must get her a passport and a visa and take her away. I must take Annie away and look after her.

When Lydia returned to the Highgate house, Marjorie was standing outside her front door with a bunch of dahlias in her hand. 'You've missed Sonia and the children. Where on earth have you been?' She turned away and went inside without waiting for an answer. Lydia found her in the kitchen making a pot of tea. 'I take it you've enjoyed your day,' she said. 'You smell of drink.'

'Mum, I must talk to you.'

'If you've been drinking, Lydia, I'd prefer you went to bed. You look dreadful. Do you want a cup of tea?'

'Coffee, please. I'm dying for a cup of coffee.'

'Help yourself.'

Marjorie walked out of the kitchen. Lydia heard the television switched on for the evening news.

Chapter 21

On Sunday morning, Sonia Baird watched her husband moving around their bedroom. The new bathroom, the 'en suite', breathed out steam. Wearing a pink satin nightdress too small for her since she had put on weight, Sonia lay on her back, eyes half-closed. 'Sunday lunch,' she said. 'Mummy and Lydia. I invited Timps and Archie.'

Clive, by the dressing-table, studied a slight shaving cut beneath his chin. 'The new second fiddle. Why her?'

'Give her a bit of social life. She's only just joined the orchestra. She doesn't know a soul.'

'Who's Archie?'

'You know Archie. Archie Martin, professor of humanities at the university. Plays the clarinet.'

'What does a professor of humanities do when he's not blowing down his blower?'

'He lectures. On human culture. Literature, especially Greek and Latin.'

'Lord. A highbrow.' Clive tugged a sweater over his head. Last night's storm had cleared the heat. 'Has he got a wife?'

'Not at the moment.'

'I thought I'd go fishing and take the boys.'

'You can't. Lydia will want to talk to Adam. Go fishing where?'

'Only the Highgate ponds.'

'They're bored with that. They never catch a thing.'

Clive sat on the end of the rumpled bed. 'I suppose you're laying on a gigantic meal.'

'A roast with all the trimmings and apple tart. I've cleaned the house.'

'Good for you, darling.'

He stared at the wall above her head, frowning. Sonia asked, 'What's the matter with you, Clive?'

'Nothing, why?'

'You've been quite peculiar lately.'

'I have?' He found her foot beneath the bedclothes, pinched her toes. 'I'm no different from what I've always been. A dull old stick.'

'You're different. Are you worrying in case she takes Adam back?'

'Lydia?' A sharpness in his voice, reproach, as if Sonia should not refer to Lydia as 'she'. 'Lydia has every right to take him back. He's an Australian citizen, born out there. He's not ours.'

'Mummy rang last night. You'd already gone to bed. You go to bed awfully early these days.'

'Worn out. Heavy week.' He shifted his position on the bed, stretched his arms.

'You shouldn't have changed a personal assistant like Carol for a secretary, a child hardly out of school.'

'She's not too bad, the new one. Bad speller but

she'll improve. The young ones need to learn to read a dictionary.'

Sonia wriggled. 'You're sitting on my feet. That hurts. What made you get rid of your precious Carol?'

'Matter of cutting costs. Carol wanted a better job. More pay. The board said no.'

'Carol,' said Sonia, rolling over on her side, 'always had a yen for you. Wanted you for years.'

'You're being silly, darling. Dear old Carol? What an absurd idea.'

'She isn't old. Younger than I am, I bet. Getting rid of her to cut costs? One woman's salary? We going broke?'

'Of course we're not going broke. The company has been overstaffed for quite some time. Uneconomic, paying somebody like Carol a high salary. The young ones don't demand big money, not when they're inexperienced, and they're good on the computers. Carol loathed computers. What did your mother want last night?'

'Lydia was out all day and came back drunk. Not reeling about but smelling of drink and red-eyed. Mummy sent her off to bed. Very worrying.'

'Your mother's always worrying about drink. Just because one sherry to greet visitors is her limit, and a glass of wine at Christmas. Lydia doesn't drink.'

'How do you know she doesn't?'

'I don't, I suppose. Never thought about it. I'm going to mow the lawn.'

'Too wet, Clive, after last night's storm.'

'Must get on with something.'

'Can't you just sit and talk? We never talk.'

'Of course we talk,' he said irritably. 'What do you want to talk about?'

'You find her attractive, don't you?'

'Carol? Hard worker. Deserves a top admin job. Not that attractive. Not to me.'

'Not Carol.'

'Who, then?'

'Lydia.'

He looked at the wall behind her head and up to the ceiling. Sonia had painted the ceiling a colour she called dusty pink. 'I suppose Lydia is quite attractive. Not pretty-pretty. Different.'

'She's that all right. When we were young she was considered plain.'

'Most men, I think, would find her attractive. I didn't think she looked too well at the concert. Very thin and pale.'

'She has always looked like that. Pasty. I think we did the wrong thing, taking Adam away. Things would have worked out eventually.'

He turned to her, accusingly. 'It was your idea.'

'Yours, too.'

'Don't you want him?'

Sonia sat up in bed, leaned forward, large white breasts pendulous, overflowing the satin nightdress. 'I've got enough to do. You've got enough to pay for. When he moves up to the senior school he'll cost the earth. Why should we keep paying for Lydia's mistakes?'

'Sonia, it was you, and your mother, who were always so keen on private education. It was you and your mother who insisted Lydia was not a suitable person to rear a child.'

'If we keep him we should adopt him legally.'

'She wouldn't hear of that.'

'How do you know she wouldn't? We haven't discussed it. Or have you discussed it with her?'

He looked blank. 'How can I have? I've only seen her at that concert.'

'Really?' Sonia said. 'Really?'

'Lunch today will be the second time I've laid eyes on her since we were both in Sydney.'

'You've been to Sydney several times since we were there together. I'll bet my bottom dollar you looked her up.'

'Why would I do that without telling you? Lydia's island is a long way from Sydney. I've never seen the place.'

Sonia yawned. 'Bet she gets around.'

'Not anywhere near me, if that's what you're inferring. Australia's a massive continent, darling. Remember? You've lived there.'

'So have you.' She added, sarcastic, bitter, imitating him, 'We met there. Remember, darling? We were married there. We got around. Tip-top air services, you used to say. Lots of little planes for getting one around. Excellent safety record. Best in the world. But you wouldn't have business contacts on the islands, would you, darling?' She looked at him and smiled. 'Flying to Nodding Blue or the nearest airport to it would be a waste of time.'

'I've never been there in my life.' He pushed the

sleeves of his sweater up his arms as far as the elbows, then pulled them down until they touched his wrists.

'Don't do that, Clive. You'll stretch the sleeves. I made that for you, remember, darling? Hand-knitted. All done by me on winter evenings. How nice I used to be.'

'And very nice it is. My favourite weekend gear.' He stood up, pulling down the sweater at the waist. 'I might not be in for lunch today.'

'But Lydia's coming.'

'Won't make much difference, will it, my not being there? Don't feel very social. The professor of humanities will get me down.'

'Of course he won't. Archie's sweet and you're always in for lunch on Sundays.'

'Make a change to go fishing by myself.'

'And sail a boat on the ponds like a little boy. Clive, what on earth's wrong with you?'

'I'm sorry,' he said. 'I'm sorry. I need a break.'

'From what? Me? The children?'

'From everything. I'll be in Manchester on Tuesday. Staying overnight. Did I tell you?'

'You didn't tell me. You never tell me anything, but never mind. Going to Manchester is not a break. Why don't we leave the kids with Mummy and take a little trip before the summer's really over? Spain would be nice this time of year. Most of the tourists will have gone.'

'Can't spare the time.'

'You never find time for anything, except work and Adam.'

'I spend no more time with Adam than with the other two.'

'You spoil him. He's your favourite.'

Outraged, he said, 'I do *not* have favourites.' He stood looking at the carpet, pushing at the pile with his feet and smoothing it back again.

'Darling, you do take me for a fool.'

'I certainly do not take you for a fool, Sonia. Anything but. You say I'm peculiar. So are you.'

'You want her.'

'Want who, for Christ's sake?' He was furious, blazing.

'Lydia.'

'Now you *are* behaving like a fool.'

'I'll never agree to a divorce, you know. I'll never give this house up. I won't. I don't believe in this newfangled amicable divorce and going shares with everything. If you want a divorce you'll have to get out quick and let me have the children, my two children, and the house and every single thing that's in this house.'

'Get out?' He looked askance, colour high, jaw unsteady. 'Why on earth should I get out?'

'If you want to run off with Lydia, have the guts to admit it and go. Get out. Go. Run off with Lydia and Adam. Both of them. Just don't stand there looking like a whipped dog and calling me darling. That's all I wanted to talk about. Now go away.'

'You believe I want to run off with Lydia?'

'Don't you?'

He said, husky, as if he were about to weep, 'I'd never leave you, not unless you wanted to be rid of me. I wouldn't blame you if you did. I'm not much good to anybody.'

Sonia lay flat on the bed and stretched, wriggling her toes beneath the covers. 'I never said I wanted you to go. I said go if you want to go. That's very different. I love you.'

He looked down at her, his face red, his mouth open. 'You've never said that to me, not for years.'

'You should have known.'

'How can I know something that isn't evident?'

'It should have been perfectly evident,' said Sonia, turning over, her face against the pillows. 'One doesn't go round every day telling somebody you love them, not after living with them for years. How boring for you if I had. More boring than I am already, a dreary housewife who happens to be fairly musical. I'm no adventuress who skips around the world, befriending freaks and making films and running Pacific islands.'

'Lydia is no adventuress and I've never found you dreary.'

'No?'

'Of course I haven't. I thought we were happy. I'd never leave you, not unless you told me to get out.'

Sonia climbed out of bed. 'I might one day, do just that. If I go on feeling as I do. Clive, please be in for lunch and try to behave normally, if you wouldn't mind. I don't want Mummy all upset. Now I'm going to do something about the joint.'

She wore her old caftan over her nightdress and went downstairs without combing her hair. He

Eventide

heard her call out, waking the children. He flopped back on the bed; felt exhausted; found he was sweating; heart banging. He could hear it. Must have a check-up, lose some weight. God. Sonia called up the staircase in her normal voice. 'Breakfast, darling? Bacon? Cooked breakfast as it's Sunday.'

'Nothing cooked, thanks. Just some toast.'

'Gracious, Clive. You can't be well. Go back to bed.'

Sunday lunch at Sonia's. The house looked clean, attractive mats on the dining-table, and flowers. Sonia wore white trousers and a pale-pink shirt. Lydia wore her jeans, Marjorie an expensive linen trouser-suit in lettuce green. The red-haired woman known as Timps was dressed in a childish summer frock with a bow at the back and a big black bow in her hair. She would have passed for a teenager until one saw her face. Timps was a worn-out fifty. She praised everything, seemed nervous, anxious to please. 'Sonia! My goodness, Sonia! What a gorgeous house! I love your tiles. Italian? You laid all those yourself? How do you find the time? I'm quite hopeless in the house. Quite impractical,' and turned, gushing to Lydia. 'Lovely to meet Sonia's sister from Australia. Didn't get a chance to talk to you at the concert. I was in such a whirl. You're not at all alike.'

'No,' said Lydia.

'Nobody would take you for sisters. There's generally some family resemblance with sisters.

London, 1982

What do you think, Professor Martin? You're the expert on genetics.'

Archie Martin, professor of humanities, had a goatee beard and pale blue eyes. 'I'm not an expert. Genetics covers a very wide field indeed, including the study of heredity in animals and plants.'

'Like trying to grow blue roses,' said Timps and clasped her hands.

Clive was pouring drinks.

'Scotch for Archie, darling,' Sonia told him. 'Mummy, what about a G and T?'

'No, thank you, darling. Not in the middle of the day.'

'Sherry, Lydia? Scotch? Glass of wine? I know how the Aussies go on about their wine. Swear it's superior to our Common Market plonk. They even make champagne and think it's as good as French.'

Archie turned his pale blue gaze on Lydia. 'You a connoisseur of wine?'

'I'm afraid I'm not. No, thank you, Sonia. Soda water for me. And ice, if you have any.'

Sonia broke into a peal of laughter. 'Big sister over there has a hangover. Went out drinking yesterday and we don't know where she went, do we, Mummy?'

Marjorie sipped orange juice, murmured, 'Now, girls. Now.'

They all looked at Lydia, expectant, waiting to hear where she had been. She dug an ice cube from her soda water and sucked it. 'Seeing business contacts. What a silly fuss.'

'Do you enjoy living in Australia?' asked Archie, tactful, filling an awkward conversational gap.

'Love it.'

'What exactly do you do?' Timps twisted her fingers like an excited child. 'Sonia said something about an island. Like a desert island. No roads. Fascinating. Isn't that fascinating, Professor, meeting somebody who lives on a desert island? Do you have your desert island discs?' She looked round anxiously, waiting for laughter. Only Archie smiled.

'We have television and radio. We even have hot water. I run a small motel.'

Sonia urged everyone to sit down for lunch. As usual the children were eating in the television room, as if Sonia wanted to hide them away. Did they eat with their mouths open? Did Adam still have a tendency to throw food?

'Why don't they sit down and eat with us?' Lydia asked, and Sonia looked annoyed. 'Today's children don't sit down to meals as we had to do. They rush in and out of the kitchen and pick all day. Duncan won't touch green vegetables, so Diana says she doesn't like them. Adam does as they do. They get enough to eat, Lydia. They're perfectly healthy. You're just not used to children.'

'I get a horde of them on the island.'

'Other people's. That's very different.' Sonia's face was pink.

From the television room came a roar, a husky voice—Adam's—and the sound of something being thrown across the room. *So he still has tantrums*, Lydia thought. *How often, I wonder? How does Sonia cope?*

London, 1982

She glanced at Sonia's bright pink face.

'They've been fighting lately,' remarked Sonia. 'I suppose kids of that age always do. Almost teenagers. I expect things will get worse, from what other parents say.'

'I think they're gorgeous,' said Timps. 'Absolutely gorgeous. So well-behaved.'

'Have them for a weekend,' suggested Sonia, busy at the sideboard, face turned away. 'All yours. Feel free,' and Timps shook and giggled.

'In my teeny-weeny bedsit, Sonia? If I had the space I'd love to have them for a week.'

Marjorie sat down at the table. She unfolded her table napkin, carefully smoothing it over her lap. Clive carved the leg of lamb. 'Sundays here are so relaxing,' said Marjorie. 'Just what Sundays are meant to be.'

Lydia, far from relaxed, felt her throat contract. The old, old sensation at family meals; fear, dread, nausea. 'Sonia, give me the children's plates. I'll take them in.'

'If you want to,' said Sonia ungraciously. 'Don't let yours get cold. That's Duncan's. He only wants roast potatoes and a roll. Diana might eat a runner bean or two. One never knows.'

'What about Adam?'

'He eats most things when he feels like it. One never knows with any of them. I've given him a bit of each.'

The children knelt on the floor eating off a coffee table. Lydia sat by Adam. He cut his meat neatly; did not eat with his mouth open nor throw his food on the floor or at the wall. None of them said a word. The television set flickered in the background.

'Have you thought about coming back to Australia with me, Adam?'

He swallowed before he answered. 'Not yet.'

'Will you have a great big think this afternoon?'

'I'll try. There's no school in that place, that island.'

'There are schools on the mainland, or we could move.'

'Move where?'

'Sydney.'

'To where we lived before?'

'No. Not there.'

'Is my father in Sydney?'

'Yes.'

'He's not on TV now.'

'He's ill.'

'What's wrong with him?'

'Pneumonia, I think it is.'

'What's pneumonia?'

'A nasty illness that affects the lungs.'

'You're divorced.' Adam chewed, swallowed, balanced a runner bean on his fork. 'They said. They told me.'

'Yes.'

'Is Janno on the island?'

'Of course he isn't, darling.'

'Is he in Sydney?'

'No. He's gone for good.'

Adam asked curiously, 'Dead?'

'He might be. I don't know.'

'Why don't you know?'

'Because I never see him.'

'Is Imogen dead?'

'Of course not. She's still there and she rings me up.'

'I can't come until after skiing.'

'Come in January. High summer in Australia. Swimming.'

Bribing him. Manipulating him. Adam ate a second roast potato. 'You my real mother?'

Shocked, she said, 'Of course I am. You know I'm your mother, Adam.'

'Im could be my mother. Or Sonia. I know a boy with three mothers. He's a friend of mine.'

'I'm glad you've got friends at school.'

'Everyone has friends at school,' said Diana, her voice still thick from her cold. 'I have two best friends. I don't know which one I like best.'

'Sometimes she hates them both,' said Duncan.

'I do not.'

'You said.'

Adam put his knife and fork together. 'We had a movie at school, you know.'

'Yes?'

'On birth.'

'Was it interesting?' Lydia asked. A progressive school they went to, obviously. Nobody when she was at school had ever mentioned birth.

'It was okay. It was in colour.'

'My class didn't see it,' said Diana. 'We've got to wait till next year. Duncan didn't see it either.'

'I did.'

'You did not. You weren't allowed.'

'I saw it and all the blood. Ugh! Buckets and buckets of blood all over the sheets.'

'He's telling lies. He's showing off,' Diana told Lydia primly. 'He's never seen a movie about giving birth.'

'I saw one on the telly. The lady screamed and yelled and made awful faces.'

Adam looked at Lydia. 'Did you shout and scream when you had me?'

'I don't think so, no.'

'Some people have two mothers, a step one and a plain. You're not my step?'

'Adam, of course not. I'm the plain one. I had you just like the person in the movie you saw at school.'

'Some people have two fathers,' Diana announced. 'I want more gravy. Bread and gravy.'

'Gravy, ugh,' said Duncan.

Adam asked, 'Am I an only child? Uncle Clive and Aunt Sonia said I am.'

'I'm afraid you are, but you have your cousins and you've had a good time here with Duncan and Diana.'

Adam put down his knife and fork and placed his plate in the middle of the floor. He asked her hoarsely in his almost broken voice: 'You going to have another when you get back?'

'Another child? No, darling. I haven't got a husband.'

'Jack Gordon's mother hasn't got a husband but he got born. She never had a husband, not one.'

'Shut up. You're not supposed to say,' Diana told him. Her plate swam in gravy. She looked carefully at Lydia. 'You're not too old to have a baby, are you? Not as old as Mum.'

'I'm older.'

'Mum's fat. Fat people are old.'

'Not all fat people and your mother isn't fat. She's plump.'

'She's *fat*.'

'Grannie isn't fat,' said Duncan. 'She won't have a baby though. She's very, very old.'

'Mum's very, very fat.' Diana licked her knife. 'Have you seen her in the bath?'

'I have,' said Duncan. 'By mistake. She didn't lock the door. They have their own bathroom now and we have ours.'

'They have an on-suit.'

'Suite.'

'That's what I said.'

'You did not.'

Sonia shouted from the hall. 'Lydia, come back, will you? Or I'll have to heat your lunch up. We're almost finished.'

Returning to the table she found herself laughing. 'What's funny?' said Sonia.

'The children made me laugh.'

'Ghastly, aren't they?'

Lydia picked up her knife and fork. Clive poured more wine.

A tour of the garden after lunch; squeals of delight from Timps who had no garden, lived in a one-room flat on her own and tried hard to grow plants on her balcony. 'I talk to them. Do you talk to your plants, Sonia? I'm told they grow better if you do. I talk away to mine but they don't react. They wither away and die. Do you think they object to my practising the violin?'

'No, but the neighbours might,' said Archie, who also lived alone. His neighbours disliked the sound of his clarinet. 'I practise at the university now, not at home.' Archie had a garden. It had gone to seed since his wife left. Divorced was Archie, with two grown-up sons he rarely saw. Timps poured out sympathy. 'How sad for you.'

'I'm not sad,' said Archie. 'I enjoy it, being alone.' He began talking about fertilisers and mulch.

Clive took the children for a walk. Sonia filled the dishwasher, made coffee, handed round chocolate mints. After the inspection of the garden the silence in the drawing-room was uncomfortable. Marjorie picked up the *Sunday Times*. Timps picked up the cat, tickled it, kissed it, squealed when it nipped her finger. Archie slumped in an armchair blowing his nose. Cats gave him hay fever, sometimes brought on an attack of asthma. Sonia removed the cat. Marjorie, smoothing the newspaper, remarked that an election might be announced quite soon. Archie said he was a Labour man. Timps thought she might vote Labour this time, although her family had always been Conservatives. 'One shouldn't just follow in one's parents' footsteps over important issues. One must have a mind of one's own,' said Timps, who seemed to Lydia mindless, a giggling fool. Marjorie, staunch Conservative, voiced no opinion and turned to read the feature pages, marking books she intended borrowing from the library. Sonia flicked through the Sunday colour supplements and began talking about the next orchestral production. Lydia didn't know the people involved and had never heard of some of the composers. Sonia and Archie wanted to try out new, young composers. 'One has to give the young a chance.'

'Not easy,' said Timps. 'I find modern pieces very hard, but then I'm not much good. Would you believe I once auditioned for the BBC Symphony Orchestra but they didn't take me. Only second fiddle, of course. Always a second fiddle, silly old me.'

'You'll do all right with us,' said Archie and turned away to talk to Sonia.

At half-past three Timps announced she must be off. 'Outstayed my welcome,' she gurgled. 'So enjoyed myself I forgot the time. Such a lovely, lovely day, Sonia. I'm so full up I can hardly move. Oh, dear, the poor non-existent waistline!'

She was thin, flat as a board; a silly schoolgirl with an ageing face. Lydia glanced at her mother. *God, why can't we leave? Why doesn't this professor, the old bore, go home too?* Archie stayed on, sitting close to Sonia and from time to time turning his head and looking closely at her profile as though inspecting whether or not she had cleaned her ears. Sonia brought tea and scones and Archie told her what a wonderful cook she was and what a lucky man Clive must be. He made no attempt to leave until Clive came back with the children and offered him a scotch. 'Wonderful, wonderful day,' he said to Sonia.

'Knew he'd be a bore,' said Clive, scowling, when Archie had finally departed. 'What a pair of bores.'

'You didn't help much, going out all afternoon.' Sonia clattered to the kitchen with a tray. 'Mummy, I'll drive you and Lydia home.'

'Clive will take us, darling.'

'Clive can unload the dishwasher and feed the kids and get them into bed, for once.'

Sonia in a fury about something. Back in her mother's house Lydia read the Sunday papers in silence. Marjorie watched television. They barely exchanged a word.

When Marjorie had gone to bed she dialled Annie's number. No reply.

Happy families. Just the way a Sunday should be spent.

Chapter 22

Lying became easier with practice. Telling her mother she simply must get down to Sussex to see an old friend—such a nice person, used to be a stills photographer in Australia and had decided to retire in England, in Goring—and wrote regularly and would be so hurt if Lydia didn't make the effort ... Easy, it was. The lies flowed like a stream of milk. 'When I rang her she said I must stay the night, Mum, because the evening trains get so crowded. I'll be back tomorrow. May I ring for a cab to get me to Victoria?'

Even the facts were right. Trains to Goring-by-Sea, Sussex, left from Victoria Station. Coaches for Cromer left from the coach station at Victoria.

The coach station was jammed with people, luggage, buses attempting to reverse and officials yelling, 'Stand clear!' Her seat was at the back by an open window too stiff to close and by the time they reached the motorway it was raining hard. Rain trickled down Lydia's neck, on her shirt, her newspaper, her book. It was a long and jolting journey.

Eventide

At Cromer there were whorls of mist. Mothers with small children and spades and buckets and beach balls and crumpled sandwich papers left the bus. The driver called out, 'Have a good time!' Lydia sat in the bus shelter to wait for Clive. He was twenty minutes late. When he pulled up by the bus shelter he waved, beckoned but did not leave the car. The company car was a distinctive, conspicuous green. He opened the passenger door and Lydia climbed in and threw her zipper bag at the back. 'You're wet,' he said.

'It's raining.'

Not a good beginning. Something wrong. Smile. Touch him. Talk. She couldn't think of a word to say. She saw a seafront and lines of hotels and boarding-houses. The sea and sand were invisible, swallowed in the mist. 'Not far now,' he said, but it seemed a long way when visibility was almost nil. The company car had windscreen wipers that squeaked. 'Must get that seen to,' he said.

They turned into a street packed with pedestrians carrying umbrellas and walking in the gutter because the pavements were so narrow. She saw old buildings, shops, cottages, a church, a pub with an inn sign swinging. The area was vaguely familiar. *William and I came to Norfolk. I think we came somewhere here.* The cottage was at the top of a muddy lane hidden by bushes, trees, creepers. It was a long way from a main road, from a village, a neighbour or a shop. 'Adam's cottage,' said Clive. 'There!'

The gate was broken, the path overgrown. There was a sagging porch, windows with small diamond panes, a broken doorstep and a thick wood front door with a heavy latch. 'Sorry about the mud,' said Clive.

'How old is it?'

'Seventeen something. The previous owners renovated a bit, extended it, but a lot needs doing.'

Standing in the porch with her zipper bag on her shoulder she felt wild rose thorns scratch her arms. Inside it was dark and damp; one big room with an enormous brick fireplace, a grate with the remains of ash, a basket of logs, an old sofa, a table scratched and ink-stained with a broken leg, a rug thrown across a bare floor and dusty boards that creaked. Overhead were rough beams, blackened, ancient. A few letters lay by the door. He shut the door and gathered up the letters. 'Electricity bill. I've had that laid on. Rates.' He stuffed the letters in his pocket but not before she saw one of them, a fat one in an airmail envelope with Australian stamps. The handwriting, big, round, sprawling, was unmistakable. Imogen. Imogen Smythe writing to him here, in the wilds of Norfolk. Was this Adam's cottage or Clive's secret lair?

'Got potential,' Clive said. 'Lots of potential. Lovely little place. So many people after places like this. Can't help but increase in value.'

'Lovely,' said Lydia. 'Such low ceilings. Perfect for eighteenth-century dwarfs.'

'You don't like it?'

'Of course I like it.'

'Come and see the bedroom. Mind the step.' They ducked their heads, avoiding beams. The bedroom contained two camp beds and rolled-up

Eventide

sleeping bags. It smelled of damp. Lydia started to shiver.

'Where are we going to eat, Clive? I'm ravenous.'

'I thought right here. I got in some stuff, tinned kidneys and some rice and there's wine. You could cook up something, couldn't you, darling? Such an awful night for going out.'

'Somebody might see us.'

He looked hurt, feeling the sting. 'I don't know anybody, except the local builder.'

'Could I have a bath, Clive? I'm cold and wet.'

'The bathroom's pretty primitive. There's an old geyser. It doesn't work. I did warn you about lack of most mod cons. Couldn't you just boil up some hot water if you want to wash? The bog works all right. Chain and string. Just pull the string.'

'I hope it's not outside.'

'In the bathroom, darling. I'll light a fire, shall I? And we'll have a drink. I stocked up with quite a bit of booze.'

'You say Sonia has never been here?'

'Never. I've plans for the properties I've bought, old places that'll fetch a fortune in the future. Until Adam's grown-up I can let this as a holiday cottage or even on a long lease to retired people.'

'Not many retired people would live here, not if they were elderly. They'd have to walk two miles for a loaf of bread.'

'There's a shop and post office not that far away. Artists, painters would love this place. You can't beat a Norfolk sky.'

'Artists and painters might not pay the rent,' said Lydia unhelpfully.

London, 1982

She inspected the bathroom. Bath stained black where the tap had dripped; huge, deep bath perched on curling iron feet; wash basin cracked across the middle; lavatory stained brown with a wooden seat. Hanging on a rusty nail was one used towel. Water from the tap came out almost black.

'Why's the water such a funny colour, Clive?'

'Iron. The local water's full of iron. Very healthy.'

'Splendid for the anaemic,' said Lydia. Her teeth were chattering.

In the kitchen she found tins of baked beans, a can of kidneys in red wine sauce, a packet of rice, dried peas, an opened pack of cereal, condensed milk, tea-bags. 'No coffee, Clive.'

'Darling, couldn't you just for once drink tea? There's wine.'

'Not for breakfast, thanks.'

Under the sink two potatoes sprouted long, white tendrils.

'No vegetables, Clive.'

'There're peas, I think. Oh, darling, don't make such a fuss. I look on this place as a camping site until it's been done up.'

He lit the fire. The wood was damp and the chimney smoked. He opened a bottle of wine. He poured it into plastic tumblers that needed washing. 'Picnic stuff,' he explained, apologetic. 'But it's decent wine.'

They sat on a rug by the smoking fire. 'I've even thought of retiring here myself,' he said. 'Until Adam is old enough to take over.'

'Retire? At your age?'

'Get out of the rat race and enjoy my life.'

Eventide

'I can't imagine Sonia retiring here. She'd want to bring the Gospel orchestra with her.'

'I don't expect to be living here with Sonia.'

'You'd live here on your own? You'd go bonkers.'

'Sonia and I might not be together for much longer. We might separate. I think she's had enough of me.'

Lydia finished off her wine and held out her glass for more. *Is this what I've been waiting to hear for all these years? Is the unavailable Clive to become available at last and will I be the final choice?*

She asked, quietly, gently, terrified of the answer and unsure, if there was an answer, that it would be the truth: 'What's gone wrong between you and Sonia? Something to do with me?'

'I think she knows. I believe she's known for a long time that Adam's mine.'

'I've always told you she must know.'

'She's never said a word, never. Sonia doesn't bitch—until recently. She thinks we've been meeting when I've been away. That's what she implied. I told her I'd never been to Nodding Blue Island in my life.'

'One grain of truth in all the lies,' said Lydia.

'I never wanted to hurt her, or you, or anybody. I can't bear hurting people.'

Lydia thought: *But you do, you do, and never know it.*

'Somebody's been talking,' he said. 'Damn. Forgot to buy some bread. Somebody's seen us and talked.'

'Your ex-personal assistant, perhaps, the one you sacked?'

'How the hell did you find that out? Sonia

wouldn't have told you. She's always imagined Carol and I—'

'Did you?'

'At one time. Nothing serious. Who told you, Lydia, about Carol?'

'Annie. I went to see her on Saturday.'

'The drunken aunt. You went to Colinwood? All the way to Colinwood?' He said 'Colinwood' as if she'd had a trip to the Antarctic and back.

'I went by Underground. On the Northern Line.'

All sympathy, he muttered, 'Poor darling you.'

'Your Carol's mother was an old friend of Annie's. They nursed together in Saigon. Jeannie, her name was. She died.'

'Carol never mentioned her mother dying. I knew she and her mother shared a flat and her mother had been a nurse. Would have written her a line if I'd known, if somebody had bothered to tell me about her mother.'

'Carol told Jeannie about our trips and how she sent the telegrams from the post office so no one at your place would know.'

'Disloyal bitch,' he said. 'I trusted her. I thought she was discreet. I thought I'd taught all my staff discretion.'

'She was loyal and discreet, your Carol, until you became managing director and got rid of her. Did Sonia know her?'

'They talked on the telephone. Sonia used to ring when I was overseas to find out if everything was okay, that is if I hadn't had a chance to telephone myself. I kept in touch with the office. Had to. I think they did meet at an office party.'

Eventide

'Perhaps,' suggested Lydia carefully, 'they had lunch together after Carol left the company, and Carol spilt the beans. A woman spurned, as the saying goes. Why did you get rid of her? Because now you're based in London she might have become embarrassing? Wanting to see too much of you? Making demands? Whatever it is the other woman is supposed to do? Poor old Clive. Poor Carol.'

He took her wrist, held it hard, almost twisted it, hurt the bone. 'You believe everything that drunken woman told you?'

'I'm afraid I do. I love Annie. I always have. She'd never lie. She even told me who my real father was.'

'Christ! What a wonderful drink-sodden time you must have had on Saturday with your tipsy aunt. Bloody gossips. Carol tells her mother who tells your aunt who tells you. My God, women!'

A log in the fireplace began to blaze. Sparks flew from it, falling on the rug. Lydia moved and stamped the sparks out with her foot.

'Did you hear me, Clive? Annie told me who my natural father was. He had Indian blood. He was a doctor. Killed in the retreat from Burma. My grandmother was three-quarters Indian and Annie says I look just like her. Sonia was the Major's only child. I am my mother's half-caste bastard.'

He showed neither surprise nor interest. 'Makes no difference to you and me.'

'Aren't you interested? Don't you want to hear the details?'

'Who cares about the past? Do you feel better now you've dug out all the dirt? Proud of yourself, sneaking to a friend of Carol's, discussing me ...'

'Annie was a friend of Carol's mother. We did not discuss you. Carol, unlike some of us, must have been close to her mother and told her the office gossip. Why not? Don't get so worked up, Clive. You look as if you'll have a seizure.'

'I'll wring her neck, that Carol.'

'You won't. You'll put it all behind you, as if it never happened. You hate fuss and trouble and emotional scenes. Just send Sonia lots of roses and she'll come round.'

'Roses?'

'I know about the roses, too. Annie found out a lot about us even if she hadn't seen me since I was five.'

Lydia thought: *I'd like to tell him about Annie and Robert and my mother. I'd like to tell him everything. He wouldn't care. He wouldn't want to know. Clive only worries about Clive and keeping his own life nice and neat and tidy and not hurting people because hurting people makes him uncomfortable.*

He found a bottle of whisky and poured a large measure which he swallowed in a gulp. Clive was no heavy drinker. Spirits made his face go red. He looked red and furious. 'You going to get a meal or aren't you? Because we're not going out.'

She put water on to boil for rice. She opened the tin of kidneys and stirred in wine. She fumbled in cupboards and drawers for plates and cutlery. The plates were plastic, so were the knives and forks.

She carried the food to the sitting-room by the fire. 'I hope we don't get poisoned. Nothing's clean.'

'I told you not to expect the Ritz. The old boy who lived here was ninety. Widower. Let the place go. I bought it just as it was, broken furniture and all.'

They ate in silence. It didn't taste too bad. Lydia finished off the wine. He opened another bottle. She whispered, 'I'm sorry if I've caused trouble.'

'What?'

'Trouble between you and Sonia. I'm sorry. I never made demands. I never asked for anything. You came chasing after me.'

'You wanted me just as much as I wanted you, and you know it, Lydia. I've always wanted you, since you were a skinny little creature getting yourself engaged to a homosexual who's brought more trouble to all of us than one would think possible.'

'He's dying, Clive.'

'Good riddance.'

'I think Annie's dying, too.'

'Drunken gossip.' The level of whisky in the almost full bottle was going down.

'I'm taking Annie back with me to Australia.'

'Going to look after both of them, are you? You're eccentric, Lydia. You always were. I had better plans for you.'

'Plans?'

'What's the good of talking? You're so calm and self-possessed and sarcastic.' He sounded a little drunk.

'What plans?' Lydia sat back on her heels,

looking at the fire. She threw on another log, watched it as it started to burn.

'I thought, you see, I thought if you sold your island you could come and live here for a while, you and Adam, both of you, in this cottage.'

'You said you were going to rent it out to pensioners or artists.'

'That was my alternative plan.'

The room was almost dark, the second wine bottle empty. The whisky bottle was half empty. Clive sounded distinctly drunk. 'Adam would have you and me and Sonia and his cousins ...'

'Half-brother and half-sister, Clive. We don't have to lie. I want Adam back.'

'Sonia will let him go. Now she will.'

'She'll have to, unless you start a paternity suit or whatever people do. Blood tests to prove paternity.'

He looked startled, shocked. 'I'd never do anything like that. And she wouldn't want me to.'

'She might, now she knows for certain about you and me. Or she might be too frightened of a scandal and upsetting Mum. You would be, too. You might get written up in the *Gospel Weekly*. What would all those amateur musicians say?'

He put his hands against his face. 'Stop it, Lydia. Stop talking to me like that, as if it's all a joke.'

Lydia continued calmly, 'I'm not sure she wanted Adam in the first place, if she hadn't guessed he was your son, even if she was upset about the Janno thing. She wanted to get him away from me because he belongs to you.'

He shouted, 'She's been good to him. She's done everything for him. He's fit and well. Haven't you noticed? He was a nervous wreck. I love him. You love him. I don't know what to do.'

'Go back to her and stay there. Make her happy. Forget all your other women.'

'Lydia.'

'Mmm?'

'Darling, there have never been other women. Only you.'

'Come now, Clive. I was never the only one.'

'The others didn't matter.'

'You might have mattered a lot to them.'

'That's their own damn-fool fault.'

She had never seen Clive drunk before. Tomorrow he would probably not remember the things he said tonight; but for a split second—for the first time ever—she hated him. *Devious, delightful, disarming Clive, my sister's husband; no, half-sister's husband, father of my child. My lover. I love. I used to love. So much.*

She screamed at him, 'I hate liars.'

'I've never lied to you.'

'Perhaps you can't help it. Perhaps you always want something you shouldn't have. The grass is always greener somewhere else ...'

'Shut up, Lydia. I thought you were too intelligent to talk in clichés.'

'You *are* a bloody cliché. I knew I wasn't the only one. I never asked.'

'I never said you were the only one, and you had no right to ask. What I did in my private life when

London, 1982

I was away from you had nothing to do with us.'

She said clearly, harshly, 'I had your child.'

'An accident. You don't regret it. Nor do I.'

'How many other children have you sired by your other women?'

'None that I know of,' he said. 'Sired? I'm not a stallion.' He smiled at her. Trying to make her laugh.

'I'd never heard of Carol until last week. I did know you met Imogen in Oxford Street when you were all alone looking at the Christmas lights, but I didn't know you corresponded. When she comes over again, will you bring her here? In Adam's cottage, as you call it, where nobody will recognise you except the local builder?'

'Imogen?'

'You've just had a letter from her. You hid it, stuffed it in your pocket in case I saw. With the rates and electricity accounts.'

'Oh, her,' he said.

'Yes, her.'

'We do write occasionally. We might even meet up again if she comes to England. What's the harm?'

'How many more women have you got tucked away?'

'You introduced me to Imogen. Nice, friendly woman. She cheered me up.'

'I'm sure she did.'

'You have no need to be jealous of her, darling. She's a very pleasant creature. Amusing. An amusing sleazy tart.'

Eventide

Lydia shrieked, 'You bastard!'

'I always thought, darling Lydia, you were so restful, the only woman I've ever known who never makes a scene.'

She pulled on her sweater and crossed the room to unlatch the door.

'Where do you think you're going?'

'For a walk.'

'I'll come with you.'

'No.'

The door was heavy, the latch rough and rusted. She felt it scratch her hand. She slammed the door behind her.

A clear, washed sky after the rain, pearl-coloured, flecked with gold. Silence. Country smells. The smell of fruit, ripe apples, blackberries. Somewhere somebody was making jam.

A signpost to Blickling Hall. *William and I filmed here together*; fireplaces, tapestries, portraits, a moat and lawns and a lake; the clock tower and the Dutch-type gables like a pen and ink sketch against the sky.

The gates of Blickling Hall were shut. Clive's car pulled up behind her with a screech of tyres. He had had far too much alcohol to drive. 'Come back. It's late.' The window slid down and he shouted, 'We'll look at Blickling Hall tomorrow.'

'No, damn you. No.'

He got out of the car and took her by the arms and shook her. 'Get in, for Christ's sake. Don't make a scene.'

She climbed into the passenger seat. She cried, loudly, with fury, anguish. She could hear herself crying as if the sound was coming from someone else. 'Oh, hush,' he said. 'You know I can't bear it when women cry.'

He drove badly, too fast, round the twisting street, up the muddy lane to the cottage. As soon as he was inside he reached for the whisky. He hit his head against a beam and swore. Lydia went to the decaying bathroom to clean her teeth, stumbled to the bedroom, unfolded a sleeping bag, lay down. Her eyes ached from weeping. *Jealousy is a futile, destructive emotion. I can't help it. I am eaten up by jealousy. Like Annie's cancer, it eats me up.*

He turned the light out when he came to bed. The country night was black.

They lay far apart, a yawning space between the beds. 'Don't be angry with me, darling. I'm sorry. Don't be angry.'

Lydia did not answer. She turned over and shut her eyes and felt his hand reach out across the gap between the beds. She ignored his hand.

'I do love you, darling, I really do,' he told her in the night.

Chapter 23

I hear mice scratching in the early hours. I find mice droppings on the kitchen floor. The morning is bland and sunny. I have missed the early coach. I can catch a train at twelve.

We drink tea for breakfast. The tea-bags are cheap, disgusting, left over from the days of the widower in his nineties. Deceased estate. There is no fresh milk. The cereal is stale. Clive puts my bag in the boot of the car. There is time for a drive, he suggests. 'But only if you'd like to.'

'I'd like to get away from here.'

He looks dreadful. So do I. We drive to the coast and walk across sand-dunes, miles of loose, shifting sand that stings the eyes. Trippers have left litter on the dunes, ice-lolly sticks and beer cans and condoms; even a pair of knickers. Hundreds of people have copulated in these dunes. Nasty word, copulate. Intercourse. Sex. Wonder why people refer to unleashed lust as making love? Not me. I love. I loved. I did. All over now.

Flat Norfolk landscape, flat grey sea. The morning passes slowly. He leaves me at the station. Have I enough money on me for the ticket? Just about enough. Train fares in England are very expensive. He sits behind the wheel while I climb out of the car. He presses some lever on the dashboard to release the boot. I take out my zipper bag and slam the boot down hard.

'See you some time before you leave,' he says.

'I expect so, yes.'

He really does look ghastly. An unpleasant scene with me and far too much to drink.

The absolute finale. Curtain down. No encores. The end.

'Did you have a good time?' asked Marjorie. She was sitting in her drawing-room reading a book with a pile of library books on the table in front of her. 'Sonia's just left. Ran me up to the library. I order more books than I've time to read. You enjoyed your trip?'

'Yes, thank you, Mum. Weather wasn't all that warm.'

Marjorie took off her spectacles, looked briefly at Lydia, replaced the spectacles and turned a page. 'Had a late night, did you?'

'Not all that late.'

'You look exhausted. Very peaky. Somebody telephoned you, somebody called James. I left the number on the hall table.'

'I don't know a James.'

'It was a woman, somebody or other James, with a north country accent. I think it was north country. A regional accent.'

'I don't know who she is, but I'd better ring her back.'

The woman who answered the telephone had a

Yorkshire accent. 'Mrs Napier, I'm Carol James. You don't know me. I believe you saw Georgie Gaye last week?'

'Annie. Yes, I did.'

'She died on Sunday.'

Silence. 'Can you hear me, Mrs Napier? Georgie died in hospital at seven-thirty on Sunday evening. The cremation was this morning. She said you bought a lot of food. I've given it to the Salvation Army. I was sure you wouldn't want it back and some of it was perishable.'

'She never ate it.' A whisper, choking.

'I'm sorry, I can't hear you very well. I don't think you realised she was unable to swallow solids.'

Lydia opened her mouth. No words came.

'You there, Mrs Napier?'

'Yes.'

'Georgina was to go into hospital this week to have a tube inserted into her gullet to help her swallow. You may have noticed she was very hoarse.'

Annie coughing, Annie's rasping voice; her grating laugh.

'I went round on Sunday morning. I have a key, you see.'

'I see.' Two words, extracted like rotten teeth.

'She never cared for visitors. I used to pop over every Sunday. I had to get an ambulance. She told me you'd been there. She was quite coherent but in dreadful pain. She wouldn't have come through any form of surgery. Far too weak.'

Annie leaning against the hallway wall, lopsided; bones sticking out like splinters, face shrunken beneath that wig.

'She died quite peacefully. Under morphine, of course.'

Say something. Say anything. What should one say? Carol James, Clive's ex-personal assistant, is on the line. 'Was anyone with her when she died?'

'The nursing staff, of course. I got there about ten minutes too late.'

'I thought she might get better.'

'Not a hope. The condition was inoperable. The tube might have made her a little less uncomfortable, enabled her to get a little food inside her, if she could have stood up to the insertion.'

'She said she was having treatment.' Lydia's voice rose suddenly so that Marjorie, sitting in the drawing-room with the door open, looked up from her book. 'I was going to take her to Australia.'

Carol James said coldly, 'That would have been out of the question. The primary, which did react to treatment, had spread. The secondary was larger. Throat. Then liver. Lymph glands. Surely you noticed the hoarseness?'

'Yes.'

'A very aggressive carcinoma. I know a little about these things. My mother, like Georgie, was a nurse. My sympathy, Mrs Napier. I'm your aunt's executor. A solicitor will be writing to your mother about Georgie's house.'

'House?'

'When she made her will, which was quite a while ago, before the mastectomy, she insisted your mother should inherit the house. She said it should have been your mother's anyway. I don't know what she meant by that. I gathered she hadn't seen any member of her family for years, although she had your mother's address and telephone number.'

'I'd have liked to have been at her funeral. I've been looking for her for years. Years and years.'

'She'd been living in that house since she retired. You wouldn't have had very far to look.'

Disapproval in the woman's tone; positive dislike; the woman who sent the air tickets from the post office, ordered Sonia's roses. Clive's woman, one of them. 'I must go now, Mrs Napier. Goodbye.'

'Who was that, Lydia?' Marjorie slipped a bookmark between pages of her book. 'What's the matter with you? Have you had bad news?'

'Annie's dead.'

Just a flicker of emotion on Marjorie's face. 'Who was that woman and why did she ring you?'

'A friend of Annie's. I saw Annie on Saturday. That was where I went.'

'You went behind my back.'

'Yes.' Defiant. *She's treating me like a child*. 'The funeral was this morning.'

'You couldn't have gone. You weren't here. I certainly wouldn't have attended, even if I'd known. Sit down, Lydia. Don't stand there staring at me.'

A sudden change in Marjorie's face, a sagging. The make-up on her skin was like thin paint put hastily on flaking plaster to hide the cracks, the under layer showing through in discoloured patches. But there were Annie's eyes and Annie's nose; a glimpse into the future of how Marjorie would look if she were sick or very old.

'I said sit down, Lydia.'

'You'd never tell me where she was. She called herself Georgina. Georgina Gaye. I found her in the telephone book and I had to see her. She was sick, sick, sick. She died of cancer. She was cremated this morning and not one of us was there.'

'Will you please sit down and calm yourself.'

'She's dead.'

'Annie was only a little younger than I am. Cancer where? Did she tell you?'

'She had a mastectomy. She rang you up and warned you, about breast cancer running in families. You didn't want to know. She'd had chemotherapy and radiotherapy but it spread. Please Mum, don't keep asking questions. I don't want to talk.'

She saw not grief in her mother's eyes but fear, terror. Her mother realising her own mortality; afraid of death.

Every afternoon Lydia walked to Sonia's as Adam came home from school. They went for a walk. 'He has homework,' Sonia would say. 'Duncan and Diana must stay in and get on with their homework before they look at television. And Adam has to have his tea before I go out.'

'I'll take him out to tea.'

'If you don't want the other two ...'

'I want Adam, Sonia, on our own.'

There was so little time before she went back to Australia, and Adam was still a stranger. She needed time. She needed patience. And time to heal. Nobody mentioned Annie's death. Her mother behaved as usual. They were no closer. They never would be. Clive she saw not at all.

Two days before she was leaving, she walked with Adam on the heath. October; leaves falling, blowing, rustling; sharp, cold wind.

'Finished all your thinking, darling?'

'I had heaps of thinks.' He was friendly now, the barriers breaking down. 'I could stay with you after Austria. I want to ski. You can't ski in Australia.'

'In the mountains you can. It snows up there in winter. I'll take you one day.'

'Is there a ski lift?'

'Of course. I'll fix up a school for you at the start of the new school year, the summer term.'

'Winter term.'

'No, Adam. Remember the seasons are reversed. We'll be in the Southern Hemisphere. You'll be starting school in summer. I told you. Swimming.'

'I'm not sure how long I'll stay.'

'You can't keep going backwards and forwards across twelve thousand miles. We can't post you like a parcel.'

'No,' he said, and laughed. 'I'd cost too much.'

'We'll give it a go, Adam, and see how we get along.'

'Okay.'

Twelve years old, intelligent, but wary; suddenly more malleable. Had Sonia indicated she no longer wanted him? Had Clive? At last he seemed to like her. *Not at the beginning; wanted nothing to do with me and Sonia encouraged that, kept us as far apart as she was able. Now he talks and listens and even smiles and laughs and I think he enjoys our walks without the other two. Something has changed since Norfolk, since Annie's death.*

'I didn't really hate Australia. Only bits.'

'I'm glad, Adam. Tell me about the bits.'

'We went swimming once.' He ran ahead of her, jumping to reach an overhanging branch of an oak tree. 'In the swimming baths. I could climb that tree.'

'Not in your school uniform. Tell me about when you went to the swimming baths.'

'When you were working.'

He circled the tree, patted an enormous dog that looked none too friendly, walked back slowly along the path, kicking stones. 'We went to swimming baths in Sydney. Indoor ones. In the winter. That dog's a she, not a he. It didn't lift its leg to pee.'

'You and Imogen went swimming?'

'Me and my father and him. Not Imogen.'

'Janno.'

Adam took a piece of string from his pocket and chewed the end. 'Want to know what he did?'

'Do you want to tell me?'

'I don't mind.'

'Tell me, then.'

'He took a boy inside the shower. There are men's showers in the swimming baths and women's and a gym and the other kind of baths with steam. He never took me in the shower. I wouldn't let him. This boy didn't mind. Do you know why he didn't mind?'

'No idea,' Lydia said, with dread.

'He gave him money.'

'Janno gave this boy money? How old was the boy?'

'My age, bit older. Nine or ten. He gave him lots of money, notes, not change. Twenty dollars. He said he'd kill me if I ever told.'

'You could have told me, Adam.' Shock, fear, revulsion. She put her hand on Adam's shoulder, kept it there, held him tight.

'Couldn't tell you. He might have killed me. You were never there.'

'I was often there, working in the flat.'

'You said go away, don't worry me. If I don't work we'll starve, you said. We didn't starve.'

'No, we didn't. I was wrong.'

'He liked the steamy baths.'

'He never took you there?'

'No. Expect I wasn't old enough. Who wants to sit in a lot of steam?'

'Some people do. For their health. To lose weight.' *To pick up young men and boys.*

'You ever been in one?'

'Not me,' said Lydia. 'Not my scene.'

'Do you know what else he used to do?'

'Tell me.' *At last he's talking, freely, openly.*

'Made his nose run when he hadn't got a cold. Guess how?'

'I can't guess, not possibly.'

'He sniffed up white stuff so his nose would leak. He'd carve it on the bread board with a knife and sniff. Sometimes he put it in a spoon. Coke.'

Cocaine. The money went on dope as well as gambling.

'Once he stuck a needle in his arm. It didn't hurt him. In his place that was, not ours.'

'Did William—did your father—do things like that?'

'He went to the dogs.'

'He what?'

'Dog racing or the trots. Or horse racing. He liked dogs and horses. He liked horses best. He didn't like the white stuff Janno ... Janno sniffed.'

The name came out with difficulty; apprehensive; watching her face for a reaction.

They were coming up to Kenwood House. 'Would you like to go inside and see the paintings?'

'Been there with the school. No, thank you. I liked it better when we went to the museum.'

'The last time I went to Kenwood House was with your great-grandmother. I remember a portrait of a woman called Mary, Mary, Countess of Howe. She was very beautiful. Do you remember her?'

'No. School outings are boring but not the skeletons in the museum. Are you frightened of skeletons? I wasn't frightened. There's that dog again.'

'A German shepherd.'

'We call them Alsatians here. Will we have a dog?'

'We might. Depends where we decide to live. Adam, I want to talk to you about lots of things.'

'Now? I've got homework.'

'Not now. When you come to live with me and you're a little older. I want to tell you things about our family. I hope we'll never lie to each other or hide things from each other. Not important things.'

'I don't tell lies, not very often I don't. What sort of things?'

'I have Indian blood. Way back some of my ancestors were Indian.'

'Red Indians or Indian Indians?'

'Indian Indians. Do you mind?'

'I've never met a Red Indian. At school there are plain Indians. One's called Raj. He's all Indian. There's one called Nigel who's just a little Indian. Are you just a little Indian?'

'Just a little, but it doesn't show in you.'

'Oh,' he said. 'You sure? I haven't any Indian blood like you? Not a tiny drop?'

'You must have a drop or two because you're my son, but you look like Duncan and Diana and they haven't any Indian blood.'

'Has Auntie Sonia or Uncle Clive?'

'No.'

'Has Grannie?'

'Definitely not.'

'Oh, good,' said Adam, indifferent. 'Can I tell people I've got a drop or two?'

'If you want to, but I shouldn't go on about it when Grannie's there.'

'Grannie,' said Adam, 'hates coloured people. She said. She wants them to go home. How can they, if they live here? Raj was born here and so was Nigel. They're English really but they don't look English. There's a Greek in the coffee shop. He doesn't look English either. Heaps and heaps of people don't. If I come and live with you, will you be out working all the time?'

'I'll make sure I'm not.'

'Auntie Sonia doesn't work but she goes out. Every day.' He started chewing on the other end of the piece of string. 'All day. Grannie comes to get our lunch in the holidays. Auntie Sonia is never home unless she's gardening or changing things around the house. She told me to call her auntie. Other people don't call aunts "auntie".'

'It's a little old-fashioned. Call her Sonia.'

'Sometimes I call her Mum because I forget she isn't.'

'Do you wish she was your mother?'

'Sometimes, when she's there.'

Frank, truthful. *Swallow that one and chew on it. Imogen first, then Sonia. I don't deserve this child.*

'She's always out,' he said, disapproving. 'She likes Diana best, then Duncan, then me. Uncle Clive likes me best, then Diana and Duncan both the same.'

'Clive likes you best?'

'Sure.'

Poor Clive. He's going to lose you. I still hurt for Clive. I hurt for Annie. I hurt for me. I hurt.

'I like him much better than I like her,' said Adam. 'He's always going out, too. Everybody goes out except Grannie. She only goes out when she has her hair done. She comes to our house or we have to go to hers. She makes us do things, like washing windows. She doesn't like mess. Sonia doesn't mind a mess because she's never there.'

'Adam, Sonia's out a lot because she's busy with the orchestra.'

'She goes out with Archie. Do you know him?'

'I met him the day I came for Sunday lunch.'

'He teaches.'

'I know.'

'Not school teaching. Advanced. In the big college place.'

'The university. They play together in the orchestra.'

'Not when he doesn't bring his blower and she leaves her cello in the house. But don't you tell I said.'

Annie used to say that in India. Now, Lyd, don't you tell I said that ... Don't you tell.

'You're laughing,' said Adam in amazement.

'I do laugh sometimes.'

'I've never seen you laughing. Can I throw a stick for that Alsatian? German shepherd?'

'If you want to. Don't go too near him. They're not always friendly.'

'That one is. Come, girl! Here! Catch! Fetch! Good girl!'

Oh, Adam, I love you. I love you. I've got to make you happy. I must wipe out the past, yours and mine. You can't turn the clock back, Annie said. We'll set it forward, begin again. Will Sonia begin again with that boring Archie? Sonia, wouldn't, couldn't. Could she? What about the kids?

'People are beyond me,' she said aloud.

'What people? Where?'

'Just people. Sorry. I was thinking out aloud.'

'I don't do that in case they find out all my thinks.'
'Very wise.'
'She won't have a dog, Sonia won't,' said Adam. 'She doesn't like them. She likes the cat. Shall I tell you something else?'
'Yes, please.'
'Archie doesn't like the cat. It makes him sneeze. I don't like Archie. Do you like Archie?'
'I don't know him.'
'What shall I call you? Mother? I called you Mother, didn't I? When you first arrived.'
'Yes, you did. It sounded very cold and formal.'
'What's formal mean?'
'Almost too polite. You call me what you like.'
'Lydia,' said Adam. 'I like your name. Lydie. Is that rude?'
'Not a bit.'
Annie used to call me Lydie. I'd like to take my Lydie to Australia ... Now, Lydie, don't you tell ...
'Good-oh,' said Adam. 'Can I throw one more stick?'
'If you like.'
'Do you know where Sonia and Archie go when they go out?'
'No idea.'
'To his house or the pub. They went to the South Bank once. It's like the Bank of England, I think.'
'Actually it isn't. You can go to theatres and concerts there.'
'Don't tell I said.'
'I won't tell a soul.'

'You're laughing.'

'Yes. Yes, I am.'

'Good-oh,' said Adam again. The dog barked. The stick flew high. The dog leapt up and caught it between her teeth.

Sonia offered to drive her to the airport. She had already booked a minicab. Adam would be at school. On her last night she took him to a film—a Western made in Italy he asked to see—and out to dinner for hamburgers and chips. She took in nothing of the film and could only pick at the hamburger, pointing out to Adam the health benefits of salad instead of chips.

'When I live with you, will you go on about eating greens?'

'I won't go on. I'll just see you eat some. Doesn't Sonia make you eat green vegetables?'

'She doesn't mind what we eat. Grannie does. Sonia leaves us things to heat up in the microwave when she's out with Archie. We get take-away if Clive's not there. He hates take-away. I can work a microwave. Can you?'

'I haven't got one.'

'I'll buy you one, when I get a job.'

'That's a long, long way ahead.'

'I'll do a paper round. Nigel does a paper round in the holidays. He's the one with some drops of Indian blood. Do they have paper rounds in Australia?'

'Not on the island. The newspapers come over on a launch.'

'I'd like to drive a launch.'
'Perhaps you will.'
She made saying goodbye as casual as possible and was surprised to see tears in Adam's eyes.

'Sorry Clive couldn't get away to see you off,' said Sonia. 'He sends his best wishes, bon voyage and all that.'

The minicab stood outside Marjorie's house. They brushed cheeks, as they had when she arrived. Marjorie came out on the pavement and unexpectedly pressed her hand. 'Look after yourself, Lydia. So peaky. You must eat.'

'I will, Mum, promise.'

'We'll let you know the exact dates of Adam's flight.'

'Get him to write to me.'

'We'll all write,' Sonia said.

All over. Relief, sadness, nostalgia came at once, emotions in which one drowned. The minicab driver, a woman, was very chatty. 'What time's your plane? I've got a cousin in Australia. Like to go there myself ... Get away from the English winter ... I've got a friend who went to live in Perth. It's rather grand there, isn't it? Isn't Perth the place with all the millionaires?'

Luckily the woman didn't expect coherent answers. Yes and no were quite enough.

PART IV

Australia and England, 1982–1993

Chapter 24

Returning to the island was bizarre. The launch plunged through heaving water; it creaked and shuddered. Cyclone Edwina had passed this way and removed the motel roof. The souvenir shop and the Quickie Snax were flattened. The pool, put in so competently by Enrico—or so Lydia had imagined—leaked, trickles of dirty water seeping into floors and corners, leaving behind an unpleasant smell. The dining-room was a puddle, its sinking centre like a lake, its ceiling a gaping hole. Broken tables and chairs floated upside down. The store cupboards, filled with bedding, had collapsed. Linen, obtained through Enrico's unseen contacts, lay in heaps of sodden dirt. After Cyclone Edwina had passed, petered out, tropical rain had poured down.

'From South America the bitch Edwina came,' said Enrico. 'You didn't read? It was in the pypers she is on her way. No radio. No TV. No launches for two dyes. That one you cyme on was the first. Two whole dyes. And no insurance. We have no builder's licence, no permission from a council.

They say the plyce keep up with sticky type.'

'Who says?'

'Inspectors. Police Rescue. Council. Flimsy hardboard and sticky type.'

'Tape not type,' snapped Lydia. After nearly a month away his accent jarred.

'I said that. Sticky type.'

'The band-aid job was your idea. I could hold you responsible.'

'No contract,' said Enrico. 'I am not a licensed builder. I work for love. I help you as my friend.' Enrico had lost a layer of tan. He looked, for him, quite pale. The visitors had been evacuated a week before. Fat Dorrie and worn-out Miriam had left, heading for Brisbane and new jobs. The Vietnamese had disappeared, although Enrico had not noticed when they left. Enrico, and Maria wearing not a sarong but a thin damp blanket, were staying only until Lydia returned.

'We go to jobs in Fiji, Little Bum. Maria knows hotels that need us.'

'It was you who did a patch job and said we must open in six months. If things went wrong you'd take the rap-tit, as you called it. You'd better take the rap-tit. I can't.'

'I tyke my ten per cents.'

'I bet,' said Lydia, blazing.

'I did good work. We make good money. Now you sell.'

'Like to buy me out?'

'A developer will buy. Sell, Little Bum, while the going's good, before the market falls.'

Lydia shouted, 'What do you know about the market? Who the hell is going to buy a place like this?'

'A millionaire developer,' said Enrico. He did not smile at her or attempt to pat her bottom. 'Little Bum, you'll be okye!!'

'You sneaky Mafia pig, you've betrayed me, exploited me, and I have no proof. Not one piece of paper, not one legal document passed between us. I signed receipts. You stood over me while I did.'

A gross betrayal she should have anticipated. *Lydia, you are a fool.*

'One hundred thousand clear, as it stands,' said the manager of real estate investment and development at the bank, 'including any items that might be salvaged or sold. You have contents insurance?'

'No.'

'We have worked out your situation as accurately as possible, providing you accept this offer. We have deducted expenses, bank charges, loan and unpaid interest on your loan and termination of loan charge. That leaves one hundred thousand of our client's final offer absolutely clear. There will be tax on profits, naturally. I advise you to discuss your situation with the Tax Department. Accept the offer, Mrs Napier. Another good one may not come our way for months.'

'It's not enough. I can't buy a house for that. Prices are going up and up.'

'Depends where you choose to live. A pleasant

little unit? Or you could buy a very nice place outside Brisbane for well under one hundred thousand. A piece of land around Nambour, perhaps? And build your own place? Many home buyers are doing that. You have to be careful, naturally, of council regulations, and an architect's advice is advisable for the uninitiated.'

'Your client is a shark,' snapped Lydia.

'A businessman, Mrs Napier. The buildings, what's left of them on Nodding Blue, will be bulldozed and the area of bushland cleared.'

'I can't accept. He's buying a whole island.'

'He's thinking in terms of a four-star hotel. Something very different from your enterprise. I expect you know how beautiful some of the developed islands are these days? Millionaires' paradises. Our client has a luxury resort in mind with amenities for yachts to berth, and perhaps a little airstrip later on, or a helicopter pad.'

'There isn't space for an airstrip.'

'These problems can be solved. With the scrub cut back it might be possible for small aircraft to land. A helicopter pad would be ideal. One needs cash flow.'

'One does indeed. I have no cash to flow. I want a better offer.'

'I'll approach our client again. I have little hope your property will fetch more. I'm working very hard in your interests, Mrs Napier.'

'And yours.'

'Come, come,' he said amiably. 'The bank granted you a loan.'

'With the island as collateral.'

'I do advise you to accept the offer. Prices may fall. We must be prepared for a recession.'

Lydia signed her inheritance away.

In order to economise while waiting for the money to come through, she flew to Sydney and asked Imogen to put her up. Taking advantage of Imogen, William would have said. So what? Other people had taken advantage of her. She hoped wherever Enrico and Maria went in Fiji they might be swept away by hurricanes and floods. *Damn their sodding eyes*. Anger was sickening, brought on waves of nausea and shaking. She could hardly hold the glass of orange juice brought her by a cabin steward. The sandwich in its plastic wrapper made her retch.

Imogen was delighted to see her. 'Oh, darling, I do hope you won't be too uncomfortable. I take students now and the bedrooms are full up but you can have the sofa in the sitting-room. It extends into a sofa-bed. I've often had to sleep on it myself.'

'My sister told me about the students. Adam told her you had several husbands in your bed.'

'Oh, Lydia, how sweet. What a lovely child he was. Of course the students come and go and never knock on doors. In my bed? Dear me, no.'

Imogen looked much the same. Amusing, sleazy tart Clive had called her. Hair a little redder now, very frizzy; figure going to seed, thickening at the waist, spreading on the hips. 'Any more ads in the offing, Im?'

'Not a thing, not even a grannie spooning out cough syrup. I tried for that.'

'You don't look like a grannie.'

'Too fat to play the mum. The camera is cruel, Lydia, makes one look twice the size one is. There might be work for you. Remember the Hamley agents? William and Janno knew them well. They're looking for somebody to assess scripts. The money isn't good, well below what experienced people like you should get, but it's something. Shall I put in a good word for you?'

'You could try. Not too long hours, not with Adam coming out.'

'I'll see what I can do. Tell me, Lydia, how's that ravishing brother-in-law of yours?'

'I didn't see much of him.'

'We had such a lovely time when I was in London, a really lovely time. He drove me to the country and showed me an old cottage he was buying. We didn't go in, just drove past. Real oldie worldie English.'

'I thought you just ate a bun together in Oxford Street.'

'It went a little further than a bun, but things didn't go too far, darling. I had to find somebody to mind the kids and he is a very married man. We spent just a little time together. I thought I told you.'

'You didn't tell me. There's no reason why you should. I believe you write to him?'

'Not all that regularly. We keep in touch. I swore I'd let him know if either of the ex-husbands stand me a holiday overseas. I write to him at that country place. Wouldn't want to break up a happy home. Wives can be funny about husbands getting letters from strange women.'

Imogen's hands spread out. 'Is he happy with your sister?'

'How would I know?' said Lydia. 'I don't ask things like that.'

'William's in Sydney. In hospital again, in Darlinghurst. He wants to be buried near his parents.'

'I thought all the cemeteries were full. Tidier to be cremated. I shall be.' Voice flat and hard, eyes malevolent; Imogen startled, distressed.

'Lydia, really! The Napiers have a plot. He wants to see you, darling. I told him you were back.'

'I wish you hadn't. I can't face it, not yet. My aunt's just died.'

'Oh, sweetie, I am sorry. But William is so insistent that he sees you, while he still knows what he's doing and saying.'

'Is he worse?'

'They don't get better. A short remission sometimes and then another virus. He's in pain. It's terrible. He's on a morphine drip.'

God, she's going to weep. Shut up, Imogen. Stop talking. Stop going on. Do you ever stop talking? No, she was always like this, jabber, jabber. I can't stand staying here but I can't afford a motel. Shut up, Imogen Smythe, before I'm sick.

'He walks about on good days. Better days. He never has a good day. He tries to walk.' Imogen wiped her eyes. 'Hates the nurses helping him to shower. Doesn't like girls washing him. There are male nurses. He prefers the male nurses to help him but he tries to cope himself. The staff are very good, I mean, they don't treat him or the others like him as if they're contaminated. In some hospitals the staff resent nursing somebody like William. It's ignorance. This place is different. Some of the male nurses are gay. There's nothing wrong with them. I mean, they're perfectly healthy. They wouldn't have jobs there if they weren't. They're efficient, my God, they are.'

Lydia put her hands flat against her ears, tried to blot out the loud, familiar voice. 'I will go and see him, Im, but I must find a place to live and get a job. I must do that before Adam comes.'

'You and Adam can stay with me for as long as you like. You know you can.'

'Thanks, Im, but no. We've got to cope and on our own.'

Get up early and house hunt. She dressed in tracksuit, running shoes, scarf tying back her hair. She heated the remains of last night's muddy coffee and let herself out of Imogen's house, jogging down the lane, across a street and another street, through the shopping centre to the seafront. She headed up the twisting concrete path above the bay. Blood-red, the sun rose above the sea.

Down there in high summer the beach would be packed; sunbathers topless these days, looked stark naked, nipples pointing at the sun. Her mother wouldn't recognise the place; would hardly recognise the sandstone house where they used to live. Nice duplex. *Wish I could buy a place like that,* she thought. *Maybe it will come on the market. Never mind the Major dying there. He was nothing to do with me. Lydia O'Malley, remember. That's who you are. You were never Lydia Mary Harper. Lydia O'Malley, the failure, with a broken marriage and a broken love affair and a business wrecked to pieces by a cyclone, could never afford a duplex on Beach Road.*

Through the next suburb and up to the graveyard above the sea. Short cropped grass and a chilly wind; gorse, spiky lantana dark orange, and a neat paved path laid since she had been here last. She slowed, walked between tombstones; familiar names, so many Irish and Scottish and the dead from two world wars; sandstone figure of Christ; plaster angels with folded wings; broken angels, some of them, spotted with seagull droppings and neglected; and Italian families locked away in huge tombs with doors like little houses; plastic roses in jam jars and here and there a bunch of fresh flowers drooping in salty air. Below the graveyard the ocean beat at rocks and retreated gulping and beat again.

Sweet William's parents were buried here, side by side; Roderick Napier and his wife Ethel, dearly loved and missed ... Ethel had intended living on forever and receiving a telegram from the Queen. Ethel's tombstone still looked relatively new. Plain tombstone; no little angel guarding awful Ethel's bones. A plaster angel would have been considered common.

Above the graveyard a line of houses; nothing up for sale. *Walk, fast, to the nearest real estate agent.*

'People either refuse to live near a graveyard or

they stay there till they die,' he said. 'Wonderful position, fantastic views. If a property ever gets on the market—and it happens very seldom—it's sold below market value. Because of the graveyard. People are funny about graves. I'll be in touch.'

The house was weatherboard with a verandah, two streets back from the ocean. You could just see the graveyard and the statue of Christ and, not too far away, the sea. 'Needs a little tender loving care, the imaginative decorator's personal touch,' the Saturday newspaper advertisement read. 'Great potential, position. Owner must sell. Price negotiable.'

The owner was handling a deceased estate. He wouldn't live anywhere near a graveyard himself, not for the most wonderful view in all the world, the real estate agent confided to Lydia. Seepage. Decaying blood and bone. What a lot of rot. The agent, anxious for his commission, was helpful. The house was well above the graveyard. Blood and bones and any form of liquid cannot seep uphill. Lydia negotiated. Ninety-eight thousand, ninety-five, ninety-one, eighty-nine, eighty-five, eighty-one. It needed a new kitchen and bathroom and new windows and several coats of paint. She signed the contract. A small mortgage was not too difficult with the island money on the way, and she had a job, but the bank insisted on an inspection, for termites and cracks and damp. The bank's engineer did not mention seepage, blood or bone.

Hamley's Literary Agency was run by an earnest

myopic woman called Maisie, who had once worked for the State Film Commission, and her husband, Dave, a one-time comic in the early days of television. They rarely spoke, even to each other. Once a month they held a meeting in their dusty office piled high with scripts no one had ever had time to read and never would. The office was a shabby terrace house a short walk from Kings Cross, two up, two down and a basement. This was where they lived and worked with a cubby-hole in the basement for their assistants. Lydia worked on film and television scripts, a girl in her early twenties on novels. The basement, they told her, was hot in summer, cold in winter, as if they hoped she might turn the job down for reasons of discomfort. The basement contained two desks and chairs, a typewriter, a word processor, floor-to-ceiling shelves heaped with files, two telephones, a one-bar electric stove and a small desk fan. There was a very dirty uncurtained window beside the desks. Through this Lydia could see the legs of people in the street and the wheels of trucks and cars.

'Such an interesting area,' Imogen said. Parts of it were squalid. In the early morning there were used syringes in the gutter. After dark, young prostitutes stood in doorways in short skirts and black stockings and, as the weather grew warmer, in halter tops and tiny shorts. Some of them looked about fourteen. The food shops were plentiful, the park pleasant for a walk if one avoided looking at drunken bodies fast asleep. In Macleay Street the fountain spurted showers of sunlit water.

Most of the submissions sent to the agency were hopeless. Lydia's job was to attach criticisms to the borderline efforts, write letters to aspiring hopefuls and send the rest back with polite rejection slips. The telephones rang incessantly. The worst of her duties was to inform clients that Maisie and David were both at meetings and would ring them back. Neither Maisie nor David rang anybody back if they could help it. Pestering clients were to be avoided. Messages on the answering machine each morning were numerous and several very rude and angry. Lydia tried putting faces to the voices of frustrated writers, as she tried imagining the assortment of bodies attached to the legs walking in the street.

Imogen produced students of mixed nationalities to help decorate the house. 'No band-aid jobs,' Lydia told them. 'I've had enough of them.' The students worked weekends and evenings for five dollars an hour. The Chinese students were industrious, as the Vietnamese on the island had been. The Australians and two English back-packers on holiday needing money to get them round the country were so idle Lydia grew frustrated, angry, shouting, 'I'm not paying you to sit around and smoke.'

'Darling, they're only young,' said Imogen, who gave constant and unwanted advice like a tap left on to drip. Lydia should relax. She was so pale and thin. Why didn't she be kind to herself, spoil herself? Have a hairdo and a facial? Or sit in the sunshine sometimes and enjoy the day? Why didn't she just sit down with a glass of wine?

'The place has got to look decent for Adam.'

'Children don't notice things like dirty paint.'

'Adam notices everything. He's coming here from a luxurious home.'

'Boys don't care about luxury. Come on, Lydia darling. You're seeing things askew.'

Maybe I always have.

The hospital was a short walk from the office. Lydia went there after work.

'He's asleep, Mrs Napier. Perhaps you'd like to sit beside him until he wakes.' The gay male nurse led her down a corridor. Nice boy. Only by his voice could you guess that he was homosexual. Spotlessly clean. Spick and span white coat. 'I'm Len. We don't worry about surnames here. Help yourself to a cup of coffee any time. Here we are. Room eight.'

Flowers on the locker; a photograph of the cast of *Summer Nights* and signatures: 'All love, William' ... 'Miss you, William' ... 'Get better quick, with love' ...

Get well cards, a heap of them, toppling over in a breeze from a verandah with tubs of mixed spring flowers. Two wheelchairs; the bed opposite William's was empty; a private bath and shower. William's name above the bed and the name of his doctor, somebody called O'Connor. A drip beside him; one arm outside the bedclothes fastening him with tape to a machine on wheels.

William lying on his back; unrecognisable; scooped-out face, all bone; mouth open; breathing harsh, jerky; hair white at the roots; an old man.

Can't touch him. Bend over him, speak to him. William. William. 'William, it's Lydia.'

Eyelids flickered, bright blue eyes stared for a second, closed. Eyes still that incredible dark-sapphire blue. *William, Sweet William still has his youthful eyes. Doesn't know me. Find a cup of coffee and come back.*

Outside, off the corridor, a little kitchen with an urn and cups and saucers, teabags and tins of coffee; VISITORS PLEASE HELP YOURSELF TO TEA OR COFFEE. THE MICROWAVE IS AVAILABLE FOR HEATING SNACKS. Another room with the door half open; linen baskets and plastic bins: CONTAMINATED DRESSINGS. A noticeboard announced HAPPY HOUR EVERY SATURDAY 4.15PM. FRIENDS AND RELATIVES WELCOME.

All comforts for the dying.

She carried the coffee back to Room 8 and sat beside the bed. Again his eyelids flickered. The faintest sound. Her name? Or was he calling for a nurse?

'William.'

Trying to sit up, falling back; pushing away bedclothes and exposing white legs, thin, weak, bent, half-cooked spaghetti legs. Struggling to live, fighting; like Annie. His voice was so faint she rose and bent over him, reluctant even to touch his hand, frightened, terrified, a terrible, wicked wish to run away, never come back; run and run.

'Wanted to see you,' he said. 'Good of you to come. I have bedsores. Where's the rubber ring?'

The rubber ring, wrapped in a cotton sheet, was

at the foot of the bed. She handed it to him, but he was unable to move. His body was too wasted, no co-ordination; like a spastic. She saw a bell on the wall behind his bed and pressed it. Len appeared. Len pulled William upright. 'Would you wait outside, please, Mrs Napier, just for a minute? I'm going to change him, make him a bit more comfortable.' Len pulled curtains round the bed.

Change him? Did he wear a nappy like a baby? Was he incontinent? Was this the last stage of a terrible disease nobody really understood? In spite of all the research written up in the newspapers, articles that sounded full of hope, about new drugs being tested and some patients reacting well; about meditation and positive thinking, about change of diet and famous people who had fought for their lives and won, or believed they had, until their deaths were announced and carefully worded obituaries appeared.

The curtains were pulled back. 'That's better,' said Len, carrying something hidden in a towel. 'I'll bring his supper before I go off. Stay as long as you like, Mrs Napier. I believe you're his next of kin.'

'Ex-wife.'

'He's been asking for you. If you'd like to stay the night we can offer you a sofa just across the way.'

'I don't think I can, not today.'

'Any time you like, just ask. If I've gone off duty while you're still here, ask for Ben.'

Len and Ben. Tweedle Dum and Tweedle Dee.

She followed him to the doorway. 'How long?' she asked. They were whispering. A silence, broken by the rattle of plates and trays; a smell of food. William's supper. Can he eat?

'One can't predict how long. Hours, days, a few weeks, sometimes longer. I think with William it will be quite soon.'

'I'll come again tomorrow.'

Will I? Coward.

'Have we your telephone number? If there's any change we'll ring.'

She sat beside William until the verandah doors were closed and the night outside turned black.

'Thank you for coming,' said William clearly. He had left his supper. Ben took the tray away and the plates with their metal covers. Ben gave him soda water to drink and changed his bed again and injected something in his side. A morphine drip, said Ben who looked so like Len she knew she would mistake one of them for the other. Her eyes were blurred. A little spurt of energy rose in William just before the morphine took over, a coherent moment before drugs sent him off to sleep. He stretched out his hand. She took it, held it, tried to squeeze it. It was like a claw.

It was half-past six in the morning and the telephone had rung. She called a taxi. She stood in Room 8 beside the bed. *This is William, anonymous, inert.* The bedclothes had been changed and smoothed. He was wrapped up in white bedclothes like a mummy. She put her hand out, touched his hair, Sweet William's beautiful hair which had turned white and thin. There was a slight movement, as though he had been brushed by a passing fly. His eyes flicked open, twin globes of sapphire. 'William? It's me again.'

The eyes shone and looked straight into hers; one instant of recognition? Two bright lights searching? Lights extinguished. The eyes were open but the light had gone. She heard footsteps outside. Len or Ben, two figures in white coats bending over him. They led her away. 'We'll just tidy up a few things for him and then you can come back and stay as long as you like.'

When she went back a candle burned beside the bed and fresh flowers had been arranged. The twin globes of brilliant sapphire were covered by waxen lids. William's eyes were closed. Lydia bent over the bed, felt the warmth of the flickering candle and the morning breeze blowing through the verandah doors. She could smell the flowers. She kissed William's forehead. His skin was not quite cold.

Chapter 25

February. The summer almost over; Adam was on the beach, flying a kite. The kite, filled with air, looked like a body in a black wetsuit. Its legs swam vigorously in the sky and kicked. It had no head.

'What a disgusting object,' said Lydia. 'Been on the guillotine. Why did you buy him a body without a head?'

Imogen, cupping her hands around her lighter, tried to light a cigarette. 'It's what's called a novelty.'

'I'll give it that,' said Lydia dryly.

'If it had a head the string things probably wouldn't fit. It's a wonderful shape when the body fills with wind.'

'You have an original way with words.' Lydia grinned. 'Headless kites that look like divers when they're full of wind. Bet they're popular.'

'They are. That was the only one they had. He handles it very well. I could never fly a kite. Mine would get stuck in trees.'

'So would that, if there were trees around. Might lose a leg. Where on earth did you find it?'

'In a kite shop. A toy shop full of kites. He's happy, Lyd. Isn't it wonderful he's happy?'

'Seems he is.'

'I told you. He likes the house.'

'The kitchen and bathroom are awful, Im. I'm trying so hard to save. He says we need more furniture. He wants bunk beds so he can have friends to stay. He wants a dog.'

There will be friction. There will be arguments. I will yell at him and he will yell back and probably stamp his feet, for Adam still has a temper. But we get on. We accept each other. She believed, she hoped, they loved each other. *Nothing turns out as one expects.*

Imogen asked, 'Ever hear from England?'

'Not a word.'

'How unkind.'

'I wasn't all that kind to them.'

Imogen lay down on the sand, shading her eyes against the sun. 'Adam says he has a few drops of Indian blood. Where did that idea come from?'

'Didn't William ever tell you?'

'William never discussed you, not with me.'

'I have several drops of Indian blood. You must have guessed.'

Imogen sat up, brushed sand from her legs and looked at Lydia's profile. Lydia stared at the kite, eyes hidden behind dark glasses.

'I've always thought you were a bit dark-skinned, but not exactly foreign-looking.'

'Sonia is my half-sister.'

'Your mother married twice?'

'No.'

Eventide

'Your mother had a little flutter. Before she married? After?'

'Before. Sonia is younger than I am. What you call a flutter was a terrible mistake. My mother's never liked me much.'

'I expect it was rather embarrassing for her, in those days, and in India. Weren't they awful snobs in India about colour?'

'So Annie always said. My aunt. The one who died.'

'How absolutely fascinating,' said Imogen. 'Piece your family story together and it might make a film or telemovie. Have you told Maisie and Davie you have a plot?'

'It's not that interesting.'

'Does your sister's dishy husband know?'

'He's always guessed. He'd be irritated if I went on about it. It doesn't matter now. I used to have hang-ups.'

'You've always had those, darling. Do you love him?'

'Who? Adam? Of course I do. I dote on him. Im, you know I do.'

'Not Adam. That dish.'

'I think we ought to go. Adam will get burnt. He keeps forgetting to put sunscreen on. Come on, Im.'

'His skin must be protected by those little drops of Indian blood,' said Imogen. 'Don't worry about him. You worry all the time.'

She watched him, searching for inherited genes; Clive's eyes, her mother's and Annie's nose, the snub nose of the colonel, the boy in Annie's photograph: Ian, 1919. The stockiness, that came from Clive; the height from Grandmother Deighton-Gaye; the temper, the obstinacy? *From me? From Annie? From the O'Malleys?* Imogen was talking, asking questions.

'Did you love him, Lyd? Your brother-in-law? The lovely Clive?'

Lydia stood up, called out, 'Adam, reel that creature in. We're going.'

Her voice was lost in a gust of wind. A hot westerly was blowing up. The kite dipped and swerved. Its legs kicked out.

'Did you, Lydia?'

'Yes.' *I love. I loved. I always will.*

'Then why did you marry poor old William?'

'He'd already married Sonia.'

'Couldn't he untie the knot?'

'No.'

'He loves you. He told me—on the bun night in Oxford Street. Couldn't get you out of his system, he said, which wasn't that encouraging for poor old me, chatting him up like mad, dying for a Christmas cuddle. "She's in my blood", he said.'

'Oh, Im. Don't go on.'

'He loves your sister, too. In a different way. I think he tore himself to pieces over both of you.'

'He isn't the type to tear himself to pieces over anybody. Believe me, I know.'

'You're so wrong. He loves you. He may need other women, but he does love you. Adam looks so like him. I've always known Adam wasn't William's child.'

'I'm surprised you've never mentioned it. You

talk a lot, Im. You're a right old gossip.'

'Thought it was safer to tell lies when people asked how could Adam be William's son. Does Adam know?'

'I've told Adam everything. Whether he understands it all I'm not sure. But I've told him. We've stopped telling lies. I've been lied to all my life. I'll never do the same to him.'

Lydia walked across the sand to help Adam reel in the kite. She had a tube of sunscreen in her hand. 'Come on, Adam. I don't want you all red and peeling. We're going out to tea.'

'Hot cakes?' said Adam, 'with maple syrup? Or fruit pancakes with maple syrup and cream in that place on the seafront? Could we?'

'Delicious thought,' said Lydia. The headless kite was stubborn, difficult to control. The strings caught on somebody's beach bag. A man, who was flying a normal-looking kite, came to help. When at last they had wound up the string and folded the kite, now shrunken without its air, she tucked it beneath her arm. 'What a monstrous thing.'

'Looks indecent,' the man said. He had a pot belly and wore a peaked cap. 'Never seen one of those before.' He laughed loudly, belly wobbling. 'Funniest thing I've seen in years.'

'Thank you for helping.'

'My pleasure. See you again.'

'It is *not* a monster,' Adam said. 'It's a person with legs and arms. I like him.'

She put her arm around him. He put his arm around her waist. They struggled up the sand against the hot, strong wind. Adam smelled of sea and salty sand and active boy.

'Hot maple syrup and cold ice-cream,' he said, 'and a bit of cream, on a big, flat pancake, not the small rolled-over ones. Not the creeps.'

'Crêpes.'

'The big, thick ones. They're called American.'

'Wait till we get there and we'll see.'

'I've had a great big think.'

'Tell me.'

'I don't call you Lydie now. Have you noticed?'

'You don't call me anything at all.'

'It sounds silly. Lydie-Billy-Silly.'

'That sounds sillier.'

'I'll call you Mum.'

Lydia walked with Adam up the beach. Imogen was waving. They waved back. Walking in the hot, windy sunlight she was weak with love.

'I've always been frightened of her,' said Sonia, eating sausages and mash at the Flask in Highgate. Archie ate French bread and Cheshire cheese. There were crumbs in his goatee beard.

'Can't think why.' Archie took a swig of beer. 'Quiet woman. Hardly said a word. Doesn't play an instrument or sing. Not a scholastic type, is she?'

'She's always been clever. Devious. Watches people. Sly. Sarcastic. Can't tell what she's thinking. She's always made me feel inferior, small.'

'You're bigger than she is. Tiny little thing. Sexy. Good in bed, I'd say. Want another sausage?'

'Better not. I'm getting fat. You found Lydia sexy?'

'Very. Wide mouth. Very attractive. Passion simmers

in women with a mouth like that. Good figure, too, but they say, don't they, that generous armfuls are better than bags of bones? Not that your sister is a bag of bones. You don't look the least alike.'

'So people keep saying. Don't laugh at me, Archie. Don't sit there grinning.'

'I'm not laughing. You've wasted yourself, you know. Should have gone in for the cello professionally.'

'And be turned down, as Timps was.'

'Poor dear Timps has little talent.'

'I'm not clever, like she is.'

'Timps is far from clever.'

'Not Timps. My sister.'

Archie blinked his pale, mild eyes. 'There's nothing the matter with your brain. You've never used it. Never had to. Lucky you.'

'That's unkind, Archie.'

'You chose the amateur way because you were afraid of failure. You don't take risks. Perhaps you're right. Don't let the old brain get rusty, though. Use it. Stop feeling sorry for yourself.'

Her eyes opened wide, large and hurt. 'I'm not. I'm just confused. When she was here I didn't want her. I wanted her to go away again as quickly as possible and those three weeks dragged on and on. When she did go I felt awful. I actually missed her. I kept wishing I'd made things nicer for her, talked to her, except that she doesn't talk much, not to me. And then when Clive, well, when Clive almost let out he'd been seeing her, almost let it out but I knew anyway, I said I might leave him.'

'Very silly of you,' said Archie. 'I bet he didn't let

out anything of the kind. Imagination. You're imagining things. As for talking about leaving him, you know you never would. Want another drink?'

'Better not. I'm driving Mummy to have her hair done this afternoon.'

'You have a mother complex or she has a daughter one. She never leaves you alone.'

'She's not too happy at the moment. Frightened.'

'Of what?' asked Archie without interest or surprise.

'Dying.'

'But she isn't dying.'

'Her younger sister died in September.'

'We're all scared of dying,' said Archie coldly. She noticed for the first time how hard his face was, unemotional, a deadpan face. 'We're dying from birth. So what?'

'When someone in your family dies it's frightening. You worry in case you've inherited the same disease.'

'What can you do about it if you have? Keep going to quacks to have your insides scanned? Waste of time.'

'I've made her have a thorough check. They say she's all right but one never knows for sure.'

Archie finished off his beer, wiped his mouth and beard and yawned. She saw several metal fillings in his teeth. When he spoke again, he sounded bored. 'There are people who don't go out in bad weather. If you worried about the weather you'd never do anything at all. It's the same, worrying about dying. Nothing you can do about dying or the weather. Get on with things.'

'I do get on with things, all the time. You know I

do. You don't understand my family.'

'Not my problem. I tell my students that. If something's nothing to do with you, keep out of it. See to your own problems. Dependency. Fatal. Like you and your mother.'

'That's humanities, is it? What you teach? Inhuman lack of interest in people who care about you?'

'Nothing to do with what I teach. It's common sense.'

'It's selfishness.'

'Survival of the fittest. You'd survive without your husband or your mother. Look Sonia, I asked you out today because I've got something I want to tell you.'

Expectant, doubtful, apprehensive, she said, 'Yes?'

'I shan't be seeing so much of you. Timps has moved in with me.'

Sonia's eyes opened wider. Her mouth shook and her shoulders; a little tremor went through her body. 'Timps? Why?'

'You got us together, my dear. She'll suit me fine.'

'As what? A housekeeper?'

'As a woman. I don't think she's much of a housekeeper. She lives on frozen packaged food, when she eats at all. I don't mind that. She'll do.'

'You're going to marry Timps?'

'I'm not marrying anybody. Been there. Done that. Not even divorced from the first one yet.'

'I thought you said you were.'

'I said nothing of the kind. You rather hoped I was.'

Sonia muttered, blushing, 'I didn't give it much thought.'

'You're a liar. Where do you think you're going?'

'To take my mother to the hairdresser.'

She picked up her handbag, walked out of the Flask, walked down the road to where she had parked the car. Archie ordered another beer.

'I'd like a week or so in Spain,' said Sonia. 'Or Majorca would be nice.'

Clive was undressing, getting ready for bed. In the en suite she could hear him cleaning his teeth, running water. It took him a long time to clean his teeth. He had an electric toothbrush, a new toy.

'Overrated, the Balearics. Whole world goes there.'

'Or Minorca. There are some lovely places for holiday letting in the paper. We'd be on our own and go out for meals. We'd be together.'

'We're always together. We're together now.'

'We're not. She's always there.'

'Don't start that again.'

'She's like a ghost, haunting us. A quiet, sly little ghost with a nasty sharp tongue and those big dark eyes.'

'Lydia is not sly. She's possibly the most honest person I've ever known.'

'You'll never hear a word against her. You've always said you hardly know her. You must know her very well to find out about her honesty. You think she's honest. I think she's sly.'

He shouted, 'Will you stop it? Just stop it, or I'll go into the other room.'

'I made up a bed for you in the spare room, just in case.'

'In case of what?'

'In case we had another row.'

'Christ,' he said. 'You wear me out. I don't want to talk about Lydia. I mean that. Let's get some sleep.'

'Clive.'

'Now what?'

'Why don't we have another child?'

'For God's sake.'

'If we had another child you wouldn't grieve for Adam.'

'Grieve? I'm not grieving. The boy's not dead. He's back where he should be.'

'You'll find them. You'll go to them. You'll never give them up. If we had a child things might be better.'

'For whom? Another lot of school fees for me to pay?'

'Better for us.'

He pulled on his dressing-gown, face reddening. Fury. She wondered if he'd like to strangle her; almost wished he would. 'If you want more children, try another man, not me. Try your clarinet player. He has a yen for you. Can't keep his eyes off you. Don't know about his hands.'

'Archie is a friend. We have lunch, go to concerts. I've got to talk to somebody.'

'You discuss our private life with that bearded creep?'

'He's not a creep. He's intelligent and highly qualified. Far more qualified than you.'

'I do realise I've never been university material. I realise I know very little about anything except making enough money to keep you in the manner you expect.'

A sound like a whimper. 'Archie doesn't want me.'

'Oh? Given you the boot?'

'There was no boot to give. We didn't have an affair, like you and her and you and all the other ones I'm not supposed to know about. Timps has moved in with him.'

'They deserve each other.' A bellow of laughter. 'What a joke. Are you upset?'

Sonia began to weep, silently, face pink, shoulders shaking. 'He was my friend. I need friends.'

'You've heaps of friends—all that damned orchestra.'

'You don't understand. Archie talks to me on an intellectual level. Not just about music, about everything.'

'You know I can't stand intellectuals.'

'He said I don't use my brain. Even Archie seemed to like her, Lydia. People find her clever, interesting. I hate her.'

'No, you don't.'

He knelt beside the bed, took her in his arms. 'Darling, do stop crying. There's nothing to cry about. Surely it's not because Archie What's-it is moving in with that funny woman.'

'She has moved in with him.'

'Same thing. We'll go to Spain, if you want to. We'll go anywhere you like. Just stop these scenes.'

'You love her.'

He stood up, walked up and down the room. As if Lydia were in the room. Lydia was always in the room, in every room. In her mother's house. Everywhere at once, watching, waiting.

'She said that to me once, about you. Said "You love her".'

'When?'

'I can't remember when, or even where. I said I did.'

'She accepted it?'

'I've never known her to make a fuss.'

'And I do. Make a fuss.'

'You do rather, darling.'

'You saw her every time you went overseas.'

'Not every time. I saw her when I could.'

'Archie said he found her sexy. Said she'd be good in bed. I'm not a very sexy person.'

He looked in pain, holding his palm against his side. 'I shall never see her again. Is that enough?'

An effort, saying those words.

'If you mean it.'

'I'd hardly bump into her, would I? She's on the other side of the earth. I'm going to bed.'

Making for the door, heading for the spare bedroom, hand against his side. 'Clive, have you got a pain?'

'Indigestion. Too much pie.'

'You're always having indigestion. I won't make pastry any more, if it disagrees with you.'

'Nonsense. I love your pies.'

'You'd better see Dr Audley and have some tests. When did you last have your blood pressure checked?'

He turned back from the door, came towards her slowly as if his legs were made of stone. 'No idea.'

'I'll make an appointment for you.'

'I'm perfectly healthy. I don't need to see any doctor. Hate going to doctors. Such a bore.'

'You're going.'

She opened her arms, wide, wide. 'Come here, Clive. Don't you dare go sleeping in the other room.'

He climbed into bed beside her.

'Don't you go getting ill. Don't you dare die and leave me on my own.'

'Darling, really.'

'I mean that. I get scared.'

He held her gently, rocked her. In the middle of the night their third child, Clare, was conceived.

Chapter 26

Six years after Clive Baird's death a taxi pulled up outside Lydia's house. The driver unloaded luggage, case after case as if the passenger intended staying for months. It was early morning, an hour after the first jumbo jet had flown across Sydney's eastern suburbs, heading for Botany and the airport. Lydia, just out of the shower and wearing a towelling dressing-gown, stood on the verandah. She saw a pink-faced woman in a creased trouser-suit, white-haired, plump. 'Good God,' she said. 'You.' And thought: *Her. The widow. What can she possibly want, coming here, to me?*

Sonia paid the driver, tipped him and asked him to help carry her cases to the house. 'Hallo, Lyd. You're not going out or anything? Is it inconvenient?'

How quite extraordinary. For a second Lydia stared, then grabbed a suitcase in each hand. 'Come on in. I'm not going anywhere. It's Saturday.'

'So it is. I'm very muddled. It takes a day to get here, by the clock, but it's really two days, almost. Sorry to descend on you like this.'

Lydia and the cab driver brought the remainder of the luggage up the verandah steps into the hallway. Sonia watched them, standing with shoulders hunched, as though too exhausted to move. 'Sorry about all that stuff. I had to pay excess baggage.'

Lydia waved the cab driver goodbye and piled the cases in a corner. 'I'll see to all that. You going to stay? I mean here, with me?'

Meekly, Sonia said, 'If you'll have me. If you have room.'

'Loads of room. Adam's in Canberra. Tea? Coffee?'

'Coffee. Please. Mind if I take my shoes off? I got all swollen on the plane.'

'One does. Take off anything you like.'

Sonia's feet and ankles were puffy. Her stomach bulged. Lydia showed Sonia into the sitting-room and made a pot of coffee. They barely glanced at each other until Lydia sat down. 'Well,' she said serenely. 'Sugar? Milk? I can't remember.'

'Two sugars, please. A little milk.' Sonia looked up, looked away. 'You haven't changed.'

'Oh, I expect I have. One does.'

Lydia sat upright, straight-backed, in a deep cane armchair with attractive coloured cushions; legs crossed, barefooted, ankles neat, hair still rather long for a woman now in middle age. Face without make-up pasty but hardly lined; a few crinkles around the mouth; smooth forehead; thick hair. Still thin, good figure, the belt of the towelling dressing-gown tight around her waist. Sonia looked again at Lydia as she gulped hot coffee, then her gaze roved around the room. A room with character, not luxurious, nothing ostentatious; tidy, clean, simple; splashes of colour, apricot and green but colour understated. 'Nice,' she said. 'Weatherboard.'

'It's not sandstone like our old place.'

Sarcastic, as always? Sonia said, 'Weatherboard's hard work, isn't it? All the painting.'

'Not really. Adam's done a lot.' Lydia, very calm, brows raised, blowing on her coffee.

'I see you still have Mummy's pictures.'

'About all I had, when I first moved in.'

'It must have been awful for you, losing the island.'

'Not a bit of it. I found a job.'

'You still work?'

'I'm afraid I do.'

'What exactly do you do?'

'I'm a partner in a literary agency. The elder partner retired and I took his place.'

Eagerly Sonia asked, 'And is it fun?'

'Sometimes.'

'I wish I worked.'

'You never tried. I take it you haven't come here to look for work? The recession is as bad as everywhere else.'

Sonia shook her head, putting down her cup, spilling coffee in the saucer. 'I was left—well, provided for very adequately.'

'I'm sure you were.' A faint smile, not unkind.

'Clive left quite a bit of property. And the London house. And shares. He had shares in the company, of course.'

'Of course.' Again, the faintest smile, a lifting of the eyebrows.

'The reason why I didn't write or telephone was I wasn't sure you would want me. I thought if I just turned up and you were away or said I couldn't stay with you I could go to a hotel.'

'You thought I'd shut the door on you? What an extraordinary idea.'

'We knew you had a house but we didn't know how big, what it was like. I must say it's very pleasant. I like your colour schemes. I love those plates up on the wall.'

'Found them in a market. Dirt cheap.'

'Thought you disliked shopping.'

'Oh, I do. I never browse, except in bookshops.'

'I remember.'

'If I want something I buy it. If I don't need it I come away. I needed something on those walls. I expect you'd like a rest. I'll make you up a bed.'

'Oh, no, don't worry. I don't mind where I sleep.' Flustered, Sonia reached for her coffee cup. 'Do you live alone?'

'Adam comes home when he's on leave, when he isn't staying with friends. He comes and goes.'

'On leave?'

'He's in the army. In Canberra at the moment.'

'You never wrote to say what he was going to do when he left school.'

'He went to Duntroon.'

'To what?' asked Sonia.

'The military academy.'

'Oh,' Sonia said. 'Adam in the army. Does he like it?'

'Loves it, so he says. He wanted to go into the police at one time and then it was the army. Duntroon was no bed of roses but he didn't complain. Seems to enjoy everything he does.'

Sonia took a deep breath and asked, 'So you only live with Adam, when he's on leave?'

Another little lifting of the brows. Lydia's secretive look. 'No live-in lover, if that's what you want to know. No live-out one, either.'

Sonia blushed. 'I wasn't prying.'

'How's the baby?'

'Clare isn't a baby now. She's nearly nine. Mummy's got her at the moment but Mummy gets so exhausted. That's one of the reasons why I'm here.'

'Because Mum's exhausted?'

'Her arthritis is much worse. She can't stand another English winter, she says. She must be over seventy.'

'I suppose she must be, but that's no age these days,' said Lydia lightly.

'She was wondering if our old place was up for sale, or something like it. She always liked that house, except for Daddy's moods when he'd been drinking. I think people leave their moods behind in houses, don't you?'

'Like ghosts? No, I don't believe they do. The old house is a two-storey now. They've stuck a bit on top.'

'Does it look awful?'

'It's rather nice.'

Sonia said, diffident, 'Would it be difficult immigrating? Surely not, if you bring in money and don't sponge on the government and have relations here who would sponsor you. I've heard you have a lot of Chinese but young people in Britain can't get permanent residence, only temporary visas—and they need so many points and qualifications if they want to stay. I don't really understand but I thought you might be kind enough to help.'

'I could sponsor you, I suppose. What about the children? Do they want to come here and leave their friends behind?'

Sonia looked uncomfortable. 'Clare won't be a problem. The other two will be a different matter. They worry me to death. They wouldn't go to university. Not that they'd ever have been accepted. They wouldn't work at school. They won't look for decent jobs. Say there aren't any jobs. I can't do a thing with either of them. Diana wanted to be a model once but it appears living on me is easier. And she's mad on men.'

Lydia nodded, suddenly aware of Sonia's stare, her assessment. The thick hair fell almost to her shoulders. Not a grey hair showing, Sonia noticed. Does she have it tinted? Spend a fortune on touching up regrowth? And no worries about Adam, apparently. Adam, with a decent career.

'The young,' said Lydia cheerfully, 'are always mad on sex. Hormones. One can't do much about one's hormones until they die down with age.'

'I'm sure I had no trouble with hormones when I was young. We didn't know what hormones were.' Sonia sounded prim.

'I knew all right.' Lydia, grinning.

'Mummy never discussed the facts of life. Now they're taught everything at school.'

'All about condoms and drugs and AIDS. Good

thing, too.'

No emotion, not a twinge.

'William died of AIDS, didn't he?'

Lydia leaned her head back against blue and green striped cushions. 'Oh, yes. He must have been HIV positive for years. Nobody knew much about AIDS then. It was just another sexually transmitted disease.'

'I remember Mummy going on about getting Adam tested—and you. She was worried stiff.'

'I don't suppose they even knew what they were testing for. William must have been one of the first to admit he was homosexual. One of the first in Australia to be diagnosed as having AIDS. I don't think the term AIDS was used at the time William died.'

'I'm sorry, Lydia. The way the press got at him was awful. The gay plague, they called it.'

'I don't think he minded the press. He and Janno used to bend over backwards for publicity.'

Sonia looked faintly shocked. 'What happened to that person?'

'I've no idea.'

'Lydia.'

'Yes?'

'Mummy was very upset about you going behind her back and talking to her sister.'

'Upset about Annie dying or about the past, out in the open at long, long last?' asked Lydia crisply.

'She shouldn't have told you all that about the O'Malleys or whatever their name was. Mummy told me everything after you left and she cried and cried. She told me everything I hadn't guessed before. It must have been very hard on her. Why shouldn't poor Mummy have had a good time in India when she was young? She fell in love.'

Lydia smiled. 'And didn't much care for the result. You did all right.'

'You might have thought so. I always just got by.'

'You were considered a raving beauty.'

'I got by.' Sonia sad, tearful. 'You get on all right with Adam?'

'I think so. We're friends.'

'It's dreadful when children can't wait to leave home and just stay because they can't afford to go away. One wonders what one's done.'

'Nothing. One does one's best. It's good for them to be independent.' Lydia, practical, down-to-earth. She lit a cigarette.

'Is it? I think it's painful when they want to leave home and only lounge around because there's nowhere else.' She was again staring hard at Lydia. 'Do you still smoke like a chimney?'

'I smoke. Does it worry you?'

'No, no, of course not. Is Adam very independent?'

'Very.'

'So were you. Lydia, Mummy wants to live near you. Isn't that something after all these years? I don't mean we want to live in your pocket, but for the whole family to be in the same hemisphere and see each other, for birthdays and Christmas, like other families do.'

'It doesn't always work,' said Lydia, wry. 'I know people who dread the annual family gathering for Christmas and New Year. The suicide rate goes up at Christmas.'

'A typical cynical Lydia remark,' said Sonia, bitter.

'Sorry. It wasn't meant to be.'

Sonia stifled a yawn. 'Think I'd better have a snooze, if you don't mind.'

Lydia led her to the spare bedroom, made up the bed—pretty sheets, a quilt to match the curtains; venetian blinds; a fan. She helped Sonia unpack, put a jug of iced orange juice on the bedside table; checked there were several coat-hangers in the cupboard.

'You've become very domesticated. Quick and competent.'

'Because I can make a bed?'

'I've always imagined you in rented places, struggling.'

'Surrounded by freakish friends.'

'Something like that,' Sonia admitted, blushing.

'One adapts. Bathroom first door on the right. Have a shower or a long hot bath.'

'A bath would be lovely.'

Lydia produced clean towels.

'Nice bathroom, Lyd.'

'It was awful when I bought the place. Don't believe the previous owner ever washed. Help yourself to anything else you need. I'm going out to get some food. I won't be long.'

'Don't lay on anything special just for me.'

'I won't. Sleep tight. Get up when you feel like it and I'll cook a meal. No hurry.' Lydia spoke softly, kindly, from the doorway.

'Thank you,' said Sonia. 'I'm very grateful. Thank you very much.'

Australia and England, 1982-1993

Lydia pulled on jeans and T-shirt and reversed her car out of the garage. She headed for the shops and thought: *Most peculiar. Why on earth do they want to live near me? We've not written to each other more than once a year. Once a year, at Christmas.*

Chapter 27

'Delicious,' said Sonia.

'An ordinary chicken casserole.'

'Lovely flavour. What herbs?'

'Basil and other bits. I throw in everything I can find.'

They sat on the verandah after dinner, drinking wine. Sonia tucked envelopes of photographs in her bag. Snap after snap of Clare; tubby child, fair, Clive's features. All Clive's children took after him.

'I see you've taken to gardening, Lydia.'

'Not on your life. Put down paving. I wanted to make it look a bit like Mum's patio used to be, only it's much smaller. I buy things in pots and tubs. Not green-fingered like you.'

'Remember the tubs outside Mummy's house?'

'Still there, are they?'

'She's getting rid of a lot of stuff, if she comes out here. The tubs are very heavy.'

'I'd have them. Rather fond of them. They were there in Grandmother's day.'

'I'll tell Mummy when I write.'

'You can't cart too much across the world. I'm very surprised you want to come yourselves.'

Sonia nibbled the end of her thumb. 'I've got to make Duncan and Diana see they'll never get jobs or get anywhere if they continue as they are. They won't do anything except go out and never tell me where. I'm so tired of London and everything's expensive and the winter goes on and on and the central heating bills are awful and Mummy never feels well. I want to start again.'

Lydia asked curiously, 'What makes you think the children might do better here?'

'It would be a challenge. A new country. I want to get them away from their dreadful friends. I can't control them. They've been appalling since Clive died. Diana stays out all night. She goes out with a West Indian, a Jamaican. I don't mind him, but when Mummy saw him she had a fit.'

'Good at cricket, they are, West Indians.'

'It isn't funny. I've been a hopeless parent. It isn't easy, on one's own.'

'No.'

'What's that sound? Not frogs?'

'Cicadas. The sound of summer. Don't you remember how they scream? They scream when they're mating and then they die.'

'Lucky things. I wanted to die after I had Clare.'

Lydia asked abruptly, 'Why?'

'I was very ill. Too old to have another, I suppose, and I knew Clive didn't want more children. He was all right once Clare was born but when I was having her he was very odd.'

'I expect he doted on her when she arrived.'

'I don't know. He was always out, working, going to meetings, so he said. I had Clare as a way of hanging on to him, I think I did. That's not fair, producing a child when a man's had enough of you. It wasn't fair, the way I had Clare on purpose and said it was a mistake. It's not that I don't love her. I love them all. I've never faced facts, Lydia, never. I've skirted round hard facts. Head in the sand.'

'Like Mum,' Lydia said blandly, nodding in the darkness. The dark came suddenly; a blazing sunset and then night full of insects and scents and the gulping tide. 'See that star? Adam and I used to watch it rising. He swears it's Venus and I say it's Mars. Neither of us knows a thing about astronomy.'

Sonia continued talking, dreamy, half-asleep, anaesthetised by wine. 'He'd played tennis in the morning. Going through a keep fit phase. Said he was putting on too much weight. He had pains he said were indigestion. He wouldn't see a doctor. After lunch that day, it was a Sunday, he insisted on mowing the lawn. He died, just like that. Massive coronary. Too young to die. And I felt guilty. Guilt is worse than grief. Isn't it strange? We're both widows.'

'I never think of myself as a widow. We were divorced quite a time before William died.'

'Did you see him?'

'When he was ill, you mean? Twice. At the very end. I was there when he died.'

'Did he know you? Was there time to say goodbye?'

'We said goodbye when he was alive and well—presumably well, although he couldn't have been—through solicitors, an amicable divorce, as they call it. Did he know me? The night before he died he did. I don't know after that.'

But she remembered his eyes, twin globes of sapphire light, for an instant burning; gone.

'It must have been painful,' said Sonia, helping herself to wine, 'even if you were divorced.'

'For some reason it was. Very.'

'Poor Lyd.'

'Not poor. Quite happy.'

'What do you do with your life?'

Lydia said pleasantly, 'What thousands of other people do. I have a few good friends. Theatre, concerts, opera sometimes, although I prefer opera on the radio. The plots annoy me, heroines singing away for ten minutes when they've been stabbed or dying of TB. Go out to lunch, to dinner, see a movie, look at TV, clean the house, wash, iron, cook vast meals for Adam when he's home. Go to work, come home again.'

'No men?'

'Celibate as the Virgin Mary.'

'Do you mind?'

'Mind no man around? Not one bit, not now. I'm over fifty!'

'Lydia, Clive and I were so unhappy towards the end. We had no chance to say goodbye.'

'Dreadful shock for you. And Clare so young.'

My fault. I made them both unhappy when I loved.

'I'm not blaming you,' Sonia said quickly. 'I'm not, please don't think I am. It was me. I went overboard.'

'Jealousy?' Lydia spoke the word very softly, wrapping it in cigarette smoke, in darkness.

'No. Overboard over someone else. Not physical.

I'm not a physical person. I never have been. That must have been hard on Clive.'

Lydia could hear her breathing. She thought: *don't tell me. I don't want to know.*

'I was very lonely. I needed a friend. Archie became more than that and I think, I believe, the physical would have followed. He was nothing to look at. I think you met him. Had a beard.'

'The clarinet player who came to lunch? I remember he kept staring at you. Looked as if he was peering into your ear.'

'I got a bit too keen. When he threw me over I hated him. I even noticed he had quite a lot of fillings in his teeth.'

'Oh, dear,' said Lydia. 'You'd have got used to them. Better than a plate or gaps.'

'Clive laughed at me, like you do.'

'I'm not really laughing, Sonia. I think it's rather sad.'

'Clive wasn't jealous. He had no right to be jealous, had he?'

'I suppose not, no.'

'Archie used to consider me worth talking to.'

'Did you imagine that you weren't?'

'I've never had your confidence, your self-possession.'

'My what?' Lydia sat bolt upright and lit another cigarette. 'Don't be absurd. I had no confidence whatever. You used to make heads turn.'

'Only at what I looked like. Not because of me, of what I am inside.'

'What are you? I don't think I've ever known,'

and Lydia filled up their glasses.

'Have you ever felt that you want to grab what's going, take it all while you can, in case nothing goes right again?'

'Used to. Constantly.'

I took and took; Sydney and Singapore, Bangkok and New Zealand. I loved and loved and destroyed us all.

'I felt like that with Archie. He didn't want me. Timps went to live with him.'

'That funny woman who dressed like a little girl? I remember her.'

'It didn't last. After Timps left him, he disappeared. Never even rang me up to say he was going away. I felt rejected. You wouldn't know the feeling.'

'Wouldn't I just,' said Lydia.

'By then I was pregnant with Clare. Never got my figure back. After Clive died I kept eating. Consolation, I suppose.'

Sonia was wearing a loose cotton dress Lydia had lent her. Her clothes were crushed, she said, and it was far too hot to iron. The dress looked tight. She was a rounded mass, a smudged outline in the darkness, sprawled in a canvas chair. She had removed the combs and slide from her hair, sat twisting them in her lap, her hair loose around her face, a white untidy cloud.

'Mummy will come in January with the children, if she finally makes up her mind. Could we find something nice for her to rent until she sees a house she likes?'

'I should think so.'

'Unfurnished. She has so much stuff. My cello's coming out with the furniture. Are there retirement places here?'

'Retirement villages, yes, lots of them, and medical attention handy, if it's needed.'

'I think she might like to live in one of those eventually, if they're big enough for her favourite things.'

'You wouldn't all live together?'

'No. Archie talked to me about dependency. I've always been like that. I depended on Clive for everything. And Mummy. I never appreciated Clive when he was alive. I didn't love Clive, you see, not at the beginning. I was fond of him but I didn't love him. I loved the idea of being married.'

Lydia sat listening, absorbing, silent. Cicadas screamed. Finally she said, 'I think all our generation was a bit like that and our mothers encouraged it. You made a good job of being a wife.'

'I didn't really, Lydia. People thought I did but it was a facade. Mummy went on about how wonderful I was. She wouldn't face the fact that I wasn't wonderful at all.'

'Clive thought you were wonderful.'

'He did not. He always wanted you.'

Somewhere along the seafront a band was playing Christmas carols. 'Salvation Army band,' said Lydia, standing up, looking over the verandah rail.

'I never enjoyed Christmas much,' said Sonia. 'I did all I could to make it nice but Clive hated all the fuss and the mess the children made and the wrapping paper all round the house and the tree dropping pine needles and all the food. Couldn't wait to get back to the office after the Christmas break. Clive needed peace and quiet. I think the only times he felt peaceful must have been with you.'

Don't. Stop. The last time wasn't peaceful. I screamed and yelled and he drank too much.

Sonia said sleepily, 'Bit early for carols, isn't it?'

'They always come round well before Christmas. We must give them some money. They do a wonderful job.'

'Preaching,' said Sonia.

'No. Giving. Caring for the poor and sick.'

Like Annie who loved the poor and sick and nursed them and broke her heart.

'I'd like to go to India, Sonia, just a trip to look around.'

'To trace the O'Malleys or whatever their name was?'

'Look at records, try to find their graves. Annie said everything has changed, but I still want to go there.'

'You can't remember much. You were only five. I don't remember anything at all.'

'What I've always remembered is like pieces of a jigsaw all mixed up and I couldn't put the bits together. Now I can.'

'I'll come with you, so long as we stay somewhere civilised. We could go on a coach tour. Or will you go with Adam?'

'If Adam ever gets to India it will be with a rucksack on his back and about a dozen friends, not a coach tour with middle-aged retirees and pensioners.'

'I'd feel safer with retirees and pensioners. Would you like me to come with you?' Pleading. 'It might be fun, Lydia. I hope by the time I've been here a few months we may be friends.'

Sonia pushed herself out of her chair and stood beside Lydia, looking out across the graveyard to the sea. Lydia felt Sonia's arm across her shoulders. 'Would you like me to come with you?'

'If you think you'd enjoy it, of course I would.'

The band was moving slowly along the seafront, no longer singing carols; saying goodnight.

'Lyd, please don't cry. Was it because I talked about Clive?'

'No. Nothing to do with anything you said.' Lydia's lips were moving. 'Listen.'

... Fast falls the eventide;
The darkness deepens; Lord, with me abide ...

In the purple night with a thousand stars and the hum of insects the band, marching beside the ocean, played 'Abide With Me'.